A DIFFERENT WORLD

By Judith Lennox

Reynardine
Till the Day Goes Down
The Glittering Strand
The Italian Garden
The Secret Years
The Winter House
Some Old Lover's Ghost
Footprints on the Sand
The Shadow Child
The Dark-Eyed Girls
Written on Glass
Middlemere
All My Sisters
A Step in the Dark
Before the Storm
The Heart of the Night
Catching the Tide
The Turning Point
One Last Dance
The Jeweller's Wife
Hidden Lives
The Secrets Between Us
Summer at Seastone
A Different World

A DIFFERENT WORLD

Judith Lennox

First published in 2025 by Headline Review
An imprint of HEADLINE PUBLISHING GROUP LIMITED

1

Cataloguing in Publication Data is available from the British Library

ISBN 978 1 0354 0880 1

Typeset in Joanna MT Std by Palimpsest Book Production Ltd, Falkirk, Stirlingshire

Printed and bound in Great Britain by Clays Ltd, Elcograf S.p.A.

Headline's policy is to use papers that are natural, renewable and recyclable products and made from wood grown in well-managed forests and other controlled sources. The logging and manufacturing processes are expected to conform to the environmental regulations of the country of origin.

HEADLINE PUBLISHING GROUP LIMITED
An Hachette UK Company
Carmelite House
50 Victoria Embankment
London EC4Y 0DZ

The authorised representative in the EEA is Hachette Ireland, 8 Castlecourt Centre, Dublin 15, D15 XTP3, Ireland (email: info@hbgi.ie)

www.headline.co.uk
www.hachette.co.uk

To Sheila,
and in memory of
my dear friend Julian Rizzello.

Acknowledgements

Heartfelt thanks to my agent, Margaret Hanbury, and to everyone at Headline, in particular my editor, Clare Foss, for her patience and incisiveness. Thanks also to my copy-editor, Jane Selley, for her meticulous work. Any errors remaining are mine alone.

I am grateful for the support given to me through the years by Bettina Feldweg and Martina Vogl at Piper Verlag. Huge appreciation is also due to my translators, especially Mechtild Ciletti who has worked on so many of my books.

Lastly – thank you, friends and family and, most of all, Iain, for your help and encouragement.

PART ONE

Chapter One

1939, London

One afternoon, Olivia Goodland was sent by her employer to deliver a new gown to a client, a Mrs Ruthwell. She left the small, stuffy back room in which she and three other girls sewed for the spring sunshine, and headed for Hinton Place, in Mayfair. There, the windows of the large, splendid buildings looked out onto a central garden square of shrubs and mature trees.

As she approached the house, a boy ran out of the door and dashed down the stone steps towards the road. Olivia called out a warning as a cyclist cursed and a van's horn blared. Grabbing the boy by the shirt collar, she tugged him back onto the pavement.

A woman in a cyclamen-pink dress appeared in the doorway. 'Frankie, Frankie, you must be careful!' She ran down the steps and put her hands on the child's shoulders. 'Darling, please! You could have been hurt.'

'It's a Hispano-Suiza, Mama!' The boy's gaze was fixed on a large cream-coloured motor car parked on the far side of the street.

'But Frankie, you must mind the traffic.' The woman spoke

to the cyclist. 'I'm so sorry. I hope he didn't give you an awful fright.'

The cyclist grumbled and pedalled off.

'I can't thank you enough,' Frankie's mother said to Olivia. 'My name is Grace Ruthwell. This is my son, Frankie.' She ruffled the boy's curls. Mother and son were strikingly similar, both good-looking, with even features, sapphire-blue eyes and golden hair.

Olivia introduced herself. 'Mrs Beaumont sent me with your gown, Mrs Ruthwell.' She held up the brown paper parcel.

Grace Ruthwell beamed. 'So you're the new girl! Violet has told me all about you.'

'Yes, madam, I started with Mrs Beaumont last month.'

Twenty-five years ago, Olivia's mother and Violet Beaumont had been school friends. Since then, they had both married and been widowed. Violet Beaumont had no children and had established a successful dressmaking business in Knightsbridge. 'Vi will keep an eye on you,' her mother had said, as Olivia had packed for her journey to London. 'Have a wonderful time, darling. Remember to keep your stitches small and neat, and promise me you won't go into a public house or smoke cigarettes.' Olivia had promised.

As Frankie chattered about the motor car, Mrs Ruthwell ushered her inside the house. The hallway was the size of Olivia's room at the hostel, which she shared with three other young women. White tulips spilled from the glass vases on the side tables and light from two tall, narrow windows scattered on the marble floor tiles and gleamed on the sleek gold picture frames. Mirrors on opposing sides of the room reflected Mrs Ruthwell herself, her sheeny pink dress and her necklace of sparkling yellow stones.

A tall young man appeared. 'Grace, I'm so sorry,' he said. 'I just couldn't stop him.'

'No harm done, but Rory, you must keep a closer eye on him. You know how impetuous he is.'

'I'll keep a better watch, I promise.' Rory spoke with a soft Scots lilt.

'Let me introduce you to Miss Goodland,' said Mrs Ruthwell. 'She works for my dressmaker, Mrs Beaumont. Miss Goodland, this is Frankie's tutor, Rory Madden.'

Frankie said, 'It wasn't Rory's fault, Mama. I can run as fast as the wind.'

'Yes, dearest. Get along now and finish your lessons. How is he doing today, Rory?'

'We've started a new reading book.' The tutor smiled at the boy. 'You're working hard, aren't you, Frankie?'

The man and the boy disappeared down a corridor. Olivia said to Mrs Ruthwell, 'What a delightful child. How old is he?'

'Frankie is eleven years old. Rory's very good with him. Some of the others, they hadn't the patience . . .' Mrs Ruthwell's smile faded.

Olivia was unsure of the protocol. Should she wait for Mrs Ruthwell to unwrap the parcel and inspect her gown? Or, having safely delivered it, should she slip away?

Mrs Ruthwell solved her dilemma by saying, 'Shall we take a tiny peek? It's so thrilling when one has a new gown, isn't it? Let's go into the morning room. We won't be disturbed there.'

In the morning room, dappled light fell onto apple-green walls and a rose-pink carpet. A glass-paned door lay open, letting in cool air from the outside and permitting Olivia a glimpse of a back garden in which narrow paths wound between silver birches and box hedges.

Mrs Ruthwell said, 'Have you always been fond of sewing, Miss Goodland?'

'Yes, madam. My mother taught me.'

'Do I detect a West Country accent?'

'I come from Somerset, from a village near Crewkerne.'

'I do love the country. We have a house in Staffordshire. To begin with I'm always delighted to go there because it's so quiet and blissful, but after a week or two I yearn for the hurry and variety and utter *wickedness* of London. Oh, look at this. Isn't it simply divine?'

Olivia had unwrapped the parcel Mrs Beaumont had entrusted her with. Mrs Ruthwell rubbed a piece of mauve devoré velvet between finger and thumb and gave a sigh of pleasure.

But she had been mistaken in assuming they wouldn't be disturbed in the morning room. As Olivia shook out the gown, the cook appeared with a query about dinner, then the telephone rang. Shortly afterwards, a slim, beautiful girl of around Olivia's own age put her head round the door.

'Mama, Summers has put out my lilac silk gown and I don't want to wear it.'

'But Alice, you look so sweet in it.'

'I hate it.' The girl was a paler version of Mrs Ruthwell and Frankie. Her shoulder-length hair was silvery blonde, and her eyes were a very light blue, as glassy and translucent as a chalk stream. Her prettiness was marred by the sulky downturn of her mouth.

Later that evening, in her cubicle in the women's hostel in Earls Court, Olivia wrote her nightly letter to her mother. She described the Ruthwells' house, with its high ceilings, shining surfaces and flickering shadows on rose-pink carpets.

As she wrote, she recalled Mrs Ruthwell's kindness and charm and the beauty of her daughter. And the sweetness of Frankie's smile, and the handsomeness of his tutor.

Late the following afternoon, she returned to the house in Hinton Place. 'Mrs Ruthwell seems to have taken a shine to you, Olivia,' Mrs Beaumont told her. 'She has asked me to send along "that charming girl" to alter a seam in her new gown.' Olivia was flattered that the elegant Mrs Ruthwell considered her to be charming. She was tallish and slender, with narrow shoulders, and her eyes were a very dark brown. After a memorably disastrous perm, she had given up trying to wave her straight dark hair and wore it pinned in a bun or plaited at the nape of her neck. She got on with most people and aimed always to be cheerful and hard-working.

A maid led her upstairs to Grace Ruthwell's bedroom. The large, airy room was at the front of the house. Yellow flowers bloomed on the wallpaper and the curtains were of chartreuse shot silk.

Mrs Ruthwell was standing beside a Chinese screen decorated with red and gold dragons. She was wearing the mauve devoré velvet gown.

'Olivia! I may call you Olivia, mayn't I? What a pleasure to see you again. What do you think?' She twirled, and the handkerchief hemline spun out. The sinuous lines of the gown emphasised her height and statuesque beauty.

'It suits you so well, madam.'

'The neckline is a little loose. We need a tiny tuck here and here.' A slim hand with glossy scarlet nails indicated the shoulders of the gown. 'Could you do it for me now, do you think? I know, I'm as bad as Frankie, so hopelessly impatient, but I do so *yearn* to wear it tonight.'

Olivia checked and measured the shoulder seams. Her fingertips brushed against Grace Ruthwell's soft white skin; she breathed in her expensive perfume. When the pins were in place, the maid, a sallow, fair-haired girl, unzipped the gown. The fabric rippled and the crystal beads sewn on the godets sparkled, catching the light. Beneath, Mrs Ruthwell was wearing cream-coloured silk undergarments made to accommodate the gown's low back.

She indicated a small, round table for Olivia to sit at and sew. 'Summers, fetch Miss Goodland a tray of coffee. Or would you prefer lemonade?'

'Coffee would be marvellous.'

The maid, Summers, left the room. Mrs Ruthwell put on a red satin kimono while Olivia threaded her needle. Velvet was a tricky cloth to sew. The stitches must be tiny and hidden, the alterations invisible to the onlooker.

Mrs Ruthwell stood at her shoulder. 'You are so clever. Did you always want to be a dressmaker?'

'I would have liked to go to art school, but we couldn't afford it. I do so enjoy sewing, though.'

Mrs Ruthwell sat down at the dressing table. 'Did you know that in London there are evening schools where one can study art? The daughter of a friend of mine, Sally Chichester, attends one. If you like, I'll ask her about it.'

'Thank you, Mrs Ruthwell.' Olivia felt herself flush. 'That's very kind of you.'

'Grace. Do please call me Grace. Dressmaking is an art too, of course. One must have an eye for colour and the knack of choosing the right fabric for a gown. Perhaps I should ask you to make something for my daughter, Alice. She was presented at court last month. I have an idea for a simple gown in a dark red. With her fair colouring it would look so striking. A girl needs to stand out.'

Olivia recalled the pretty, sullen-looking girl she had glimpsed the previous day. 'I'd be delighted to.'

'I wonder whether I might ask you to do me a favour, Olivia.'

Knotting her seam, she looked up. 'Yes, of course . . . Grace.'

'Would you deliver this for me on your way home?' Mrs Ruthwell held out a letter to her. 'The house is only a few streets away, so it shouldn't be too far out of your way.'

Olivia tucked the envelope into the cloth bag in which she kept her sewing things. She heard footsteps approaching the room. Mrs Ruthwell lowered her voice. 'Make sure to deliver it to Mr Ellwood in person. To him and no one else. And if you wouldn't mention it to anyone . . .' The door opened and Summers came in with the tray of coffee.

Half an hour later, her task complete, Olivia was shown downstairs. In the distance she heard voices – Frankie's, she thought, and one of a lower timbre, the tutor, Rory, perhaps. She was in the hall, buttoning her raincoat, when the front door opened and a man came into the house. He was around forty, tall and well built, his sandy hair swept back from his brow. Beads of rain glistened on the shoulders of his mackintosh. When he glanced in her direction, she saw that he had the same ice-blue eyes as Alice Ruthwell. He did not acknowledge Olivia in any way; his pale gaze drifted over her with utter lack of interest, as if she was an inanimate object, like an umbrella stand or one of the glass vases.

At the corner of Hinton Place, Olivia glanced at the envelope Grace had given her. It was addressed to S. Ellwood Esq., of South Audley Street. She asked a passer-by for directions and set off. A light rain glazed the pavements, and during the hour she had spent in the Ruthwells' house, the sky had turned ink blue. The trees and shrubs in the garden squares had become intricate black cut-outs against the terraced houses surrounding them. The air was fresh and scented with blossom.

Half a dozen stone steps led up to the front door of Mr Ellwood's house. Behind the window blinds, shadows danced. A maidservant opened the door and Olivia was enveloped in a blare of music and chatter.

'Yes, miss?' said the maid. She was a pert, round-faced girl.

'I've a letter for Mr Ellwood.'

'I'll take it.'

'I was instructed to deliver it to Mr Ellwood by hand.'

The maid glared at her. 'Wait here.'

In the hall, a stuffed animal – a cougar or a puma – bared its teeth on a black marble side table. White gardenias spilled from a green bowl, their heady scent mingling with cigarette smoke and an exotic, earthy perfume.

Open double doors revealed to Olivia the room in which jazz music was playing. Guests were milling around, cocktails in hand, and couples were dancing. Waitresses in black dresses and white aprons circulated with trays of food. Olivia's foot tapped to the rhythm of the music. She loved to dance. A few days ago, she had gone dancing at the Locarno Ballroom with some of the girls from the hostel. They had had a high old time.

More guests arrived; people spilled into the hallway. A woman in a white bias-cut gown spoke to her. 'You don't happen to have a light, do you?' Olivia apologised and the woman wandered off.

A red-haired man with a vol-au-vent in one hand and a cocktail glass in the other bore down on her. 'Have you seen Kit?' Crumbs sprayed onto his waistcoat.

'I'm afraid not.'

He slumped against the wall, looking disconsolate. 'She *was* here, I'm sure of it. She is so bloody elusive.' He stared at her. 'Do I know you?'

'No, I shouldn't think so.'

'There's to be a conjuror later. Sammy is partial to conjurors. Does unspeakable things with snakes, apparently. Don't you sometimes think . . .' his small hazel eyes raked round the crowds, 'that all this – alcohol, snakes, sex – is to take our minds off what's about to happen?'

Without waiting for her reply, he went back into the room where the guests were dancing. Olivia supposed he had been referring to the likelihood that Britain might soon be at war. In March, Hitler's armies had invaded what remained of Czechoslovakia. The prime minister, Mr Chamberlain, had since given Poland a guarantee of support should Hitler try to invade there next. In this fine late spring of 1939, most people seemed to think war was inevitable, though Olivia's mother, who was a pacifist, continued to fire off letters to newspapers and journals in the hope that conflict might be averted.

With a friend from the hostel, a tall, intense girl called Louise, Olivia had recently attended a political meeting. Some of the men had been in uniform and several women had spoken of taking their children to the countryside in case of air raids. Husbands, brothers and boyfriends were joining the RAF or being conscripted into the army.

Her wristwatch told her that a quarter of an hour had passed since she had entered the house. Perhaps the maid had forgotten her. She wondered whether she should plunge into the seething mass of people in the adjoining room and seek out Mr Ellwood herself. 'Anything Goes' was playing; her lips formed the words.

A voice said, 'I'm sorry to keep you waiting. There was someone I couldn't get away from. I'm Sammy Ellwood.'

He was tall and elegantly dressed, his complexion dark, his hair black and tightly curled, his coal-black eyes amused. Olivia introduced herself. 'Mrs Ruthwell asked me to deliver a letter to you, Mr Ellwood.'

'Ah, the divine Grace.' He smiled, tore open the letter and scanned it. 'Thanks,' he said. He put it in his pocket. 'Appreciate it.' He took out a couple of coins. 'For your trouble.'

Startled, she said quickly, 'No, thanks.'

'I'm sorry, Miss Goodland, I don't mean to offend you.'

'I'm not offended.'

'Then perhaps you would accept this?' He took three white gardenias from the green bowl, then cocked his head as he ran his gaze over her. 'Or maybe you'd like to stay for the party.'

She laughed. 'I don't think I'm dressed for it, Mr Ellwood.'

His craggy features broke into a broad smile. 'I shouldn't worry about that,' he said, with a bark of laughter. 'Tommy Fitzalan once turned up in a tutu.'

Olivia walked back to the hostel to save the bus fare. Was that what Grace Ruthwell had been referring to when she had spoken of *utter wickedness*, parties like Sammy Ellwood's? It would have been fun to have stayed, and a part of her regretted not having done so, but she was wearing an old mackintosh over a hand-knitted short-sleeved jersey and a skirt she had made herself from an offcut of fabric. And she suspected that different rules applied to her and the man in the tutu.

She supposed that Mr Ellwood was Grace's lover, and that was the motive for her secrecy, though she wondered why she hadn't asked her maid to deliver the note. Grace and Mr Ellwood would make a striking couple, she so fair, he so dark, she so sparkling and he louche, possessed of a pantherine watchfulness.

Back at the hostel, she put the gardenias in a jam jar on her small chest of drawers. They gave a dash of exoticism and glamour to her cubicle. She was too late for supper and ravenously hungry, so she ate the last slice of a fruit cake her mother had sent up to her. Then she lay back on the bed, closed her eyes and imagined herself at Sammy Ellwood's house, dressed in a purple devoré gown, dancing to 'Anything Goes' with Rory Madden.

As the maid showed Olivia into the Ruthwells' house a week later, Frankie dashed into the hall. 'Hello, Olivia. Would you like to see my schoolroom?'

'I'm calling on your mother, Frankie. She asked me to bring her some new dress designs.'

Rory appeared. 'I'm afraid Mrs Ruthwell had to go out, Miss Goodland. You're welcome to sit with us in the schoolroom until she gets home.'

Laughing, she allowed herself to be tugged along the corridor by Frankie. The schoolroom was at the front of the house and was well proportioned and decorated in light, fresh colours. On a round table were textbooks, an exercise book, pencils and crayons.

Frankie peered out of the window. 'Rory, the Bentley's back,' he said. 'Look, Olivia, I've drawn it.' He fetched a sketchbook and turned the pages for her to look at. On each one was a drawing of a motor car.

'They're awfully good,' she said.

'Frankie, come back to your books now,' Rory said. 'Miss Goodland, please forgive us. Take a seat.' He drew out a chair for her.

Reluctantly, Frankie sat down. He and Rory bent over the reading book. Though the story was simple, a lacklustre tale about a rabbit who wanted to be an engine driver, and was surely aimed at a much younger child, progress was slow because the boy read haltingly. When he stumbled, Rory helped him sound out the letters. Throughout, the child fidgeted, picking up the inkwell, twiddling a pencil and writhing round in his seat to peer beneath the table or out of the window. It shocked Olivia to realise that at eleven years old, Frankie Ruthwell, who had surely had every advantage in life, could barely read. She wondered what had happened to make him so behind with his books.

And yet her gaze kept drifting to Rory, taking in the firm line of his shoulders, the symmetry of his profile and the wave of his chestnut-brown hair. It was a pleasure simply to listen to him as over and again he patiently returned Frankie's attention to the book. She could have sat there for hours, luxuriating in the sound of his voice.

Just as with much squirming and sighing on Frankie's part and encouragement on Rory's the end of the story was reached, Grace Ruthwell opened the door to the schoolroom. She peeled off her gloves and greeted them. She was wearing an aquamarine two-piece in a fine knit. A matching hat, a jay's feather in the band, perched to one side of her blonde head.

Rory told her that Frankie had finished the reading book. Grace hugged her son. 'A whole book in one day! How clever of you.'

'Will Father be pleased with me?'

'I'm sure he will. Rory, why don't you take Frankie out to the garden? He could do with some fresh air and the sun's still shining. Olivia, please come with me.'

In the morning room, Grace closed the door behind them. 'Thank you for delivering my letter last week. I do hope Sammy behaved himself. He can be rather a tease.'

'He was most civil. He gave me some gardenias.'

'Did he now? He told me he thought you were a very pretty girl.'

Olivia blushed. Grace took the folder of dress designs from her, then slid out a couple of envelopes from beneath the blotter on the desk. 'Could you post these for me on your way home?'

Olivia put the letters in her pocket. She and Grace had returned to the hall when the sandy-haired man she had seen on her previous visit appeared. His pale blue gaze alighted on Grace.

'You have remembered we're to dine with the Lamberts?'

'Naturally, Claude. I'm going to play with Frankie for half an hour and then I'll get ready.'

'Don't be late.' His voice was sharp.

There was a postbox at the end of the road. Dropping the letters into it, Olivia felt honoured that Grace entrusted these little tasks to her and showed her such warmth and amiability. The things she had seen these past weeks! London's great buildings and Sammy Ellwood's racy party and the heavenly gowns they sewed at Mrs Beaumont's establishment. Her narrow world had opened up. Back there, in the Ruthwells' schoolroom, she had felt as if she were almost part of the family.

A fortnight later, Summers let her into the house once again. Olivia followed her upstairs. It was a hot day, and beneath her white cap, tendrils of the girl's hair had darkened with sweat and clung damply to the back of her neck.

In the bedroom, Grace was seated at her dressing table, patting powder on her nose. She rose, flashing a smile, as Olivia came into the room. Brisk and businesslike, she inspected the fabric samples Olivia had brought with her, selecting the blue-flecked tweed rather than the green, the yellow silk instead of the fuchsia for the wrap skirt that would go over white cotton piqué beach shorts.

When they were finished, she took a handful of bracelets from her jewellery box and sighed. 'Oh dear, I have a very dull luncheon engagement with an extremely dull man. What wouldn't I give to spend an hour in the garden with Frankie or drive to the coast and lie on the sand, soaking up the sun. Help me out, please, darling. Which one should I wear?'

'This one.' Olivia picked out a silvery bangle with cabochon stones in boiled-sweet colours of red and purple. 'It's beautiful.'

'Isn't it? It's a favourite of mine. Here, try it on.'

Olivia slid the bangle onto her wrist. The metal felt cool against her skin and the jewels seemed to trap the sunlight pouring through the window.

'It suits you,' said Grace. 'You have such slender hands.'

'Thank you.' Olivia gave the bangle back.

The order complete, she offered to show herself out. As she went downstairs, a sound caught her attention.

Someone was crying, a series of loud, desperate sobs. She thought at first it might be Frankie. Along the corridor, a door stood a few inches ajar. She paused and tapped lightly, then opened it.

Inside the room, Alice Ruthwell was curled up in an armchair, weeping.

'Are you all right?' Stupid question, Olivia thought immediately. The girl's face was blotched scarlet, her eyes swollen, her hair dishevelled.

She took a few steps into the room. 'Would you like me to fetch your mother?'

'No . . . *no*.' Shaking her head violently, Alice sat up, rubbing her eyes with her sleeve.

Olivia offered her handkerchief to the girl.

'Thanks.' Alice pressed it to her eyes.

'Are you feeling unwell? Or has something happened?'

With a gasp, Alice flung herself out of the chair. 'Nothing has happened! And now nothing ever will! Oh God, it's so awful! I hate it! I hate that I should be treated like a . . . like a *toy*, to be fooled around with, to be passed from pillar to post as if what I want doesn't matter at all!' She began to cry again.

On the sideboard there were silver chargers and dishes and a silver tray on which stood a jug and half a dozen glasses. Olivia poured water into a glass and put it in front of Alice.

'Take a sip. Is there anything I can do? Sometimes talking helps.'

Alice frowned. Her strange, cold eyes settled on Olivia. 'I expect you mean to be kind, but I really don't know why you're here. You're my mother's errand girl, aren't you? I'd like you to go. It's none of your business.'

Olivia left the room. *You're my mother's errand girl.* For a while, Alice Ruthwell's judgement of her rang in her ears, but once out in the street, hurrying back to Mrs Beaumont's premises, she was soon delightfully distracted by the bright shop windows and the rush and churn of London.

As each of the items in Grace's order was completed, Olivia took them to the Ruthwells' house. It was a pleasure to escape the stuffy workroom. Grace herself seemed busy and their interactions were brief, but on the day Olivia delivered the final item, the yellow silk wrap skirt, she asked her to take another note to Mr Ellwood.

This time, the South Audley Street house was quiet. As before, Olivia waited in the hall while the maid fetched Sammy. Though it was four in the afternoon, when he appeared he looked as if he had just got out of bed. His hair was tousled, and he was wearing a maroon silk robe over what appeared to be paisley pyjama trousers. The robe revealed a triangle of tanned, muscular chest.

He slit open the envelope and scanned Grace's letter. Then, with a slightly mocking bow, he took a pink rose from a vase and offered it to Olivia. 'Thanks, sweetheart.'

Olivia had left the house and was hurrying back along the road when she heard someone call out her name. Rory Madden was striding across the street towards her.

'Hello, there!' He caught sight of the rose Sammy had given her. 'What's that?'

'Oh, someone gave it to me.' She knew she was blushing and quickly added, 'Someone I had to deliver something to.'

'Are you often paid in roses?'

She laughed. 'No, not often. Where's Frankie?'

'Grace is taking him to the dentist. I've a couple of free

hours and thought I'd take the chance to get outside. Where are you headed?'

'Knightsbridge.'

'May I walk with you?'

'Please do.'

The walk through Hyde Park, which she must have taken a dozen times before, instantly became a delight. In Rory's company, she felt herself part of the great city instead of standing on the perimeter, at the centre of the story instead of occupying a superfluous role. She revelled in the heat of the sun; she enjoyed hearing the conversation and laughter of the small groups of young people, office workers and shop assistants, who had settled in twos and threes on the grass.

She broke the silence by asking Rory whether he had been Frankie's tutor for long.

'Six months. I'm from Ullapool, on the north-west coast of Scotland. I graduated last summer from the University of Edinburgh, then I travelled round Europe for a while. When I got home, I was at rather a loose end. I met Grace through a mutual acquaintance, and she asked me if I'd consider teaching Frankie.'

'Do you enjoy it?'

'I do, yes. It's hardly an onerous position. Frankie's a good lad.'

'He seems a dear little boy. Does Grace not want to send him to school?'

'She doesn't think he's ready for it.' They threaded round three nursemaids, talking to each other as they pushed prams. 'You must have noticed,' Rory said, once they were side by side again, 'that his reading isn't up to scratch. Boarding school is the usual thing for a boy of Frankie's age. If it wasn't for his problems, he'd have gone to school years ago.'

'I wondered whether he'd been unwell, whether that's why he's so behind.'

'His health isn't the best – he suffers from asthma – but no, I don't think so. To tell the truth, I've struggled to understand it. He can't seem to remember the sounds of the letters and yet I've been through them with him repeatedly. There's nothing wrong with his sight or hearing, Grace has had that checked. And I don't believe he lacks intelligence, though that's what Mr Ruthwell thinks.'

Olivia remembered the sandy-haired man who had addressed Grace so brusquely. Rory said, 'It's Mr Ruthwell's opinion that boarding school would sort Frankie out, knock him into shape. Toughen him up, you know, all that.'

'What does Mrs Ruthwell think?'

'She doesn't agree.'

'And you, Rory?'

'The right sort of school, one that would recognise the boy's qualities and give him extra help with his reading and writing, that might work, but not the usual brutish English public school. I can't imagine Frankie thriving somewhere like that.' Rory frowned as he looked out over the vista. 'It's frustrating, I thought I'd have him up to Common Entrance level after a month or two, but we're nowhere near that. I've suggested sending him to a day school, but Mr Ruthwell insists that he boards, and I suspect he gets what he wants. Frankie is his son and heir, no matter how unsuited he is for the role.' He squinted in the sun. 'The truth is that if the government speeds up conscription, I may not have much more time with the Ruthwells.'

Dark scars sliced through the green grass, trenches dug

the previous September at the time of the Munich crisis, when Britain had teetered on the edge of war. In her room in the hostel, a gas mask hung on the end of Olivia's bed. There were rumours of air-raid drills.

'If there is a war, my mother will want me to leave London,' she said. 'Is it dreadful of me to resent Hitler for that? It is, isn't it? You must think me very shallow.'

He laughed. 'Maybe a wee bit. I don't blame you, though.'

'Maybe it won't happen. Maybe Hitler will be satisfied with what he's got.'

They had stopped in the shade of a horse chestnut tree. Sunlight piercing through the leaves cast darting patterns of light and dark on Rory's features as he said softly, 'I can't see any endgame other than facing up to Hitler and beating him fair and square. Sorry to be blunt, Olivia, but I'm afraid that's how it is.'

On the ground floor of the Ruthwells' residence servants bustled about, carrying vases of flowers and stacks of linen. Maids wielded feather dusters and polished window panes. Olivia passed a dark green room where manservants were inserting leaves into an enormous dining table. Two other men were raising to the ceiling a sparkling glass chandelier. Along the corridor, in a larger room, the furniture had been cleared back against the walls and a grey-haired woman was slowly progressing across the floor on her hands and knees, polishing the boards.

Ahead of her, Alice Ruthwell stood poised in a doorway. 'Daddy, Mrs Mortimer has phoned and invited me to lunch, but I don't know whether . . .' The door closed, cutting off the rest of her sentence.

The morning room was in disarray, the small desk littered

with papers, some of which had slipped to the floor. Grace was standing by a side table on which stood an overflowing ashtray and a tray of coffee things.

'Olivia, how good of you to come. Always such a pleasure.' She twisted her hands together, frowning. 'I wondered whether I might ask you . . . but now that you're here . . . I should hate you to think I'm presuming on our friendship.'

Her use of the word 'friendship' warmed Olivia's heart. 'I would never think that.'

A shadow of a smile crossed Grace's features, then vanished. 'Something has happened,' she said. 'A letter of mine is missing. It should be in the bureau, but it's gone.'

As she gestured towards the desk, the balloon sleeve of her blouse caught the tray, sending the coffee cups and jug crashing to the floor. She gave a little gasp. Quickly, Olivia stooped to pick up the fallen items.

She cradled in her hands a tiny pink and gold cup. 'Oh dear, the handle's broken.'

'Oh, how infuriating!'

Olivia dabbed at the spilt coffee on the carpet while Grace rang for the maid. Summers appeared and Grace showed her the damaged cup.

'You must find someone to repair this.'

'Mrs Clarke says I must help with the ballroom floor. Elsie's had a funny turn. It's not right, madam, polishing floors isn't a lady's maid's work.' The girl sounded resentful.

'I'm afraid we all have to muck in today, what with the dinner party this evening.' Grace's voice took on a cajoling note. 'I'll make sure you have an extra afternoon off, Summers.'

The maid sniffed. 'Sneddon is good at repairing china, ma'am.'

'Very well, send him to me. And the carpet must be cleaned.'

'No one's free, madam. We're all behind like the cow's tail.' Summers left the room.

'That coffee set was a wedding gift.' Grace spoke quietly to Olivia. 'Though why I should care about *that* . . .' Her lips pressed together, and she shook her head.

Gently Olivia prompted, 'The letter you spoke of . . .'

'It was a very personal letter.' Grace looked away. 'I'm afraid there were certain details . . .' Moments passed, and then she cried out, 'The thought of a life without love, without passion, is unbearable to me!'

Olivia remembered the thrill she'd felt walking with Rory in the park. 'I understand,' she murmured.

Grace grasped her hand. 'I knew you would. Without feeling, without love, one may as well be dead! I'd sealed the letter, but I hadn't addressed the envelope. I had to leave the room – Frankie was upset – and when I came back in here after he had calmed down, it had gone!'

Someone tapped on the door. Grace let go of Olivia's hand. She raised her voice. 'Come in.'

The man who entered the room was young and dark-haired, good-looking in a florid, fleshy way. His gaze moved from Grace to Olivia. 'I've been sent to repair some broken china, madam.'

'Yes, Sneddon.' Grace gave him the cup and the handle. 'It's a clean break. Can you repair it?'

'I'll make it look as good as new, madam.' His upper lip twitched into a sneer. 'Will that be everything?'

'Thank you, yes. Have Mrs Clarke send up another tray of coffee. With two cups.'

Once the door had closed behind him, Grace said in a

lowered voice, 'He is Claude's valet and a perfectly vile man. It's horrible to think that anyone would steal my private correspondence, but Sneddon is more than capable of it. And I wouldn't put it past Summers either, the sly little thing.'

'But why would she do that?'

'For Claude.' Grace turned to Olivia. 'After all, he pays their wages.'

'You believe your husband has stolen your letter?'

'I'm certain of it.'

She had been slow to grasp, Olivia realised, that though the Ruthwell household seemed serene and enviable, dark undercurrents seethed beneath the surface.

Grace sat on the sofa. She patted a cushion and Olivia sat down beside her. 'I see the way Claude looks at me,' she said softly. 'I see the triumph in his eyes. He wants to divorce me, you see, and my letter gives him the ammunition he needs. I wouldn't mind a jot. I'd be happy never to see him again.' She gave a short, humourless laugh. 'It's only that I fear for Frankie. Claude despises him.'

'But Frankie's his *son*!'

Grace crushed her cigarette in the ashtray. 'Frankie isn't the son Claude wanted. He isn't a son Claude deems worthy of the Ruthwell name and inheritance – what remains of it. He has certain words for him. *Backward . . . halfwit . . . defective*. I've heard him use worse, Olivia. I'm afraid that he wants to divorce me so that he can remarry and sire another heir.' Despair etched itself into Grace Ruthwell's beautiful features. 'And now, because of my stupidity and carelessness, nothing will stand in his way.'

Olivia's mind raced. She thought of Frankie's endearing liveliness and enthusiasm. And how, at eleven years old, he stumbled through a reading book meant for a six-year-old.

Grace's eyes were the same hard blue as the sapphire pendant she wore at her throat. 'If Claude divorces me for adultery, he will show me no mercy. He will take me to court, where he will expose my private life to public view. He will ensure that my character is displayed in the worst possible light. You must believe me, Olivia, that if the contents of my letter were to be made public, I would be an object of gossip and contempt in every household in London.' Her voice lowered. 'I would have no further say in Frankie's upbringing. I would be unable to protect him. Claude would send him to a boarding school, and Frankie . . . His health is delicate. I'm afraid he wouldn't survive.'

Tears glittered their path down her cheeks. Outside in the garden, manservants were placing wrought-iron tables and chairs in the shade of the birch trees.

Olivia said, 'What will you do?'

Grace took a deep breath, then sat up straight. 'I must get my letter back. I suspect it's in Claude's study. He keeps the door locked and only he has the key. That wretch Sneddon is forever snooping about, spying on me. I dare say you saw the insolent way he looked at me just now.'

'I'm sorry.' Olivia felt the inadequacy of her words.

'I won't let him win.' Grace rose to her feet. 'I can play the game every bit as well as he. Claude has secrets too – there are things I know about him, shameful things. I'm not speaking of his squalid little mistresses. He has views . . . *opinions* . . . that I know he would wish to keep hidden at a time like this.'

The door opened and a maid came in carrying a tray of coffee things. It occurred to Olivia that in this large, luxurious house, Grace had little privacy. The most intimate conversation could be interrupted by one of the very servants she mistrusted.

The men had gone from the garden, so Grace suggested they take the coffee outside. They sat in the shade of an apple tree. Overhead, twigs and leaves made a green mesh against a forget-me-not sky.

She handed Olivia a cup of coffee. 'In the twenties, Claude was an admirer of Mussolini and became involved in one or two of the English fascist groups. I thought them silly little secret societies at the time, set up to amuse disgruntled landowners, eccentrics and inadequates. For a while, he was a supporter of Oswald Mosley, until he too fell out of favour. Claude considers Mosley to be too soft.'

Grace spoke quietly, as if unseen listeners might be hovering behind the open upper-storey windows.

'I've heard him speak with admiration of Hitler. Not openly recently, not since the man's utter wickedness was exposed, but I'm sure his views haven't altered one iota. Claude is a member of the Anglo-German Fellowship. Have you heard of it, Olivia?'

'I have, yes.' The Anglo-German Fellowship had been mentioned at the political meeting she and Louise had attended. Though its members described it as an association to promote business links between Britain and Germany, some at the meeting had considered it to be a conduit between the Nazi Party and British sympathisers.

Grace stirred sugar into her coffee. 'There are men who share his loathing of the current government, and they also share his admiration of Hitler. He dines regularly with bores like Hugh Grosvenor and Lord Brocket. Sammy has seen him in the company of George Pitt-Rivers and Barry Domvile.' Her lip curled. 'If I'm to outmanoeuvre Claude, then I must find out what his intentions are. That will be my only chance of protecting Frankie. Don't you see, Olivia?

Claude won't want his allegiances with fascists made public, not now, when at any day we may declare war against Germany. He will recognise the danger to himself should his loyalty to his country be in doubt.'

Olivia grasped the enormity of what Grace was implying. 'Do you believe that Mr Ruthwell is capable of betraying his country?'

'Betrayal is such a strong word. But yes, it's possible.'

Sunlight tumbling through the leaves cast shifting shadows on Grace's face, as Olivia found herself saying, 'Is there anything I can do to help?'

Chapter Two

1939, London

You're my mother's errand girl. It was hard to disagree with Alice Ruthwell's statement. Olivia delivered her parcels of fairy-tale gowns enfolded in whispering tissue paper; she took *billet doux* to Grace Ruthwell's lover.

And yet now the nature of her errands had altered. Within days of Grace confiding in her, Olivia found herself standing in the shade of the trees that grew in the green square in Hinton Place, waiting until Mr Ruthwell came out of the house. Her heart gave a little ripple of anticipation as she watched him stride along the pavement. She followed him, keeping out of sight, until he entered a glittering establishment in Piccadilly or St James's. Then she turned for home as the day faded to dusk.

It was only when she rose early the next morning to get ready for work that her behaviour troubled her. She had drifted away from the irrefutable code of her childhood that had been drilled into her by her mother. Always tell the truth, never do anything you might later regret. Grace was hoping to blackmail her husband and Olivia had volunteered to help. She herself was abetting a venture that could be considered, if you looked at it dispassionately, despicable. In taking a lover, Grace, too, was guilty of betrayal.

When she stepped out into the sunshine to walk to work, these scruples fell away. If Mr Ruthwell really was a Nazi, then wasn't it her duty to expose him?

One afternoon, delivering fabric samples to Hinton Place, Grace handed Olivia a parcel. 'I wondered whether you might like this, dear. I wanted to say thank you for everything you're doing for me. My silly daughter refuses to wear it and you are about the same size, I think.'

When she was out of sight of the Ruthwells' house, Olivia peered beneath the wrapping and glimpsed the gleam of lilac satin. Back at the hostel, she spread out the evening gown on the bed. It was exquisite, and in perfect condition apart from a small tear in the hem, though that could easily be fixed.

She scooped up her hair and knotted it at the back of her neck. Dressed in Alice Ruthwell's lilac satin gown, she looked older, no longer one of the sewing-room girls, but a woman, a woman who might do anything and who might become whoever she wanted.

On Thursday evening, Mr Ruthwell hailed a taxi. Hidden beneath her mackintosh hood and umbrella and elated by her own daring, Olivia walked past him as he gave the address to the taxi driver.

'Paper Buildings, Inner Temple.' His commanding voice cut through the drizzle.

She made it her mission to share this piece of information with Grace as soon as she could.

A few weeks later, Olivia was in the sewing room, attaching a lace panel to the front of a sleeveless blouse, when she caught sight of Grace Ruthwell making her way to the fitting room. Now and again the familiar warm, cultured voice floated through the open door.

On leaving work, she headed along the pavement and noticed a black car parked along the street. Grace was sitting in the driver's seat. She opened the window.

'Hello, Olivia! Would you like a lift home?'

Olivia climbed into the car and sank into a seat of soft, luxurious caramel-coloured leather as Grace pulled out into the traffic.

'Such a stunning new dress Violet is making up for me. But dear me, I'm quite worn out with all the fittings.' As she braked for the junction with Cromwell Road, she turned to Olivia and smiled. 'So clever of you to find out about Paper Buildings, darling. Sammy had a word with one of the porters. A man called Wyndham Cotter rents a flat there. Sammy says he gives a supper party every Thursday night, a private event by invitation only.' She gave a throaty laugh. 'I imagine canapés followed by, no doubt, a patriotic beef Wellington. Drinks and toasts and the odd Nazi salute. What wouldn't I give to be a fly on the wall at one of those parties! I had the idea that I would disguise myself as a waitress so that I could eavesdrop. Dear Sammy is trying to talk me out of it. He says Claude would recognise me.'

'I expect he's right.'

'He probably is. Such a bore.'

Office workers were streaming along the pavements. Two young women, arm in arm and wearing matching pink and navy-blue outfits, strolled, chatting. A black man in sailor's uniform carried a parrot in a cage. Olivia loved London, the busy variety of its inhabitants, the zing of infinite possibility.

The car glided smoothly into Earls Court Road. 'It's just here,' she said.

Grace glanced across the road to the soot-stained red-brick building. 'Is that where you room? It looks rather grim.'

Olivia wished, then, that she had asked to be dropped off at the corner of the road. Seeing her home through Grace's eyes was discomfiting; it reminded her of the gulf between them.

'It's quite comfortable,' she said quickly. 'The girls are very friendly.'

'Friendship . . . that's what matters most.'

An idea occurred to her. 'Mr Ruthwell wouldn't recognise *me*. I could engage myself as a waitress.'

Grace frowned. 'No, I couldn't possibly consider it.'

'Please, Grace, let me help.'

'Sweet of you, but I'm not sure you understand . . .'

'When I was younger, I had a Saturday job at a hotel in Crewkerne, so I've waitressed before.' The more Olivia thought about it, the more the plan excited her. 'A girl I know at the hostel works for a catering agency in the evenings, to earn extra money. She told me that they're always short-staffed.'

'No.' An emphatic shake of the head. 'No, it's too risky.'

'Mr Ruthwell has never spoken to me. And I'm hardly likely to be recognised by anyone at the party.'

'The dress shop . . . Violet's clientele. There are female fascists too, Olivia.'

'I don't have much to do with Mrs Beaumont's clients. It's usually the more experienced assistants who help in the fitting rooms. Besides, I'd make myself look different, I'd curl my hair and borrow a pair of spectacles. And I'd be wearing a maid's uniform. People never notice the servants.'

Grace's gloved hand drummed the steering wheel. 'But why would you do this for me?'

'I want to help you and Frankie if I can. And you've been so kind to me, Grace.'

'Oh, my dear . . .' Pressing her lips together, Grace looked away. Then she said briskly, 'I must go. We're to take the sleeper train to Scotland tonight. I'll be so relieved when Alice's engagement to Ivo Mortimer is announced, and we're no longer obliged to attend these frightful house parties.' She sighed. 'I don't know. To tell the truth, it makes me nervous. If I could only think of another way.'

'Let me do it, Grace.' Olivia climbed out of the car. 'Let me help you, please.'

'Name?' At the entrance to the flat in Paper Buildings, a tall, balding man in butler's uniform of tailcoat and boiled shirt peered at her.

'Nellie Jones.' Olivia attempted a cockney accent.

The butler studied a list. 'Jones . . .' He put a tick against a name. 'Hurry up, then.'

'Where should I leave my things?'

He made an impatient gesture. 'Down there. Servants' room.' He barked directions at her.

In the end, it had been surprisingly easy. Mr Ellwood had found out the name of the agency supplying serving staff for Mr Cotter's parties and had written a glowing reference for the maidservant Nellie Jones, asserting that she was conscientious, hard-working, honest and clean. Grace had procured a parlourmaid's uniform: black dress, white apron and a cap that refused to stay securely in place. A friend who belonged to a drama society lent Olivia a pair of plain-lensed horn-rimmed spectacles, and her roommate, Louise, pin-curled her hair and crimped her fringe. Now and then she breathed in a whiff of singed hair. When she had peered into the mirror before leaving the hostel that evening, an unfamiliar woman had looked back at her.

A short, plump gentleman was standing near the door to a drawing room, pumping the hand of a newly arrived guest. His dark hair was smoothed slickly back from his forehead, which gave him the look, she thought, of a self-important seal.

Catching sight of a maidservant carrying a tray of empty glasses, Olivia followed her through a green-painted door. There, in a low-ceilinged room, barmen made cocktails and maids jostled each other as they exchanged trays of empty glasses for others bearing drinks.

'Are you Nellie?' A freckle-faced girl with a heavy jaw was addressing her.

'Yes.'

'At bloody last. I'm Dora.' A tray of cocktails was thrust at her. 'As soon as you've finished, come back here for the next lot. Don't forget to collect the empties for washing or we'll run out.' Protruding eyes the colour of oysters examined her. 'You need to straighten up your cap or Finchie will have a go at you.'

In the corridor, Olivia balanced the tray against a bookcase and tried to sort out her starched white cap. A slight, dark-haired girl in maid's uniform, coming from the direction of the party, smiled at her.

'Here, may I help?' She tweaked the corners of Olivia's cap. 'There, that's better. Are you new too? It's my first time waitressing and I'm all fingers and thumbs. I'm Rebecca.' She had a faint accent.

'Nellie. Thanks. I'm pleased to meet you. Will we be serving dinner tonight?'

The girl shook her head. 'There's to be a private supper later for Mr Cotter and a few special guests. Mr Finch and one of the barmen are to serve it. We girls only do the drinks and canapés.'

'Is Mr Finch the butler?'

'That's right. One of the other waitresses told me he has a temper.'

'I'll keep out of his way, then.'

Olivia took her tray into the drawing room. The air was thick with cigarette smoke; voices echoed off the wooden panels. Offering round cocktails, she wove in and out of the clusters of guests. There were women as well as men, the older ones with their ropes of pearls and ostrich feathers occupying the comfortable chairs at the perimeter, the younger women in paler colours, their filmy silk overdresses embroidered with flowers or encrusted with beads. Though she searched through the crowds, she couldn't see Claude Ruthwell.

Every so often the butler, Mr Finch, stood in the doorway and announced a new arrival. 'Mr Bartholomew Fitzgibbon! Captain Reynold Strathclyde-Morris!' Olivia memorised the names.

The guests' conversation did not pause as they took their cocktails from her, and she listened out for scraps of dialogue that might be useful to Grace. Once the tray was empty, she gathered up discarded glasses and took them to the scullery. There was still no sign of Claude Ruthwell. Perhaps he wasn't coming tonight after all.

Back in the drawing room, she offered drinks to two men standing in a corner. She took her time collecting up the empties from a nearby side table so that she could eavesdrop. It was all going rather well, she thought. She had filed away in her memory a dozen names and had discovered that some at this gathering had higher status than others.

Someone tapped on her shoulder, making her jump. It was the butler, Mr Finch. 'Get a move on, girl. The canapés should be out by now.'

Olivia headed back towards the servants' quarters. But as she approached the corridor, Claude Ruthwell emerged from a side door. She passed him so closely they almost touched.

'Where is Finch?' she heard him asking someone. 'I need him to run an errand for me.'

Inside the servants' room, tray after tray of canapés was thrust into waiting hands. Olivia took one. Pink peeled prawns nestled in puff-pastry beds.

Claude Ruthwell stood sentinel-like at the entrance to the drawing room, surrounded by half a dozen other guests who hung on his every word.

Olivia carried her tray into the room. As the grim social event rolled on, she began to look forward to being back at the hostel, curled up on her bed with a book or chatting with her roommates, doing something *normal*, with nice, normal people. It occurred to her that she had been wrong in assuming that helping Grace retrieve her compromising letter was the most important matter. The stakes were far higher than that.

As the guests started to leave, she was instructed to gather up the empty glasses.

Approaching the corridor, she saw that the door to a side room was ajar. She might be able to hear the conversation within. Yet the thought of being caught made her stomach turn.

From a tray abandoned on a bookcase, she grabbed a cocktail and downed it in two gulps. The fiery liquid scorched her throat and she had to stifle a cough, but it gave her Dutch courage. Mr Finch was no longer at his post in the hallway; instead, a bored-looking manservant was showing the partygoers out.

From inside the room, she caught the sound of Claude Ruthwell's dry upper-class drawl. 'Chamberlain and his ship of fools will be susceptible to Jewish influence. They rely on Jew money. We must be prepared, if war is declared, with our response. You will make yourselves ready. When the time comes, I will inform you of your individual responsibilities.'

'If war is declared, then surely we'll have failed.' The speaker sounded hesitant. 'All our efforts to keep peace with Germany will have been in vain.'

'You dolt, Gordon. How long do you think our defences will hold out if faced with the might of Hitler's forces? We will crumble, we will be destroyed. If an invasion of this country were to take place, we need to make sure our voices are heard. We must be ready to take on whatever role destiny demands of us.' Claude Ruthwell's voice hardened. 'Cotter, you've left that damned door open.'

'Sorry, Claude.'

The scrape of a chair being drawn back. Olivia darted deeper down the corridor.

With a soft click, the door closed. She hurried back to the drawing room. One thing was now clear to her. Claude Ruthwell didn't merely belong to the inner circle: he was its leader.

The next hour passed in a blur of tiredness, but once the drawing room was clear and the kitchen clean and tidy, Mr Finch paid the maids and barmen, and Olivia was free to leave. Outside, the lamps and trees pasted black and white shadows on the lawn. As she hurried through the garden, she saw that someone was walking towards her. The yellow flare of his cigarette lighter illuminated his face, and to her horror she recognised Mr Ruthwell's valet, Sneddon. She fought the impulse to turn and run, and instead stooped and pretended to lace up her shoes. As he passed, her heart thudded.

The front door opened, and as soon as Sneddon had entered the building, Olivia tore off her starched cap and began to run.

Chapter Three

1939, London

At the hostel, she wrote a letter to Grace, giving an account of the evening while it was still fresh in her memory.

Days then passed, and as Thursday approached, Olivia was relieved not to have been asked to return to the flat in Paper Buildings. She never wanted to see those people again.

But when another week went by and there was still no word from Grace, she began to feel uneasy. Could it be that Mr Ruthwell had intercepted the letter she had written her?

A client of Mrs Beaumont's, a society girl, was to marry at six weeks' notice, so everyone was hard at work making the wedding gown and trousseau. 'Sounds like someone's jumped the gun,' one of Olivia's colleagues sniggered. A nice, motherly seamstress whose twenty-year-old son had recently been called up, scolded her, and said she expected the groom was joining the forces, poor fellow.

Olivia had been assigned the task of sewing frills onto the scooped backs of the bridesmaids' dresses. The fabric was a slippery slate-blue satin, which slithered through the fingers. Towards the end of the afternoon, she was told to bring her work to Mrs Beaumont's office so that it could be checked.

'Very neat.' Mrs Beaumont peered closely at the frill. 'You will take care round the fastening, won't you?'

'Yes, Mrs Beaumont.'

Olivia made to leave, but Mrs Beaumont stopped her. 'I've been meaning to have a word with you, dear. Close the door.' Frowning, she pushed her spectacles to the top of her head, where they balanced precariously on her silver-streaked brown curls. 'Grace Ruthwell is one of our most valued clients,' she said. 'She is also a dear friend of mine. A woman in her position has a busy life. I hope you appreciate that.' The myopic blue gaze settled on Olivia.

Bewildered, Olivia said, 'Yes, Mrs Beaumont.'

'I wouldn't want to have to worry that you were overstepping the mark.'

What had she heard? Could she have somehow found out about the errands Olivia ran – her visits to Sammy Ellwood . . . or even Paper Buildings?

'Of course not,' she murmured.

'I've been told you accepted a lift in Mrs Ruthwell's car.'

Olivia recalled the evening when Grace had picked her up outside the shop and driven her to her home. 'Yes, but I didn't . . .' she began.

'Mrs Ruthwell is a kind and generous woman. It would concern me if I thought you were taking advantage of her good nature.' The telephone rang; Mrs Beaumont's hand hovered over it, and she went on blandly, 'Do you understand, Olivia?'

Flushing, she muttered, 'Yes, Mrs Beaumont.'

Her employer picked up the receiver. Olivia went back to the sewing room. Her fellow workers were discussing who was the more attractive, Cary Grant or Clark Gable. *Overstepping the mark . . . taking advantage* . . . She burned with humiliation and anger. One of her workmates must have seen her getting into the car with Grace and told Mrs Beaumont.

Six o'clock arrived and Olivia hurried out of the premises. As she walked home, she realised that she was heading in the direction of Hinton Place. Climbing the steps, poised to ring the doorbell, she was suddenly nervous. Perhaps she had presumed too much.

She rang the bell. A maid opened it – and then the sight of Rory, slinging on a jacket as he crossed the hall, cheered her instantly.

'Olivia!' He smiled at her. 'Grace is in the country, I'm afraid.'

'Oh! It doesn't matter.'

'I was just going out to post these.' He had a bundle of letters in his hand, and a copy of André Maurois' *Ariel* was peeking out of his jacket pocket. 'What about you? Are you free? Yes? Splendid.'

He tucked her hand into his arm. Her heart lifted as they made their way down the street.

Rory had spent the last fortnight with the Ruthwells at Corfield, their country house in Staffordshire. They had intended to stay there for only a few days, but then Frankie's asthma had flared up. He was on the mend now, but the doctor had been called several days running; for more than a week, Grace had slept in her son's room.

The Ruthwells had since moved on to the Mortimers' place in Hertfordshire. Alice Ruthwell was now engaged to be married to Ivo Mortimer. 'Lots of fuss, you can imagine,' Rory said, with a touch of cynicism. 'Mr and Mrs Ruthwell are as happy as Larry.' Rory had been sent back to London to run errands for Grace before her return to Hinton Place tomorrow.

Olivia's spirits lightened now that she knew why Grace hadn't contacted her. Relief put a smile on her face and a spring in her step.

'Are you enjoying *Ariel*, Rory?' she asked.

'Very much. Have you read it?'

'Not yet.'

'I've only a few pages left. If you like, I can lend it to you. Are you hungry, Olivia?'

'Ravenous,' she said.

'Do you like Italian food?'

'I've never tried it.'

'No time like the present, then. I know a decent little Italian café in Soho. Do you fancy going there?'

The café was shaded by green and white striped awnings; scarlet geraniums flourished in pots by the front door. Waiters hurried between the small tables. The menu was in Italian, so Rory offered to order for them both. As he spoke to the waiter, Olivia looked round the room. The posters on the walls were of Italian cities; a Puccini aria was playing on the gramophone.

All the diners were young. Rory told her that the café was popular with students. The men wore corduroy trousers and shirts or jerseys that had gone through at the elbows, while the girls were scruffily chic in hip-hugging skirts or slacks and short-sleeved hand-knitted jerseys in subtle colours. They wore their hair in blunt fringes or casually swept back beneath a bandeau. She would make herself a pair of slacks, Olivia decided; she would knit a mustard or lichen-green short-sleeved jersey.

Rory must come here often, because a stream of people stopped to chat with him. He introduced them to Olivia. 'Alf's just back from Spain,' he explained. Or 'Johnnie and I were at school together,' or 'Vicky and I hiked in the Dolomites last summer.'

Their food arrived. 'Like this,' Rory said, helping her twirl the long strands of spaghetti round her fork. 'You're nimble-fingered, Olivia, you'll have the knack of it in no time.'

The food was delicious, the red wine they drank tart and heavenly. 'There aren't any Italian cafés where I live,' she said.

'That's Somerset, isn't it? The Scottish Highlands aren't exactly teeming with them either.'

'You've travelled a lot, haven't you, Rory?'

'A fair bit. It's funny, though, I still sometimes feel as if I'm on the outside, looking on. As if I haven't got away from being that lanky lad living in the middle of nowhere and impatient to see the world.'

'I wouldn't have thought someone like you would feel like that.'

He grinned at her. 'Maybe everyone does. Maybe it's a disease of the young.'

She smiled. 'Maybe when we're middle-aged, we'll know exactly what we're doing.'

She loved the broad sweep of his forehead and the fall of his chestnut hair. For the first time she noticed that his grey eyes were flecked with a darker shade, like sea-washed granite.

A slim, pretty girl wearing a beret rakishly to one side of her head came into the café and cried out, 'Rory, darling!'

'Hello, Paddy.'

Paddy waved her cigarette at Olivia. 'Who's this?'

'This is a friend of mine, Olivia Goodland. Olivia, meet Paddy Stephens.'

Hellos were exchanged. Resting her hand on Rory's shoulder, Paddy stooped close to him. 'Give me a light, darling,' she murmured. 'I'm clean out of matches.'

Rory lit Paddy's cigarette. After more smiles and pouts, Paddy drifted off to another table. They had seemed very intimate together, Olivia thought, and it was a few distracted, jealous seconds before she could focus on what Rory was saying.

'When we were in the country, some of Claude Ruthwell's chums came to Corfield. The after-dinner conversation, once the women had left the table . . . it sickened me. They see Stalin as the real threat. In their eyes, we're heading into the wrong war; we should be fighting the Soviets, not the Germans. The "Russian menace" was the phrase they used.' He twisted his mouth to one side. 'I grant you we're being forced to choose between a rock and a hard place. You'd prefer not to be bedfellows with either dictator.'

Tripartite talks were currently going on between the Russians, the French and the British. In the mornings, hurrying to work, Olivia scanned the newspaper hoardings. These days, they walked a knife edge.

She said, 'Did you say anything?'

'I said that if Hitler and Stalin were to make an alliance, then God help us all.' Rory laughed drily. 'They told me I was a fool, an ignorant youth who didn't understand the situation. And I let it go.' The humour drained from his eyes. 'It was cowardly of me.'

'You did your best.'

'No, I don't think so. I should have tried harder.' He

stabbed his fork into the pasta. 'People like the Ruthwells, like their friends, have influence. They have a *voice*. What troubled me most was their defeatism. Mr Ruthwell and his circle have friends in Germany. They'll be passing on the message to Hitler that if it comes to war, Britain will throw in the towel. And I'm afraid that will only embolden him. He may come to believe that if he sparks off a war in Europe, he'll have a free hand.'

Olivia thought of Wyndham Cotter's supper party. Should she confide in Rory? Should she share what she knew, that Mr Ruthwell and his compatriots were already planning the peace negotiations that would follow defeat?

But she kept her counsel. Only once she was sure that Grace had retrieved her compromising letter would she be able to talk freely.

And anyway, Rory was saying apologetically, 'Sorry. Gloomy subject. Girls tell me off all the time for being too serious. Ice cream and coffee?'

After they left the café, they walked through Haymarket and Whitehall to Westminster Bridge. He put his arm around her waist, and she leaned her head against his shoulder. She felt the warmth of his body and his cheek brushed against the crown of her head. If she had ever felt a little envious of couples strolling in the evening sunshine, she was not now; instead, she was blissfully happy because she was with the nicest and handsomest man in London.

'Don't you love it here?' he murmured.

'It's so perfect. Just look at it.'

The view from the bridge was breathtaking. Sunlight flashed on the waters of the Thames and on the many windows of the Houses of Parliament. It was growing late, and only a handful of people wandered along the span.

When he kissed her, the city retreated, and it was as if she and Rory were alone in this magical place that hovered between land and water.

The following morning, attaching the final frill to a bridesmaid's dress, she joined in the sewing-room chatter and told her colleagues about Rory taking her to the Italian restaurant. 'Olivia's got a boyfriend!' sang one of the girls, and for once she didn't even blush. It was true. Rory had kissed her, and it had been divine. Before they had parted, he had asked her to accompany him to a dinner and dance. He would write to her as soon as he knew the details. She pictured the two of them circling the dance floor. She would wear the gown that had once belonged to Alice Ruthwell, and the lilac satin skirt would flare out as they twirled.

At a quarter to six, Mrs Beaumont beckoned her out of the room. 'Have you finished that dress?'

'Yes, Mrs Beaumont.'

'Thank goodness. I'll be relieved when this order is off my hands. If you would take this round to Hinton Place . . .' A parcel was thrust at her. Mrs Beaumont said stiffly, 'Grace saw this silk wrap last time she was here, but she wasn't sure about it. She has just telephoned, asking to wear it tonight. She's giving a reception to celebrate her daughter's engagement.' Her eyes evaded Olivia's. 'She was most insistent you bring it.'

'Yes, Mrs Beaumont.' Olivia tried not to sound triumphant.

Outside, she made for Mayfair. In the warmth of this August afternoon, the sunlit gardens were heavy with leaf and bloom. Clematis spilled over the walls, and the pinks in the pots on the doorsteps gave off their heady perfume. She smiled at the thought of seeing Grace again. She might see Rory, too. She revelled in the memory of how neatly his hand had rested on her hipbone and the cool, dry touch of his lips.

A harassed-looking maid showed her into the house and directed her upstairs to Mrs Ruthwell's bedroom. Servants bustled up and down, carrying buckets and brooms; some distance away, a raised voice called out for cream to be fetched from the dairy.

Grace rose from her dressing table as Olivia came into the room. She was wearing her red silk kimono. Olivia gave her the parcel, but Grace put it on a side table without opening it, then gestured to Olivia to shut the door behind her.

In a low voice, she said, 'I have the key.'

'The key?'

'To Claude's study.' The older woman's expression was jubilant. 'We returned from the country this morning. Claude went out after luncheon. An hour ago, I was passing his bedroom and I saw that the door was ajar. His keys were on the table. It was the work of a moment to slip the study key off the chain.'

'Do you have your letter?'

'No.' Grace's eyes flicked to the door. 'I don't dare. The servants, they're everywhere today. I feel them watching me.'

'How horrible.' Olivia felt a pang of pity for Grace, locked in conflict with the man who should love and protect her. 'Perhaps if you tried at night-time?'

'I thought of that.' Grace gave a conspiratorial smile. 'I imagined myself tiptoeing downstairs in the dark, dressed in black like a cat burglar. But I'm afraid to leave it so late. The longer I wait, the more likely it is that he will notice the key has gone.' As she spoke, she paced back and forth.

A spot of scarlet bloomed on each of her pale cheeks. 'I'm so close. I can't fail now. This may be my only chance. And then I thought of you.'

'If there's anything I can do . . .'

'You'd do that for me? You'd get my letter back for me?'

Olivia had thought Grace might ask her to take another note to Sammy, something like that, and Sammy would come to the party and sneak into Mr Ruthwell's study. But that was impossible. Sammy Ellwood was Grace's lover. Mr Ruthwell would never let him into the house.

Grace must have seen her hesitate, because she said, 'I'm sorry, forgive me. I shouldn't have asked you.' She pressed her hands together. 'Help me choose my jewellery, please, Olivia. You are so clever at that sort of thing. This is the gown I shall be wearing tonight.'

She gestured to the cocktail dress of gold lamé, burnished with a pattern of ivy leaves, that hung on the wardrobe door.

Olivia sighed. 'It's exquisite.'

'Isn't it? It was made for me in Paris. What do you think? This one – or this?'

Olivia pointed to the simpler of the two gold necklaces Grace held up. 'I'll do it,' she said, and suppressed a stab of fear. 'I'll get your letter for you, Grace.'

'Are you quite sure?'

'Yes, I'm sure.'

'Then thank you.' The words were soft and fervent. 'Thank you, my dear.'

'What about Mr Ruthwell?' The thought of him coming across her rifling through his study made a chill run down her spine.

'The reception is to be held outside, in the garden. Claude

and I will be receiving our guests. The servants will be occupied with the drinks and canapés. I've told Summers that as we're short-staffed, she must give a hand too.'

'Mightn't Mr Ruthwell notice the key is gone when he comes home?'

'Then I shall be done for, I'm afraid. All I can do is hope for the best.' Grace glanced at her watch. 'He's cutting it fine. He'll be in a hurry to dress for the evening, especially with Sneddon away. Sneddon's mother is ill, so he has gone to be with her, in Wales. If my luck holds, there should be no reason for Claude to go to his study.'

That Mr Sneddon was far from London was a relief. Olivia recalled the valet's handsome, dissolute face and the fear she had felt in the garden of Paper Buildings, kneeling among the roses.

Together, they planned. Olivia would wait in Grace's bedroom until half past seven. If anyone came across her, she would say that she was repairing an item of Grace's clothing. No one would notice that she hadn't left the house, and by the time she went downstairs, the party would be in full flow.

'I shall stick to Claude like a *limpet*.' Grace flashed a smile at her. 'I shan't let him out of my sight, I swear to you!' She ran her fingertips over a tray of rings. 'If you have any qualms at all . . .'

'I don't.'

For a moment Grace shut her eyes. 'To tell the truth, I'm at my wits' end,' she murmured. 'I shouldn't ask this of you, Olivia. But there are so few people I can trust. I thought of begging Rory to help me – I count him as a friend – but I can't bring myself to. The truth is that I'm ashamed of this silly mess I've got myself into. I'm not sure a man would understand how I feel. I believe that men and women feel differently about love, that *our* feelings are stronger and deeper.' Her voice lowered to a whisper. 'We women have so much more to lose.'

Olivia helped her into the gold lamé gown, which fell with a soft susurration over her ecru silk petticoat, and clasped the chain round her neck. A pair of gold sandals, a spray of Shalimar, a dash of scarlet lipstick.

'How do I look?' The older woman studied her reflection in the cheval mirror.

'You look magnificent.' Olivia had never seen Grace Ruthwell appear more imperial, more mesmeric.

'You are a true friend to me. I will never forget this.' Grace clasped Olivia's hands in hers, then left the room.

Alone, Olivia waited. As the strains of violin and cello murmuring the sweet, liquid tones of the latest Ivor Novello song drifted from the garden through an open window into the bedroom, the nugget of fear hardened inside her. The hum of conversation rose as the Ruthwells' guests arrived. She heard the distant pop of champagne corks and the chink of glasses, and she saw clearly all the ways in which this plan of Grace's, conjured up on the spur of the moment by a desperate woman, could go wrong. Mr Ruthwell might think to fetch something from his study. He might leave the garden for the house, for whatever reason, just as Olivia was unlocking the door to his private domain. The letter might not be in his room. It might have been lodged with his solicitor weeks ago.

Time seemed to have solidified. It crawled, sluggish and aching, so that when she glanced at her watch, she was shocked to see that it was only ten past seven. She longed for this ordeal to be behind her. She would have liked to cut short her rising anxiety by heading downstairs immediately, but she must not, she must wait, as Grace had instructed her to. On the surface of the dressing table were crumpled tissues, spilt powder and half a dozen Elizabeth Arden lipsticks, some fallen on their side. Summers would have tidied the room, Olivia thought, had she not been consigned to handing round drinks in the garden.

Too restless to be still, her fingers trailed over a satinwood side table, a velvet cushion. Grace's perfume lingered in the air. A sound made her retreat and hide in the folds of a chartreuse curtain, her heart beating wildly. The footsteps faded. From this viewpoint, a corner of the garden was visible, and the idyllic scene distracted her a little from her anxiety. The chiffons and taffetas of the women's gowns fluttered as they moved, echoing the quivering leaves of the birches. Sunlight glittered on diamond necklaces and on a narrow rill of water. Olivia imagined Grace standing at the central point where the paths met, a flaring column of gold, everyone's eyes on her.

Might Rory be in the garden, too? Or was he ensconced in some distant corner of the house, playing snakes and ladders with Frankie? If only he were here with her! Then she would feel sure of herself, then she would no longer be haunted by the fear that in doing this for Grace, she was making a mistake. It was not true, what she had said earlier to Grace, that she had no qualms. It was a low and sneaky thing, to search through a man's private papers, however despicable that man might be. Six months ago – a month ago – she would never have contemplated taking such a risk.

Grace had said nothing to her about the party at Paper Buildings. Had she even read the letter that Olivia had written with such care? The silk wrap remained on the table, still in its brown paper wrapping.

She could leave now, walk out of the house, never look back.

And yet she had promised. She recalled Grace's feverish disquiet, her terror that she might be separated from Frankie. The older woman was possessed of a single-minded determination, but she had good reason for that. Her obsession was understandable: she was driven to protect her child. *We women have so much more to lose.* It mattered, what happened to Frankie. How lost he would feel, and how despairing, abandoned in an unfamiliar place among strangers!

Twenty-five past seven. Heat was gathering in the bedroom, and Olivia pulled at the collar of her blouse. She went over the plan in her head. Grace had warned her to look out for stragglers. From the top of the stairs, she would be able to hear any late arrivals to the party. The letter would be easy to pick out because Grace always used the same pinkish-buff stationery. She herself had delivered the thick, watermarked envelopes the colour of blush roses to Mr Ellwood's house.

Half past seven. Olivia checked the key was in her pocket and left the room, closing the door with a soft click. She stood on the landing, looking down. She could see no one. She heard only the distant tapestry of sounds from the garden.

Silently she made her way downstairs before heading along the corridor to Claude Ruthwell's study. Her hands, slippery with sweat, fumbled, and as the key struck the marble floor, the clang seemed to reverberate in the silent corridor like a gunshot. She scooped it up, throwing a fearful glance along the passageway. Her hand shook violently as she unlocked the door. And then she was inside, her mouth dry, her heart hammering.

Bookcases, armchair, fireplace. The desk was beneath the window. She hoped the slatted blind hid the interior from the pavement beyond. Above the surface of the desk were slots for stationery and an alcove containing an inkwell and fountain pen and several little drawers with tiny brass knobs. An unfinished letter lay on the sheet of blotting paper on the desktop. She couldn't see a blush-pink envelope. Anxiety flooded through her. Perhaps Grace was wrong, perhaps the letter wasn't here. She reached out her hand to a drawer.

She heard a sound behind her and spun round. Mr Ruthwell's valet, Sneddon, was standing in the doorway. A sneer played on his full red lips.

'Well, well,' he said. 'May I help you?'

'I'm not . . . I wasn't . . .' Frozen by fear, she could not have run even if he hadn't been barring her way.

'I expect you're looking for this.' He took something out of an inner jacket pocket. He held up a pink envelope.

A sound escaped her. Sneddon cocked his head to one side. 'What a versatile little girl you are. Sewing . . . waitressing . . . and now a spot of thieving. It's a bad habit of yours, isn't it, Olivia Goodland, or Nellie Jones, or whatever you're calling yourself today. I'm going to teach you not to snoop into other people's affairs.'

Stepping forward, he pinned her against the desk. Though she tried to pull away, he was stronger and held her in an iron grip. His hand fumbled beneath her skirt; she gasped.

'What are you going to do?' he murmured. 'Scream? I don't think so.'

'Let me go!' His fingers were kneading the top of her

thigh. She heard herself pleading with him. 'Please . . . Please don't!'

'Why not? It's what you deserve. You're a naughty girl, aren't you?'

He shoved his body hard against hers. She couldn't breathe.

A bell rang – voices, chatter and a loud peal of laughter. More guests were arriving. Sneddon released her. 'Keep your nose out of other people's business,' he murmured. 'Next time, I promise you I'll finish the job. Now get out.'

He dragged her from the room and flung her out of the front door. It slammed shut as she stumbled down the steps.

Olivia tugged down her skirt and tried clumsily to tuck her blouse back into the waistband. Passers-by gave her curious stares. Blindly she made her way to Hyde Park, where she found a quiet spot behind some shrubs and fell, shaking and nauseous, to the grass. She hadn't realised she was crying until she put her hand up to her face and discovered it was wet. The nightmare voice echoed in her head – *I'm going to teach you not to snoop into other people's affairs . . . It's what you deserve.* She still felt Sneddon's hands on her, roughly probing.

Eventually the sickness retreated. The grass was dotted with courting couples. Though it was a warm evening, she felt cold inside. She ran her hands up and down her arms to rub away the chill. Then she rose, straightened her stockings, smoothed down her clothing and headed for the Underground station.

Back at the hostel, she found a vacant bathroom and scrabbled in her purse for the three pennies needed to use it. She soaked for a long time in the hot water, scrubbing herself over and over, scouring off Sneddon's imprint. Eventually another girl hammered on the door and asked her how much longer she was going to be. Olivia clambered out of the water, wrapped herself in a towel and went back to her cubicle.

Louise had to shake her awake in the morning. Olivia dragged herself out of bed. Buttons slipped; stockings laddered as she dressed clumsily.

And yet there was relief in being at work, in hemming skirts and pinning darts, in undertaking familiar tasks she had known since childhood. The trousseau was almost complete. The wedding was to take place the following day, Saturday, at St Margaret's in Westminster. Two of the sewing-room girls were planning to wait outside the church to see the bride and groom. They asked Olivia to come with them.

'Do you good. You look peaky.'

'I've a headache, that's all. I'll be at work tomorrow.'

'Oh, bad luck.'

The afternoon dragged on. Though she felt tired and dull-witted, some things slotted into place. Sneddon had recognised her at Paper Buildings. He had told Mr Ruthwell that she had been there. His mother had not been unwell, of course, and he had not gone to Wales: that had been a lie hatched by Mr Ruthwell to put Grace off her guard. He had intentionally left his bedroom door ajar and his keys on the table, and Grace had fallen straight into his trap. With bleak understanding, Olivia saw that Grace had never had any hope of retrieving her letter, and so her husband would get his way. He would divorce his wife and Frankie would be sent away to school.

At half past four, while she was tidying up the rails of clothing in the shop, one of the other girls told her that Mrs Beaumont wanted to speak to her. Her nerves jangled.

What if she was asked to deliver a gown to Hinton Place? She couldn't possibly go back there.

In the office, Mrs Beaumont was on her feet, putting the final touches to a tissue-paper parcel.

Olivia said, 'I've finished the hemming, Mrs Beaumont.'

'Good, good.' Her employer's back was to her as she tweaked the loops of a pink silk bow. 'I sent for you because with the Portman order complete . . . well, unfortunately, I'm afraid I'm going to have to let you go.'

She had felt all day as if she was walking through a thick fog. She couldn't seem to follow what Mrs Beaumont was saying, and repeated confusedly, 'Let me go?'

'I know this must be a disappointment to you, Olivia, but you must understand there's always a lull after the summer.'

With slow comprehension, she realised she was being given the sack. She said, 'Is it my work?'

'No, no. Your sewing is perfectly competent.' The short-sighted eyes evaded hers once more. 'I was clear to your mother when we spoke in the spring that I could only take you on for a trial period. The summer wedding season is almost over. We don't have work for an extra girl.' An envelope was thrust at her. 'I've paid you until the end of next week. You need not come in tomorrow. I wish you well, dear. You may go.'

'You want me to leave now?'

Mrs Beaumont returned to the parcel. 'I trust you'll find employment suited to you. Please pass on my compliments to your mother.'

Olivia fetched her bag and cardigan from the cloakroom and went outside. The hot sun burned, and her feeling of disorientation persisted. She walked aimlessly along unfamiliar streets and alleyways. Eventually she found herself in the Strand, where she went down dusty steps to a basement café.

A cup of tea revived her, but in her mind she kept going through Mrs Beaumont's words, her evasiveness and her lack of sincerity, and it came to her that Sneddon's assault had not been her only punishment, and that someone – Mr Ruthwell, presumably – had instructed her employer to sack her.

Olivia found a job in a café in Earls Court, preparing sandwiches for the midday office workers' rush.

A fortnight passed. She heard nothing from Grace and nothing from Rory either. One afternoon, after work, she walked to Mayfair and stood at the far corner of Hinton Place, looking at the house. No one went in or out. The blinds were down, giving the building a secretive look.

At the café, boiling eggs and chopping cress, she wondered whether Grace had been punished by her husband and forbidden to make contact with her. And as for Rory . . . Had she meant anything to him all? Or had she mistaken a flirtation for love?

At the hostel, Olivia's nerves were starting to fray. The wireless set spoke of German troops massing on the Polish border; then, in the latter part of August, news broke that Germany and the Soviet Union had made a pact between them. In the event of war, neither country would attack the other. The alliance that everyone had feared had taken place, and there was on the streets and in the shops and buses an air of horrified disbelief. Parliament was recalled and army reservists called up; notices were pasted to walls, instructing the public in what to do in the event of a gas attack. Workmen piled sandbags against London's great buildings and strangers talked to each other in bus queues as ammunition lorries pounded along the arterial roads.

Out for a walk one evening, Olivia caught sight of a young woman on the far side of the street. Small and slight, her fair hair peeked out from beneath the brim of a straw hat, but Olivia recognised her immediately as Mrs Ruthwell's lady's maid. Darting across the lanes of traffic, earning hoots and curses from drivers and cyclists, she called out, 'Miss Summers?'

The maid turned and waited for her. 'Miss Goodland.'

'How are you?'

'I'm very well, thanks. You?'

'I'm well too, thank you. How are things with the Ruthwells?'

'I wouldn't know. I was given the sack.'

Shocked, Olivia said, 'I'm so sorry.'

'I'm not.' Miss Summers shook her head, making the artificial cherries on her hat quiver. 'Best thing that's ever happened to me. I'm joining the ATS, aren't I? Tomorrow morning I start my basic training. Food, clothing and bed all in. They'll teach me a trade, that's what they told me. Catering . . . clerking . . . driving a lorry, even.' Her head was held proudly. 'I've had enough of being treated like dirt. You won't catch me plumping pillows and bobbing curtseys to high-and-mighty ladies ever again. I tell you, Miss Goodland, I can't wait. People like the Ruthwells, they're going to have to do their own hair and button their own frocks now, aren't they?'

PART TWO

Chapter Four

1943, Wiltshire

Hugh had said he would wait outside the house, but he wasn't there, so Olivia propped her bicycle against a tree trunk and stayed outside, admiring the spectacular view. As far as the eye could see, the Wiltshire plains and hills swelled and dipped in smooth sage-green curves, while a distant narrow road laced like a dark ribbon between fields and trees. As time passed, she prised out soil from under her fingernails, but gave up after a while: it was too deeply ingrained.

From the entrance gate, the manor house was visible only in patches through the thicket of hazel and birch that surrounded it: red-brick walls, the window panes criss-crossed with tape. Partygoers arrived, cycling or on foot, and she wondered whether to join them. But the chap whose engagement celebration it was – she couldn't remember his name – was one of Hugh's fellow officers and she doubted if she would know anyone.

Four months ago, Hugh Redmond had made a beeline for her. He belonged to a Scottish regiment currently stationed on Salisbury Plain. They had dated several times before they had gone for a night to a little hotel he knew. Hugh was tall and loose-limbed, with feathery light brown hair and grey eyes and smile lines permanently incised to either side of his mouth. Charming, exuberant and good fun, he was popular with everyone.

A footfall made her glance up. A man in army officer's uniform approached the gate. Seeing Olivia, he called out, 'Hello! Have you come for the party?'

'Yes, I'm waiting for my boyfriend.'

He came to stand beside her. 'I like the twilight, don't you? Interesting things happen at twilight.' He offered her his hand. 'George Flynn.'

'Olivia Goodland.'

'Goodland . . . that's a Somerset name, isn't it?'

Black hair, high cheekbones and hooded eyes: his was a remarkable face, vivid and expressive, worthy of a second glance. He looked immaculate in his uniform. Still, she sensed something unruly about him.

She said, 'How did you know that?'

'I have a magpie brain.' He leaned against the gatepost. 'I store up all sorts of snippets, a great many of them of no practical use whatsoever. I've been stationed round here for a while, and when I get the chance, I like to go and look round. Stone circles . . . hill forts . . . old churches – I had a prowl round a churchyard in Somerset once and found a fair few Goodlands buried there. Are you a Somerset Goodland?'

'I am, yes.' She told him the name of the village in which she had been born.

He offered her a cigarette. Olivia thanked him but refused. He asked her where she was stationed.

'I work on a farm near Winterslow.'

She and her friend Louise, from the Earls Court hostel, had attended an interview for the Land Army at the Ministry of Agriculture and Fisheries in Smith Square three days before Britain had declared war. She did not know how she had got through it, still lurching between numbness and rawness in the aftermath of Sneddon's attack and Grace and Rory's desertion of her. But they had taken her on; she supposed the need for volunteers had been urgent.

'Is it a good posting?'

'Really good. It's mixed arable and livestock and the family are nice.'

He struck a match. 'Which was the worst?'

That was easy. She didn't even have to look back over the three and a half years of her career in the Land Army to know the answer. 'My first one,' she said. 'It was in the Lincolnshire Fens. We got there mid morning, my friend Louise and I, and I was sent to muck out the pigsties and barrow the stuff onto the fields for fertiliser. I slipped and fell flat on my back in the pigsty. The old bloke who'd been working there for decades roared with laughter. I thought I was going to cry, and I wanted to run back to London.'

'But you didn't.'

'No. I got up, smiled, dusted myself down and set to work again. It was a close call, though, and my goodness, I stank something awful. And no bath till Sunday. Anyway, I couldn't have left Louise. We helped each other stick it out.'

'Sounds rather a baptism of fire.'

'It was.' He had an elegance, she thought, but it wasn't a studied, self-aware elegance. She had an urge to reach out and touch the brown hand that rested on the gate, to feel the ripple of bone and tendon beneath her palm.

Disconcerted, she looked out to the road. *Where the hell are you, Hugh?* She should go into the house, she thought, but did not.

She said, 'We slept in our overcoats. Straw mattresses in an attic. Sometimes we thought we'd die of the cold and the wet.'

Perhaps she was boring him. Everyone had their war stories. He might have been at El Alamein or Dunkirk, considerably more awful than a chilly farm in the back of beyond.

But he said, 'It must have had its compensations.'

'Honestly, in the spring, it was so lovely there, I wouldn't have wanted to be anywhere else in the world.'

The rumble of an engine made them both glance up to the Plain. She wondered whether he was waiting for someone too. A lorry drew up and disgorged half a dozen men and women, who hurried down the path to the house, talking and laughing. Hugh wasn't among them.

George Flynn said, 'Farm work's tough.'

'Have you done it?'

'I have, yes.'

'Are you from a farming family?'

'No, not at all. My father owned a jeweller's shop in Manchester, but I've always loved the countryside. After Oxford, I worked on a farm in Nottinghamshire for six months. I wanted to know what it felt like, living somewhere remote.'

'Why?' she asked, picturing him as one of those back-to-the-land students, a townie who saw rural life as a curiosity to dabble in and tell funny stories about to his intellectual friends. She wished Hugh would hurry up.

'When I was a boy,' he said, 'I'd cycle out to the

countryside most weekends – evenings, too. The Trough of Bowland . . . Alderley Edge. If I had a couple of days, I'd head off to the Lakes, camp out, sleep under a hedge.' His eyes shone. 'Visiting a place and living in it are very different. It's no good claiming to love the countryside and evading the tough bits. Rural life isn't all flower-filled meadows.'

Her fleeting coolness towards him vanished. The distant music stopped for a while. In the quiet, he glanced up at the sky. The first stars had come out.

'There might be a frost,' he said. 'Are you cold?'

She was wearing her khaki uniform coat over the lilac satin dress that had once belonged to Alice Ruthwell. 'Not at all. There was a frost on the grass in the orchard this morning.' It had been a cold May.

He dropped his cigarette end in a rut. 'Tell me what you did before the war.'

'I was a dressmaker. Bridal gowns and evening frocks mostly, which hardly lent itself to anything military. I liked the Land Army uniform. It's practical, you can do things in it. I can't say I chose it from any noble motive.'

'If we're being honest, I volunteered for the army because I can't stand planes and I get sick at sea.'

'What were you before?'

'A poet.'

This surprised her. He was one of those wiry, capable-looking men. He had an aura of barely suppressed energy, a quick fluency of movement. It was easier to imagine him pitchforking hay or stoking a firebox than hunched over a notebook.

'Were you . . . are you . . .' She was wary of unearthing sensitivities, puncturing his ego.

'Published? Yes, a few months before the war. One slim

volume, as they say. Though it's not that slim. Rather chunky, in fact. But just the one, so far.'

'Congratulations. And did it . . .' Again she floundered.

'It didn't do too badly.'

'You must be very proud.'

'I am, yes.'

Suddenly frowning, he tipped his head towards the trees and put a finger to his lips. Treading softly through the fallen leaves, she followed him. It was darker here, and it took a moment for her sight to accustom itself to the lack of light. He touched her elbow and pointed, and she saw through the narrow columns of coppiced hazels a small, circular pond. The full moon, fractured by filtering branches, glimmered on the black water. A roe deer, antlers lit up by the moonlight, was standing on the bank. They watched as it bent to drink from the pond, Olivia hardly daring to breathe. Then the deer, catching their scent perhaps, turned in a single lithe movement and disappeared into the trees.

'"They flee from me, that sometime did me seek",' George Flynn murmured as they went back through the trees. His words, and the moon and the pool and the deer, seemed to imprint themselves on her mind, like the after-image of a bright light, and she shivered. Emerging from the woodland, the gate and the house seemed unfamiliar, as if they had been away for hours rather than for a moment: a strange alchemy.

'I like to think I'm still a poet,' he said. 'In spite of, well, everything. There's a fine tradition of soldier poets. Edward Thomas . . . Rupert Brooke . . . Wilfred Owen. Not that I'm claiming to be in their league yet.'

She noticed that 'yet'. She wondered whether he was

conceited and ran her mind over their conversation, but it seemed to her it had gone pleasantly back and forth, that he had not hogged it. She glanced at her watch. It was gone nine. It might be sensible to give up on the party and cycle home, but she found that she wanted to stay there, by the gate, with George Flynn. Eventually he would say, *Well, I'd better go in and join the fun*, or something like that, and head off, and she would, she realised, miss him.

She said, 'I wonder whether Hugh has forgotten.'

'Might he?' His eyes met hers. She had assumed them to be brown, but she now saw that they were a deep greenish blue.

'He might, yes.'

'I should give it a while. It's a fine night. You've already seen a deer drink from an enchanted pool. Who knows what else might happen? I expect he's been held up, that's all. You're hardly the sort of woman a man would forget.'

She looked out to where bruised shadows pooled in the valleys. The air smelled fungal and brackish and of the first new growth and the last frosts. Powdery green lichen from the gate smeared the sleeve of her coat; she brushed it off.

She said, 'I don't know about enchanted pools. I'm in the Land Army. I look at a pond like that and wonder how long it took some poor soul to dig it out. Or whether the water will last through a drought.'

She sounded flippant, she thought, and was irritated with herself. It had become a habit of hers to shy away from deep emotion. She was not the only one; they all did it. It was the war, of course, the relentless routine, the physical labour and the need to suppress worry.

'It's funny how we adapt,' he said. 'The nonsensical rules and regulations . . . the underlying barbarism of army life . . . I should hate it all – and I do, I've always detested physical violence and brutishness. And yet sometimes, dashing about on a training exercise, I feel a sense of exhilaration.'

He came to stand beside her. She could almost feel the heat of his body and inhale the scent of his skin. It was as if he had run his fingertip down her spine, firing her nerve endings into action. She wanted to rest her head against his shoulder – he was a couple of inches taller than her – and for him to put his arm round her waist. That they did not touch made her ache inside.

He said, 'What gets my goat is the churning mess the armies have made of the Plain. It's a trampled colony of bee orchids or a man taking a potshot at a songbird for fun. Should it be that which enrages me most? I'll see things differently when we get to France, I know I will.'

'We all have to hold on to optimism, don't we?'

'We do indeed.' His gaze rested on her as he smiled.

The music had stopped again; she heard a buzzing noise, like a bumble bee burrowing into a flower. 'Something's coming,' she said. 'Sounds like a motorbike.'

She walked to the verge and made out the pale glow of a dimmed headlamp as it traced a path over the curving landscape before disappearing beneath the brow of the hill. Returning, it flickered through the tall trees that hedged the approach to the house.

The driver brought the motorcycle to a halt and swung off. She recognised Hugh.

'Sorry I'm late, Livvie!' he called out. Then, as he flung his arm round Olivia's shoulders, 'George, how are you? Congrats and all that. Where's Cecilia?'

'In the house, surrounded by well-wishers.'

'Then for pity's sake, man, what are you doing out here? Someone will run off with her.'

'I've enjoyed talking to you, Olivia,' said George. 'I'll see you in there.' He walked away, down the path.

Hugh put his hands on Olivia's hips and kissed her. His lips were cool against hers and he smelled of fresh air and the night. A hint of petrol, too.

As they headed to the house, she said, 'Who's Cecilia?'

'George's fiancée. Didn't he say? This is their engagement party. Cecilia shares this house with some other girls. We'd better get in or all the booze will have gone.'

They headed up the path, arm in arm. The house was square-fronted and pretty, roses scrambling up the brick walls. Guests crowded into a large room at the back, all the men in uniform, a mixture of army and RAF, while most of the women were wearing party frocks. A few lumps of coal gleamed in the fireplace, and someone had covered the lampshades with pink tissue paper. The gramophone was playing 'Boogie Woogie Bugle Boy' and the floor was jam-packed with couples jitterbugging. The dancing was wild, and shrieks and laughter filled the air. One day there would be a last party; one day the men would be shipped out across the Channel to France.

Hugh was a good dancer. He held her tight, his jaw strong and firm, like a chunk of granite against her cheek. Yet she found herself searching through the throng for George Flynn. She spotted him on the far side of the room with a small, pretty girl with sharp, vivid features – Cecilia, she assumed. Cecilia was wearing a red frock and had a silk flower in her brown hair. Honestly, he should have told her that this was his engagement party. Perhaps he had assumed she knew – but no, gut instinct told her that was not the case and that there had been intention in his omission. She felt at a disadvantage for having been wrong-footed.

There was a howl of approval as an American airman tipped a bottle of brandy into the punch bowl. The dance ended and Hugh fetched them both drinks. Browning slices of apple bobbed in the mixture, but it had a kick.

When Olivia came back from sorting out her hair in a bedroom, Hugh and his friends were discussing a motor car they were fixing up. She hung round for a while, then moved away, feeling bored and dissatisfied. Though she liked Hugh and was attracted to him, she did not feel deeply for him. When he was away, she didn't think a great deal about him at all. Sometimes she had to rack her brains to remember when she had last heard from him.

'It's a bit of a crush, isn't it?'

A voice snapped her out of her reverie. George Flynn was standing beside her.

'Masses of people,' she said. 'You must be very popular.'

'Most of them are Cecilia's friends. They're talking wedding plans. I wondered whether you'd like to dance.'

What would it be like to be held by him? A longing to find out leaped into her heart, but then she heard Hugh bawl out her name. He had detached himself from his friends and was beckoning to her.

'Sorry,' she said, smiling at Hugh. 'I'd better go. Enjoy your party, George.'

Coming home from work one evening shortly after the party, Olivia scooped up her post. There was a small package, wrapped in brown paper, addressed to her.

Gussie, one of the three Land Girls with whom she shared the cottage, was in the sitting room, standing in front of the mirror, doing something to her hair with a home-made concoction. She called out a hello as Olivia flung herself into an armchair and began to peel away the parcel's brown paper wrapping.

'What's that?'

'A poetry book.' It was entitled *Poetry of the English Renaissance*. The spine was coming away in a spider's web of threads.

'From Hugh?' Gussie daubed a curl with crimson paste. 'How romantic.'

The label on the back of the parcel gave the sender's name, rank and regiment. It wasn't from Hugh; it was from George Flynn. Olivia didn't correct her friend. It seemed too complicated.

The book fell open where a scrap of paper marked a page. Seeing that he had written on it, she snapped it shut.

She nodded at Gussie's hair. 'What's that you're using?'

'Beetroot, with just a teeny spoonful of sugar and flour. It's supposed to give the hair a coppery sheen.' Gussie peered in the mirror, chewing her lip. 'Do you think it looks coppery?'

'It's rather pink, to be honest, Gus. Pretty, though. Goodness, I need a wash. Are you in for supper?'

Gussie shook her head. 'Geoff's giving me a lift to a dance at Tidworth. You could come along if you like.'

'Thanks, but no. I've things to catch up on.'

Olivia boiled up water and scrubbed away the day's grime. She and Kay shared a bedroom; Kay wasn't back yet, so she had it to herself. She took a proper look at the book George Flynn had sent her. It was well thumbed, the corners folded over and pencil notes in the margins. She turned to the page he had marked and read what he had written on the scrap of paper.

I've had this poem in my head ever since we met. It's such a fine poem. So much passion, so much pain, still there after four hundred years.

She knew that he was remembering the hazel grove where they had seen the pond and the deer with its moonlight-silvered antlers. She herself had recalled that scene so many times. If it had been a length of fabric, she would have worn it thin by now. The touch of his hand on her elbow. *You're hardly the sort of woman a man would forget.* She remembered how the shadows had fallen on his features and his quick, lithe movements through the trees. His air of finding amusement and interest in everything and how he had whisked away their conversation into engrossing byways. All those things.

She, Olivia Jane Goodland, who had little talent for falling in love, had been captivated by a man she had spoken to for barely an hour, a man who was promised to someone else and whom she might never see again.

Propping herself up on the pillows, she began to read.

They flee from me, that sometime did me seek,
With naked foot stalking in my chamber.
I have seen them, gentle, tame and meek,
That now are wild, and do not remember
That sometime they put themselves in danger
To take bread at my hand; and now they range
Busily seeking with a continual change.

She kept the poetry book on top of her chest of drawers, where it seemed to smoulder, snaring her line of vision. She spent ages deciding how to pitch the letter she wrote to thank George Flynn for the book. She didn't want to sound breezy, but nor should she gush. In the end, she told him that she had loved English literature at her girls' grammar school but had not come across Sir Thomas Wyatt.

He didn't write back. Every evening, returning to the cottage after work, she hoped there might be a letter or card, but searching through the post, she found nothing. What had he intended with this gift? Was he in fact warning her off? Had she, during their conversation, given away too much? Had she made a fool of herself, looked at him too intently, laughed too shrilly, concurred with him too often or done any other of the silly, embarrassing things girls did when they were attracted to a man? George Flynn was good-looking and charming; he would be used to women losing their heads over him. Perhaps he was weary of them.

Then, on the last day of June, a letter arrived.

I'm glad you liked the poem, George wrote. *Wyatt was a diplomat and a courtier. A political prisoner too. He'd have learned to watch his step, to say only what his betters wanted to hear. It's a handy thing for a poet, to be able to hold two views at once. You can't be sure whether the lover in the poem is flighty, as he implies, or whether it's he, Wyatt, who is hopelessly self-pitying. A mixture of both, perhaps.*

You could have said that his letter contained nothing personal, except that at the foot of the page he had included eight short lines, signed with his initials. George Flynn's poem was slight, but it had an incantatory power, as if he was trying to magic something into existence.

Her heady joy at hearing from him kept her going for weeks. Once more she wrote back, and once more there was no reply. And really, she thought, she should expect no reply, because after all, what of Cecilia? She and George might well be married by now. Couples didn't wait long in wartime. She pictured the pair of them, united in bliss. Cecilia would have found a couple of rooms and made them into a home. She had looked a stylish sort of girl who would be good at making a comfortable home out of nothing much.

She had a week's leave and went to see her mother. Josephine Goodland had put the entire garden over to soft fruit and vegetables, ruthlessly unearthing shrubs and dahlias. One rose remained, a pink rambler that Olivia's father had planted more than twenty years ago, a memento of love. She had a lie-in each morning, which let her catch up on sleep after years of rising early on a farm. She and her mother ate outside because the weather was fine, and it saved on clearing up.

They had always got on; theirs was not one of those warring mother and daughter relationships. From the outside they must seem close, and in most ways they were, yet there were great areas of experience they had never shared. Fearful of picking at scars, Olivia had never asked her mother about her father's last few months. She herself had given only a brief account of what had happened in London with the Ruthwells and Rory, partly because she did not want to worry or upset her mother, but also because she was ashamed of what had taken place. Nor did she mention George Flynn. After all, nothing had happened.

Chapter Five

1943–4, Wiltshire

The rain fell more heavily as Olivia cycled back from the farm to the cottage. Turning the corner of a narrow lane, her bike lurched as the rim of the wheel struck a large flint. Muttering a curse, she slid to a halt.

The front tyre was as flat as a pancake. She laid the bicycle on the muddy verge. Rain streamed from her sou'wester as she fumbled for the puncture kit. She was struggling to lever off the tyre when a jeep overtook her. She shrank away from the spray, then saw that the vehicle was reversing back towards her.

A door slammed and a man climbed out. In a dry-mouthed moment (every other part of her was soaked through), she recognised George Flynn. Her heart hammered in chorus with the rain, and she dashed water from her face with the back of her hand.

'Olivia?' he said. He came towards her, curtained by the rain, gaining substance as he reached her. He crouched to inspect the bike. 'Puncture?'

'The blasted tyre lever keeps slipping in the wet.'

'Good thing I was passing by, then. I'll give you a lift.' He nodded towards the jeep. 'Get in out of the rain.'

She climbed into the passenger seat. In the rear-view mirror, she watched him lift the heavy bicycle into the back of the vehicle.

Jumping in beside her, he asked, 'Are you heading home?'

'Yes.' She gave him directions to the cottage.

'Take this. Dry your hair with it.' He unwound his scarf and gave it to her. It smelled of tobacco and the outdoors and of him.

It was disorientating to be in the jeep with him. She had thought about him so often over the last six months that he scarcely seemed a real person, but almost a figment of her imagination. She had forgotten the curl of his eyelashes, the angle of his cheekbones and the solid brown muscularity of his hands. They were a soldier's hands, not a poet's.

She said, 'Thanks for the book. If you'll hang on a mo when we get to the cottage, I'll give it back to you.'

'No need for that. I want you to keep it.'

'Then thank you, George.' She rubbed the scarf's scratchy khaki wool between finger and thumb. 'I liked your poem, too.'

'Verse,' he said, flashing her a smile. 'That fragment I wrote for you is mere verse. Cecilia is disdainful of rhyme and calls that sort of thing my juvenilia, but it's all I've been capable of these last few months. All I've done is haul myself up mountains and wade through bogs and eat and sleep. That verse was my single flicker of creativity.'

'How is Cecilia?'

'She's very well. She's gone back to Oxford.'

'Are you married now?'

'No.' The windscreen wipers whizzed back and forth, and she saw in each momentary clearing of the glass how the wind tore the red-brown leaves from the beeches.

'Cecilia's father has been taken ill,' he said. 'We've put the wedding on hold.'

'I'm so sorry.'

'Robin's been ill before. He always seems to pull through.' He did not sound overly concerned.

'Is that where you two met, at Oxford?'

'Yes, in the early thirties.' Which made him, she calculated, around ten years older than her. 'Cecilia's a poet too,' he said. 'She's rather good. She had the sense to go into teaching after university, but she still writes.'

'What sort of poems?'

'They're very contemporary. Comments on modern issues. She likes to spring off what's happening here and now.'

'Different to you?'

He laughed. 'Very different. She accuses me of being a traditionalist, a Victorian. There are themes that resonate through the ages, don't you think?'

'Love and joy,' she said. 'Loss.'

The rain had drawn a veil over the surrounding countryside so that they travelled through a shimmering silvery tunnel. The lane they headed down scarcely accommodated the width of the jeep. Dripping branches thwacked the bonnet.

He said, 'How's Hugh?'

'Fine, as far as I know.' She gripped the edge of the seat at he swung the vehicle round a tight corner. 'I haven't seen him for ages. We finished.'

'I'm sorry. That's too bad.'

'Not really. We both felt the same.' There had been no tearful parting, no difficult severing of ties. Hugh had been posted away. She had not written. There was nothing more to it than that.

'Still,' he said, 'one's always searching for connection.'

The rain began to pound against the windscreen with renewed ferocity, obliterating the road. 'Can't see a thing,' he muttered. 'I'm going to have to pull in till it eases off.' He braked in the shelter of the hedgerow. 'And there's another thing . . .'

'What?'

He made a vexed sound. 'Cecilia and I, we can't agree where to live. After it's over, I mean. Assuming it's ever over.'

By now, by these drenched, cold months that made up the dregs of 1943, they all found it hard to believe the war would ever end. The Americans had entered the conflict on the Allied side after Pearl Harbor, and over the course of the last year, vast numbers of US troops had been shipped to Britain. Accents from New York, from the Midwest and the Deep South spilled from Hampshire village shops and pubs in once isolated Dorset valleys. In Russia, the Germans were in retreat following their defeat at the Battle of Stalingrad. After their successes in North Africa, the Allies were engaged in fighting a series of fierce battles to take Italy. The spark of hope Olivia every so often felt when news was broadcast of a battle won or town taken seemed almost more difficult to bear than the relentless defeats and retreats of the earlier years of the war. Though she longed for it to come to an end, to speak of it felt like tempting fate.

She said, 'Where does Cecilia want to live?'

'Oxford. She's never wanted to be anywhere else. To her, it's the centre of the universe. She'd be close to her family and friends.'

'But you don't want to live there?'

'I had enough of it when I was at university. I found it too confining. A little smug. All that weight of tradition stifled me. If I were to live in a city, I'd prefer London, but Cecilia dislikes London.' He beat his palm against the steering wheel. 'It's always been a problem with us. Cecilia believes she should have the greater say in the matter as she's likely to spend more time in the home, and that's fair enough, but I'm afraid . . .' He broke off.

'Afraid of what?'

'That I wouldn't be able to *write*.' He laughed. 'I am aware that sounds so bloody pretentious. The tortured poet drawing inspiration from the daffodil fields. I didn't write any poetry while I was at Oxford. I only began writing again when I was working on the farm. Cecilia can work anywhere, on buses and trains, in cafés, but I've never been able to. I must have . . .'

'Peace and quiet?'

'I'm too easily distracted, Olivia, I know that. If we were living in Oxford, quite apart from the fact that the place oppresses me, Cecilia's family and friends would visit, and . . .'

'You would feel obliged to be sociable.'

'I enjoy company. I'm not good at resisting it.' His blue-green gaze fell on her. 'Do I appal you?'

She shook her head. George sighed. 'It's a barrier between us and we can't seem to find a way over it. It was why we split up after we graduated.'

'You mean Cecilia didn't fancy living on some farm in the middle of nowhere?'

He gave a bark of laughter. 'That's exactly what I mean. I can't blame her.'

'When did you get back together again?'

'About a year ago. I'd heard that she was nearby, sharing a house with Helen and Anna. I marched up there one evening and knocked on the door.'

The rain having eased a little, he started up the jeep again. She should have been longing to get back to the cottage, to strip off her wet clothes and heat up water for a bath, but she had to acknowledge the truth: that she wanted to remain sitting beside him in the chilly jeep while a gale howled, because doing so, she felt blissfully content.

They headed off down another narrow lane. Yellow-brown water puddled to either side of a central grass strip and the jeep bounced on the flints. A flash of lightning revealed a larger stretch of water ahead and she saw that the lowest part of the incline had flooded. She called to George to watch out, but the jeep plunged into the water, sending up waves to either side of it before coming to a halt. Another wave washed over the bonnet.

'Damnation.' He tried the accelerator, but the vehicle didn't move.

'I'll get out,' she said. 'It'll be lighter then.'

She jumped out and waded through the puddle. George followed, then crouched to inspect the wheels. The front left one was wedged in tight between two large rocks. They worked to free it, hauling the stones out of the rut onto the verge.

'We'll give her another go,' he said. 'Can you drive?'

'Yes, of course.'

'I'll push, then.'

Olivia had learned to drive on a farm where everyone, from the twelve-year-old daughter to the great-grandmother in her eighties, knew how to drive a tractor and a van. She knew everything there was to know about getting tractors out of mud. She slipped off her oilskin coat and handed it to him, then climbed into the driver's seat while George laid his jacket and her coat in front of the wheels to give traction before going round to the rear. The rain pelted down. When he thumped on the roof, Olivia pressed the accelerator. At first she thought it wasn't going to work, but he gave another hard shove and the vehicle moved forward, out of the deepest water. She drove to a higher patch of ground before pausing to test the brakes.

George threw their muddy garments into the back of the jeep. Olivia shifted over to the passenger seat. They were both laughing with relief.

'Damn this weather.' He looked at her. 'You poor girl, you're drenched.'

'I was drenched already.'

'Here, put this round you.' From the back, he dug out a grubby jersey, which smelled of oil. 'Give me your hands.'

He rubbed her cold hands, trying to bring them back to life. And then seamlessly, as if there was an inevitability to it, they were kissing. She tasted the rain on his lips and felt the flick of his wet hair against her face. She closed her eyes, hungry for him, lost, drowning. She breathed in the salty scent of his skin and the wet dog smell of soaked khakis and heard the rain batter on the roof. And then even that retreated, and all that mattered was the touch of his hands and the taste of his mouth.

Suddenly she pulled away from him. 'George.'

Wild-eyed, he stared at her, then abruptly looked away. 'I'm sorry,' he muttered.

'You're engaged to be married!'

'I know, but . . . Olivia, I can't help it! I can't stop thinking about you. I've tried to, but I can't.'

'Oh, George . . .'

'It may sound corny, but it's true.' He became a little calmer. 'That first time we met, outside Cecilia's house, I felt drawn to you. I've tried to fight it. I didn't contact you for months, though I longed to, I can't tell you how much I longed to. I thought it would wear off, but it hasn't. And Cecilia and I . . .'

'I won't be a party to you breaking off your engagement. I won't be party to a *betrayal*, George, I absolutely won't, do you understand?' She heard the tension in her own voice.

'Yes, of course.' His tone was bleak. 'I see that.'

They drove the rest of the journey in silence. Where the path branched off to the cottage, he parked at the side of the road. They both got out. There were more painfully awkward moments when he lifted her bicycle out of the jeep and handed it to her. She pushed it up the hill, which seemed steeper than usual, and as the jeep's engine faded into the distance, she found some small relief.

She knew she was as much at fault as he was. He would not have kissed her if she had not wanted to be kissed. The book he had sent, the letter and the poem he had written – they too had been a betrayal, every bit as much as the kiss, because they had contained an intimacy that in her heart she had always recognised. She could not claim innocence; she should have known better.

A fortnight later she took the train to London, to stay with her old friend Louise, who had recently had a baby. Louise had left the Land Army during their posting to the Lincolnshire Fens, after badly injuring her hand on a bill-hook. She had returned to London, where she had found an office job at Whitehall and met Malcolm Grey. The couple had married a year ago. Within days of their daughter's birth, Malcolm had been sent to the Scottish Highlands for training. Olivia had a week's leave owed and had offered to come and help.

The baby, a girl, was called Sarah. Cocooned in layers of white knitting, only her face showed, like a bud coming into bloom. Louise's flat was in Earls Court, a few streets away from the women's hostel in which they had shared a room before the war. Olivia's kitbag was in the spare room, and she had made tea and was sitting in an armchair cuddling the baby, who smelled milky and delicious.

Louise lay on the sofa opposite, hands wrapped round her mug. She was pale and thin and there were shadows beneath her eyes. Lank strands of her long dark blonde hair tumbled over her shoulders.

'You could have a nap if you like, go to bed,' Olivia said. 'I'll look after her.'

'I'd rather talk. I'm so desperate for a conversation with a normal person, not a midwife or doctor or someone sent to check on the baby.'

'She is utterly gorgeous.'

'Isn't she? I know I'm biased, but I do think she's a particularly beautiful baby.'

'I think so too.' Gently, with the tip of her forefinger, Olivia stroked the soft, velvety cheek. 'Was it awful?'

'The birth? Not too bad. I'm rather anaemic, though. The midwife told me I must eat calves' liver. At least I get extra ration points because I'm a nursing mother.'

'How are you managing with shopping?'

Louise took a mouthful of tea. 'Gladys across the landing has been a huge help. I managed to get out to the shops for the first time this morning.' She gave a croak of laughter. 'You wouldn't believe how long it took me. I spent simply ages getting Sarah ready, and then I had to change her nappy again. When I got downstairs, I realised I'd forgotten my purse. I didn't dare leave her in the pram – the man in the downstairs flat makes a fuss about me leaving it there anyway – so I had to get her out and carry her back up two flights of stairs.' She made an exhausted gesture. 'I feel as if my brain is full of feathers. I can't seem to remember anything for more than a couple of minutes. It's hard to believe I once had a decent job, doing quite clever things. But some nice women in the butcher's let me go to the front of the queue, so that was all right.'

'I'll do the shopping and cooking,' said Olivia. 'You have a rest.'

'It's so lovely that you're here.'

'You must miss Malcolm awfully.'

'All the time.' Louise's brow furrowed. 'He doesn't know if he'll be coming back to London, not till it's all over. He hopes he'll get leave, but he can't be sure at all, and if he does, it'll only be for a night or two.'

'Oh, Lou.'

'Susan has asked me to go and stay with her.' Susan was Louise's elder sister. She had spent the duration of the war in a cottage in south Wales.

'Will you?'

'Malcolm wants me to. Sue has her two, and Dolly – you remember, her home help – has a little boy, and they're all there. It would be company.'

'I didn't know Dolly was married.'

'She isn't. She met this soldier at a dance, and he scarpered, leaving her pregnant. Her Donald's about the same age as Sue's Mikey; they're like brothers.' Louise hauled herself into a more upright position and winced. 'It'll be fine. It'll be fun being with Sue and Dolly. It's just that . . .' She glanced round the room. 'This is our home. Mal and I, we've had such happy times here.'

'It won't be for ever,' Olivia said gently.

'I know. And there are the bombs. When it was just Mal and me, it didn't seem to matter, we just went down to the shelter when there was a raid, but it's different now I've got Sarah. I don't want Mal to worry about us.'

'When will you go?'

'Soon. It's not going to get any easier, is it?'

'I'm afraid not.'

'It's just the journey and everything. If it takes me an hour to get out to the shops . . .'

'I'll help you pack. And I can book your train ticket for you.'

'Thank you, darling, you're a brick. How's she doing?'

'Still sleeping.' The baby squirmed, screwing up her face, and Olivia rocked her until she calmed and settled. 'I'm so envious of you, Lou,' she said.

'Nonsense. I bet it isn't long before you have one of your own. Have you met anyone since Hugh?'

'Not really.'

'Olivia?'

On the mantelpiece were framed photos of Louise and Malcolm, looking handsome and carefree. Louise was wearing a man's Aran knit jersey, presumably Malcolm's. Though the windows might be taped up and the furnishings worn, the room had a settled atmosphere. It spoke, Olivia thought, of a happy marriage.

'There's no one,' she said. 'For a while, for a very short while, I thought there might be, but it didn't work out, and actually it can't work out because he's engaged to someone else.'

She had not heard from George Flynn since the day of the storm. It was a good thing he had not tried to contact her, and yet part of her still wished he would.

This week in London would cheer her up. She would feel better for the change of scenery. She needed to make herself forget that he had said *I can't stop thinking about you*, because then she would not feel so torn to pieces. At the end of the day, it had only been a kiss.

Louise had closed her eyes. Olivia put the baby in her Moses basket and tucked a knitted blanket over her, then went into the kitchen, where she tidied and washed up and began to make supper, slicing liver and sprinkling it with flour.

A few days later, she walked to Paddington station to check the timetable and buy train tickets for Louise. There had been a raid the previous night, bombs falling on Shepherd's Bush and North Kensington, so she took a circuitous route. She would see Louise onto the Swansea train on Friday morning and then she herself would catch an afternoon train back to Salisbury from Waterloo.

The tickets purchased, she left the station and walked to Oxford Street. Gaps like crevasses in a mountain range showed where the great department stores had been bombed. Fire had reduced John Lewis to a blackened husk, but she was able to buy a reel of thread in Selfridges. Louise had a piece of brushed cotton that Olivia planned to make into nightgowns for the baby. Brought up in a progressive, socialist family, Louise couldn't sew to save her life. That morning, she had asked Olivia to be Sarah's godmother, and Olivia had been thrilled to accept.

Funnelled through the streets by bomb craters and barriers, she passed parties of labourers clearing the roads and pavements. She edged round a wheelbarrow and a huge metal bucket, shiny black with tar, whose pungency overlaid the acrid odours of brick dust and wet cement. These streets had once been familiar to her, but now, battered out of recognition by the Blitz, she struggled to find her way.

As she turned a corner, she looked up. 'Watch your step, love!' one of the workmen called out. Jarred and disorientated, she caught herself on the verge of stumbling into an open drain, water gushing in its depths.

She was in Hinton Place, but it was a reduced, distorted version of the grand square she had once known. She couldn't at first work out on which side of the square the Ruthwells' house should lie, and for a moment she was unsure what she wanted to find, whether she would have preferred the house and all the violent emotions associated with it gone for ever, destroyed in the Blitz.

But it had survived and appeared undamaged, rising proud and dignified out of the chaos. It was possible that everyone she had known all those years ago had been dispersed to the four winds. She remembered how she had sat in the schoolroom as Rory had helped Frankie through his reading book. It had been the first time she had felt powerfully drawn to a man. When she looked back, it was clear to her that she had never been uppermost in Rory's mind, that his focus had been elsewhere. She might always make the mistake of falling for a certain type of man, who for one reason or another was unobtainable.

Leaving Hinton Place and its memories behind her, she headed for the Underground station.

A chill winter was followed at last by the first bright signs of spring. Long convoys of military vehicles clogged the narrow country lanes. Cycling to and from the farm, Olivia hauled her bicycle onto the verge to avoid the thundering columns. Soldiers wolf-whistled and waved to her, calling out greetings in accents from all over the world: American, Canadian, Polish, French. They were heading for encampments near the southern coast of England, where agricultural land had been requisitioned for training and preparation. They were heading for the Second Front.

Towards the end of March, she had a Saturday afternoon off. She and Kay were in the cottage garden, pegging out sheets on the line, when her eye was caught by movement at the far end of the path that led down between the fields to the road. A lorry pulled up and a man climbed out of it.

She walked out of the trees to the top of the path and looked down again. As she headed down the hill, a feeling of serenity washed over her. She noticed the shoots of wheat showing in the fields to either side of her, and the hedgerows hazed white with blackthorn blossom.

When he was within earshot, she called to him. 'Hello, George!'

'I'm sorry to turn up out of the blue.'

'It's all right.' And, seeing him, it was. 'How are you?'

'I'm very well. And you?'

'Fine, thanks.' Reaching him, she nodded to the lorry parked on the road, idling its engine. 'I'm guessing this is a flying visit?'

'I'm afraid so. I hoped we could talk. Cecilia has broken off our engagement. I came here as soon as I could.' He looked thinner than when she had last seen him, and deeply tanned.

She saw in his eyes a vulnerability as he added, 'I thought that if I wrote, you might rip up my letter.'

'I might have. What's happened?'

'Cecilia has been seeing someone else. I had no idea.' He

gave a lopsided smile. 'It has been going on for months. He – Philip or Patrick or whatever he's called – lives in Oxford. She met him last spring, before our engagement party, she said, but they were just friends back then.'

'Gosh,' she said. 'I'm sorry.' She thought what a muddle it all was and how hard to know quite the right thing to say.

'She didn't want to tell me when I was away on training because she thought I might be upset. She felt obliged to tell me in person.' George picked an ear of corn and rubbed it across his palm. 'Cecilia has never been one to duck out of a difficult conversation. She can be quite blunt. She told me it would never have worked out between us because I have my head too much in the clouds. And I wasn't sufficiently committed.'

'Crikey. That is blunt.' Bordering on brutal, thought Olivia.

'I can hardly blame her. Maybe she sensed, after our engagement party, that my thoughts and feelings were elsewhere. Olivia, dear Olivia.' Gently he touched her cheek. 'I was afraid you might have forgotten me.'

Shaking her head, she put her arms round him. 'I could never forget you.'

She pressed her face against the rough khaki cloth of his uniform and closed her eyes. He stroked the back of her neck, and she raised her head. His lips brushed against her forehead, and then they kissed.

The lorry hooted its horn. 'You'd better go,' she said. 'I'll wait for you, George.'

'Will you?' Hope flared in his eyes.

'I will, yes.'

They walked arm in arm to the road. Before he climbed into the lorry, he turned to her. 'I love you. I've loved you since the first moment I saw you, standing at the gate. I love you so much. I promise I'll never let you down.'

'I love you too.'

There was such release and delight in saying the words, in admitting their truth. The lorry pulled away from the verge. Olivia waved until it turned a corner and was lost in the folds of hedgerow and woodland.

Chapter Six

1949, London and Devon

Olivia's dear friend Caspar greeted her at the door of the flat, which was behind Victoria station. As she took off her raincoat, she heard a loud roar of conversation, underpinned by piano music. Caspar hugged her and told her that George was already there, which was a relief, because it meant that he had returned safely from roaming the moorlands of Devon.

A fog of cigarette and pipe smoke blurred the sitting room. A friend of hers called Maudie Gresham collared her as Caspar thrust a glass of cider into her hand. With some more friends, Olivia and Maudie were setting up a babysitting circle.

As they talked, Olivia took a quick look round the guests. She picked out the top of George's head, on the far side of the room. Always, when she saw him again after a parting, her heart lifted.

'I thought we should have a points system and you would be the best person to keep track of it.'

Maudie's voice captured Olivia's attention. 'Me?'

'You're so organised.'

She wasn't, she thought; she lived in chaos. All mothers of two very small boys lived in chaos. 'I'd be happy to,' she said. 'Maudie, I should go and say hello to George. We haven't seen each other for days.'

'I've bought a notebook,' Maudie said earnestly. 'I thought that would be helpful. I could pop round with it tomorrow. I'd have to bring the twins, though, and Alison has a bit of a cold. Is that all right?'

'I shouldn't worry, Gareth has a snuffle.'

Maudie had a difficult marriage to a husband who gave her little help with their three-year-old girls. Olivia knew that she was so lucky to be married to George, who was a kind and affectionate father and a practical and capable one, too. He changed nappies, gave baths, repaired second-hand tricycles and constructed playhouses out of orange boxes. He had the patience to head off Lorcan's temper tantrums and distract Gareth from teething pains.

She wound between the guests. Beer glasses and ashtrays perched beside stacks of books and literary journals. George was standing among a circle of people, his back to her. He had a talent for making new friends and keeping in touch with old ones. Acquaintances from Manchester and Oxford and from his army days and the arts world turned up at all hours at their flat in Fulham to drink coffee and talk until the early hours. The men he was with now Olivia recognised as London literary friends – poets, novelists and reviewers.

He had a beer in one hand and a cigarette in the other. He looked a little dishevelled, she thought affectionately. His dark curls were wild, and he had torn a hole in the elbow of his russet-coloured jersey.

As she drew closer, she heard him say, 'I finished the book. Oh, and I've bought a house.'

She stopped so suddenly she jolted the arm of the woman beside her. Cider splashed. 'Sorry, so sorry,' she murmured as she found a hankie and mopped up. She must have misheard. George couldn't have said that, could he? He wouldn't have *done* that . . . would he?

Olivia had married George in September 1945. It had been a perfect day, the church in Somerset crammed with their friends and decorated with yellow and gold chrysanthemums, grown by Olivia's mother. Her wedding dress had been made from a length of snow-white silk taffeta sent to her by Violet Beaumont – hoarded, presumably, from before the war. It had crossed her mind that this was a peace offering, reparation for her sudden dismissal that hot August day in 1939. But no matter, that was in the past, and she had felt beautiful in the gown, which was gorgeous, romantic and floaty and heavenly to wear and as different from the bottle-green and buff utilitarianism of her Land Army uniform as was possible.

Since then, they had lived in a succession of London bedsits and flats. Four and a half years after the end of the war, rosebay willowherb grew lustily in the bomb sites that pocked the streets, and many of those houses that still stood, shoddily built in the first place, remained uninhabitable.

She said, 'George,' and he spun round.

'Darling, I didn't see you.' He kissed her. 'How are you? How are the boys?'

'We're all very well. Did I hear you say you'd bought a house?'

Though his smile remained, he flushed. George wasn't given to drinking too much, so it must be the crowded room or his long, rushed journey back to the capital. Not guilt or shame, because he wasn't much given to those emotions either.

'I'd meant to get home first so that I could tell you all about it, but then the blasted train was delayed.' He added, 'You'll love it, Olivia.'

'You bought a house without me seeing it? Without even asking me?' The other men were melting away.

'I had to. Sweetheart, it was up for auction. If I hadn't made a decision, it would have gone.'

'In *Devon*?'

'Yes.'

'Do you mean you've actually paid for it?' She had to be clear.

'It's ours, yes.' His eyes gleamed. 'If I'd hung about . . .'

'Was it expensive?'

'Not for what it is, not at all.'

'George?'

He admitted, 'My savings are pretty depleted.'

George had bought a house in Devon. Olivia had not imagined herself living in Devon. She'd had her fill of remote rural West Country spots during the war and had pictured herself bringing up her family in a nice house in a quiet street in London. She would have shops and a park and a decent school for the boys nearby, and maybe a part-time job for her when eventually family life permitted. What if she hated this house he had bought? What if she felt lonely living hundreds of miles from her friends? What about Louise, whose flat in Earls Court was just a short Underground journey away – Louise, whose husband, Malcolm, had been in a parachute regiment, and who had been killed on the first day of the D-Day landings. How could she possibly desert her friend and her god-daughter? Sarah was nearly six years old now and a delightful little girl. Olivia was especially fond of her.

And knowing George, the house he had purchased on a whim was a romantic old ruin in the middle of nowhere.

'Even if it was sold at auction, you could have . . .' Her sentence faltered. What might he have done? They hadn't a phone, and a letter or postcard wouldn't have reached her in time. She saw that, but it didn't make it any better. She felt hot with dismay.

He said, 'It's a few miles from Honiton.'

She stared at him. 'A few miles? Do you mean two miles, George, or twenty?'

'Three or four . . .' he said vaguely. 'Look, love, the flysheet's in my rucksack, I can't wait to show it to you. I can see this has been a bit of a surprise, but—'

A voice called out, 'George! Hey, George Flynn!' and they both looked round. A red-faced, beefy-looking man was bearing down towards them. George raised his voice. 'Brian!' Then, quietly, he said to Olivia, 'There's woodland and a stream – this morning I saw an otter. Trust me, you'll love it.'

Going home on the Underground, Olivia reminded herself that George had two sides to his nature: the sociable one, which thrived on company, and the contemplative one, which craved solitude. The births of Lorcan towards the end of 1946, and then, less than two years later, Gareth, had changed their lives utterly. George had wanted a family every bit as much as she, and to support them, he wrote poems and articles for journals and literary periodicals and took teaching jobs. He was currently teaching English part-time in a crammer in Bayswater, which paid the rent and the bills. But teaching sucked up the time and energy he longed to give to poetry. Their search for a decent place to live, and their failure to find it, had taken its toll too. Their flat was small and there was nowhere for George to work. He found it hard to shut out the prattle and shrieks of the children and the clatter of pots and pans.

Ten years after the publication of his first collection of poems, he had not yet completed his second. A few months ago, he had been deeply despondent about his future. 'Who's going to remember one modest success a decade ago?' he had said. 'What if Faber drop me? What if I end up spending the rest of my life drilling Shakespeare and Shelley into dim-witted spoiled kids? In a couple of years, I'll be forty. I lost six years with the war. Newer, younger writers are snapping at my heels. Soon they'll devour me.'

They had agreed that he should cut down his teaching hours; since then, he had taken to escaping to the hills and moorland he loved for two or three days at a time. They had dipped into his savings to pay the bills so that he had time to write, and it had been worth it, because he had achieved far more than he ever had when working in a public library or his shared study at the crammer. The poems he had composed perched on a Dartmoor tor or camping by a chalk stream in Wiltshire were the finest he had written.

The train rattled to a halt at Walham Green, where they alighted. As the crowds swept them down the platform towards the exit, George took her hand.

He said, 'I finished the poem. "The Snow Leopard". I found a spot under a hawthorn tree in the Blackdown Hills and sat down and wrote the entire thing in a couple of hours. It was effortless. It almost wrote itself.'

'And that means the book's finished?'

'Yes. I know, I can hardly believe it. I'll type up the poem over the weekend, then I'll deliver the final section to Neville on Monday.' Neville was George's editor at Faber & Faber.

In the pool of light that fell from a street lamp, they kissed. 'I'm sorry for jumping at you,' she said.

'No, I'm sorry. You shouldn't have found out like that.'

'It was just such a shock.'

'I know, I know.' He held her close to him. In his arms she felt safe and consoled. 'It'll be all right, love, honestly.'

The rain had stopped, and the light from the street lamps gave the wet pavements a satiny sheen. 'After I finished the poem,' he said, 'I hiked back to Honiton. There was a poster up outside an auction house, so I had a dekko. One lot, Goldscombe Farm, caught my eye. I went into the pub to see if I could get something to eat, and I had a chat with the landlord. He knew the house. He told me it had been empty for some time but was good and solid, stone-built with a slate roof. It had been a working farm, but the land was sold off between the wars. He was a decent chap – he'd gone over to France on D-Day, too – and when I asked him if he could lend me a bike to have a look at the place, he offered me his van. It was dark out there, but I hardly needed my torch because the moon was full. One of the back doors was on a rather mouldy sort of bolt, so I fiddled around with it and managed to get inside. There are four decent bedrooms. Sweetheart, imagine!' Their current flat had just the one bedroom, which they all shared. 'And the kitchen,' he added, 'it's enormous. Olivia, you'll love it.'

They reached the flat. After paying the babysitter, they went into the bedroom, tiptoeing round Lorcan's little bed and Gareth's cot, which were squeezed into opposite corners of the room. Gareth was a light sleeper and took ages to settle if disturbed. Since he had been born, this flat had been too small for them, but it was still hard to accept that she must uproot herself to Devon.

The tenderness with which George stooped to kiss their two sons touched her. They were unalike in looks and character. Lorcan's curls were dark, while Gareth's fine hair had a reddish tinge. Lorcan had a fierce and unfaltering will; Gareth was more biddable. Tucking in her boys, Olivia breathed in their sweet, powdery baby smell.

She sat down on the bed. George passed her a piece of paper from his rucksack. *Goldscombe Farm*, the flysheet was headed. *Five and a half miles from Honiton. Seventeenth century with late-nineteenth-century additions . . . Four bedrooms and extensive attics . . . Garden of a third of an acre laid to productive south-facing vegetable plot and orchard. Well and septic tank.*

Would there be a school nearby? How far away was the nearest shop? Was the water piped or must she cope with a hand pump and buckets? There was no point in asking any of this. It was done.

She whispered, 'I wish there was a photo.'

'I drew it.'

'In the dark?'

She heard amusement in his soft voice. 'You know I can see in the dark.'

The house in George's sketchbook was long and low and clung to the earth. His pencil hinted at stone walls and roofs of varying levels, barns to one side and trees and a stream and the shallow sloping arms of hills. Our future home, she thought. How odd, and despite her initial reservations, how exciting.

He sat down beside her. 'I won't need to go away from home because I'll have a place to write. And you'll have a garden, love. You've always wanted a garden. Think of the space and freedom the boys will have. You won't ever have to worry about them running out into the traffic again. You must want to be shot of this flat too.'

'Oh God, yes, George, of course.'

He unbuttoned her blouse, then kissed her stomach. Desire uncoiled inside her. He eased down the zip of her skirt, and she wriggled out of it. They made love urgently and quietly, so as not to wake the sleeping children. Afterwards, she lay with her head on his chest, and he stroked her hair and caressed her. 'Forgive me,' he murmured.

Of course she forgave him. How could she not? She ruffled his curls.

'I love you,' she said. 'Is it a wreck? Honestly, George?'

'Not at all.' He gathered her in his embrace. 'You'll love it, sweetheart, I promise you.'

On moving day, the Flynn family took the train to Exeter and stayed there overnight. In the morning, George and Lorcan travelled on in the removal van while Olivia and Gareth took a train to Honiton. From there, they caught a bus, which dropped them off near the narrow lane that led the quarter of a mile to Goldscombe farmhouse. Gareth had dozed off in the pushchair, and a light rain was falling as Olivia, following the map that George had drawn for her, first saw their future home. The house squatted like a toad in the dusky gloom, surrounded by a brown blur of mud and backed by looming hills.

The dark oak front door was ajar; she stepped inside. The house was cold and the rooms she walked through smelled of cobwebs and damp. She found George and Lorcan in the back yard, filling buckets from the hand pump. George scooped up Gareth in his arms and they all went indoors.

Olivia made sandwiches for the boys' tea and then tried to light the cast-iron range in the kitchen. Coming indoors, George crouched down beside her and peered into it.

'It's clogged up with soot,' she said.

'I'll have a go at it. Can you manage without it tonight?'

She would have sold her soul for a pot of tea. She made up the beds and Gareth's cot, then brushed the boys' teeth in a grim bathroom that someone had decades ago painted an ill-advised shade of green. She put Lorcan and Gareth to bed with jerseys over their pyjamas because of the cold. She and George had a skimpy supper, then he went back to the range while she unpacked boxes and put plates and saucepans in the cupboards. It felt unsettling the boys being so far away; she was afraid she wouldn't hear if they cried in the night.

She had thought she would lie awake listening to the hooting of the owls and feeling homesick for the London life she had left behind her, but instead she fell asleep straight away. When she woke, George was already up, and a shimmering winter sunshine was pouring through the window. She dressed and went downstairs to the kitchen. The room was warming up now, and she registered that its aspect was enchanting. Through the wide windows she could see how the green hills rose, cradling the farmhouse.

Lorcan was sitting on the floor, playing with his toy cars. Gareth was in his highchair, getting porridge everywhere. George nipped away from the range to slip a spoonful into his son's mouth.

'Cup of tea, love?'

'You've got it working?'

'It only needed a bit of love and attention.' He gave the stove an affectionate pat.

'When did you get up?'

'About four, something like that.'

She hugged him, then brushed back his curls from his forehead and kissed him. 'You're wonderful.'

After breakfast, while George took the boys outside for a ramble, Olivia explored the house. Corridors lurched off at unexpected angles; a run of steps led into a small chamber tucked beneath the eaves. There were two sitting rooms, both of a good size and with large open fireplaces and dark oak floors. Upstairs, despite the peeling wallpaper and grimy window panes, she was able to picture how attractive the bedrooms would be once she had decorated them and replaced the old hangings with cheerful curtains and cushions. It might take them a while to transform this unwieldy, neglected building, but she could already see its potential. In her imagination, it had become a warm, welcoming home.

A narrow staircase led up to an attic divided into a succession of little rooms. George had parked his notebooks, pens and pencils and poetry books in one, so this must be where he intended to work. Brown patches on the ceilings and walls showed where rain had come through the roof. Olivia looked out of the narrow window. She couldn't see George or the boys.

She went outside. A glass lean-to ran along the rear of the house. Though there were missing panes and a great deal of clutter – chipped plant pots, empty tin cans and a rusty water barrel – the structure appeared intact and would be perfect, she thought, for tomatoes and cucumbers. To the far side of the cobbled yard was a stone barn. She went inside, where she peered up at the high, arching roof beams. A dark scurrying among the abandoned hessian sacks and mouldering hay bales prompted her to make a mental note to get a terrier, a good ratter.

As she walked through the garden, she envisaged how glorious the orchard would look when it bloomed in the spring and turned over in her mind what produce she would grow in the vegetable patch. An expanse of rough grass sloped upwards, and she saw how the clouds that hung over Goldscombe lightened to silver far away, where they met the hills.

She followed the path that three sets of footsteps had made through the wet grass. George was carrying Gareth on his shoulders. She watched him for a moment, thinking how much she loved him, and then called out to them. Lorcan ran towards her, throwing himself at her, his arms looping her neck, and she hugged him. He showed her his finds – fir cones, an old red rubber ball, a disintegrating bird's nest. Gareth slithered off his father's shoulders and grabbed the ball, and Lorcan pushed him away. Gareth fell over and cried, and Lorcan snatched the ball back. He threw the ball down the slope and Gareth tottered after it, chortling.

George put his arm round her shoulders. 'I've had an idea, love. I could run a poetry workshop here. It's the perfect place and it would earn us some money. I could use the barn for teaching. It needs a bit of work, but that won't take long. If we get a move on, we could put on the first workshop in the summer. What do you think?'

Chapter Seven

1950, Devon

In this, the height of summer, Goldscombe valley was lush and humid, the green darkest, almost black, beneath the trees, and a touch of bronze where the ferns thickened amid the narrow slashes of silvery white birches. You could get lost in such beauty, thought Olivia as she gazed up at the hills, hypnotised by it.

Because it was a fine, warm evening, she and George had decided to give the final dinner of the first poetry workshop outside in the courtyard. The event was also a belated celebration of the publication four months earlier of *The Snow Leopard*, George's second collection of poetry. His agent, Selwyn Paley, and his editor, Neville Clarke, had travelled from London to join the party.

Selwyn was a short, stout, cheerful-looking man. He came to speak to Olivia as she smoothed cloths over the trestle tables.

'On the whole, I don't approve of the countryside – I'm a city person – but for this place I can make an exception. A lot of work, though, I imagine.'

'A fair bit. George and I are so pleased you could come, Selwyn.'

A fair bit. As she shook out a tablecloth, Olivia reflected on the months of labour they had both accomplished to make this event a success. She thought of George balancing precariously on the roof as he replaced tiles blown off in a gale, or poring over manuals borrowed from Honiton library so that he could work out how to rewire the building. She herself had scrubbed floors clean of decades of dirt, painted bathrooms and made curtains, and had enjoyed decorating the bedrooms in which the attendees would stay, keeping them fresh and simple in style. Together they had transformed the barn, wheelbarrowing heaps of wet straw and rubbish to the bin and compost heap. Tables and chairs had been sourced from auctions and junk shops.

The shared project had brought them even closer together. Late into the night they had planned menus and discussed the programme of lectures and seminars. Olivia had raised pots of pelargoniums and pinks in the greenhouse; she had still been arranging them outside the house and barn as their first guests had arrived. Now, surveying the courtyard, she felt the pleasure and satisfaction of a worthwhile task well done. George's passion had infected her, and she was thrilled that this joint endeavour had gone off with hardly a hitch.

The sight of his empty glass seemed to take Selwyn by surprise. 'I'll go and find a top-up. May I fetch you one?'

'No, thanks.'

He lumbered off, breathing asthmatically. Olivia counted knives and forks. Neville appeared. He was tall and thin, Selwyn's opposite. He kissed her cheek.

'I think of this place as George Flynn's Camelot. What a marvellous setting.'

'Isn't it? We've been so lucky with the weather.'

'May I help, Olivia? Make a salad? Do the table?' He took the cutlery from her. 'Sylvie tells me I'm good at salads and table-laying.' Sylvie was Neville's wife.

'How are Sylvie and the children?'

'Very well, thank you. Sylvie's teaching art in an evening class. And you? Are you well?'

Olivia was five and a half months pregnant, the baby due towards the end of November. 'I'm fine, thanks, Neville.'

'Exhausted, I should think, with all this.'

'It's been a hectic few days, but honestly, it's been great fun.'

Neville pulled out a chair for her. 'Sit down.'

She sat. Neville polished the knives with a tea towel. The workshop was almost over, and their guests would go home tomorrow. Though she and George looked forward to having Goldscombe to themselves again, there had been such pleasure in inviting people to share it with them. She sensed that some might remain friends for life.

Neville said, 'Do they help much, your budding poets?'

'Most of them are perfectly sweet. So helpful and appreciative.'

'All this must interrupt George's sylvan idyll.'

'Oh, Neville, he's loved every minute of it.' She must ask George to gather their guests at the table. She scanned the courtyard, looking for him, and caught sight of him outside the barn, in conversation with one of the workshop participants, a girl called Lena Prescott. Lena, who was in her early twenties, was small and slight and had a square, exquisite face as vivid and perfect as a pansy.

'George is good with an audience,' said Neville. 'That isn't necessarily a common quality in a poet, but it's a fine and useful one for his publisher. He gives an excellent interview.'

'He told me he's been asked to appear on some wireless programme.'

Neville's narrow, patrician features broke into a smile. 'Olivia, my dear, I think you're referring to his discussion with Cyril Connolly on the Third Programme. It's rather a coup and, of course, will help *The Snow Leopard*. Which, by the way, is doing marvellously well.'

'Is it? That's great news. George hasn't said much about sales.'

'They're excellent. Beyond expectations, in fact. Your lives are going to change, Olivia. When the royalties come in, you'll be able to have gold taps in the bathroom.'

She laughed. 'A new oven would be nice, Neville, honestly. Does George know about the sales?'

'Not yet. I'm the bearer of good news. I have the figures here.' Neville patted the breast pocket of his linen jacket. 'Can you see him? I haven't said hello yet.'

'He's over there.' Olivia pointed to the barn door. 'Talking to the girl with the purple bandanna.'

Lena Prescott's yellow gingham dress showed her narrow waist to advantage. Olivia had felt huge almost from the start of this pregnancy. The midwife had told her that her third child was going to be a big baby. She was sure she was having another boy. People assumed that after two boys she would be desperate to have a daughter, but that wasn't so. Naturally, she would love to have a girl, but she would love another boy just the same.

Neville said, 'If you lend me a pinny, I'll help you serve.'

Hearing a peal of silvery laughter from across the courtyard, Olivia looked up. Lena was smiling at George. After five years of marriage, she had become accustomed to the fact that women were attracted to him. And when she looked at the pair, she could tell that he was trying politely to disentangle himself from the conversation.

George woke her as he came into their bedroom. Squinting in the darkness, she asked him what time it was.

'Gone two. They've all gone to bed at last, thank God.' He peeled off his shirt. 'I can't wait for the lot of them to head off and leave us in peace.' He hung his trousers over the back of a chair. 'Neville said that Faber are going to make an offer for another two books.'

'*Two?*' She was suddenly wide awake.

'An anthology of essays and another collection of poems.'

She sat up. 'George, that's wonderful!'

'It is, isn't it?'

'You're going to be famous.'

He laughed. 'I doubt that.'

'I always knew you'd do it.'

They kissed. Then she said, 'What were you and Lena talking about?'

'She wanted me to introduce her to Selwyn.'

'Did you?'

'I did. Selwyn's no fool and I knew he'd make short shrift of her.' He climbed into bed beside her and lit a cigarette. 'She's missed half the sessions and hasn't finished a single piece of work. Claimed she had a headache or was starting a cold or whatever and expected me to be sympathetic. I can't stand her calculated neediness. I like my women tough and self-reliant.'

She snuggled up to him. 'Is that how you see me? Tough?'

'As old bricks.'

'I love you.' She twined her arms round his neck.

'I love you too.'

Three months later, shopping in the nearby village of Loxleigh, Olivia reached out to take the string bag of vegetables from the greengrocer and felt it, that powerful and painful hardening of the belly she'd experienced twice before in her life. She couldn't possibly be in labour because it was only late October, and she still had a month to go with her pregnancy. Lorcan had been late and Gareth bang on time, so it must be a practice contraction.

Once the pain eased off, she shepherded Gareth back into the pushchair, hung the shopping bag on one handle, then coaxed Lorcan to hold on to the other, and steered them all out of the shop. It was raining, a soft Devon rain that looked like it might go on for ever. The pushchair threatened to overbalance with the weight of the bag.

There was a café along the road, staffed by twin sisters in their sixties. Olivia went inside and ordered a cup of tea for herself and an iced bun for the boys to share. It was a relief to sit down. She was eight months pregnant and had a four-year-old and a two-year-old and a big house and garden to look after. George had left for London the previous afternoon, where he was to attend a swanky literary party.

Neville had been right when, in the summer, he had told her that their lives were going to alter. With the first royalty cheque they had bought a new sofa and a second-hand Morris Minor. Now that they owned a car, Goldscombe seemed less isolated, and shopping for food and trips to the library in Honiton were far easier.

There were other changes. A journalist from a popular women's magazine had travelled all the way to Devon to gather material for an article. Photographs had been taken of the house and garden. George never turned down a request for an interview or an invitation to a social event. He enjoyed company and was invigorated by his trips to London and the attention and adulation he received. The fact that he hadn't completed a single full-length poem since the day he had sat under the hawthorn and written 'The Snow Leopard' didn't seem to deter him.

Olivia was chatting to the boys when another contraction started. She put down her teacup, pressed her hands together and tried to quell her rising alarm. Remember to breathe. *Breathe.*

'Mummy?' said Lorcan.

'It's all right, darling.'

It was annoying, she thought, as the pain ebbed, how one forgot what labour was like, only to remember when it was far too late to do anything about it. She gathered up boys, bags and pushchair and they made their laborious way back to the car. As she unhooked the shopping bag and made to open the boot, she gasped at the fierceness of the pain. At not quite thirty-seven weeks, she was going into labour.

She wasn't ready. She felt a rush of panic. She had urged George to go to London when he had suggested postponing his trip. 'Don't be silly, I'm not due for several weeks,' she had said. 'You'll be back in a trice.'

George had added, 'At least Dinah and Charlie will be around to keep an eye on you.'

Dinah was a friend of George's from Oxford, who had been staying with them for the past month, and Charlie was Dinah's seventeen-year-old son. Charlie seemed to sleep most of the time and, if she was being honest, Olivia found Dinah, who spoke three languages fluently and worked as a freelance translator, quite intimidating.

Lorcan said, 'Mummy, can I sit in the front?'

'No, darling, I want you to go in the back with Gareth.'

'I don't want to.'

She wrestled both boys into the car, then fumbled in her bag for the Lincoln biscuits she always carried with her as a bribe.

'Sit quietly, be good, eat those. Lorcan, keep an eye on Gareth for me. I need to make a phone call.'

There was a phone box at the end of the street. Olivia called the midwife and told her that she was in labour. Then she phoned her mother in Somerset. Josephine, calm and capable, promised to hop on a train straight away and be at Goldscombe in no time. Lastly, she tried George's hotel. He wasn't there, but she left a message for him.

She drove home along the winding single-track roads. Perhaps the contractions were lessening in intensity. They might fade away completely if only she were able to lie down and have a rest. Then she would have a few weeks' respite and have time to get everything ready for the baby's arrival.

In the back, Gareth was trying to take Lorcan's Dinky cars and Lorcan was protesting. Olivia persuaded Lorcan to give his brother a car and then tried to distract them by singing nursery rhymes, while all the time a different verse beat through her head, the poem that had given George the title of his collection, which was selling in the tens of thousands. It was about a female snow leopard giving birth alone in her den. George said it was about creativity, but Olivia felt it was about the creation of new life itself. It was George's poem, but that didn't mean it meant the same to everyone.

When she reached the house, she went to open the

passenger door for the boys, but the ferocity of the contraction forced her to lean against the vehicle, resting her head on her forearm, her eyes screwed shut, gasping for breath. This baby wasn't going to wait long enough for her mother to arrive.

A voice from behind her called, 'Olivia, are you all right?'

'Oh, Dinah, the baby's coming. The midwife's on her way.'

'Let's get you upstairs.' An arm round her shoulders, steering her away from the car. 'Lorcan, Gareth, out you come. Charlie wants to play soldiers with you. Olivia, it's going to be all right.'

Dinah had a pleasant, posh, confident voice. When she said things, you believed her.

'I haven't got any baby things ready.'

'The baby won't mind if we wrap it in a towel,' said Dinah firmly.

Her third son was born in a rush twenty minutes after the midwife turned up. The midwife told her he was a fine, big baby, just over nine pounds; wrapped in a clean towel, he was placed in her arms. As Olivia gazed into his tiny face, she realised how lucky she'd been to have Dinah's reassuring presence throughout.

But the pain was still alive in her, and through a fog of exhaustion and confusion she felt the midwife take the baby out of her arms and say sharply to Dinah, 'Can that boy of yours drive? Yes? Then go and get him and tell him to drive as fast as he can to Loxleigh and phone for an ambulance. Then come straight back here and look after the baby for me.'

When Olivia opened her eyes, she was lying in a hospital bed, tubes coming out of her. George was sitting beside the bed, holding her hand.

She whispered, 'The baby . . .'

'He's fine. Doing very well. Your mother is looking after him, and Dinah's taking care of Lorcan and Gareth.'

Olivia couldn't disentangle the order of events. She had given birth to the baby and then something had gone wrong. How could George be here? How many hours or days had she lost?

He stroked her cheek. 'You and the baby are both going to be fine, love. You had a haemorrhage. You're doing well. The doctor told me I should be able to take you home by the end of the week.' Gently he squeezed her hand. 'I'm so sorry I went away. I shouldn't have.'

'It's okay.'

'I'll never go away again, I promise you, love.'

She closed her eyes. When she woke, minutes or hours later, George was still there, still holding her hand. She murmured, 'His name . . .'

'We've plenty of time to think about that.'

'I want him to have a name.' Life seemed so fragile. They had narrowly escaped disaster. It seemed to her that a name would tether her child to the earth.

'Caradoc?' he said. 'Or Malachy? Malachy was an ancient Irish king.'

'Thomas.' She wasn't going to saddle her son with Caradoc or Malachy. 'He's to be called Thomas, after my father.'

He nodded. 'Yes, of course, Thomas.'

'And please, George, would you ask Dinah if she would be his godmother.'

'Yes, good idea. I'll have a word with her.'

She whispered, 'I thought . . . I thought the baby . . .'

'Love, he's doing so well. He's a fine big boy. Your mother

is out there in the car, waiting with him. Would you like me to bring him to you, so you can hold him?'

'Will they let you?'

'I'll smuggle him in under my coat.'

And he did. And he became Tom there and then, as she cradled him in her arms, her third and last child.

Chapter Eight

1959, Devon

After dinner, their guests lounged on the sitting-room sofas: the archaeologist John Farley and his wife, Caroline; a young musician called Desmond Murphy, who had brought his girlfriend, Zoe Cooper, who was an actress; and the Flynns' old friend Dinah. Dinah and Olivia had bonded with each other after Tom's dramatic birth, and had since become close friends. Tonight Dinah had brought with her a new husband, a cheerful, portly man called Anthony Clairmont. Heather Osbourne, George's latest protégée, sat cross-legged on the rug, waving away offers of a seat.

Olivia was showing Dinah and Caroline the damaged curtain. 'It was Gareth's idea,' she said, 'but all three of them were involved. They were trying to make a rocket propelled by lighter fuel.'

'Good Lord.' Caroline inspected the scorched and shredded lower half of the fabric. 'Little blighters. They are terrifying, aren't they? Children, I mean. Perfectly sweet a lot of the time, but now and then utterly terrifying.'

'Thank God George smelled burning. Do you think the room still smells of smoke?'

Dinah sniffed. 'Maybe a little. George must have been furious.'

'He's told them they have to wash up the dinner things for a fortnight. But I think a part of him thought it was funny. It was the sort of thing he'd have done when he was their age.'

Olivia stole a glance across the room. George was still deep in conversation with John Farley. Heather Osbourne was laughing at something Desmond had said. She had a loud, playful laugh, which would have made Olivia smile had she not noticed on Heather's previous stays at Goldscombe how George's eyes followed her round the room. She had seen them coming out of the barn together earlier that day, George's hand resting on the small of the young woman's back. Heather had turned her face to him and laughed; throughout the rest of the day, the sound had echoed in Olivia's mind.

'At least it gives you the excuse to buy new curtains,' said Dinah.

'But they're such a gorgeous colour,' Heather said, joining in the conversation. 'You have such marvellous taste, Olivia.'

The curtains were turquoise blue with a small cream print. They were one of the first pairs Olivia had sewn after they had moved into Goldscombe. She had chosen the fabric in a shop in Honiton and George had carried the heavy parcel home on the bus. When she looked back, she remembered how happy they had been, sharing the excitement of a new chapter in their lives.

'Rather dated now, perhaps,' she said.

'Beautiful things never go out of date.'

'Nonsense, Heather, the ideal of beauty changes all the time.' This was Desmond. 'Think of all those heavy-jawed

Edwardian beauties. You look at pictures of them now and you think, good Lord, what were they thinking?'

'That's because they're old photos, surely, Des. They can't really have looked like that.' His girlfriend, Zoe, wiggled her jaw from side to side and Heather laughed again.

George had been mentoring Heather for the last six months. She had attended the most recent poetry workshop. George thought her to be very talented, though she was not yet published. She was very pretty, with tumbling chestnut curls and a full figure.

Caroline was speaking again. 'Annabel and Christine don't tend to set curtains alight, but my goodness, they do other awful things. Last week, Annabel borrowed my diamond earrings without asking me. I was furious with her.' She scrabbled in her navy leather handbag, brought out a packet of cigarettes and offered them to Olivia.

'No, thanks.'

'How good you are.' Caroline's sharp little hazel eyes studied her. 'Don't you get fed up with all these people hanging round your house? I would. All that extra cooking and laundry.'

'Not at all. I like the company.'

This was true, though seven staying overnight at the farmhouse was a lot even for the Flynns. The Clairmonts and the Farleys were in the new guest rooms that had recently been built in the barn. Heather and Zoe had been squeezed into the attic and Desmond was sleeping in Gareth's room, while Gareth himself had a mattress on Lorcan's bedroom floor. Tom was in his own little bedroom. Thank heavens for Janice Turner, who cycled from Loxleigh four mornings a week to help with the washing and ironing.

George and John were standing at a side table, examining

the Neolithic flint axes that John had brought with him. George was holding one, testing its weight.

Caroline lowered her voice. 'How long can they go on gassing about a few lumps of old flint?'

'You must have known what John was like when you married him.'

Caroline sighed. 'But when you're in the first flights of love, everything they say sounds fascinating, doesn't it? I must have heard his pet theories a hundred times. Tell me honestly, Olivia, don't you find it utterly tedious when George wants to read you a poem?'

Though Olivia smiled and said she didn't think so, she found, with a tugging of unease, that she couldn't remember when George had last asked her opinion of a piece of work. During the early years of their marriage, he had read to her every evening; sometimes only a line or two, but at other times, when he'd had a good day, an entire poem. When had they stopped doing that? After the birth of one son or other. After the success of his career had stepped up its demands on him.

Caroline said, 'You teach, don't you, Olivia?'

'Part-time at the primary school in Loxleigh, yes.'

'Sounds exhausting.'

'Honestly, I love it. The children are a delight.'

'Oh, come on. Some of them must be little horrors.'

Olivia smiled. 'I have a soft spot for the little horrors.'

Now and then she came across a child who reminded her of Frankie Ruthwell. A boy – it was usually a boy – who was bright and fun and endearing but who struggled to learn to read. A boy who couldn't sit still in class and who wriggled and jiggled throughout the lessons, and who stayed at the starting blocks while his classmates surged ahead. She tried to help these pupils, to find ways of encouraging them to achieve what came so effortlessly to the others. In the small amount of spare time she had, she was trying to research what lay at the root of their problems.

'I envy you, having a proper job.' Caroline flicked her lighter. 'I'm stuck with John's secretarial work. It bores me stiff, and I don't get paid, of course.'

George called out, 'We could do with some coffee here, love.'

'Let me do it.' Heather went to the door. 'You sit down, Olivia. That was such a delicious meal.'

Dinah offered to give Heather a hand, but Heather said there was no need. She left the room.

'What a sweet girl,' Caroline said approvingly. 'And such a pretty blouse. I would look washed-out in that mushroom colour.'

Desmond moved along the sofa, making space for Olivia. George ran his palm over the polished surface of the axe. He had not looked up once as Heather had offered to make coffee and then left the room. It was all right, Olivia told herself, relieved. She was just being silly. It was a fault of hers, this lamentable lack of trust. She felt lighter now, and able to enjoy this pleasurable occasion with old friends and new.

John Farley said, 'So little survives from the Neolithic period. The few artefacts we have would have belonged to exceptional individuals. How society functioned, what the day-to-day life of the average Neolithic man consisted of and how he spent his time, we know almost nothing of that. Archaeologists have a bad habit of inferring a great deal from very little evidence.'

'I see that as the gap that poetry can inhabit.' George

refreshed his guests' wine glasses. 'That's why I lured you down here, John, to pick your brains about the past.'

'How's it going, George?' Anthony Clairmont asked. 'The new book. Finished it yet?'

'Not yet.'

'I thought you said September, that you had to wrap it up by September.'

'The end of September.' George gave a stiff smile. He always hated talking about a work in progress. His fourth collection of poems had been due at the beginning of April, but Neville had agreed to extend the deadline by six months. The tension that George felt as the date approached had pervaded the house. He had never been good at keeping his moods to himself.

Anthony ploughed tactlessly on. 'Better buck up, George. Just scribble something down. Tell you what, I'll give you a hand.' He roared at his own joke and squeezed Dinah's knee. 'That would soon polish off his career, wouldn't it, sweetie?'

'Oh, do shut up, Tony,' Dinah said mildly. 'What will the book be called?'

'*Flint and Bone*,' said George.

Rising, Olivia rested her hand on his shoulder. 'I'm going up to check on Tom,' she murmured.

She left the room. She could hear Lorcan and Gareth fooling around in the kitchen. She went upstairs. Moonlight slid through the windows, softly illuminating the house's quaint nooks and crannies, and on nights like this, the magic of the old building revealed itself.

Tom was fast asleep, the blankets thrown off, his limbs sprawled out like a starfish. He had slept like that as a baby. All three of her sons had recently recovered from chickenpox, but Tom, who was eight years old, had been the most unwell. She smoothed his straight dark brown hair back from his face. He had had a fever for night after night, but his forehead was now cool and the rash had healed over.

Tom was quieter than his elder brothers, more reserved, competent and cautious. He liked to read and cycle and make things. Like his father, he enjoyed solitariness, but unlike George, disagreements upset him.

She picked up his *Biggles* book from where it had dropped to the floor, replaced it on the shelf and switched off the lamp. Closing the bedroom door behind her, she went to the landing window and looked out. Night had draped itself across the barn roof and the hills beyond. From downstairs, she heard the sitting-room door open with a creak. Then George's familiar tread along a corridor.

His third collection of poems, *The Blue Hare*, had been published three years after *The Snow Leopard*. It had sold well, even better than its predecessor, cementing his reputation. The annual Goldscombe poetry workshop had become an established date in the literary calendar. Would-be poets enthusiastically attended it and established ones vied to tutor sessions. George was in demand as a speaker at conferences and a guest of honour at literary dinners. The previous month he had for the first time appeared on a television programme, *Monitor*.

She had everything a woman could wish for – a happy marriage to a loving, successful and celebrated man, three fine sons and a beautiful home with modern conveniences. As well as Goldscombe Farm, the Flynns now owned a flat not far from Russell Square, bought with the royalties from *The Blue Hare*. George, who disliked hotels, stayed there when he was in town.

And yet tonight her thoughts ticked away, their beat jarring and their tune unsettling. She hadn't heard George return to the sitting room. Nor Heather, come to that. Where were they?

She went downstairs to the kitchen. Heather wasn't there, though the kettle was on the hob and cups and saucers were lined up on the dresser. Perhaps she had gone upstairs to fetch a cardigan, something like that – but the attic room she was sleeping in was directly above Tom's, and surely Olivia would have heard her moving around. Olivia felt hot, suddenly, and frightened.

'Mum, we've finished,' said Lorcan.

'Well done, both of you.'

She hugged both boys, and after they left the room, she began to dry dishes from the teetering tower on the draining board. A light tread on the flagstones and Heather appeared with an empty tray.

'That's the coffees done,' she said. 'Just the teas to go. Has the kettle boiled yet? Sorry it's taken me a while, Olivia. The floor was awash, so I gave the boys a hand. I hope you don't mind, but they were making rather a meal of it. Let me help with the drying.'

'No, it's fine, thanks, Heather, that's good of you.' Relief and a measure of guilt made her say conspiratorially, 'To be honest, I wouldn't mind grabbing the chance to have a few moments to myself. I'll make the tea. You go and sit down with the others.'

'Neville and Sylvie have asked us to dinner on the second,' said George. 'You'll come, won't you?'

The Flynns were in the kitchen. It was late afternoon and Tom and Gareth had come home from school. Lorcan, who now attended a secondary school in Honiton, was expected shortly. Olivia and George were checking their diaries, except that George didn't use a diary because he claimed he could keep track of all his engagements in his head. This was manageable only because he made no attempt to recall doctor's appointments, school term dates, rugby fixtures and music lessons. Those were Olivia's department.

'I can't, I'm taking Lorcan to the dentist that afternoon. And I teach on Friday mornings.' She cut a fruit cake into slices and offered it to the boys. 'Do you want some, George?'

'No, thanks.' He lit a cigarette, looked at it, then stubbed it out. He was trying to give up. He said, 'I'll be staying at the flat that weekend.'

'Must you?' She took a bottle of milk out of the fridge.

'I've to give that talk at the dinner on the sixth.'

'Which dinner?'

'I told you.'

'It's not in my diary.'

He waved a hand. 'You must have forgotten. There could be some useful people there.'

Olivia spooned rice and sugar into a bowl for a pudding. How many more *useful people* did he need? You'd think he'd have enough by now.

George picked up on her lack of response. 'I don't do these things for *fun*,' he said irritably. 'I do them for us, for our family.'

'Look, there's Lorcan. Could you make sure he takes off his shoes before coming into the house or I'll have to mop the floor again.' It had been raining all day. Whenever it rained, the track from the bus stop to Goldscombe turned into a mire.

Lorcan tugged off his shoes, the laces still knotted, on the back doorstep. Olivia called out, 'Hello, love. Good day?' and he grunted.

'Where's your cap?' He was bare-headed, his damp curls standing up in springy tufts.

'My bag, I expect.'

Olivia dropped a knob of butter onto the rice pudding, which went in on the lowest shelf of the oven. Lorcan hurled his wet coat onto the pulley clothes airer hanging over the stove, then burrowed through his satchel, looking for his cap. Exercise books, stubs of pencil and a protractor stuck together with tape slipped to the floor.

George said, 'Nowadays it isn't enough to write the bloody poems, no, a poet is expected to prance round like a performing seal.' Giving up smoking hadn't improved his mood. Nor had his imminent deadline.

'I just wondered whether you'd think about coming home for the weekend, and then going back to London on Monday morning. It would mean we could have the Gerrards over for supper on Saturday.'

'Oh God, no.'

'Where's that cap, Lorcan?'

'It's here somewhere . . .'

'Did you have it when you came out of school?'

'I think so.'

'You *think* so? You haven't left it on the bus, have you?'

'If we're to have people to supper, for Christ's sake let it not be the Gerrards.'

'I thought you liked them.' Olivia felt hurt. Sally Gerrard was a friend of hers. They taught at the same school.

'*She's* all right, but *he's* as dull as ditchwater. And I can't be rushing up and down to Devon all the time, not when

I've a book to finish. It'll be more convenient to stay at the flat.'

Convenient for what? she wondered. And for whom? George had never in his life cared about convenience. The thought that Heather Osbourne lived in London flashed into her mind. She pushed it away.

The pages of her diary were patched like a moth-eaten jersey with the criss-crosses that indicated George's absences. 'Look!' She flicked through the pages. 'Honestly, George, just look at how often you've been away these past couple of months.'

He made a furious sound, then flung open the back door and went outside. Olivia started on the dishes. She pictured Heather at Waterloo station, waiting for George's arrival and greeting him off the train with a soft, bosomy, enveloping embrace.

Gareth said, 'Lorcan, you idiot, it's in your pocket.'

Olivia looked up to the airer. Lorcan leaped up to tug his cap out of the pocket of his mackintosh and items of clothing tumbled to the floor.

Tom had left the room. Olivia felt a flicker of dismay. Good parents kept their differences to themselves, they did not inflict them on their children. What were they coming to, that they had ended up disagreeing in front of their sons? What George had said was true, that writing great poetry wasn't enough to maintain a career, and that he must promote his work as well. She would never want to be the sort of clingy wife who complained of her husband's absences, and nor would she wish to restrict his freedom.

And what had they really been quarrelling about? Nothing much. An unfounded fear on her part and his habit of making plans without consulting her first.

Lorcan was standing back from the overhead dryer and flinging the fallen garments at it. 'Lousy aim,' said Gareth.

'*Lorcan*,' said Olivia.

'Sorry, Mum.' His cheeky grin melted her heart, and she laughed.

She went outside. The drizzle shimmered over the hills, making them insubstantial and hemming the farmhouse into the valley. George was smoking, the tip of his cigarette shimmering orange in the drizzle. She put down his moodiness to the pressure of completing the book. His dejection was visible in the angle of his head and the way he stood.

She put her arms round him. 'Sorry, love.'

'It's okay.' He rubbed her back. 'If it's what you want, I'll come home that weekend.'

'No, don't, you don't have to. It was silly of me.'

He drew her close to him. The warmth of his body comforted her, as always, but she felt the tension that quivered through him, as if he was an overstretched string.

Chapter Nine

1959, London

They were running late because George had spent most of the afternoon with his agent, Selwyn Paley. He had returned to the Bloomsbury flat after six and hurled on his evening clothes, and now they were heading at pace to Bedford Square. Olivia was wearing the new red patent-leather heels he had bought for her that morning.

As they walked, George said little, and his expression was morose. 'We could skip the party if you don't feel like it,' Olivia suggested. 'Go somewhere for a drink instead.'

'Cyril said he'd be there. There are people I need to catch up with.'

'Did Selwyn say anything?'

'Nothing much.'

He strode over a zebra crossing. She scuttled after him. Soon he was some way ahead, the gulf between them widening. It was half term; leaving the boys with her mother, Olivia had travelled up from Devon the previous afternoon to join George at their London flat. The plan was to have a few days on their own, shopping and catching up with London friends.

The party was at a house in the centre of a fine Georgian terrace. They were late, and by the time they were ushered into a grand room on the first floor the reception was in full swing. A glass chandelier suspended from the ceiling splintered the light into jewelled shards. The walls were hung with paintings of vases of frilly tulips and gloomy, mountainous landscapes. In a corner of the room, a man in a white evening jacket crooned a Dean Martin song over the echoing chatter and laughter.

A voice called out, 'George! Over here.'

Olivia said, 'Give me a minute. I'll catch up with you.' She found a quiet place, then took off her shoe and ran a finger round the inside. The heel had rubbed a hole in her stocking.

The crowds shifted and she saw a woman she immediately recognised. Though twenty years had passed since she had last seen Alice Ruthwell, she recalled clearly the cool, crisp angles of her features and her moonlight-fair hair.

She wound through the crowds to Alice's side. 'Excuse me,' she said.

'Yes?' Pale blue crystal eyes turned to her, a hint of irritation in them.

'Alice Ruthwell?'

'Alice Mortimer, actually. I'm sorry, but I don't think I . . .'

'I knew your family before the war. I worked for your mother's dressmaker, Mrs Beaumont. I'm Olivia Flynn now, but I was Goodland then.'

Grace's daughter narrowed her eyes. 'I remember.' She let out a trill of laughter. 'Goodness me, that was a long time ago!'

'I hope your parents are well.'

'Quite well, I believe. I haven't seen Mummy for a while. She lives abroad.'

'And you, I hope . . .' But what did she hope for Alice, whom she had once found sobbing in the Hinton Place breakfast room and tried to comfort? 'I hope you're well too,' she finished, rather lamely.

Alice's male companion spoke for the first time. 'Alice is always in robust health. She only looks pale and consumptive because Ivo insists she wears black in the evenings. He admires the way it contrasts with her hair.'

'Do shut up, Christopher,' said Alice.

Ivo Mortimer had good taste, Olivia thought. Alice's simple, narrow black silk cocktail dress emphasised her unusual beauty.

Alice ran a palm down her waist and hip. 'I like black. It means I don't have to think about what to wear. I can't stand girly pastels. At least Ivo and I agree about that.' This time, her laughter was sour. Her gaze returned to Olivia. 'How extraordinary, that we should meet again after all these years.'

'I came with my husband, George Flynn.'

'George Flynn the poet?' said Christopher.

'Yes.' This happened quite often.

His smile charmed her. 'Then I'm thrilled to meet you, Mrs Flynn.' He offered her his hand. 'I'm a great admirer of your husband's work. It's a shame I must dash off, because I would beg you to introduce me to him.'

Alice said, 'I'm afraid I don't know anything about poetry.'

'That's because, sweet Alice, you are a Philistine.' This was said teasingly, with an affectionate pat on Alice's arm. 'I must go. It's been a pleasure, Mrs Flynn. Alice, will you and Ivo be at the Savoy?'

'I will, I expect. I can't speak for Ivo.'

Christopher left. Through the sliver of silence that fell between the two women, Olivia heard, some distance away, George's familiar roar of laughter. She said, 'How is Frankie? I hope he's doing well.'

Alice's expression altered. 'Frankie died.'

Olivia stared at her in shock. 'Oh no.'

'I'm afraid so. It was a long time ago.'

'How awful. Oh, I'm so sorry.' Though she tried to collect herself and offer condolences in a coherent manner, she struggled to take in the news. For a moment she wished that on recognising Alice Ruthwell she had avoided her.

Alice said, 'I'd forgotten you knew him.'

'I remember what a sweet boy he was.' How horrible and jarring it was to hear of the death of someone so young. 'You said he died some time ago?'

'Yes, in the last winter of the war.' Alice looked at her cigarette, which had burned down to a stub, then dropped it into her empty glass. 'I'd started to hope he was going to get through it.'

Amid the hubbub of the party, Olivia strained to hear the muttered words. 'Get through the war, you mean?'

Alice stared at her. 'No, no, boarding school. He absolutely hated it. He was thrown out of one, and one of the others closed down, and I remember there was another he left for some reason. And then he ended up in a frightful place in Yorkshire.' She paused. 'He died of an asthma attack. I'd meant to visit him, but I never did, and I've always regretted that. The school was so far away. I wasn't well, and you know how difficult it was, travelling then, but I ought to have gone.' Looking down, she added, scarcely audibly, 'Ivo tells me I'm selfish.'

Olivia spoke gently. 'Poor Frankie. But poor you, also, to lose a brother. I didn't mean to upset you. I'm sorry.'

'No, it's all right, honestly. I like to talk about him.' Alice gave a small smile. 'He died so long ago, and Mummy and Daddy never mention him. No one talks about him. It's as if everyone's forgotten him. It's almost as if he never existed.'

'Do you know what happened to Frankie's tutor?'

'Rory? Oh, he left.'

'Do you mean he left after Frankie was sent to school?'

'No, it was earlier than that. Daddy told me he just walked out. Maybe he got fed up with us all.'

The man at the microphone was singing 'Blue Moon'. The joyful strains soared above the commotion.

'My father has a temper,' Alice said suddenly. 'That awful engagement party they held for me. I'd never seen him so angry. It frightened me. I've sometimes thought it cursed me and Ivo, but that's nonsense, of course.'

'I'm sorry,' Olivia said. 'Did your parents divorce?'

'Yes, quite soon after my engagement. Daddy is married to someone else now.' Alice's mouth made a contemptuous shape. 'Celesta is such a tedious woman.'

'What about your mother?'

'She lives on her own, in the south of France. She travels a lot and goes to stay with her friends. I visit her most summers.'

A genial-looking man came to stand at Alice's side. Some years older than her, he had receding brown hair and kind eyes. 'Michael, thank goodness,' said Alice, and Olivia saw for the first time a softness in her expression. 'Olivia, this is Michael Hain. Michael, this is . . . forgive me, I've forgotten your surname.'

'Flynn. Olivia Flynn.' She shook Michael's hand.

'Michael, darling, could you get me another drink?' Then Alice clutched the sleeve of his jacket. 'No, don't bother. Let's go.' She turned to Olivia. 'It was good to talk to you. I'm so pleased you remember Frankie.'

Alice and Michael's fingers threaded together as they left the room. Olivia retreated to her spot by the wall, where she slipped off her shoes and wiggled her toes. Her encounter with Alice Ruthwell had shaken her.

In the years that had passed, she had almost forgotten about the Ruthwells. It saddened her now to think of Grace living alone. She wondered whether Claude had another heir now, a healthy son to replace the sickly one. A son to inherit his fortune and status.

George reappeared. 'Once Ken starts talking, it's hard to get a word in edgeways,' he said. 'Let's go.'

They went downstairs and Olivia waited for George to collect their coats. Perhaps she had no right to feel upset. But the news of Frankie's death at school had had time to sink in.

A brisk wind tugged leaves from the branches of a gingko; they stuck to the damp pavement, a scattered handful of miniature golden fans. They were heading for a jazz club in Soho, where they were to meet friends.

'So did you have fun?' asked George.

'I bumped into someone I used to know.'

'Really?'

'She used to be Alice Ruthwell. I knew the Ruthwells before the war. Alice married a man called Ivo Mortimer. I got the impression that the marriage isn't very happy.'

'I shouldn't have thought it would be.' They crossed a road.

'Do you know him, George?'

'I've run into him a couple of times.'

'What's he like?'

'Wealthy. Good-looking. A snob, and sarcastic as hell. The man-about-town type – too much money and a crowd of hangers-on, most of them fawning young men. I'd always assumed he was that way inclined.'

George was implying that Alice's husband was attracted to men. Olivia wondered whether Grace, who had been a sophisticated woman, had known that when she had chosen Mortimer for her daughter.

'Poor Alice,' she said.

'I doubt she wants for anything.'

'Except love, perhaps.'

'Yes. Except for that.' He drew her to him, looking down at her, frowning. 'Is something wrong? You've seemed a bit distant lately.'

'I don't mean to be.'

'I need you, Olivia. I need you so much. I always thank God I found you.'

They kissed. She felt as if they were repairing something she had only recently realised was easily breakable.

On the fringes of Soho, the streets were busier and more colourful. Tattered posters advertised revues and calypso evenings; car horns blared.

She said, 'Was Selwyn well?'

'Selwyn?'

'Didn't you say he was seeing someone about his cough?'

'Yes . . . yes. I don't think he's had the appointment yet.' Then George said, 'By the way, it doesn't look like we'll be seeing much more of Heather. A friend of hers has started up a writers' retreat in Fife and has asked her to work there with him. She's always wanted to do something like that.'

'That's marvellous,' Olivia murmured. She felt her spirits lifting and she looked forward enormously to the rest of the evening.

A rumble of car engines and shrieks as half a dozen people spilled out of a pub. Girls in black polo necks and angora skirts hung outside the entrance to the jazz club in Dean Street, waiting for their boyfriends, and the distant strains of music made Olivia want to dance.

'I've been thinking,' George said. 'Would you mind if we went home tomorrow?'

'If you like.' In the shadowy corridor she could not read his expression. 'I thought you had things you needed to do?'

'Nothing is more important than spending time at home with you.'

They went inside the auditorium and were enveloped by music. Couples swayed on the small dance floor. Olivia caught sight of their friends, sitting on the far side of the room, and waved, and then George took her in his arms and pressed his cheek against hers as they danced.

Chapter Ten

1965, Devon and London

By half past three that December afternoon, the sky was resolutely darkening. Sorting laundry in the lean-to, which housed the washing machine, Olivia's breath made cloudy puffs in the chilly air as she checked pockets for forgotten items and divided the clothing into whites and coloureds. She was in a rush because she needed to put a casserole in the oven for supper and peel potatoes and prepare vegetables. If she got a move on, she would have time to weigh out the ingredients for the Christmas pudding and start it steaming. She was looking forward to going to London in a couple of days' time, where she would stay in their Bloomsbury flat and visit friends and pick up last-minute presents.

She extracted a crumpled piece of paper from the pocket of George's brown corduroy trousers and smoothed it out. Sometimes she had to rescue fragments of poems from his garments.

It wasn't a poem. It was a bill from a hotel in Marylebone. She was at first bewildered. Why would George have an invoice from a Marylebone hotel?

She abandoned the laundry on the slate floor and hurried to the kitchen, opened her diary and checked the date on the bill, a Saturday at the end of October. George had been at a dinner in Manchester that night. She remembered asking him about it. 'It was fine,' he had said. 'It went well.' The entry told her that Lorcan had been using their London flat that weekend because he had been meeting his girlfriend, Tyra, at the Troubadour. There were two bedrooms in the flat, so there would have been plenty of room for both George and Lorcan. There should have been no need for George to stay in a hotel. Suspicion uncoiled like a serpent inside her. And anyway, he was supposed to be in Manchester.

Unless. She pushed back her hair from her face. Tom came into the room, searching for something to eat. Olivia looked out of the window at the misty opalescent green of garden and hills, then back at the kitchen, at its beloved familiar objects and furnishings, and at tall, skinny, fifteen-year-old Tom, who was prising open the biscuit tin. And she was afraid that they were teetering on the edge of a precipice, about to tumble over, and soon nothing would ever be the same again.

The phone was in the kitchen, and Tom was in the kitchen, scoffing the contents of the biscuit tin. Whenever Lorcan had tried to ring Tyra today, someone else had been around, Tom or Mum or Dad or Janice, who came in the mornings to help with the housework, or that odd bloke, a poet, who was a friend of Dad's and who had been staying with them for the last few weeks. Gareth was in earshot just now, and Lorcan certainly wouldn't try to call Tyra when his brother was around.

A month had passed since he had last seen her; a fortnight had gone by since they had most recently spoken on the phone. Tyra lived in a shared house in Earls Court and wasn't easy to get hold of. In term time, Lorcan lived in Oxford, where he was reading English language and literature. In September, he had been staying with a friend in London when he had met Tyra at a folk night in a pub in Rathbone Place. Languid and slender, she had long, straight brown hair and had been wearing a loose black sweater and narrow blue jeans, which emphasised her slim legs. Her black eyeliner and mascara had been so heavily applied they had seemed to weigh down her lids, so that her dark eyes gleamed like narrow chips of asphalt, which added to her aloof air. He had thought her incredibly sexy.

He had bought her a drink and they had chatted, their conversation sporadic because of the need to pause to listen to the singers on the small stage. Lorcan had discovered that Tyra had moved to London from Lincolnshire eighteen months ago, and that she worked in a fashion boutique in Kensington High Street. Though she was enjoying London, she wanted one day to live in Italy. She had a passion for Italian food, music and films and was going to evening classes to learn the language. Later, parting outside the pub, they had kissed.

He had seen her several times since then, in Oxford and in London, where they had gone to the Troubadour. As they had left the folk club at the end of the evening, he had mentioned casually that because his father was in Manchester he had the flat to himself. And she had turned to him and said, 'Lorcan, you're very sweet, but this is just for fun, you do know that, don't you? As soon as I can fix up work and somewhere to stay, I'm going abroad.'

'Of course,' he had said with a smile. 'Just for fun.'

Yet now he yearned to hear her quiet, breathy voice. Tom

was still polishing off the Rich Teas and Gareth was reading in the front room across the hall. Lorcan's gaze settled on the Morris Minor in the courtyard. The last time he had borrowed the car, his father had made a ridiculous fuss about a tiny scratch on the bonnet. His parents were upstairs. He could hear the distant rumble of voices; they were arguing.

He said to Tom, 'I'm going out. Need to make a call. I'll be about half an hour.' Grabbing his jacket and the car keys, he left the house.

When Olivia went up to the attic, George was sitting at his desk, pencil in hand. The single small window was dappled with condensation. She dropped the piece of paper in front of him.

She said, 'What's this? What is it, George?' She saw him make the effort to emerge from his inner world. 'Let me help you,' she said. 'It's a hotel bill. I found it in your trouser pocket.'

Expressions flickered across his face. She could almost read, written on his features, his panicked search for an explanation. George had a marvellous imagination, but even he couldn't come up with a convincing reason for taking a room in a hotel when he had a perfectly good flat a mile away, and when he was supposed to be in Manchester.

She said, 'Why were you staying in a hotel that night?'

'I can't remember. It's a while ago . . . I'd need to . . .'

'Perhaps you needed privacy.'

'Olivia . . .'

'What's going on, George?'

The fragment of silence before he began to bluster told her everything. Her surge of fear made her feel breathless.

'Who was it? What was her name?'

After another silence, he mumbled, 'Nadia Lessiter.'

'Nadia Lessiter?' Her mind went blank. 'Who is she? One of your students?'

'She's a poet. I met her at a party.'

'I don't care where you met her!' She looked away, through the window, unable to bear his furtive, cornered expression. 'How long?'

'Sweetheart, it's over.' He half rose from the desk, but she backed away. 'It's been over for weeks. I am so, so sorry.'

'How long?' The repeated words were a whisper.

George covered his face with his hands. 'Three or four times, that's all.'

Three or four? Didn't he *know*? Couldn't he *remember*?

'Olivia, I'm so sorry.' The muttered words were barely audible through the lattice of his fingers. 'It was never serious.'

And that makes it better? Quickly she left the room and hurried down the attic stairs.

Gareth was in the sitting room, reading *Dune*, when he heard his mother descend the stairs to the hall. He had heard the raised voices from the attic. He called out, 'Do you want a cup of tea, Mum?'

'No, thanks, darling. Just going to check on the hens.'

Gareth listened as the front door opened and closed, then he rose and went into the kitchen. Tom was in there, looking out of the window. They both watched their mother cross the courtyard, her face a streak of white in the drizzle.

Tom said, 'What were they arguing about?'

'Dunno.' Gareth had been unable to pick out words, only the timbre of his parents' voices, his mother's bewildered and upset, his father's alternately pleading and defensive. He considered running after her, but then thought she might prefer to be alone.

Tom said, 'Lorcan's gone out. He's taken the car.'

'Did he say where he was going?'

Tom shook his head. 'He said he needed to make a phone call.'

'Tyra, I expect.'

'He said he'd be back in half an hour.'

Gareth looked round the kitchen. There were carrots, celery and onions on the work surface and stewing steak, its paper wrapping unpeeled, on the marble chopping board. Mum seemed to have forgotten about supper, and that bothered him. Storms might rage through the Flynn household, but meals generally appeared on time.

He decided to go ahead with making the casserole. He chopped the onions, blinking fiercely, while Tom volunteered to prepare the carrots and celery. Gareth tossed pieces of stewing steak in flour and seasoning, like his mother always did, and put them in the pan to brown. He liked cooking, the ritual of it. He kept looking out of the window to see whether Mum was coming back yet, but there was no sign of her. She was obviously doing something other than checking on the hens.

He made a pot of tea and took a cup upstairs to his father's study. 'Thought you might like a tea, Dad,' he said.

His father said nothing. His mouth stretched in something that might have been intended as a smile, and after a beat Gareth left the room. That was what struck him most as he went downstairs: that his father, who generally had plenty to say about absolutely everything, had said nothing at all.

Tom said, when he came back into the kitchen, 'Is Dad all right?'

'He's fine.'

'Is he coming down?'

'I don't know. Have you finished the vegetables?'

Tom passed him a saucepan. Gareth dropped the carrots and celery into the casserole along with the sizzling meat and onions and gave everything a vigorous stir.

In Loxleigh, Lorcan queued in the rain for the phone box. Through the walls of the kiosk issued a muffled version of the present occupant's conversation. *I know . . . I know. Jean, I know, lovey*. He was starting to get anxious about Dad noticing he'd borrowed the car, but then the caller put down the receiver and emerged from the box. Lorcan thanked her and went inside.

He fiddled around with buttons and money. Tyra answered on the third ring.

'Lorcan! How lovely to speak to you. How are you?'

'Marooned in deepest, darkest Devon. I wish I was in London with you.'

'What are you doing in deepest, darkest Devon?'

'Nothing much. Reading.' He was ploughing through *Beowulf*. And Virginia Woolf, for contrast. 'I've been on a few hikes,' he said 'and I might go camping for a couple of nights. But I could come up to London. We could go and see a film or something.'

'Lorcan . . .'

'A concert, if you prefer.'

'Sweetheart, I'm off to Italy.'

He heard himself repeat blankly, 'Italy?'

'The teacher at my evening class put me in touch with a family in Florence. I'm going to work there as an au pair. It's all arranged.'

'Oh.' He knew he needed to add, 'That's marvellous, Tyra.'

'Thanks. I'm so excited. I can't wait.'

'When are you going?'

'In a couple of weeks, straight after Christmas. Look, I must go, I'm meeting some friends. Look after yourself, won't you, love? I'll send you a postcard.'

He murmured a goodbye and put down the phone. He couldn't face going home yet, so he went into the pub along the road. A log fire smouldered in the inglenook fireplace, warming the cosy, attractive room with its blackened beams and ochre-coloured plaster. Lorcan lit a cigarette and chatted to the friendly barmaid, Linda, who had been in the year above him at school. A game of dominoes was going on in one corner, bar billiards in another.

He was sipping his second pint, and he and Linda were discussing their Christmas plans, when he remembered the car. Dad would be furious if he found out he'd taken it without permission. When he glanced at the clock, he saw to his horror that an hour and a half had passed since he had left the house.

He downed the rest of his beer at speed and walked back to the Morris Minor. Starting up the engine, he acknowledged that he had not really taken Tyra's ambition of going to Italy seriously. He had thought it a fantasy, a pipe dream. Though he admired the tenacity with which she had pursued her objective, all he could think of was how much he would miss her.

He headed out of the village. In the countryside, the trees and the high banks to either side of the unlit single-track roads cast soot-black shadows. The Morris Minor clunked and leaped in the potholes, and as the wheels rushed through puddles, they cast up a tsunami of spray. The night and the rain made it hard to see the road ahead, so he rubbed at the inside of the windscreen with his handkerchief.

Just then, a rabbit dashed across the lane, feet away from the bonnet. Lorcan slammed on the brakes so as not to hit the animal and lost control of the vehicle. There was a *thunk* as the nose of the car slammed into the clay bank. The impact knocked the breath out of him. *Shit, shit, shit* . . . he muttered. He heard the high-pitched call of a little owl as the engine cut out, immersing him in darkness.

Tom said to Gareth that it was supposed to clear later. He went upstairs to do something with his telescope, which he kept in one of the attic rooms. This was one of the many distinctive things about Tom, Gareth thought, that he always knew what the weather was going to be. He himself never thought about weather from one moment to the next. If he got soaked, then he got soaked.

He scrubbed the potatoes and put them in the stove beside the casserole, then glanced at the clock. He went outside. It was pitch dark now, but Tom's prediction had been correct: the rain had cleared at last and a few stars sprinkled the sky. His mother wasn't at the henhouse, so he walked through the garden, past the apple and pear trees and the raised beds that contained the mid-December blowsy cabbages and the dripping brown skeletons of tall, thistle-like plants.

He caught sight of her coming down the slope of the hill. He went to meet her, and they walked back to the house together. Her wet hair clung to her face like seaweed and even in the poor light he could tell she had been crying.

He said, 'What's up, Mum?'

'Nothing important. Just a silly quarrel with your father.'

'Are you okay?'

'I'm fine, darling, I just went for a walk.'

In this weather? He said, 'I put the casserole on.'

She gave him a quick, startled glance. 'Oh! Thank you, love.'

She was so plainly not okay. Gareth tried to think of the right thing to say and at the same time thought perhaps he shouldn't say anything at all.

Instead, he said, 'Lorcan's not back yet.'

His mother's gaze swung to him. 'I didn't know he'd gone out.'

'He's gone to Loxleigh to phone Tyra, I think.'

'Tyra? But he could have phoned her from the house.'

'He said he'd be back in half an hour.'

'You mean, he's taken the car?'

'Yes.'

'How long has he been gone?'

'A couple of hours.'

They had almost reached the house. The Morris Minor wasn't in the courtyard. Gareth matched his pace to his mother's as she quickened her step.

As the train pulled out of Honiton a few days later, Olivia felt she could finally breathe again. She needed the time and peace to think, but also to protect her boys from the horrors of warring parents. Despite the row she and George had had, when Lorcan had been found to be missing, nothing else had mattered. George had cycled off in the rain to find him and had returned with Lorcan, who was badly bruised and shaken. He'd handled the situation admirably, not even mentioning the damage to the car, which was probably a write-off. At one point Olivia had felt tempted to forgive him, and yet deep down she knew she had to get away. The train flew through the countryside; sitting in the carriage, she pictured herself staying in the capital, licking her wounds, for ever. But what then of Lorcan, Gareth and Tom, whom she loved beyond anything?

When they had first bought the London flat, Olivia had imagined that she would transform it into a charming pied-à-terre. But she had never got round to it, and George, who used it far more than she, didn't care about such things. The rooms were echoing and unfamiliar. The flat, so masculine in character, was George's territory. It occurred to her that they had not merely grown apart; some of the time, at least, they had come to live in different worlds.

She put her small suitcase in the bedroom, then tore off all the bed linen and flung it in a heap in the second bedroom, where he worked, before making up the bed with clean sheets. Then, though she had told herself she wouldn't do this, she walked towards George's desk. Still wearing her coat, the kettle not yet boiled, the cold of the streets and the clamour of a crowded Waterloo station clinging to her, she searched through the items in the desk drawers. Then the filing cabinet, and then George's books, turning them over and flipping through the pages to see whether any receipts fell out.

Her gaze moved slowly across the papers on the desk, over the small, lined pages torn from notebooks on which he had scribbled a phrase or a single word, then the royalty statements and compliments slips and the scribbled notes for an article or a radio broadcast. On the desk were the folio notebooks in which he wrote the first drafts of his poems, always in pencil. She turned pages darkened by multiple crossings-out and amendments in the margins. The special stationery, obtainable only at Smythson in Bond Street, the 2B pencils, sharpened to a point, and his refusal to use a typewriter or even an eraser struck her now as pretentious.

She had a fierce urge to crumple everything up and set fire to his words. The revenge might be fleeting, but it would be pleasurable.

Assiduously, she went through the invoices. The bills were for secretarial services and stamps, not for hotel rooms. If they had written to each other, George and his lover, their letters were not here.

The burst of energy drained away and she stood at the window, watching the afternoon darken. She pushed back her hair from her face and rubbed the tears from her eyes. She should unpack, she should dig out a warmer jersey, she should hang up the dress she had brought for going to the ballet with her god-daughter, Sarah; she should phone her London friends. But she remained at the window, looking out.

'How long have you known?' Louise asked.

They were in her Earls Court flat. Louise moved about the rooms with her customary efficiency and elegance, cooking supper and mixing gin and tonics and changing the record on the gramophone.

'Three days,' Olivia said.

'Olivia, I'm so sorry.' Louise put a glass in front of her.

She looked down at it. Slices of lemon – Amalfi lemons, Louise always bought Amalfi lemons – bobbed in the bluish gin. Her mind jerked away at a tangent and she felt envious of Louise for buying plump yellow lemons from a Soho delicatessen rather than purchasing uninspiring, wizened little fruits from the greengrocer in Loxleigh as she herself did.

She told Louise the whole story, punctuating her phrases with gin, which blurred things: a relief.

Louise sat down on the sofa, one long, slim leg tucked beneath her. 'Do the boys know?'

Olivia shook her head. 'I couldn't bring myself to tell them; especially after Lorcan's accident. Though I do wonder if they might have guessed something's wrong.'

She had always been the person who mended and fixed things, but there had been moments during these few days when she had wondered whether the fabric of her life was beyond repair. She ran her gaze round the room. Louise had recently had it papered with a design of pale coral flamingos amid wafting reeds. She would have liked to fly away like a bird, to take to the sky with a spring of step and flap of wing.

She said, 'Once I knew Lorcan was all right, all I could think of was coming up to London to be on my own at last.' She considered what she had just said to Louise, who had spent so much of the past twenty-five years on her own. She groaned. 'I'm sorry. I shouldn't inflict this on you.'

'Why not?' Louise raised her eyebrows at her. 'Don't be silly. This is what friends are for.'

Before she had left the house yesterday morning, George had said to her, *You will come home, won't you?*

I don't know, she had said. And had added, *You don't imagine, do you, that we'll just go on as we are?* She had not spoken to him since. She wanted him to think it all over too. The phone in the flat had rung several times, but she had not answered it.

Louise said, 'Who is she?'

Olivia sighed. 'She's called Nadia Lessiter. She's a poet.'

'I don't think I've ever seen a female poet who dressed well.'

'I'm trying not to go to Hatchards and look for her photo on the back of a book.'

'Don't.' Louise glowered at her. 'Promise me you won't. It doesn't help, to feed one's paranoia.'

Louise always had a boyfriend, someone to take her out to dinner and the theatre. They never lasted, these men, though quite often she remained friends with them afterwards. Olivia wondered whether any of Louise's lovers were married. Personable, interesting single men must be thinner on the ground once you were in your forties.

She said, 'George said it was over; that it hadn't been serious.'

'Do you believe him?'

'I don't know. Sometimes I even wonder if I care. I don't seem to be certain of anything much. I feel . . . at a loss. Until I found that wretched bill, I had no idea. Oh, Louise, how could I have been so *dim*?'

How could she not have guessed at what might go on behind the convenient facade of interviews, dinners and poetry readings? George was often away from home, and frequently surrounded by admiring women. Even if this time she forgave him, the life he led put temptation in his way and he might stray again.

What hurt most was that he had chosen to be with Nadia Lessiter rather than with her. Though he had told her they had slept together three or four times, even she wasn't naïve enough to believe that. She expected they had tumbled into bed whenever the opportunity arose.

She remembered the time she had come to stay with Louise just after Sarah's birth. She had been so desperately in love with George then, torn apart with longing for him.

The conversation turned to mutual friends, and then Louise went to check on supper. Olivia followed her into the kitchen.

Louise said, 'You're seeing Sarah, aren't you?'

'We're going to *The Sleeping Beauty*. Her choice. I can't wait.'

The tickets had been booked months ago for her annual Christmas treat with her god-daughter. Ballet – the music and spectacle of it, emotion unmitigated by words, pure and raw – had always touched her soul, but the crisis with George so occupied her mind she wondered whether she would be able to focus on it.

The words burst out of her. 'Louise, I don't know what to do.'

'You don't have to do anything. Not now.' Louise hugged her. 'You need to give yourself time to think, to listen to your heart. Work out what *you* want. And if you ever need to get away, you know where I am.'

Olivia asked after Louise's latest lover, who worked in the Diplomatic Service.

'He's being sent to the Far East,' Louise said.

'Lou, I'm sorry to hear that. You like him, don't you?'

'I'm fond of him, yes, and it's a shame, but if I'm honest, I'm not broken-hearted.' She peered into a saucepan. 'The truth is, I never am. I expect an analyst would tell me I'm frightened of falling in love in case something awful happens again, and they wouldn't be completely wrong. But it's not only that. I'm too damn fussy, and anyway, I like being free to do whatever I want.' She drained the potatoes into the sink. 'The only thing is . . .'

'What?' said Olivia.

Louise sighed. 'I do sometimes wonder if it's rather cowardly of me. And then I think, why not? I'm happy living on my own.'

The next day, Olivia visited Maudie Gresham. Maudie's marriage had broken up several years ago. Olivia waited in for a plumber to repair the broken boiler so that her friend could go to the shops and catch up on buying Christmas gifts, and afterwards they had supper together.

The following morning, shopping in Knightsbridge and Piccadilly, she found, rather to her surprise, that she had regained her energy and was getting into the swing of things. The bag she deposited in the Royal Opera House's cloakroom after meeting Sarah for lunch was crammed with Christmas treats, chocolates from Fortnum's and new shirts for the boys from Selfridges.

She and Sarah sat side by side in the darkness and brilliance of the upper circle of the auditorium. Some distance away on stage a succession of princes vied for Princess Aurora's hand in marriage as Tchaikovsky's music swirled around the vast theatre. Olivia stole a glance at Sarah and smiled. She felt pride and pleasure in being with such a poised and intelligent young woman.

The curtain came down on the second act. The auditorium filled with applause and Olivia and Sarah joined the crowds filing out of the upper circle. In the bar, Sarah offered to go and get drinks. They had the usual tussle, Olivia saying no, she must get them, and Sarah pointing out that Olivia had bought the tickets. Quite soon she gave in. As Sarah disappeared into the melee around the bar, Olivia stood to one side of the room. Today she had felt an unexpected lightening of spirit. Of one thing she was now certain: if she and George were to continue to have a shared future, then it must be different from what had gone before.

Loud voices from not far away caught her attention. Half a dozen men and women of around her own age were making an uproar about a glass someone had dropped on the floor. One of the women, Olivia now saw, was Alice Mortimer.

Alice seemed to see her at the same time. She gave the man who was making the most noise a little shove and picked her way through the glass splinters towards Olivia. She was wearing a short dark blue satin sack dress and low-heeled, mid-calf white boots.

'I thought it was you. I saw you from our box. I said . . .' Alice waggled a forefinger, 'I said to Rudy, I know that woman. How are you?'

'I'm very well. And you, Alice?'

'I'm celebrating. My decree nisi came through this morning. Don't feel sorry for me.' She gave a brisk shake of the head. 'I couldn't be more delighted.'

'I'm happy for you, then.'

'We never had children, and I suppose that made the divorce simpler.' From beneath her fringe, Alice peered at Olivia. 'I'm sorry telling you all this, but you see, I'm rather drunk. You mustn't mind me.'

'Are you enjoying the performance?'

Alice gave a low, frowning nod. 'It's hard to concentrate because the people I came with are such bores and they fool around. Michael is away. He's a circuit judge, did I tell you? He's circuiting in the north.' With exaggerated care, she drew a circle with her fingertip.

Olivia remembered the kindly-looking man from the party in Bedford Square, and how his fingers had threaded through Alice's as they had left the room.

'When he comes back to London,' Alice went on, 'we're going to look for a house.'

'You're getting married?'

'As soon as my decree absolute comes through.'

'Congratulations. I hope you'll be very happy. Where will you live?'

'In the countryside. We both prefer the countryside. Michael comes from Hampshire, and he loves it there. I want to keep horses.' Alice sighed. 'I can't wait. Michael's the sweetest man and I adore him, and he adores me. He's the only person in the whole wide world who thinks I'm adorable. I don't blame them, I can be a complete and utter bitch, and really, I . . .' She broke off, then said softly, 'I'm a better person when I'm with Michael.'

For a moment Olivia envied Alice Mortimer. Did being with George make *her* a better person? It had once.

Alice said, 'It's funny that I should run into you, Olivia. Guess who I saw a few weeks ago? Rory Madden. You remember, he was Frankie's tutor.'

'I remember.'

'We were on the same Underground train. I looked along the carriage and there he was. He hadn't changed a bit. I told him about Frankie.' A man carrying a tower of ice-cream tubs apologised as he stepped between them, and Alice gave him a chilly smile.

'Does he live in London?'

'Yes, he said so.' Someone called out to Alice, who looked back at her friends and made a shooing motion. 'I told him I'd bumped into you at that party, Olivia.'

'Did he remember me?'

'More than that. He asked after you specifically. I said you'd married a poet.'

Sarah appeared with the drinks. The bell rang, signalling that the interval would shortly be over. Olivia said goodbye to Alice, then she and Sarah returned to their seats for the third act.

As the wedding of Aurora and her prince was celebrated, Olivia's mind drifted to her younger self, nineteen years old, living in London and falling in love for the very first time. More than twenty-five years had passed since she had last seen Rory Madden, and yet however hard she tried to concentrate on the events on stage, her thoughts kept returning to the handsome Scotsman she had met at the Ruthwells' house.

Olivia and Dinah Clairmont were in the ladies' fashion department in Liberty. Apart from her work as a freelance translator, Dinah also ran a small business helping to choose clothes for a select band of wealthy women. One of her clients was a doctor, another a politician, a third a socialite. Another hated shopping and was bored by it. Olivia had been on these expeditions before and always enjoyed them, and Dinah admired her taste.

Every now and then Dinah, burrowing along a rail, would pull out a garment. 'Anita will adore this,' she would say. Or 'Marjorie has asked me to look for an evening top.'

She held up a jacket. 'Don't you think this would be just the thing for Rosemary?'

Rosemary was the doctor. 'It's very smart,' Olivia said. 'And practical.'

'Yes, all those pockets. How are you enjoying London, Olivia?'

'Much more than I thought I would. It's funny, isn't it, how one can divide oneself into separate pieces.'

'It's a useful skill.' Frowning, Dinah inspected a tweed pinafore dress, then put it back. 'Charlie was such a tiny little thing when Miles left me.' Miles had been Dinah's first husband. 'I used to allow myself to have a good howl while Charlie was having his afternoon nap, and then the rest of the time I made sure to be cheerful. And the more one pretends, the more one actually is, don't you find?' She pounced on a pink blouse. 'Marjorie will like this. Though those buttons . . .'

'You could change the buttons. Pearl ones, perhaps.'

'Such a darling neckline.'

'I've been trying to think what to do. Sometimes it seems quite impossible, the idea of staying with George, and sometimes I think, well, doesn't this sort of thing happen to lots of couples, one way or another?'

'More than you'd imagine, I suspect.' Dinah draped the pink blouse over her arm. 'Olivia, George has been a complete and utter scoundrel. You're entitled to feel angry with him.'

'When you found out about Miles and Jen, did you know then, straight away, that that was the end?'

'No, I don't think so. What about this?' Dinah held up a dress against Olivia, made a face, then put it back. 'You put so much into a marriage, don't you, so much love and energy, and it's hard to accept that it's over. But eventually I came to accept that he was in love with Jen, and that was the clincher. Sex is one thing, but emotional commitment is quite another. For me, anyway. All marriages are different. What one couple can tolerate is an insurmountable hurdle for another. Oh, Olivia, you must try that on.'

Olivia had taken from the rail a pillarbox-red cashmere jersey. 'Such a gorgeous colour,' she said.

'It'll look so striking with your dark colouring. Do you think George is in love with the wretched woman?'

'No, I'm sure he isn't.'

An assistant came and took the garments from Dinah, carrying them to the counter. Dinah said to Olivia, 'Thank goodness I met Tony. Mind you, it took me more than a *decade*. I said to myself that I thought it would be confusing for Charlie to inflict a stepfather on him, but when I look back, I think the truth is I found it hard to trust a man again. But Tony is such a dear and devoted chap.' She gave Olivia a sympathetic look. 'In the end, what matters most is whether you still love him.'

In the changing room, Olivia tried on the red jersey. Glancing at the price tag, she felt fleetingly stunned, but bought it anyway, with a surge of exhilaration as she wrote the cheque.

Gareth said, 'Why don't you go and see her, Dad?'

'What?' George was wandering round the kitchen, putting things in the wrong place. 'Who?'

The Queen? Joan Baez? Wasn't it obvious? Gareth said patiently, 'Mum, of course.' Tom, who was by the back door, digging mud out of the soles of his boots with the tip of a screwdriver, looked round.

'You mean go to London?' George said.

'Yes.'

'And leave you two?'

'*Dad*,' said Tom. 'I'm *fifteen*.' He gathered up the lumps of dried mud and put them on a flower bed.

Gareth went back to scraping solidified scrambled egg off the bottom of a saucepan. Mum didn't go away for days and days on end and not phone. She just didn't. And it would, frankly, be a relief not to have his father around, attempting to cook supper and then kicking off because he couldn't find the whisk and burning the eggs. Tom didn't even *like* scrambled eggs because of the gloopy bits. Gareth didn't say any of this to his dad because he felt sorry for him. Whatever he had done that had annoyed Mum so much, he looked miserable all the time and was frankly rather useless without her.

'I suppose I could,' George said.

'There's a train from Honiton to Waterloo at five to eleven.' Tom was the only person Gareth knew who memorised train timetables.

George looked at his watch. 'Good idea, chaps. I'll throw a few things in a rucksack.' He put a handful of banknotes on the table. 'Cash for food.' Then he went upstairs.

Gareth let out a breath. *Thank God.* He waved a five-pound note at Tom. 'Cycle to Loxleigh and get whatever you want,' he said. 'Crisps, Maltesers, I don't mind.'

When Olivia returned to the flat after having coffee with Caroline Farley, she saw that George's black coat was on a peg in the hall. His rucksack lay beneath the console table.

He came out of the kitchen as she was unbuttoning her coat. She said, 'Why are you here, George?'

'To talk to you, if you'll let me.'

His clothes were messy, his curls tangled, and he needed to shave. It crossed her mind that the *distrait* look was intentional, to get sympathy, but then he said:

'I wasn't going to come. I understand that you need time on your own. I just . . . I couldn't bear it any longer. I phoned . . . I wrote . . . You didn't answer.'

She had put his letters in the bin without opening them and had taken the phone off the hook. 'I didn't want to speak to you. You're so good with words, George. I didn't want you persuading me to do something I didn't want to do.'

'I would never do that.'

'You would.'

'Come home, please, Olivia. The boys miss you.'

She looked at him, raising her eyebrows and widening

her eyes, and he held up his palms and made a hissing sound. 'Yes, okay, that was underhand of me. But it's true. They miss you, and I miss you so much. I don't deserve to miss you, but I do. That's what I came here to say. I'll do anything to win back your trust.'

'I don't know whether that's possible.' She hung up her coat. 'I'm not saying that to put the knife in, George, it's just how it is.'

She went into the sitting room. He had put on the gas fire and the room was pleasantly warm. She sat down and stretched out her hands towards it. Every muscle ached. She had been holding herself in tension for days.

He said, 'Do you want a drink?'

'Please.' She watched him take out glasses, unscrew a bottle of whisky, then she said, 'Why did you do it?'

Moments passed before he answered. 'Because I could. I mean, it was possible.'

'Dear God, George.'

'I know, I know. I'm sorry, but I'm trying to be honest. There were, I suppose . . . contributing factors. There was a piece in *The Times* – that creep Finley Palmer wrote a skit making fun of *Flint and Bone*.'

'You didn't say.'

'I couldn't bear being ridiculed.' He handed her a drink. 'I'm not good at *failure*.'

'So you had an affair because your ego was bruised,' she said coldly.

He sat down, then let out a breath. 'It was an element,' he acknowledged.

She sipped her whisky and ginger. Twenty years, she thought. When exactly, during the twenty years of their marriage, had passion and kindness slipped away and been replaced by carelessness? Or had he already been primed for betrayal when they had first met? After all, he had been engaged to another woman.

He said, 'A couple of engagements had fallen through. Last-minute cancellations. I didn't know whether they were because of the thing in *The Times*, but that's what I assumed at the time. I was at rather a loose end when Nadia called me, and I . . . well, I . . .' He broke off. 'Sorry,' he muttered. 'I'm so sorry. But that's the truth.'

If he had blamed Nadia Lessiter, she would have despised him. 'The night in the hotel must have taken some planning,' she said.

He looked away. Silence stretched between them. 'It was stupid and selfish,' he said.

'Were you in love with her?'

'*No*.'

Glaring at him, she gave a small, questioning shake of the head.

'I was flattered to have a young woman interested in me. I'm fifty-four. I thought I'd gone off the boil.'

She leaned forward. 'I can't think,' she said softly, 'why you, of all people, should need a boost to your confidence. You are constantly surrounded by admiration, by *adulation*.'

'You know it isn't like that. You know there are always disappointments, let-downs, that there's always some young chap coming up behind me, the latest thing, fresh off the starting blocks, implying that writers like me are too hide-bound, too earnest . . . too *old*. I fear . . .' He paused. 'Redundancy. Being past it.'

She curled into the hollow of the armchair. 'The trouble with you, George, is that you think you can have everything.'

'No, that's unfair.'

'What, then? Is it me? Are you fed up with me?' She was not, she thought, blameless. There must have been signs, indications that she had ignored, through either choice or heedlessness.

'I could never be fed up with you.' He took out a packet of cigarettes. 'Do you mind? Shall I top up your drink?'

'Better not. It's rather going to my head.'

'Have you eaten?'

'No, not since breakfast.' She had not had lunch, only the coffee with Caroline.

'I'll see if I can find something.'

'I'm ravenous, but there's nothing in the pantry and I haven't shopped for food.'

He smiled. 'I don't think we can have this conversation in a restaurant.'

She gave a dry laugh. 'I don't think so either. I bought some boxes of chocolates in Fortnum's the other day, for gifts. We could open one.'

She put a box of chocolates on the table between them. He said, 'There are times when you're so taken up by the boys it's as if you're not there, not there for me.'

'That's not true! How can you say that?'

'It's better that I say how I feel. We need to work out how we got here.'

'We got here because you were fooling around with that . . . that *tart*!' She had been reaching out for a chocolate, but now her hand fell back into her lap. 'I *mean* to have time for you,' she muttered.

She was always busy, she thought with a pang. There was never a morning, afternoon or evening when she was not busy, with teaching and the boys and housework and gardening and entertaining.

'It's just that I need you so much,' he said.

In the silence, she heard the whirr of traffic in the street outside and the ticking of the clock. She tried to draw back the conversation to something she could bear.

'The boys are okay, are they? They haven't noticed we've fallen out?'

'They're fine. Lorcan has gone camping with that friend of his.'

'Which one?'

'The red-haired lad, Alex.'

'Alec. Will they be all right on their own, Gareth and Tom?'

'Janice said she'd keep an eye on them.'

'That's good of her.'

'And those two are our sensible sons.'

'I don't know where they get it from,' she said. The whisky had warmed her. 'Neither of us has much sense.'

'You are the most sensible person I know. I'm a complete, utter idiot, I grant you that.' He went to stand at the window. 'The house feels hollow without you,' he said. 'There's no life to it.'

'I need time to myself, George.'

'I see that.' He gave her a questioning look.

'I'm getting there,' she said. 'Some things are clearer.'

'You'll come home for Christmas, won't you?'

'I don't think I have a choice.' Despite everything, she felt the pressure of the season. Her mother, who was now in her early seventies, always stayed with them over Christmas. A stray cousin of George's, a friend of Lorcan's whose parents lived abroad and a poet or two who had nowhere else to go: all these and more would join in the Flynns' festivities. And then the boys. She could not rip to shreds this fabric they had woven.

He moved about, looking for something. 'Where are the ashtrays?'

'In the kitchen, on the drainer. They were grubby and I washed them. I'll come home, yes. But we can't go on as we are, George.'

He left the room. Her life had been moulded into shape by the needs of her family. She never minded that because it was what she had chosen, but if their marriage was to have meaning and value, George must make sacrifices too.

She went into the kitchen. He was standing, his back to her, by the sink, his head bowed. She put her arm round him.

'I'll never do anything like that again, I swear to you,' he said. He sounded distraught.

'I'm not going to leave you. But there's a condition.'

He swung round to her. 'Anything.'

'We start again; we move back to London.'

'And Goldscombe?'

'We sell it.'

'Sell it?' She read the shock on his face.

Somewhere in these last days – perhaps during her conversations with Louise and Dinah, or perhaps it had been just this moment, seeing him again, touching him, remembering how she loved him – she had made up her mind. She had been afraid to test him years ago, when they had left London for Devon, but if they were to have a future, she must not be afraid to test him now.

'I don't want to live there any longer,' she said. 'The isolation . . . is destabilising. If you want us to try again, George, then that's my condition.'

Chapter Eleven

1970, London

The sale of Goldscombe attracted only a trickle of prospective purchasers. One sale fell through, then another. Frustrated, George sold the Bloomsbury flat, then scraped together what savings they had and bought a dilapidated four-storey Georgian house a short distance from Upper Street in Islington.

They moved back to London during the summer of 1967. Once again Olivia was living with the percussion of hammers and electric drills and the earthy smell of drying plaster. Because they had used up their cash on the purchase of the house, they did much of the work themselves. George's absorption in the task pleased her. He had always loved a project.

It took them almost two years to find a buyer for the Devon house, and the evening the sale went through they celebrated by cracking open a bottle of champagne. They had decided to make the front room into a grown-up sitting room, and Olivia had swatches of fabric, samples of wallpaper and trims spread out on the floor, which they planned to sand and varnish. Their glasses chinked as they drank a toast to their new home.

She took a full-time teaching job at a local school. The pupils were a mix, some from working-class families who had lived in the Islington area for generations, others the sons and daughters of young professionals who, like the Flynns, had bought houses to renovate. Still others were from families who had come over from Jamaica and Trinidad and British Guiana in the late forties and fifties to work in the hospitals and on the transport systems.

Lorcan had graduated in 1967 and then embarked upon a succession of short-term jobs in the media before starting at the BBC as a trainee. Gareth studied engineering at Imperial College, and in 1968, Tom started at Sussex University, reading maths. He chose Sussex because of the proximity of the South Downs. He liked to go out for a day's cycle ride or a hike on the chalk hills. He cycled the fifty-five miles from Brighton to London and arrived red-faced and sweaty in the afternoon, giving Olivia a quick hug before he jumped in the shower.

George still liked to throw a party. Any excuse – a birthday, a graduation, a publication, a professorship to be taken up at the other end of the country or on the far side of the world. In June 1970, when Labour lost the election to the Conservatives and Edward Heath became prime minister, they cheered themselves up by inviting their friends round. Drinks were poured, quiche and cheese and wine offered, and party workers who had spent the last six weeks leafleting and knocking on doors were consoled.

It was on that occasion that Olivia and George met Lorcan's new girlfriend for the first time. Iris Jackson was a delight, polite, friendly and helpful. Her short, wavy fair hair framed her heart-shaped face. She was studying for a PhD in biochemistry at Cambridge. It touched Olivia to see her son in love again. Love seemed to soften him, to rub off the sharp corners.

Two months later, on a hot and dusty August afternoon, Lorcan waited for Iris at King's Cross station, then they walked to the Flynns' house in Islington.

Iris said, 'It's so good of your parents to put on a party for us. And at such short notice. Are you sure they don't mind?'

'Not at all,' said Lorcan. 'Any excuse, Dad throws a party.'

'And they're happy that we're going to get married?'

He had proposed to her a week ago. Without any hesitation, Iris had said yes. Today, on the train journey to London, she had worried that Lorcan's parents might think their engagement rushed, or that she might have said something tactless to them the previous time they had met, or that she had neglected to be as appreciative as she should have been. All her usual anxieties.

Four months ago, in Cambridge, she and Lorcan had both been among the spectators at a charity cricket match. She had noticed him because a stray ball had hit him on the nose. It had bled dreadfully and the crowd of male friends he was with had roared with laughter and failed to do anything helpful. A few months earlier she had completed a first aid course, so, murmuring apologies, she had made her way along the seats, then got him to tip back his head while she pinched the bridge of his nose and mopped up the blood with her hankie.

Though it must have hurt a lot, Lorcan's strongest emotion appeared to be embarrassment, both at failing to catch the ball and at ruining her cream-coloured linen dress. He brushed away her suggestion that he go and get checked out at the hospital and said why didn't they go for a drink instead. She agreed, partly because she wanted to make sure he was all right, but also because by then she knew she was attracted to him. In the Eagle pub in Bene't Street, she discovered that Lorcan lived in London, where he shared a flat with a couple of friends and worked for the BBC. She also found out that he had two younger brothers, and that his father was the poet George Flynn.

A few days later, a parcel arrived for her. Inside it was a frock to replace the wrecked, gory linen one. It was from Biba, and made of plum-coloured crêpe, and was, Iris thought, the most lavish gift anyone had ever bought her. *I guessed the size*, Lorcan had written in his note. *If it fits and you like it, perhaps you'll wear it to dinner with me.*

Iris did not come from a family given to extravagant gestures. Her parents were both scientists; practical, gentle people, emotionally contained and, though comfortably off, frugal by nature. That the dress both fitted perfectly and suited her impressed her, and she accepted Lorcan's dinner invitation. Cautious by nature and never confident about her looks (she was too short, too plump and disliked her nose), she hadn't planned to end up going to bed with Lorcan Flynn that night, nor to fall in love with him, but both of those things happened. She loved his smile, which was warm and broad and a little piratical, and she loved him for his generosity and thoughtfulness.

Lorcan said, 'Mum and Dad are delighted. They really like you.'

'And I'm very fond of them.'

Iris liked all the Flynns. Gareth was funny and charming; Tom, the youngest of the three, was quiet and clever and had a dry sense of humour. She had noticed that Lorcan was closer to his mother than his father. She sensed some reservation when he spoke about his father.

Lorcan had told her the reason for that the morning after she had accepted his proposal of marriage. They had been in his flat in Ealing, in bed. 'When I was a kid,' he said, 'my father used to go away for weeks on end, touring countries to promote his latest book. When he came back, he'd tell us stories about the amazing places he'd been to and the famous people he'd met. He'd bring us back presents – weird American sweets and T-shirts and toys. When he went to Australia, he brought us back a boomerang. But . . .'

'What?' Propping herself on an elbow, she had a good look at him. 'Love, whatever it is, you don't have to talk about it if you don't want to.'

'I want to. A few years ago, I thought my parents were going to break up. It was just before Christmas and Mum went to London, to the flat we had then, and stayed there for a week. She never did that, never left us. They'd had a row before she went. I'd missed most of it as I'd crashed the car, but she left as soon as she knew I was okay. And I wondered whether Dad had done something. Whether he'd done something that upset her.'

'Oh.' She studied him. 'You mean . . .'

'I wondered whether he'd been unfaithful.'

She squeezed his hand. 'Oh, Lorcan.'

'As soon as Christmas was out of the way, Mum told us we were moving back to London.' Lorcan rolled onto his back, cushioning his head on his hands, looking up at the ceiling. 'I think Mum gave him an ultimatum.'

'Lorcan, are you sure? Have you talked to your parents about it?'

'No, of course not.' He looked horrified.

'Just a thought, darling,' she said gently. 'And your brothers? Have you spoken to them?'

'What would be the point? I might have got the wrong end of the stick.'

There was so much she might have picked apart in these phrases, but she could see that he found the subject deeply upsetting, so she kissed him instead. He took her in his arms and they made love again.

Iris had never loved a man like she loved Lorcan. It made her so happy to know that he felt the same about her. They would never be unfaithful to each other, and they would never have rows. They felt the same about everything of importance, they admired the same books and had similar tastes in music. They both voted Labour and believed in the redistribution of wealth. They agreed that married couples should share equally the housework and the bringing-up of children, and that whatever you chose to do with your life, you should do it with honesty and integrity.

They turned into the road where the Flynns lived, which swung gently uphill. Lime trees cast blue-black shadows on the pavement. Someone had tied two red balloons to the lantern beside the front door; they hung limply in the August heat.

'Right. Here goes.' Lorcan squared his shoulders. But before he went into the house, he embraced her. 'Thank you.'

'What for?'

'For agreeing to marry me. For putting up with me and my family. For being you. For being everything to me.'

Olivia had risen early that morning to pick flowers from the garden. Stocks and snapdragons, roses and love-lies-bleeding spilled from the vases she had scattered round the house. Over breakfast, tasks had been divided up. George was responsible for the barbecue; she sent Gareth and Tom to the off-licence to buy wine, beer and mixers. She herself whizzed round with the vacuum cleaner and Vim before concentrating on the party food.

As the first of their friends and neighbours arrived, she darted out to greet them before dashing back to the kitchen to finish the salads, decorate the trifle and Black Forest gateau and count out plates and bowls. The sun and blue skies were, she felt, a good omen for Lorcan and Iris, whom she had loved from their first meeting.

'Olivia?'

She looked up. A young woman had put her head round the door. Olivia recognised her as the girl who had arrived with their neighbours Colin and Angela. She was slender and striking, and her straight, heavy hair, which framed a fine-featured, golden-skinned face, was almost blue-black in colour.

She came into the room. 'May I help? I thought perhaps you could do with a hand.'

'Oh! Thank you. How kind. I'm sorry, but I'm afraid I've forgotten your name.'

'It's Cleo Charlton. You have such a beautiful home.'

'Thank you, Cleo.'

'If you like, I could fold the napkins.' She gestured to the bundle on the pine table.

'That would be marvellous.'

'Why don't I wrap up a knife, fork and spoon in each one? That'll make it easier for the guests. Do you have any string?'

'String?' Her fingers sticky with glacé cherries, Olivia gestured to a drawer. 'There should be some in there.'

Cleo burrowed through a tangle of rubber bands, safety pins, almost-finished rolls of Sellotape, stubs of wax crayon and suchlike. How had they accumulated such stuff? Olivia wondered. She remembered the huge clear-out she had accomplished before the move from Devon to London: attics emptied, the barn sorted through and swept clean of clutter, toys and cot bedding, and grown-out-of clothing taken to Oxfam shops or binned. It had taken months. And yet here they were again, cupboards and drawers bursting with odds and ends.

Cleo found a roll of twine and a pair of scissors. 'Would you mind if I took a few leaves from your garden? I promise I won't pick any flowers.'

Olivia put the trifle in the fridge. Cleo came back into the kitchen with a handful of bay leaves. Whipping cream, Olivia watched her wrap up a set of cutlery in one of the Flynns' ageing napkins, then tie it with a length of twine into which she tucked a sprig of bay. Once, she might have thought of doing that herself. Once, she had prided herself on sewing a fine seam and keeping up with her mending. Violet Beaumont's distant voice returned to her: *You're a good little worker*. She would replace the heap of crumpled, fraying napkins as soon as possible, she resolved.

'So neat,' she said admiringly. 'What is it that you do, Cleo?'

'I'm an interior designer.'

Of course you are. Olivia saw her home through the eyes of this confident and beautiful young woman: the heaps of newspapers, journals and books on windowsill and dresser, the mismatched plates and bowls and the spatters on the hob from the morning's cooking. She hoped the disorder might seem a part of the charm of the Flynn household; she was afraid it would not.

She asked Cleo about her work. 'An interior designer based in Chelsea has taken me on as his assistant,' Cleo said. 'Colin and Angela are family friends, and they've let me stay with them while I find somewhere to live. How many guests are you expecting, Olivia?'

'Somewhere between twenty-five and thirty. But Lorcan has invited a lot of his friends, so I suppose there could be as many as forty. It's rather an impromptu party. We thought it would be nice to welcome Iris to the family.'

Many of the Flynns' parties were impromptu. Other people planned social events weeks in advance, so maybe other people didn't end up staying awake till midnight to bake a Black Forest gateau. It was a hot day, and heat was gathering in the kitchen, which was at the rear, south-facing side of the house. Olivia pushed back her damp fringe from her face as she glanced at her list of tasks.

'I'll do forty, then,' Cleo said. 'Just in case.'

'If you run short of spoons, just shout and I'll send Tom to borrow some from the Taylors. For some reason it's spoons that go missing.'

Cleo was looking out of the window, frowning.

'What is it?'

'Those lanterns . . .'

Olivia went to stand beside her. George was stabbing glass lanterns suspended on tall hooks into a flower bed. 'Just a suggestion,' Cleo said briskly, 'but perhaps they'd be nicer scattered round the perimeter of the garden instead of all in a clump at the front? I'll go out and give him a hand.'

Lorcan went from guest to guest, greeting them and thanking them for coming. He loved a good party, and the Flynns knew how to give a good party, even if they were, he thought, pretty rubbish at some other things. He liked the way the best parties mixed people together so that new connections were made. He liked conversations that, though they might start haltingly, when oiled by good company and alcohol moved from work and family to politics and films and then to philosophies of life and all sorts of other interesting topics. At his own parties, Lorcan barbecued on a scrubby patch of shared garden. At his parents' house, Dad took charge on the terrace at the back.

A couple of Iris's girlfriends had arrived and were shrieking admiration of the diamond engagement ring that Lorcan had given her. There were times when he couldn't believe his luck in having met her, when he had to pinch himself to make sure he wasn't dreaming that she'd agreed to marry him. Iris was beautiful. Her eyes were of such a deep blue that in a bright light they seemed tinged with violet. She was about a foot smaller than him, so fitted neatly into the crook of his arm when they walked. Though she fussed about her weight and talked often about going on a diet (she never did), she was the perfect size and shape.

The restlessness that so often plagued him vanished when he was with her. He could lie on a beach with her and not feel the need to go off scrambling over rocks or scaling a cliff. If he took her out to dinner and the food or service was below par, he laughed about it instead of getting steamed up.

He could talk to her about anything – almost anything. His gaze moved back to his father, who was wearing jeans and a checked shirt and gesturing with a toasting fork while he held forth to half a dozen of his acquaintances.

There was one incident he would never share with anyone, not even the woman he loved. Shortly after he had first come to work at the BBC, Lorcan had spent three months working as a research assistant on an arts programme. He hadn't told anyone about his connection to George Flynn – Flynn was a common enough name, and no one put two and two together. He wanted to succeed (or fail) on his own merits. The topic of the final programme had been contemporary poetry, and his father had featured heavily. Afterwards, to mark the wrapping-up of the series, he and the rest of the crew had gone off to a pub to get drunk. Lorcan had been about to head home when he had overheard the assistant producer and the cameraman talking to each other. 'They're all the same, those old goats,' the assistant director was saying. 'Their behaviour is totally unacceptable.' Lorcan had stood frozen, listening to the two men talking about his father, laughing about his reputation with women.

Afterwards, mulling it over, he had questioned what he'd heard. It hadn't been an enjoyable programme to work on – the director and the assistant director were constantly at each other's throats – but he had stuck it out because he had wanted to gain a toehold in a competitive field. The assistant director was the sort of person who liked to brag about being in the know.

And yet the phrase – *those old goats* – had clung in his mind like red Devon clay to the soles of a pair of walking boots. However hard he tried, he could not quite shake it off.

Gareth emptied bags of crisps into bowls and put them on the dining-room table, then went out to the garden, where the guests were dispersed in pairs and groups, sitting on benches or sprawled on the grass, chatting and laughing. He wondered whether he should have invited Janie. He had not done so because he had known she would read too much into it, an invitation to the family home.

His father was preparing his speciality, marinaded chicken, turning over the pieces on the metal rack.

'All right, Dad?'

'Nearly there. Tell Mum I'll need the plates soon.'

Catching sight of Iris, Gareth waved and crossed the lawn to her. She was the first of Lorcan's girlfriends he thoroughly approved of. All her predecessors had been hopeless in some way, self-absorbed or fussy about food or reduced to panicked silence by the rumbustious Flynns.

He kissed her cheek. 'Can't see what you see in him, but welcome to the family. Congratulations, brother of mine.' He gave Lorcan a punch, then a hug, and then, hearing a chime, went into the house, looking into the kitchen on his way to the front door so that he could give his mother the message about the plates.

In the kitchen, the radio was humming away and the large pine table was covered with bowls of salad and platters of bread and cheese and ham. A girl in a green dress was standing at the table. Her straight, glossy hair was the colour of a raven's wing.

'Plates are on the dresser, love,' Olivia said.

'Okay, thanks, Mum.'

The girl in the green dress looked up, spoon in hand. Gareth gave her his warmest smile, then went to answer the front door.

Iris's parents had arrived. Gareth welcomed them, sorted out somewhere for them to put their belongings, then showed them to the kitchen so that his mother could greet them. The girl in the green dress was no longer there. He took the plates outside and put them on the trestle table near the barbecue. Though he scanned the garden, she had vanished. It was almost as if he had imagined her, and yet her features were burned into his vision like the after-image from a bright light.

One of Dad's poet friends tapped his shoulder and told him there was beer all over the dining room. Gareth found Tom mopping the floor and table.

'Someone brought a Party Seven and tried to open it with a screwdriver,' he said.

The large metal keg was spewing beer. Gareth tucked it under his arm and carted it outside while Tom finished mopping.

'Put it on the lawn,' a voice suggested. 'It won't do any damage there.'

Looking up, he saw her, the girl in the green dress. 'If you stick it under that shrub, it won't be in the way,' she said.

Gareth did so. The keg fizzed over the grass. She fetched a jug and he squatted, catching the erupting beer.

'I'm Gareth Flynn,' he said.

'Cleo Charlton. You have beer all over your shirt. Do you want to go and get changed? I'll keep an eye on this, make sure it doesn't explode.'

Gareth went upstairs, where he washed and changed into a denim shirt. By the time he returned to the garden, the barrel had stopped fizzing, the beer was decanted into jugs and pitchers on the dining table, and Cleo Charlton had disappeared again.

He had a quick glance round the house between letting in latecomers and making sure everyone had a drink and something to eat and the reserved people had someone to talk to. He couldn't find her. Perhaps she had gone home. His mother called him to tell him that there was a phone call for him, and he had the ridiculous thought that it might be her, the elusive Cleo Charlton, but it wasn't, it was Janie, and he found himself embroiled in a long and emotional conversation that ended only when Janie, her tears audible over the line, put down the phone.

Guests were still arriving, the younger women in bell-bottomed jeans and Biba T-shirts or rainbow-coloured hippy clothing, Indian-print maxi dresses or cheesecloth skirts that swept the ground. Their feet were bare or in flip-flops, and their bangles and the tiny brass bells on their necklaces jingled. The women of Olivia's age wore cotton or linen frocks with pearl necklaces or silk scarves and heeled sandals. Youth Dew and Aqua Manda scented the air.

In a lull, Olivia beckoned to Lorcan. 'Could you find Gareth and ask him to check the wine? He's to go to the off-licence if we're running low. And tell him to see whether we could do with more crisps. Or Tom can do it if you can't find Gareth.'

'Lorcan and I can go to the off-licence,' Iris said.

'Certainly not. This is your party and I want you to be with your guests.'

The two of them were at that stage of being in love, she thought, when the only thing they wanted was to be with each other, and when anything the other said or did was entrancing and perceptive. Walking to the off-licence would have seemed a treat to them.

A gaggle of poets turned up. 'Olivia! Looking stunning as usual.' A hug, a wispy grey beard brushing her cheek.

Maudie Gresham appeared with her daughter Alison and her five-week-old grandson. Cradling the tiny infant in her arms, Olivia felt a warm glow of happiness. She scanned the garden, her gaze alighting on their guests – Dinah and

Tony, the Farleys, Louise and her latest chap, and all the others. This was what they had created, the Flynns, despite the flaws and the faults, this edifice of family, friendship and love.

As she went back into the house, she parried snippets of conversation and smiled her thanks at compliments. Indoors, she felt relieved at having escaped the heat of the sun. Wasps crawled round the necks of the bottles and feasted on smears of food on abandoned plates. She shooed them away, then poured herself a glass of wine, though the beginnings of a headache beat at the back of her skull. She drank, topped up her glass, then went back outside.

There was a small, shady patch of garden to one side of the house, by the kitchen door, a place of bins and abandoned plant pots. Gareth grabbed some scraps of food and sat down on a decaying wooden bench. Some of Janie's phrases lingered. *You were never serious, were you . . . ? Everyone said you're never serious, but I didn't listen.* He felt fed up with himself.

Cleo appeared, a wine glass in each hand. 'I thought you might need a drink, Gareth.'

'Thanks. You keep disappearing.'

She sat down beside him. When she took off her sunglasses, he saw that her eyes were greenish-grey and fringed with thick black lashes. The Flynns had once had a cat with eyes that colour.

She said, 'I have to pop back over the road now and then, to the house where I'm staying.'

She didn't explain why. Maybe she didn't like parties. Maybe the Flynns were a bit much for her. Gareth said, 'How long will you be staying with Colin and Angela?'

'Another week or two, I should think. I'm starting a new

job. They're letting me stay with them while I look for somewhere to live.'

'Have you had any luck?'

'I think so. I went to see a place in Bayswater yesterday. It's only five minutes from the Underground station. What about you, Gareth? What do you do?'

'I'm an engineer. I finish my MSc in a couple of months' time, then I've got some work lined up.'

'What sort of engineering?'

'Civil engineering. I want to build houses.' Gareth believed that the house shaped the people living inside it. Decent housing produced decent people. Buildings and their surroundings formed character. He was aware that such pronouncements might sound idealistic or even half-baked, and he was also aware that once he got going on his subject he sometimes talked too much. He didn't want Cleo Charlton to think he was a bore.

He said, 'A house should blend into the landscape. It should be warm and light while using the minimum amount of power. We have North Sea oil now, but it won't last for ever.'

She stood up. 'I'd better nip back,' she said.

'Why? What are you doing?' He shouldn't have asked. She might have some embarrassing medical condition.

But she said, 'I'm baking a fruit cake for Colin and Angela, to say thank you for putting me up. I've never made one before, and honestly, I thought it would be ready hours ago. It's taking for ever. I'm not much of a baker.'

'I'll give you a hand if you like. I enjoy cooking.'

'How liberated of you, Gareth.' She put her head on one side, considering him with her grey-green gaze. 'Thanks, that's good of you. So long as you don't mind me dragging you away from the party. To tell you the truth, I could do with some expert advice.'

Tom, who intended never to give a party of his own in his entire life, spent the afternoon directing guests to the food and drink and rescuing glasses abandoned in flower beds and beneath shrubs. At around six o'clock, when the party-goers began to drift away, he helped them extract jackets and bags from the heap on the spare bed.

He ran errands because he would rather do anything other than engage people he hardly knew in conversation. He was fine talking so long as it was with a person he had an affinity with, and he had something to talk *about*. Faced with a stranger and zero common ground, he felt bored and anxious both at the same time but was incapable of finding an escape route. A girl he had liked had once said to him disparagingly, 'You're such an *introvert*, Tom.' He had known that already, of course, because introverts like him were not without self-knowledge and he had researched it in the psychology section of the library. *Requires quiet to concentrate . . . likes to reflect . . . feels tired and needs to be on his own after spending time in a crowd.* Spot on, he had thought. There was nothing wrong with being introverted, though people incorrectly assumed it meant you were dull or shy or stand-offish. The girl's expression and tone of voice had made clear to him that she hadn't been paying him a compliment.

His problem was that he was an introvert in a family of extroverts. All the Flynns, including his mother, could blather on for ages about nothing at all. Crowds didn't seem to bother them in the least. He suspected that his brothers' hearts did not sink when his father said, *We should celebrate*, and his mother added, *What do you think, a party or a dinner?*

Friends were enthusiastically invited, wine and beer purchased, vol-au-vents and cheese-and-pineapple hedgehogs made. Tom was certain that this afternoon not one of the other Flynns would search out a quiet corner and think, as he did, *How many more hours until I can slip away and get back to my book?*

His mother said that he took after his grandmother, and it was true that when he went to stay with Grandma in Somerset the two of them could happily occupy themselves for an afternoon doing bits of gardening and reading and hardly talking at all. Tom liked listening to music, he liked reading and going for long hikes, and caring for his indoor plants, and cooking, and finding an elegant solution to a mathematical problem, and having deep, quiet, interesting conversations with friends who were neither attention-seeking nor loud, about subjects that engaged him.

By now, after hours of socialising, his brain was as scrambled as if he'd drunk a gallon of coffee. Though he tried to picture himself in a tranquil wood on the South Downs, listening to birdsong and the buzz of bees, his thoughts skittered in an agitated way.

His mother called out to him. Tom went into the kitchen. 'I thought I might go out for a cycle ride,' he said.

'Good idea.' Mum waved at him a plate bearing a slice of Black Forest gateau. 'Do you want this before you go?'

He took the plate and stood at the sink, eating cake, looking out to the garden. The party had been going on, by his calculation, for five hours and twenty-seven minutes. Through the window, he could see Lorcan and Gareth and his father. They were all still talking. Tom finished the cake, stuffed his paperback of *Under the Volcano* into his jeans pocket and went to the garage to fetch his bike.

Even after the shadows lengthened and the lanterns were lit, a few stragglers remained, lounging in the garden, or sprawled in the back room of the house. Through the open window, Olivia could see Lorcan and Iris talking to the Clairmonts. A young woman had picked up a guitar and was singing 'The Water is Wide'. The plaintive lyrics were familiar to her; she had known them since she was a girl. Her mother had sung the song to her.

Love is handsome and love is blind
Gay as a jewel when first it's new
But love grows cold, and waxes old
And fades away like the morning dew.

There was no one in the front room. Olivia ambled around collecting abandoned mugs. This room, her favourite, was north-facing and remained cool on the hottest of days. She had enjoyed choosing the William Morris wallpaper and the two large Habitat sofas and had made the blue velvet curtains herself. Two of the walls were lined with bookshelves on which every inch of space was taken up. Books stood upright, they were stacked on their sides, they lay on top of other books.

She ran her thumbnail along the sofa's dark brown corduroy upholstery. They had done an excellent job restoring the house, but her error, she thought, had been in thinking that the move to London would be a cure for her marriage. For a while she had told herself it was working; not any longer.

The realisation had been gradual, and she had at first resisted it. Since Nadia Lessiter, George had become more careful. So, no more hotel bills in trouser pockets, but she was astute enough to be aware of the signs that indicated the ebb and flow of his entanglements. When they had first moved to London, he had restricted his social and work events to the capital. Over the past few months, though, he had been away more often, sometimes for a week or two at a time.

Now, she pictured him earlier that day, standing at the barbecue, laughing at his own funny stories, his *joie de vivre* a warning light. They still had their good times, she and George, but it seemed to her that they came further apart. All the boys had now left home, adding to her sense that an era had come to an end. The phrase 'empty nest' was a cliché, which diminished how bereft she had felt when Tom, her baby, had gone away to university. She knew that George, too, found it hard to get used to how the big house echoed with the absence of their sons. The change had brought out the restlessness that was innate to him, while she herself flailed, searching for a purpose to match the intensity of the years devoted to the boys' upbringing. She had joined a choir, she had taken on new responsibilities at the school where she taught, she read voraciously. Having not gone to college or university, too often she felt ignorant and un-informed, and she was trying to make up for that.

The front door opened and closed as more guests took their leave. Lorcan stuck his head round the door to say that he and Iris were going to the pub, and would she like to come?

'I'll join you in a while. I'll finish up a few things here. I should hang on till everyone has left, but you head off and I'll see you both later. Have fun.' Olivia blew him a kiss. 'Is Dad going with you?'

'He's already gone out somewhere.' Lorcan came into the room to hug her. 'It's been a great day. Thanks, Mum.'

Olivia went into the kitchen. She flicked on the radio and ran hot water into the sink. Her headache was still brewing, and she rubbed at the tendons in her neck. As she washed up, the radio rattled on, a discussion about the political situation in the run-up to the Second World War.

There were plenty of fascist groups in this country in the 1920s. The main difference at that time between us and Germany was that we hadn't suffered defeat in the First World War.

Olivia stiffened as she recognised the Scottish lilt in the man's voice. The party – George – everything else was forgotten as all her attention centred on the radio programme.

The mediator, a wordy chap, spoke for a while, then said, 'Thank you, Professor Madden, that's most illuminating.'

Olivia rested her back against the sink, listening. Thirty years had passed since they had last spoken, she and Rory. *I'll see you soon. Thank you for a lovely evening.* Their final conversation must have gone something like that. And then he had said, *If you'd like to borrow this.* And he had given her his paperback copy of *Ariel*. She had never forgotten that evening.

Dinah came into the room. 'Are you okay, Olivia? You look like you've seen a ghost.'

'I have, pretty much.' She nodded towards the radio. 'Not seen, but heard. That chap who's talking . . . I knew him years ago. Are you leaving?'

'I'd better drag Tony away or he'll talk all night. Do you need a hand with anything more before I go?'

'No, it's almost done. Thanks for your help.'

They hugged. 'Marvellous party,' Dinah said.

By the time Olivia returned to the kitchen after seeing Dinah and Tony out, the programme had wound up. She switched off the radio, then dried the wine glasses and arranged them in the dresser. So many years had passed, so much had happened since then, and she was under no illusions that if they were to meet again, she and Rory would share any common ground.

But there were questions she would like answers to, loose ends to tie up. Ghosts to lay to rest.

In the front room, she searched through the shelves, looking for a book she had borrowed thirty years ago and had not yet returned. It took her the entire next day to find *Ariel*, and she began to think it had been lost in one house move or another, but eventually she discovered it in a little attic under the eaves, jammed into a cardboard box along with a set of children's encyclopedias. Dusting it off, she turned the leaves until she saw, the ink now faded, Rory's signature.

Chapter Twelve

1970, London

On a trip to Foyles, Olivia discovered two books written by Rory Madden, both on topics of twentieth-century history. The biography on the back cover told her that he was a professor of history at University College London. The husband of one of her fellow teachers worked at UCL, and when the three of them had a drink together one evening, Olivia discovered that he knew Rory by sight. The idea of phoning him out of the blue did not appeal to her, so when her friend's husband mentioned that Rory was giving a series of public lectures that autumn at Westfield College in Hampstead, she decided to go and see him there.

The first one she was free to attend was in early November. On a chill, misty evening, as she sat in the theatre listening to him lecture on the Treaty of Versailles, her doubts accumulated. It was very likely that he would have forgotten her. Even if he remembered her, he would likely regard her as a minor detail in his life. And in truth, why was she here? The motives that at first had felt compelling – to return the book, to talk to him about the past, to satisfy her curiosity – now seemed flimsy.

Superficially, he appeared little altered. His frame had thickened slightly, and his hair was longer, though still plentiful. He had not lost his focus and, just as she recalled, he conveyed his passion for his subject in vivid terms. But as the lecture went on, she saw the changes in him, that he was more confident, and that there was in his delivery something of the showman, an expectation that he would be listened to. He had become a glossier, better-dressed, more authoritative version of his younger self. He was still attractive, and she could understand why the alchemy of energy and grace and charisma had once drawn her younger self.

He moved on to discussing the aims and policies of Lloyd George, Clemenceau and Woodrow Wilson. Though Olivia tried to stop her mind drifting, the preoccupations that constantly swirled around her intruded: she must remember to complete her lesson plans and to change the sheets on Tom's bed, because he was coming home for the weekend. She must write a shopping list and ring Iris's mother about the wedding, which was to take place the following May. And were Gareth and Cleo Charlton going out together? She couldn't make it out. Gareth always played his cards close to his chest and she wouldn't have dared ask Cleo flat out. She liked Cleo but sensed her need for privacy. Though the young woman was beautiful and talented, well organised and capable, Olivia nevertheless detected a brittleness about her. Gareth seemed keen on her, but Olivia found it hard to tell whether Cleo was seriously interested in him. She mustn't feel put out about that. She mustn't fret that Cleo would break her boy's heart, and nor must she be the sort of mother who assumed her adult sons to be perfect. Even though she was.

A ripple of applause jerked her out of her thoughts as Rory wound up the lecture. He answered the audience's questions with clarity and concision, and when they dried up, he brought the event to a close. People began to button their coats and pull on knitted hats and head out of the auditorium.

Olivia made her way down the central aisle to the podium. Half a dozen attendees were clustered round Rory. Most were young women, and their compliments were enthusiastic, their questions designed, she thought, to catch his attention. He dispatched their remarks with a cool effortlessness.

Olivia waited until the others had drifted away, then said his name.

He looked round. 'Yes?'

She held out the book to him. 'This belongs to you. I'm sorry for hanging on to it for so long.'

He took it from her. He turned it over in his hand, flicked through the first few pages, then glanced at her sharply. 'Olivia Goodland. Good grief! Olivia? It is you, isn't it?'

'Olivia Flynn now, actually.'

'Yes . . . yes, of course, I remember. I bumped into Alice – Alice Ruthwell – a while ago. She told me you were married.'

'It's good to see you again, Rory.'

'And you too.' Smiling, he waved the book at her. 'Thank you for this. I'd completely forgotten about it. Tell me what you're doing with yourself. Are you still a dressmaker?'

She shook her head. 'I teach at a primary school.'

He was stuffing his lecture notes into an overfull briefcase. 'You enjoy it?'

'Very much. The children are lovely, and I'm particularly interested in the ones who struggle to learn to read. Some of the teachers write them off. Sometimes even their parents write them off. There's a condition called dyslexia that I've been trying to find out about so I can help them.'

Rory scooped up several pieces of paper that had fluttered to the floor. 'You're thinking of Frankie Ruthwell.'

'Frankie was dyslexic, I'm certain of it.'

'If you've spoken to Alice, you'll know what happened to the poor lad.'

'Rory!' A cry from the auditorium interrupted their conversation. Rory looked up to where a woman in a violet-coloured coat was marching down the aisle towards them.

'You were supposed to have wrapped this up half an hour ago!' she called out. 'I've been waiting outside. You said half past eight. Our table . . .'

'Sorry, Marie, almost there.' Rory nodded to Olivia. 'Thank you for this.' He tried to squeeze *Ariel* into the briefcase too.

A man in a brown cloth coat, a janitor presumably, came into the lecture theatre, jangling a bundle of keys. Marie paused a few steps from the foot of the aisle to check her watch. Rory was putting on his coat. Olivia saw her chance slipping away.

She said quickly, 'I wanted to ask you something, Rory. I wondered why you left the Ruthwells. I wondered why you walked out.'

'Walked out?' he repeated. 'Who told you I walked out?'

'Alice.'

His expression cooled, his eyes seeming now to contain the dense pallor and chill of a frozen sea. 'No,' he said. 'It wasn't like that.'

'Rory.' Marie spoke sharply. She tapped her watch.

Olivia gave her an apologetic smile. 'I'm so sorry for holding you up.'

'Come on.' Marie extended her hand to him.

There seemed nothing more for Olivia to do but to head up the aisle and out of the lecture theatre. The temperature had fallen, and once she reached the pavement, she turned up the collar of her coat. It took her a moment to reorientate herself, to let the events of the last hour and a half sink in, before she headed off for the Underground station.

Hearing footsteps behind her, she looked back. Rory was running to catch up with her.

'Your wife . . .' she said, as he drew level with her.

'Marie isn't my wife, she's my sister. Or my gaoler, sometimes I'm not sure. She thinks she needs to keep an eye on me, make sure I eat my greens, that kind of thing.' He glanced back to where the violet-coated woman was making tetchy beckoning gestures. 'She's a good soul and I love her dearly. Mind you, a couple of minutes late and she gives me a piece of her mind. I wanted to give you this.' He handed Olivia a scrap of paper. 'That's my phone number. Do please give me a ring. I'd like to talk to you about the Ruthwells. I'd like to set the record straight.'

At home, she hung up her coat, then went into the kitchen. George was there, making a sandwich.

'Hello, love,' he said. 'Working late?'

'No, I went to a lecture.'

'Tea? Sandwich?'

'A glass of wine, thanks.'

As he uncorked the bottle, he said, 'Selwyn's just told me there isn't going to be an American tour.'

'You mean, for the new book?'

'It looks like my US publishers are going to pass on it.'

'Oh, George.' She hugged him. 'I'm sorry.'

'My contract with them has run out. They reminded Selwyn of that. The bloody nerve of it. All they do is waffle on about sales and changing tastes. After all this time, after everything I've done for them, and now they're dropping me. It's outrageous. Selwyn tried to call Bernard, but guess what, he wasn't available.'

He was furious, Olivia realised. She sipped the wine, enjoying the way its warmth ran through her and how it steadied her nerves, which were still on edge. She had thought she might tell George about the lecture, and about Rory, about the intermittent awkwardness of their exchange – she might even turn Marie's arrival into a funny story to distract him from this setback. But as he continued to talk, full of wounded pride as he described at length a series of phone calls and his American editor's lack of availability and obduracy, she knew she would not. He would not care. He might fall silent while she spoke, but he wouldn't listen and would return to his outrage at the first opportunity.

She murmured consoling remarks and hugged him again. Morosely, he ate the sandwich while she poured herself another glass of wine.

'I need to phone Iris's mother about the flowers.' Olivia left the room. In the hall, she took the piece of paper Rory had given her out of her pocket. As she unfolded it, she realised that she was smiling, and it was a long moment, standing there, before she picked up the receiver and dialled the Jacksons' number.

She met Rory again a week later, in a café in Camden. During the days that had passed since the lecture, the dry, cold weather had intensified. Hurrying along the pavement, her breath made cloudy puffs in the still air. Her boots crunched on the fallen leaves, each one of which bore a frill of frost. She had been held up after school, a parent worried about her daughter's progress, and had had to rush to avoid being late.

A blast of warm, humid air hit her as she opened the door

to the café. Most of the tables were occupied by women, who had propped their shopping bags by their chairs. What looked like a mother and daughter were having an intense discussion, their heads bent over a list. The older woman was saying, 'What about Graham? I bought him hankies last year.'

Catching sight of Rory sitting by the window, Olivia wound between the tables. He waved away her apologies and offered to get coffees. As she sat down, her reflection in the window told her that her hair was wind-blown and her cheeks pink from the cold and the rush. She smoothed her hands over her hair and reapplied lipstick while Rory stood, his back to her, at the counter. He had taken off his corduroy jacket and slung it over the back of his chair, and was wearing jeans and a navy-blue shirt.

As he put the drinks on the table and sat down, she said, 'It's rather prim, isn't it? I thought it would be easy for you to get here.'

'It's fine,' he said. 'Perfect.'

The tables were covered in gingham cloths, the walls hung with prints of Victorian London. Olivia saw Rory take a mouthful of coffee and give a slight frown.

'Not good?' she said.

'Nothing wrong with lukewarm instant. You might want some of this to cheer it up.' He passed her the sugar bowl. 'I can see how it must have looked, me upping and leaving, abandoning Frankie. But it wasn't like that at all. Claude Ruthwell threw me out. He and that man of his literally manhandled me out of the house and threw me down the steps.'

She stared at him, horrified. 'Why? Why did he do that?'

'Because he was beating Grace to a pulp and I tried to stop him.'

She put her hand over her mouth. 'Oh, Rory.'

'I thought he was going to kill her. He didn't care for me sticking my oar in. He would have had me horsewhipped if I'd gone back there. I never saw Frankie again.'

'Were you hurt?'

'A whack on the head and a couple of cracked ribs.'

She shouldn't be shocked because she knew what Sneddon was capable of. 'That's appalling. I'm sorry if I thought . . .'

'Olivia, forget it. I've been trying to remember exactly when that happened. It must have been a week or two before war broke out. As soon as my ribs knitted together, I joined the army. Truth is, I couldn't have stayed much longer with the Ruthwells anyway.'

The mother and daughter were gathering up their shopping bags and leaving the café, for a final assault on the shops, perhaps. Rory went on, 'I was in my room, and I heard Grace screaming. Claude was yelling at her. I'd heard them quarrelling before, but this was different. I went downstairs to see if there was anything I could do, whether I could calm things down. I wanted to check that Grace was all right. They were in the hall. The funny thing – it had a certain incongruous humour – was that the pair of them were still dressed up to the nines. Ruthwell was in his dinner jacket and Grace was in some sort of gold get-up.'

Olivia remembered the cocktail dress of gold lamé with its pattern of ivy leaves. How she had helped Grace slip it over her head. The scent of her perfume and a drift of melody through an open window as the musicians in the garden tuned up their instruments.

She said, 'That must have been the night of Alice's engagement party.'

He knitted his brows together. 'I'd forgotten the party. I'd forgotten about Alice getting engaged.'

'Alice told me she'd heard her parents rowing that night.'

'Alice . . . she was a tricky customer. Sometimes she'd be friendly to me, but at other times she treated me like the hired help. I spent that evening with Frankie, playing board games and listening to the wireless. After he went to bed, I went to my room. It must have been later, ten or eleven maybe, I can't remember, when it all kicked off. Claude was accusing Grace of all sorts of things. I have to say, I admired her. She didn't let him frighten her. She tried to give as good as she got. And being the brute that he was, he didn't like that. He put his hands round her neck. I had to drag him off her.'

'Oh God, that's horrible.' Olivia looked outside, to where the icy weather was causing a final flurry of papery yellow leaves to fall from the sycamore in the square opposite. The nightmarish memories of that night were still able to conjure in her a hot, panicked fear.

He touched her wrist. 'I'm sorry, I don't mean to upset you. You were fond of Grace, weren't you?'

'I think she was one of the most charming women I've ever known. She made me feel special. I think I was easily influenced, but she made me feel that I mattered, that I might be an interesting person.' Olivia put down her cup and looked across the table. She noticed, as she had done years ago, the flecks of dark grey against the lighter shade of Rory's eyes. There were laughter lines to either side of his mouth and furrows deeply incised across his brow.

She said, 'I used to run errands for her. I used to deliver her love letters to a man called Sammy Ellwood. I wondered afterwards whether I shouldn't have got involved, whether I might have only made things worse for her.'

'Why do you say that?' He didn't give her time to respond.

'Whatever you did, Claude Ruthwell bears responsibility for his own behaviour. And you were very young, Olivia.'

She remembered the anguish that had followed that night and her initial disbelief as, over the ensuing week, it had become clear to her that both Grace and Rory had severed contact with her. She had understood for some time now why Grace had made that decision. Her priority must always have been Frankie's welfare. But Rory's desertion had at the time hurt her deeply.

'I lost my job too,' she said. 'My employer gave me the sack.'

'I didn't know that.'

'Why didn't you contact me? Was it because you'd been injured?'

'I . . .' He looked sheepish. 'The truth is, I thought . . .'

'What?'

'Claude said that his manservant – I can't remember his name . . .'

'Sneddon. His name was Sneddon.' She suppressed a shudder.

'He said that he'd found you in Ruthwell's study, going through his desk. And I . . .'

'Oh my goodness.' Understanding dawned. She stared at him. 'You thought I was *stealing*. You did, didn't you, Rory?'

'Sorry,' he muttered.

The café door opened, and two women came in, both wearing identical Persian lamb coats and carrying black patent leather handbags. Rory shuffled his chair so that they could take the other window table. No wonder, after all that had happened that night, he had walked away not only from the Ruthwells but also from her. He must have longed to shake the dust off his feet.

He said ruefully, 'I had a horrible habit of thinking I knew it all back then.'

'I was in Claude Ruthwell's study, that's true, but I was trying to retrieve a love letter that belonged to Grace. She had asked me to help her get it back. It was hers, it was private, and her husband had taken it from her and was going to use it against her so that he could divorce her.' She felt a chill as the café door opened and shut again. 'But I bungled it. I made too much noise and . . . well, you know the rest. But I wasn't stealing.'

'Honestly, I can only apologise.'

'Rory, it's okay, it doesn't matter.'

'Facts matter. Interpretations matter. I tell my students that all the time.' He gave a wry smile. 'My ex-wife, Imogen, once told me I dealt with emotions as if they were mathematical equations.'

'How long have you been divorced?'

'Twelve years.'

'I'm sorry, Rory. That must have been hard.'

'It's okay now. We make sure to stay on passably good terms because of Naomi, our daughter. Imogen remarried quite some time ago.'

'And you?'

He shook his head. 'No. I've had relationships, but none has lasted. My fault, I daresay. I'll tell you Imogen's most cutting verdict on me. She said that when we talked, she could tell I was always thinking of something else. That I was permanently distracted. She had a point. I recognise that about myself now. I get absorbed in my subject, in my work.'

'How old is Naomi?'

His expression softened. 'She's just turned eighteen. She

lives with her mother in Richmond upon Thames. I'm tutoring her for Oxbridge entrance.'

He took a photo out of his wallet and showed it to her. Olivia admired the smiling, attractive girl who looked back at her. She extracted from her purse the snapshot she always kept with her.

'These are my sons. That's Lorcan, that's Gareth and that's Tom. It was taken in the summer at Lorcan's engagement party.'

'Three boys . . . They must keep you busy.'

She laughed. 'They do, yes.'

'I'm glad it's worked out well for you.'

She didn't respond. 'Olivia?' he prompted. He frowned. 'You're happy? Your marriage . . .'

'I don't want to talk about it. Not now.'

'Sorry. I didn't mean to . . .'

'No, it's okay.' She replaced the photo in her bag, then said, 'George and I . . . I'm trying to work things out.'

'I wish you luck, then.'

'When I look back, I can see that I didn't understand a fraction of what was going on in the Ruthwells' house. I can see that I was utterly out of my depth.'

'Marriages are complicated. Families are complicated too.' Glancing out of the window, he shrugged. 'Maybe good marriages are straightforward enough. I wouldn't know.'

'The Ruthwells' marriage was poisonous, I think.'

'True. I'd have thrown in the job anyway, even if Claude hadn't chucked me out.'

Poor Grace, she thought.

He said, 'Claude Ruthwell has done rather well for himself, did you know that? Half a dozen profitable directorships on the boards of various financial institutions. Trusteeships of well-known charities and art galleries. He has the London house and a place in the country. He's a respected member of society and not short of a bob or two – a man of influence, you might say.' The expression in Rory's eyes was one of chill contempt.

'Alice told me he'd married again.'

'Yes. His wife is wealthy and well connected. They have a son.' His fingers drummed the tabletop. 'Ruthwell has made sure to bury his unsavoury past deep, where no one will uncover it. The thing I noticed when I was working for them – and it took me a while to recognise this – was that he had the knack of making his views sound reasonable. And that's dangerous. A rabble-rouser is easier to spot. It was a nice enough job tutoring Frankie; he was a good kid, and I enjoyed being in London, and Grace treated me like one of the family. But it began to make me feel uneasy, living there, dining at Claude Ruthwell's table, taking his money. I felt . . . I felt there was something off about it.' His frown tightened. 'I felt that I was acquiescing. That I was *collaborating*. I only stuck it out for as long as I did because of the boy.'

'Frankie was a sweetie.'

'He was a handful.' Rory smiled. 'He couldn't sit still. He'd get upset about something, some bit of nonsense you or I wouldn't have thought anything of, and Grace or I would have to spend hours calming him down.'

She glanced at her watch. 'I'm going to have to go. It's been so good to talk to you, Rory.'

As they left the café, he said, 'There's something I've never forgotten. Claude Ruthwell hardly ever spoke to Frankie. He never looked into the schoolroom to see how he was getting on. You can say that's how it was then among their class, and that back then a distance between fathers and sons wasn't uncommon, but it was more than that. The couple of times I saw him address the boy, it seemed to me that he felt only contempt for him.'

'He disliked his own son.' This tied in with what Grace had told her.

'Yes. I'd do anything for Naomi, anything at all. I wouldn't have to think twice. You'd be the same, wouldn't you?'

As she walked away through the cold evening air, Rory's words echoed in Olivia's head, and a thought came to her, chilling in its simplicity. Had Claude Ruthwell intended Frankie to die? Had he known that in sending his fragile son away to a boarding school, one that was far from home, he might not survive? Surely not, she told herself. Surely even he wasn't capable of that. That would be monstrous. Yet the suspicion, once lodged in her mind, could not easily be brushed aside.

This is what happened, she thought as she made her way home. Sneddon had found her in Claude Ruthwell's study and had told his master, who had taken out his fury on Grace. The next day, someone, either Claude or Grace, had told Violet Beaumont to sack her. No . . . Claude Ruthwell would have *instructed* Grace to tell Mrs Beaumont to sack her. He would have forced Grace to promise to break off all contact with her. After the brutal scene Rory had described, Grace must have been afraid for her own safety and Frankie's and would have done as her husband demanded. The three of them – Rory, the lady's maid Summers, and Olivia herself – had been barred from the Ruthwell household. Violence and manipulation had severed Grace from anyone who could have helped her and had ultimately led to her being separated from her son.

All this their conversation had revealed to her, and yet as she walked on, her mind veered away from the past, and she thought instead of Rory standing at the counter in the café. She recalled the line of his shoulders and the easy grace of his limbs. The touch of his fingertips on her wrist. The spark in his eyes as they had talked. And she became aware of an excitement she had almost forgotten, a sloughing-away of an old, dull, constricting skin, and a glimpse of something bright, new and glittering beneath.

A couple of days later, the phone rang. 'It's Rory,' he said, and a thrill of pleasure ran through her.

'I had an idea, Olivia, but you might think it a nerve. I've a book coming out next week and I wondered whether you'd like to come to the launch. I'll understand completely if you've had enough of book launches.'

Olivia shut the door to the living room, muting the sound of the television. 'Send me an invitation. I'll come if I can.'

'I warn you it'll be a modest affair. A couple of dozen people in a left-wing bookshop, a few sausage rolls and a glass of Blue Nun.'

'Sounds perfect.' As she put down the phone, she felt a tingle of excitement at the thought of seeing him again.

The interior of the Pimlico bookshop was a maze of wall-to-ceiling shelves, crammed with volumes, some new, others second-hand. The scent of musty cobwebs and dusty floors and old paper accompanied her winding path through stacks of Marxist texts and dense tomes by fashionable French philosophers.

A hum of voices and clink of glasses led Olivia to where the launch was taking place at the rear of the shop. Outside, it was drizzling; the icy spell had come to an end and the damp embroidered Afghan coats of the young people who had crowded into the small space gave off an animal smell. The air was grey with smoke from cigarettes and pipes. Many of the attendees were students, she guessed, though others were of a similar age to her, late forties to early fifties, the men moustachioed, bespectacled and corduroy-jacketed, the smaller scattering of women clad in A-line skirts and roll-neck jumpers.

Someone offered her a glass of wine. Flakes of pastry sprinkled across a plate were all that was left of the sausage rolls. At George's most recent launch in Piccadilly, they had drunk champagne from Fortnum's and eaten tiny, perfect little canapés.

Smiling and murmuring apologies and hellos, she made her way to a small table where Rory was signing books. His white shirt, paired with Levi's, emphasised his lean form. His book was called *Aspects of Resistance*, and he signed the copies with a neat flourish, smiling and chatting to each guest as he did so.

Olivia congratulated him. He rose and kissed her cheek, and she breathed in the clean fragrance of his laundered shirt and the spicy tang of his aftershave.

'Glad you could make it.'

'You promised me sausage rolls.'

'This lot are like gannets. They've scoffed the lot. Perhaps, to make up for it, you'll let me buy you supper once this is over.' There was amusement in his eyes, and something else as well. Delight, and a tension – and a challenge.

'I might keep you to that,' she said lightly.

A woman in a pink Laura Ashley frock attracted Rory's attention and he murmured an apology. Olivia found a space by a wall between a heap of old *Oz* magazines and a stack of tattered Alistair MacLeans. Cold air leaked through the small window behind her; in a tiny office to one side of the shop a man with a grey ponytail was plugging in a kettle. The posters on the walls were of Che Guevara, or muscular tractor drivers and factory workers. A Cyrillic slogan ornamented the image of a woman in a red dress brandishing a hammer and sickle. Conversations rose and fell. *The cover's very striking . . . I loved his last one . . . It's finding the time to read . . .*

She and George had quarrelled that morning. He had been packing a suitcase to leave for a fortnight's residency at a writers' retreat in the Lake District. It had been their usual argument, nothing new, the conflict fired by her insecurities and his resentment of her suspicions. His parting shot, that if it had not been for her teaching job she could have come with him to the Lake District, had infuriated her.

But she regretted that they had not made it up before the taxi had arrived to take him to the railway station. A year ago, six months ago, she would have phoned him and patched up the quarrel, no matter who was in the right or wrong. Tonight, she felt no urge to do so. At best, they would brush it under the carpet, their vulnerabilities unstated, the most dangerous subjects skirted round. At worst, the disagreement would simmer on. One of them would say something that lacerated, or they would retreat into silence.

She drank another glass of wine. The thought of returning to the empty house was unenticing, and yet neither did she belong here, with these people. They were not her friends, and my goodness, she'd had her fill of book launches. Why had she come here? In her heart she knew why, and the acknowledgement of her attraction to Rory Madden made her question whether she should stay. She had begun to zip up her black midi coat in preparation to go when he glanced up from signing a book. Their eyes met and he smiled, and any impulse to head away was snuffed out in an instant.

The guests began to drift out of the shop, their egress marked by wafts of cold air as the front door opened and closed. The man with the grey ponytail put the empty bottles into a cardboard box, then tipped the contents of the ashtrays into a bin before wiping his hands on faded loon pants.

Rory said, 'Adam, I'll help you clear up.'

'No sweat, man. I'll finish it tomorrow.'

'Not at all. Are you okay to wait for a few more minutes, Olivia?'

'I'll give you a hand,' she said.

Glasses were stacked on a draining board in a tiny, freezing kitchen, and plates piled into the sink. As Olivia and Rory left the bookshop, they talked about the evening. He was pleased that a decent number of people had come. His fear that no one would turn up had proved unfounded. Several dozen books had been sold, and Adam, who owned the shop, seemed happy with the sales.

'Adam used to lecture at SOAS,' Rory said. 'That's how I know him. He scrambled his brains with acid and dropped out. He's back on an even keel now. It was good of you to come, Olivia. I hope you didn't find it too tedious.'

'Not at all.'

He gave her a sideways glance. 'Honestly?'

'Honestly, it's been fun. I usually enjoy George's launches too, though they're quite different.'

'Not so much warm white wine and fewer sausage rolls?'

She laughed. 'Something like that.'

'Shall we get something to eat? You don't have to hurry home?'

'George is away. Guest of honour at a writers' event in the Lake District.' Her good humour evaporated.

He glanced at her. 'What?'

'Nothing. Oh . . .' Briefly she told him about the quarrel. Then she said, 'Sometimes I wonder what happened to us, to our generation. Sometimes I think we ended up in uniform just as we were trying to work out what to do with our lives, and that messed us up in some way. Then I think maybe I'm just looking for an excuse.'

They paused by a shop window. Tinsel glittered in the light from the street lamps; a porcelain Mary gazed down benevolently on the child in the manger, which was surrounded by half a dozen brightly coloured baubles.

He said, 'You and I, we had to witness the disintegration of our world. And when the war ended, we had little option but to do our best to live in a different one.'

He put his arms round her. She rested her forehead against the hollow of his shoulder, and he enfolded her in the warm woollen flaps of his coat. She should say something, she thought, she should explain that she and George were going through a bad patch, a long bad patch, and she needed to find a way of mending it.

Instead, she tilted her head so that he could kiss her. The rain fell and spray blew up from the wheels of passing cars. A fire lit inside her as he drew her against him, and she felt his body, hard against hers.

He said, 'My flat's a couple of streets away. Shall we go?'

She nodded. 'Yes, let's go.'

'You're sure?'

'I'm sure.' Arm in arm, they walked away, through the night.

Chapter Thirteen

1970–2, Sussex and London

With his friend Dan, who was also reading maths at Sussex, Tom was walking in the South Downs, heading up the broad sweep of hillside that led to Cissbury Ring. Dan was talking about his pet subject, algebraic topology, coming up with increasingly ridiculous equations to represent the curves and hollows of the countryside that surrounded them. It had rained all morning, and it was still raining, quick, sharp little drops making pinpricks on their faces. Much of the time they squelched through chalky mud, so that their boots became heavier with each step. When they came across a large stone or a wall, they stopped to scrape it off.

Sparrows chirped and fussed in the brown tangle of hedgerows, and a rabbit darted across their path. A golden-brown fox loped round the perimeter of a field. Tom told himself that when they reached Cissbury Ring he would feel on top of the world. If the sky cleared, he might be able to see the roll of the hills and valleys as far as the Channel. Though it didn't look as if it was in the mood for clearing.

Speaking to his mother on the phone last night, she had seemed happier – which meant, he hoped, that she and Dad weren't arguing so much. Tom hated quarrels. Raised voices and harsh words made him feel sick inside. He was choosy about the friends he made and avoided the company of those people who enjoyed conflict and revelled in making a scene. Dramas made him long to beat a rapid retreat, and he valued his small group of friends, none of whom wore their emotions on their sleeves. When Dan, for instance, was really annoyed, he resorted to a little light sarcasm.

The only thing to mar his pleasure in the day was the pain in his guts. It had started the previous evening. He had been deciding what to have for supper, cheese on toast or tomato soup, when he had discovered that he didn't feel like eating anything at all. It wasn't agony, but neither was it a niggle. In the end, he hadn't bothered with supper and had put the upset down to having drunk about a gallon of coffee while he finished his statistics paper. The pain had eased by the time he had gone to bed, and he had forgotten about it, only for it to rear its head again halfway through the walk. Every step seemed to jar something tender inside him.

He tried to distract himself by listening to Dan, who had stopped making up equations and was suggesting that the two of them skip Christmas entirely and spend the festive season walking the Pennine Way. Tom knew this wasn't an option for him. It would be fine for Dan, who was Jewish, and whose parents didn't bother much with Christmas, but if Tom were to tell Mum and Dad he was going to do the Pennine Way instead of coming home for Christmas, they would be upset. They wouldn't say so – in fact, they would be supportive and offer to buy him new waterproofs and help with the train fare – but they would hate it.

None of the Flynns were very religious, but Mum and Dad attended Midnight Mass each year and they expected Tom and his brothers to come along as well. He always helped Mum ice the Christmas cake, had done so since he was a little kid. He had never admitted to his mother that he disliked fruit cake, especially Christmas cake, with its mingling layers of icing and marzipan. Dutifully he waded through a slice each Christmas teatime.

Grandma always spent the festive season with them. Though Lorcan and Gareth were also supposed to be around, Tom knew he couldn't rely on them. Lorcan would escape whenever he could to see Iris, and Gareth had a way of having a lengthy list of social engagements that took him out of the house. Lorcan had told him that Gareth was chasing after that girl, Cleo Charlton. The thought of his parents spending Christmas Day with only Grandma and a handful of Dad's weirder friends, the ones with nowhere else to go, made Tom feel miserable, so the Pennine Way would have to wait.

When he looked up, he saw the tufts of wind-stunted trees that marked Cissbury Ring. Dan was trudging ahead of him, up the final stretch. Half a dozen other walkers in soaking anoraks and muddy boots were already standing on the summit in the lashing rain. They chatted to each other, comparing routes, drinking tea from Thermos flasks, exhilarated at having reached their destination.

Dan chucked him a Kit Kat. The sight of it made him feel nauseous, so he stuffed it in his pocket and told Dan he was going to try and get some photos. And miraculously, as he perched on the highest ground and looked out through the lens of his Minolta to where murky greens and browns spread themselves out over the Sussex countryside, the clouds thinned and split, revealing an arrow of bluish-white sky, and he saw in the distance a grey shimmer of sea. And the thing, the gut-rot, whatever it was, retreated, and he was suddenly ravenous.

Sometimes it was as if she was watching herself from the outside, this stranger, this other, changed Olivia Flynn, who went to work, who held up word cards for six-year-olds in the classroom, who showed them how to stick coloured paper jewels on cardboard crowns and who coaxed wise men, angels and sheep not to forget their lines. And who sometimes, at the end of the school day, found her way to Rory Madden's flat, where they made love.

His rooms were crammed with books and photos and drawings and academic papers and cardboard boxes, because in the New Year he was to head off to France for a six-month sabbatical to research the book he was planning to write about the Maquis. His flat was to be let out to a visiting American academic. His bed, which was also surrounded by books and boxes, was made up with white cotton sheets and a tartan eiderdown and a very scratchy blanket, bought in Egypt during the war. All the rooms were cold. The radiators rarely seemed to be on. When they had torn off their clothes that first time she had gone to his flat, after the book launch, Olivia had steeled herself against the chill, but had immediately forgotten about it because she had wanted him so much.

She was fitting a love affair into the run-up to Christmas, and though she supposed she should have felt guilty and anxious, instead she was blissfully happy. Write a list – *butter, mixed fruit, candied peel, caster sugar* – then dash out to the shops, all the while thinking of the way he liked to trace the hollow of her spine with his fingertip. Join in the social chit-chat at a neighbour's cheese and wine party and, turning away to refill her glass, recall the heat of his body and the roughness of his chin against her cheek. Sit cross-legged in the little sloping-roofed attic room at the top of the house, surrounded by Sellotape and ribbon and offcuts of paper, wrapping Christmas presents while remembering their last, brief, joyful meeting in the park. The soupy grey December light and his embrace as they had kissed beneath leafless, dripping trees. The warmth of his arms and the scent of his skin, and how his very first touch had conjured up desire in her. He had stroked her damp hair, rubbing it between forefinger and thumb. 'Like silk,' he had murmured.

One evening she was making marzipan, pummelling ground almonds and sugar, squeezing the paste between her fingers. She looked back over the dribs and drabs of the affair, the snatched moments and interruptions and intrusions – half an hour in a café, a ten-minute stroll in the park, an hour in his bed. It amounted to so little, she thought. In only a few weeks' time he would leave for France. This brief liaison was hardly worth risking her marriage for: she should put an end to it. She dropped the lump of marzipan onto a board and began, savagely, to roll it out.

She had the words formed on her lips when she met him the next day – *Rory, I can't go on with this* – but his kiss erased them and her resolution failed. When she was with him, she felt alive, it was as simple as that. How could she bear to return to the stale, old half-life?

Gareth, who had returned to the family home for the festive season the previous day, was in his room, buttoning up his shirt, when he heard the front door open and close.

Downstairs in the hall he found Tom standing on the doormat, rainwater dripping from his anorak and rucksack.

'You're early,' he said. 'I thought you weren't back till Wednesday.'

'There's nothing much going on at uni.' Tom unwound his scarf. 'Lectures are finished.'

Gareth gave him a closer inspection. 'Christ, you look like crap. Rough night?'

Meticulously Tom tucked his wet scarf over the hall radiator. 'It's good to see you too, Gareth. I've had a stomach bug. And it was a lousy journey. No seats on the train, and then it stopped at all these places I've never heard of. Where is everyone?'

'Dad's doing a radio programme. Mum said she was having supper with Louise.'

'Are you going out?'

Gareth took his leather jacket down from a peg. 'I'm meeting Cleo.' And then, because Tom really did look rubbish, pale-faced and holding himself in an awkward way, and because he felt mildly guilty for abandoning him the minute he had come home, he reached out for the rucksack.

'I'll take this upstairs.'

'It's soaking. It'll get the carpet wet.'

Ignoring him, Gareth carried the rucksack up the stairs and put it in Tom's room, a haven of neatly aligned posters and books arranged in order of size. Airfix model planes, expertly constructed and suspended on lengths of transparent thread, wafted as he went in and out of the door.

'There's mince on the stove,' he called out to Tom as he left the house.

Standing in the packed Underground carriage, Gareth thought about Cleo. They had been going out sporadically for three and a half months. During that time, they had had dinner six times and had been to bed together three times. After each of those occasions he had assumed that was it, they were properly a couple now, but then afterwards she had seemed to retreat. She and Jonathan, the interior designer for whom she now worked, would have a project in Gloucestershire or Northumberland and Gareth wouldn't see her for a fortnight. When once he had griped that she spent more evenings with Jonathan than with him, Cleo had been furious. 'Oh, don't be so pathetic, Gareth!' she had hissed at him, and had refused to answer his letters and calls for more than a week. When eventually she had forgiven him and Gareth had met Jonathan, a pleasant and stylish man, at a party, even he, who wasn't particularly alert to such things, had realised that Jonathan Thurlow was gay. He had felt ashamed of himself, and pathetic indeed.

Cleo was waiting for him in Trafalgar Square. Hand in hand, they strolled round the square and the roads that branched off it, admiring the Christmas tree and the coloured lights. Eventually they ended up in a basement restaurant, where a five-piece band was playing.

Gareth ordered champagne. Cleo said, 'You don't have to, you know.'

'Don't have to what?'

'Try to impress me.' She looked away. 'Sorry. I'm a bit prickly tonight. Champagne will be lovely. I appreciate it.'

After the champagne had been uncorked and poured, Gareth fished in his pocket and took out a small package. 'Happy Christmas, darling,' he said as he handed it to Cleo.

'Oh. Thank you, Gareth. So sweet of you. And so beautifully wrapped.'

'Open it, if you like.'

'Are you sure?'

'Go ahead.' He watched as she peeled off the paper. Inside the small red leather box was a gold locket.

'It's gorgeous,' Cleo said. 'Thank you.'

'Do you like it?'

'It's perfect. I love it. Do it up for me, would you?'

She was wearing a long dress of a floaty black and white spotted material. When he clasped the chain round her neck, his fingers brushed against her skin, which was soft and golden and satiny and seemed to have its own subtle, heady perfume. The locket settled into the deep V between her breasts.

The band began to play 'Have Yourself a Merry Little Christmas'. Cleo's gift to Gareth was a leather wallet and a first edition of *The Day of the Triffids*, one of his all-time-favourite books. They touched their glasses in a toast.

The waiter had cleared away the first course when Gareth reminded Cleo about the Flynns' party on 23 December. The Christmas Eve eve's party was a family tradition.

'I can't come,' she said. 'I told you, love.'

'I thought you might have changed your mind.'

'I don't change my mind about things like that. I told my mother I'd be coming home that day.'

Cleo's parents were divorced. She didn't talk about them much. Her mother lived in Andover, where Cleo had grown up, and her father had a one-bedroom flat in Chelsea, where he frequented pubs and clubs and lived, as far as Gareth was able to make out, a rather rackety existence, his third marriage recently having ended in separation.

'I wondered, if you left it just a day,' he said. 'I'd like you to come.'

She gave him a cool, appraising look. 'I know you would. You've made that very clear.'

'I only meant . . . the party should be fun.'

'I'm sure it will be. But I'm going home.'

'For *ten days*,' he muttered.

'Twelve, actually. I told you, I'm babysitting for my sister on the second of January. Jonathan is fine about me starting back at work a little late.'

A part of Gareth minded that Jonathan seemed to know more about Cleo's Christmas arrangements than he did, but he knew that was unreasonable of him.

'It's just that you don't seem all that thrilled about going home,' he said grumpily.

'They're my family. They're not perfect, but I love them.' She raised her eyebrows as she studied him. 'You're used to having things your own way, aren't you, Gareth?'

'What do you mean?'

She spread out her hands. 'I mean that you have everything. Good looks, good health, you're very bright and you have loving parents. Everything's easy for you, isn't it?'

'No, that's rot, it's not true, I—'

'You're the golden boy. I saw that as soon as I met your family.'

'How can you say that?' he protested. 'Lorcan has a first from Oxford. And Tom's cleverer than the rest of us put together.'

'Lorcan has a heart as soft as a marshmallow. And if you haven't noticed how much Tom hates all your famous Flynn parties, then you must be going around with your eyes shut.'

He began to make an angry retort but managed to bite it back. A dirge-like rendition of 'Silent Night', his least favourite carol, filled the silence. Cleo did not look angry. He had noticed this about her, that she rarely exhibited signs of annoyance or distress, that she permitted emotional disturbance to show only in a tension around her mouth, a chill in her lichen-green eyes.

'We're not perfect,' he said quietly. 'I know that. I'm not perfect, and neither is my family.'

'I don't want to quarrel. Not tonight. But there are things you need to understand if we're to go on seeing each other.'

'Cleo, please . . .' He stared at her, horrified.

'I'm serious, Gareth.'

He swallowed, then looked away to where the sequinned singer was elongating 'Re-est in heavenly peace' to unbearable lengths.

Cleo said, 'I don't get on with my mother. I never have. It wasn't until I left home that I really understood how good she is at emotional manipulation. I go and stay with her because my sister lives nearby and I enjoy seeing her and my nephews, but also because she's my mother and I love her, even though she makes me miserable. But I have to call the shots. It's the only way I can handle it. I won't be . . . I won't be caught up in her life. I'll listen when she tells me her problems, about the people who've slighted her and all the times she's been misjudged or overlooked, but I've learned not to let it touch me *here*.' She put her hand to her chest. 'Is that awful of me?'

Gareth shook his head. 'No, not at all.'

'I need to keep a part of myself separate, or I feel . . . swallowed up. I make my plans early and I tell Mummy when I'm coming home and when I'm going back to London. And I stick to that, even if she tries to persuade me to stay for longer.'

The carol ended and there was a ripple of applause. With a flurry of activity, half a dozen people squeezed onto the adjacent table. Coats and bags were hung on the backs of chairs, cigarettes lit and the waiter summoned.

'Everything I've achieved I've had to fight for,' Cleo said once the commotion had died down. 'I love my job and I've no intention of giving it up, even if, in the future, I get married and have children. And I want to travel, too. I want to go to all sorts of places. I want to see the world.'

'Okay,' he muttered. 'I'm sorry. What about your dad? Is he any easier?'

'I used to think so. I used to rather hero-worship him. He's very charming and good fun. He's an actor. He did well when he was younger, but I don't think he gets much work now. Sometimes he takes me to lunch at his club.' Cleo smiled. 'The most awful food, brown Windsor soup and stodgy suet puddings. We chat, but mostly he talks about himself. His stories are amusing, but eventually I noticed that he doesn't really listen to anything I say, and I've come to the conclusion that he doesn't find me very interesting. That's all right, I don't mind, we have lunch three or four times a year and that's fine. But I've got my life how I want it, and I don't intend to change it to suit anyone. Not for you, Gareth, nor anyone else.' She made a soft, brushing-away movement. 'I find families claustrophobic. They make me feel smothered. I hate having emotional pressure put on me. And I don't trust my parents. I haven't for a long time.'

'Do you trust me?'

When she did not immediately reply, Gareth felt as if he was poised on the edge of an abyss, his future – his happiness – teetering unpredictably. Then Cleo reached across the table and took his hands in hers.

'I like you a lot, Gareth. I think I might be able to trust you.'

'Cleo . . . I'd do *anything* to make you happy, to make you feel you can rely on me.'

'What I'm telling you is that I've no particular wish to be part of your world, the Flynns' world. Your family is perfectly delightful – your mother is very sweet, and I like your brothers. But I don't *need* to be swept up by them. That's not something I want. Families can hold you back, and I'm not going to let myself be held back. I've worked too hard to get where I am.'

Gareth registered that she had said nothing about his father. He chewed this thought over, along with the other realisation that had come to him when she had hinted that she might break it off with him: that he was in love with her and had been for months.

'I was being an ass,' he said. 'I promise I'll stop now.'

'Good.' Briskly she glanced at the menu. 'Do you fancy a pudding?'

Rory let Olivia into the flat. He nudged the front door closed with his shoulder as they kissed. 'You smell gorgeous, of winter,' he murmured. He curled his fingers round hers. 'You're freezing. Come in, sit down, warm yourself.'

In the living room, he had put on a one-bar electric heater. She spread out her hands in front of it and sipped the glass of malt whisky that he brought her. She saw that the bookshelves were bare.

'How's it going?' she asked him. 'The packing?'

'I keep changing my mind about which books to take. Do you mind if I finish this box?'

'Not at all. What about your furniture?'

'Howie's taking the place fully furnished.'

She imagined the visiting American academic who was to sublet the flat, who was called Howie Freeman and who was a historian from a university in Idaho, taking glasses out of Rory's cupboard, sitting on Rory's sofa and sleeping in Rory's bed. She thought of all the things they had not yet talked about, she and Rory, and all the things they would no longer have the chance to talk about.

She said, 'Where are you going first?'

He sealed the box with brown tape. 'Paris, to do some research, and then I'll head inland. I've arranged to rent a place in Limoges. I'll use it as a base while I travel around, maybe move on after a while.' He glanced over his shoulder at her. 'Did you say that Grace Ruthwell lives in France?'

'Alice told me so, yes.'

'I might try and get in touch with her. It could be useful if she'd talk to me about Claude. I have an idea for a book. Not this one, and I suspect not the next one. It's been brewing for a while, but I keep coming up against barriers.'

'A book about what?'

'Fascism in Britain in the run-up to the war.' He smiled at her. 'I enjoy teasing out the steps that lead to catastrophe.'

Olivia put aside the glass and unzipped one of her long leather boots. 'I imagine you'll do it meticulously, Rory.'

'I will. Fact by fact. Phase by phase.' He was watching her slip off her boots.

'Good for you.'

'I've always thought there must be quite a few people who'd prefer to forget about their past flirtations with extreme right-wing politics.'

'I imagine there would be.'

He came to sit in front of her. He ran his hand along her calf and they kissed. He unbuttoned her blouse and caressed her breasts, then they made love, hastily and passionately, tangled up on Rory's living-room rug.

She was lying in his arms and he was stroking the curve of her waist and hip when he said, 'Hey, I've an idea. Why don't you come to France with me?'

She saw it in her mind's eye: the little stone house she and Rory would rent in a village in the hills of Limousin, the job she would take in a *boulangerie*, their walks in the mountains, the air scented with rosemary and lavender. He was pulling on his jeans; as she righted the heater, which had somehow toppled over, she began to frame her reply.

They both heard the front door open. Rory grabbed his jersey and pulled it over his head as a girl's voice called out from the hallway, 'Dad, it's just me!'

A part of Tom had believed that as soon as he saw his mum, he would shake off whatever bug he'd caught that was making him feel so lousy. But Gareth had told him that Mum had gone to see Louise, so he would have to wait for her return. Once he had taken off his wet outer garments and lain down on his bed, the pain retreated. He drifted off into a shallow sleep, startling awake at a sound from the street – a shout, the blast of a car horn. He kept wondering when Mum would be back. She would know what to do.

He fell asleep again, and when he woke the pain was worse. He decided to phone Louise. He got out of bed and, moving in a crouch, made his way downstairs.

In the hall, he dialled Louise's number. Her daughter, Sarah, whom Tom thought of as almost a cousin, answered the phone. He asked for his mother, and Sarah told him that she wasn't there.

'But she's been round?' Tom said, confused.

'No, not tonight,' Sarah said. 'Are you all right, Tom?'

Fine, he said, fine. He thanked Sarah, put down the phone,

then slid down the wall to sit on the floor, where he closed his eyes and rubbed his palm against his hot, damp forehead. Pain was knotting itself like a tourniquet around his insides and he could hardly think straight.

Rising unsteadily to his feet, he shuffled to the kitchen, where he dug a bottle of aspirin out of a drawer. He leaned on the edge of the sink and choked down two tablets.

Coming home on the Underground train, standing in a crowded carriage and gazing out of the window at the alternating patches of darkness and light, Gareth reflected on his conversation with Cleo. He wasn't completely confident he had managed to pull back the evening from the disaster it had almost become. Before they had parted, he had offered to come back to her flat with her, but she had turned him down, explaining that she had an early start the next day. She had neither accepted nor dismissed his suggestion that they meet up for a quick drink before she went to Andover in a few days' time. She had said she would ring him. But she had kissed him before they had gone their separate directions at Oxford Circus, a warm and passionate kiss.

I think I might be able to trust you. Neither could he decide whether this was a positive indication of her feelings for him or whether she had been fobbing him off. It was hardly a ringing endorsement. The train drew to a halt at a station and Gareth squeezed himself against a carriage wall to permit the exit of a thickset, bald man carrying an enormous green plastic suitcase. *You're used to having things your own way*. Was that true? Forced into being honest with himself, he acknowledged that it was. He was good at reading people and skilled at getting them to do what he wanted. In this, he was different to Lorcan, who swam against the tide, and different to Tom, who stood back, keeping himself apart.

Thinking of Tom made him feel uneasy. He remembered how unwell his brother had looked earlier that evening. He had said he had a stomach ache – Tom, who never made a fuss. Gareth had always felt protective towards his younger brother, who seemed to lack a layer of armour, and yet he had gone out for the night, leaving the poor blighter on his own without even having made the effort to find out what was up with him. This thought chimed uncomfortably with Cleo's assessment of him, and once he left the train, he took the flights of steps to the surface at pace, darting round the other passengers in his hurry to get home.

During Olivia's homeward journey, her memory of the moment when Rory's daughter had turned up at his flat spooled itself over and over in her head, rerunning every appalling detail. They had been getting dressed, thank God, when a girl's voice had called out from the hallway. Rory had shouted back – 'Naomi, love!' – and then he and Olivia had stared at each other, aghast. He had pulled on his jumper, and she had scooped up the items of clothing that were scattered about and bolted for the bathroom.

There, she had dressed and hastily knotted up her hair. She had stared in the mirror, her heart pounding. The murmur of conversation from the living room had persisted – she could not remain in the bathroom for ever. Emerging, she had found a pretty, dark-haired girl sitting on the floor among the books and boxes. Rory's daughter had looked up and said, 'Hi!' to which Olivia had managed some sort of response.

Then Naomi had returned to the books. 'You can't take all of these, Dad. It's bonkers.'

Olivia had murmured, *I must dash*, or something similarly inane, and had then fled, zipping up her coat on the landing before rushing out of the building. You could have seen the funny side, she supposed, had not the episode been so excruciating, so humiliating, so lacking in dignity. All she wanted was to be safely at home. She felt dishevelled, frazzled and ashamed of herself.

She turned the corner into the street in which she lived. The cool, damp air and the quiet of the streets calmed her. A deep relief spread through her as the house came into view.

Tom heard the key turn in the lock. It took an act of will to prise himself off the sofa and make his way into the hall, bent double, one arm cradling his belly. His mother, who was unwinding her scarf, saw him.

'Tom!' She rushed towards him. 'Love . . .'

'Sorry, Mum, I've been sick . . . I tried to clear up.'

'It doesn't matter, sweetheart, I'll do it.'

'It hurts so much.'

'Hey . . .' Gently she stroked his face, then touched his forehead to check his temperature. 'Where does it hurt?'

'Here.' Tom indicated his belly. 'It started a few weeks ago,' he said. 'Just twinges, on and off. But it's got worse.'

'Okay, love, don't worry. Let's get you back to the sofa.'

'Gareth said you were visiting Louise, but—'

She interrupted him. 'Yes, and I'm sorry I was so long . . . If I'd known you were coming home, I wouldn't have gone.'

Something was wrong, he registered. Someone wasn't

telling the truth. But though he meant to explain to his mother about having spoken to Sarah, a groan escaped him instead.

When he was back on the sofa, Mum said, 'I'm going to call the doctor. Try to rest, darling. I'll be back in a moment.'

She kissed his forehead, then left the room. He heard her dial a number and speak. Then there was a mixture of other sounds: the front door opening again, and voices, Gareth's and Dad's. And the pain reared up, twisting his gut, leaving him able to think of nothing else.

Hours later, after the ambulance had taken Tom to the Whittington Hospital, and Olivia and George had followed in the car; and after Tom had been diagnosed with appendicitis and been taken into an operating theatre, and after an unbearable wait, the surgeon had spoken to them and told them he had come through the operation safely. He had been taken to a ward and was sleeping.

They returned home. It was by then half past three in the morning. George sent Gareth, who had waited up for them and who looked shaken and exhausted, to bed. Olivia said, 'I should phone Lorcan,' and George said, 'Not now. Leave it till morning. No point in upsetting him. Glass of brandy?'

'Tea, please.'

The kitchen smelled of burned mince, which at least helped to mask the faint sour scent of vomit that pervaded the ground floor. The kettle boiled; George poured water into the teapot.

She said, 'Oh God, George . . .'

'I know.' He took her in his arms. 'I know. I'm so sorry.'

'For what?'

'For not being here,' he said. 'For wasting my time with that stupid little radio programme. For being so, so *selfish*.'

'It's not your fault.'

'Oh, I think it is. I think we both know that.'

'No, no, it's mine.'

'No, love, you're not to blame.'

She had cried when Tom had been taken away to the operating theatre and she had cried with relief and shame when he had emerged from it. The surgeon had said, 'We caught it just in time. His appendix was on the point of bursting.' She wept again now.

George took her in his arms, then poured her a mug of tea. 'I'll go and check on Gareth, see if he wants anything.'

Olivia cradled the mug in her hands. The sight of the aspirin bottle, abandoned on the worktop hours ago by Tom, when he was alone in the house, made her shudder. She swallowed a couple of tablets and drank the tea.

Though she went to bed, she couldn't sleep. George came upstairs after a while and fell asleep immediately, as he always did, but every time Olivia began to doze she was jolted awake by the small sounds of the house or by her own racing thoughts. Eventually she put on her dressing gown and went downstairs and sat in the back room. Dawn was approaching, a gradual lightening of a charcoal-grey sky. She gave up trying to push away the clamour of voices in her head.

Naomi Madden, and that casual little *hi*, which had told her that it was nothing exceptional for Rory's daughter to come across a strange woman in her father's flat.

Rory's voice: *Why don't you come to France with me?* She had in that moment pictured herself abandoning George and her home and heading across the Channel, leaving her old life behind her and embarking on a new one of adventure and passion.

The folly of it. At the hospital, her thoughts had not once turned to Rory. Whatever he had meant to her – and there was love there, that she knew in her heart – it did not outweigh what she felt for her family. During those long, anxious hours she had thought only of Tom, of her beloved son, of his health and survival. How had she come to forget that the only thing of importance was the need to protect her family? They had come within a hair's breadth of disaster for a love affair built on a fragile edifice, a love affair that could never have lasted.

Tom recovered well from the surgery and returned to university in the second half of the spring term. Family events studded the remainder of that year. Lorcan and Iris were married in May. The wedding, a joyful occasion, took place in a church in the Hertfordshire village of Much Hadham, where Iris had grown up and where her parents and younger brother, Angus, still lived. Iris looked beautiful in a dress of ivory crêpe with a narrow, sculpted bodice, high neck and bishop sleeves. She carried a bouquet of carnations and stephanotis – and irises, of course – the blooms grown by both Olivia and Julia Jackson in their gardens. After a honeymoon in Crete, the couple moved into a flat in Cambridge. Lorcan commuted by train to his job at the BBC.

Gareth and Cleo became engaged in October. They threw a party at Cleo's flat, just for friends, so the Flynn family later marked the occasion by taking them out to dinner at Veeraswamy. Gareth was by then working for a property company, overseeing the work of contractors and liaising with architects. The company was owned by an Australian called Peter Ryan and was based in the east of England. Cleo's father had died earlier in the year, leaving her a sum of money, and she and Gareth were scouring Suffolk looking for somewhere to live.

Tom graduated in the summer of 1972. He immediately took up an offer of a post with an accountancy firm and rented a flat south of the river, looking out towards Battersea Park. Olivia and George helped him move in; they gave him some furniture and bought him a rug and a fridge, and he acquired a collection of pot plants, glossy-leaved palms and weeping figs. Now and then he mentioned a girlfriend, but they never seemed to last long enough for Olivia to meet them.

Her teaching career had seemed to stall once she reached her fifties. When the post of deputy head became vacant at the school where she taught, she applied for the position. She couldn't decide what annoyed her most: that she wasn't offered an interview, or that the position eventually went to an applicant from another school, a man in his mid thirties. The head of the school was male too, though nearly all the classroom teachers were women. Hot flushes made her feel that she was boiling up inside; she flung open the classroom windows and decided that it was time for a change. She enrolled in evening classes in horticulture, with the idea of starting up a gardening business.

There was always a lot going on. Her mother was becoming old and frail, her children were getting engaged and married and changing jobs and moving house. There was her home to maintain and the garden to look after. If she wasn't driving to Somerset to visit her mum at the weekend, there were dinner parties to go to and suppers when the boys dropped round. And perhaps it was this, this busyness that seemed the lot of Olivia and her contemporaries, that meant that the conversation with George, the one that started with him saying, *Olivia, we have to talk*, seemed to come out of the blue.

The significance of George's statement didn't immediately register. There were always things the two of them needed to talk about. Her car was making hiccuping noises and mould was blooming in the damp plaster beneath the living-room window, but top of the list that early evening was the washing machine, which had conked out and sullenly spewed soapy water over the cellar floor.

She scooped up potato peelings from the sink. As she took the colander out to the compost heap and tipped out its contents, she found herself thinking about the way he had said it and the way he had looked at her. *Olivia, we have to talk.*

She turned back to the house. George had come out of the kitchen and was standing in the back doorway. He had been away for a week, giving talks in bookshops and libraries in the north of England, but had returned a quarter of an hour ago, a day early, without warning her. At much the same time as he had entered the house, Louise had telephoned. Now, when she thought about it, it occurred to Olivia that George hadn't followed his usual pattern of behaviour while she and Louise had chatted, that there had been omissions. He hadn't uncorked a bottle of wine. He hadn't turned on the television and bemoaned world events. He hadn't taken his holdall upstairs or opened his post.

She crossed the lawn to him. 'Talk about what?'

'Olivia, I've met someone.'

It was October, and the days were shrinking, growing chilly. There was the irrational impulse to say, not tonight, not after I've had a rotten day and the washing machine is on the blink and I must get up early tomorrow to drive to Somerset, please, George.

'Met someone?'

'Yes. She's called Serena Ellis.'

Olivia heard the doorbell chime. It might be the plumber, to sort out the washing machine. It might be Lorcan, who had said he would drop by.

George was still talking, in calm, level-headed tones, but she seemed to hear his words from a distance. *We've both given it a good go . . . expect you'll agree that it's time to call it a day . . . I'll make sure you're all right financially . . . now that the boys have grown up and left home . . .*

The doorbell rang again. She felt as if she had had the stuffing knocked out of her. 'George?' she whispered. Then she slid past him, into the house.

From behind her, she heard him speak again.

'Serena's pregnant,' he said.

PART THREE

Chapter Fourteen

1978, Suffolk

Gareth and Cleo had moved to Suffolk a few months after they had married, and it was they who suggested to Olivia that she buy the cottage. It had unexpectedly come up for sale after the previous owner, a man in his sixties, had on a whim left the area and gone to live on the south coast. By then, the Islington house had been sold and the two mortgages George had taken out had been paid off. The profit that was eventually divided between them as part of their divorce settlement amounted to less than George had hoped, so sums must be recalculated, expectations reduced.

Greengage Cottage was next door to Gareth and Cleo's home, the Hayloft. From the Hayloft's beginnings as a modest brick and thatch barn, they had transformed it into a stylish four-bedroom residence. The two houses stood on the narrow, winding lane that led from the hamlet of Holfield St Peter to the larger village of Lavenham, four and a half miles away; there were no other buildings in sight. Built on a slight rise, they looked out across a landscape of gently rolling hills, green valleys and woodland.

Living in such proximity to her son and daughter-in-law,

Olivia was able to see her grandson every day – and indeed, being near Oscar while he was at the delightful toddler stage had been a huge incentive to purchase the house. Viewing the two-up, two-down flint and brick cottage for the first time, she had admired the kitchen, which had a Rayburn and plentiful cupboards painted willow green; but what had attracted her most and cemented her decision to leave London for the countryside had been the good-sized garden and the piece of woodland that grew to one side of it. Through all the windows trees were visible. Their leaves and branches cast shifting, speckled patterns.

Olivia had moved into Greengage Cottage in January 1974. Immediately after telling her about his lover's pregnancy, George had decamped from the Islington house to live with Serena. The divorce had been finalised in mid 1973, a year of difficulty and disruption for Olivia, during which she had moved out of the family home and back to Somerset to help care for her mother in the last few months of her life. She had returned to London briefly after Josephine Goodland passed away, renting a small flat and sorting out her remaining affairs in the capital while waiting for probate to be granted on her mother's estate. She missed her mum every day. Once she had moved in to Greengage Cottage, she comforted herself with the thought that Josephine, who had loved gardens and gardening, would have approved of her decision. She decorated the cottage, putting her own imprint on it, and Gareth helped her put up a greenhouse in the garden.

She kept the name, Greengage Cottage, partly because she had a vague memory of having been told it was bad luck to change the name of a house – or did that only apply to ships? – but also because it suited her new home. Three gnarled old greengage trees stood beside the boundary hedge; in late summer they produced sufficient plump green fruits for her to make jam. She was in the habit of walking in the patch of woodland each morning before breakfast. In spring, the chorus of birdsong lifted the heart.

With the move to Suffolk, she had given up teaching altogether and had started up a gardening business – on her own to begin with, until, at a rehearsal of the Holfield St Peter choir, she fell into conversation with a woman called Margot Packham. Margot was a widow; like Olivia, she had been a Land Girl during the war. Later, she had studied botany and horticulture. The two women had stopped talking only when the musical director, Ralph, had plunged into the intro to Mozart's 'Alleluia', but by then they had made the decision to join forces and work together. Which, Olivia thought, made everything more fun.

Both women fitted their gardening work round grandparenting duties. Margot's grandsons were scattered around East Anglia; by the late seventies, Olivia had four grandchildren. Gareth and Cleo's son Oscar was four; his sister Hazel was, at twenty-one months, a plump, beaming toddler. Iris and Lorcan had two children as well. Magnus was just four months younger than Oscar; Florence was born at the beginning of October 1977. Nothing gave her more pleasure than to spend time with them.

Cleo continued to work for Jonathan Thurlow's interior design company, though she had cut down her hours since Oscar's birth. Olivia looked after her grandchildren while her daughter-in-law was at work, and often stayed with Lorcan and Iris in Cambridge, an hour and a quarter's drive away.

From the beginning, she and George had made sure to

be civilised with each other in front of their sons. Serena, his second wife, was a perfectly agreeable woman, and if Olivia sometimes found her a little tiresome, rather shallow, it felt a matter of pride not to let that show. And George and Serena's daughter, Amelia, who was now four years old, was a delight, sturdy and bossy in the way little girls often are, with an infectious laugh and a cloud of strawberry-blonde curls.

But the separation, divorce and George's eventual remarriage had torn the family apart, and the rift it had caused had not yet healed. So much went unspoken: that Serena was almost twenty years younger than Olivia, that Amelia was the same age as Lorcan and Gareth's sons, that this had not been George's first affair. These things must be tiptoed around. And Olivia saw it as her role to do her best to ensure calm and tolerance remained in force whenever the family were reunited.

Their three sons had each reacted differently to the divorce. Gareth, ever the pragmatist and peacemaker, had continued to invite his father – and Serena – to family celebrations. Tom, too, took part in family events, though it seemed to Olivia that his natural quietness and reserve had become more pronounced since his parents' divorce, and she worried that he had become increasingly isolated as a result.

It was Lorcan who took the break-up hardest. He refused to speak to his father for more than a year. At first he turned down family events at which George might be present. Olivia talked to him, and so did Iris, and in time he modified his stance; yet though Lorcan might now tolerate George, he had certainly not forgiven him. Gareth once said to Olivia that having his elder brother to a family dinner was like having a black rain cloud parked in the corner of your living room, and she knew exactly what he meant. The animosity the situation had bred between Lorcan and Gareth troubled her. Gareth was irritated by Lorcan's inability to accept a set of circumstances that could not be altered, and in turn, Lorcan thought Gareth spineless and complacent in his acceptance of their father's betrayal.

Lorcan commuted each week-day to London to work at the BBC. Gareth's mentor, Peter Ryan, had returned to Australia towards the end of 1976, so Gareth had found a job with another employer. Tom continued to work for a top London accountancy firm and most of his weekends were spent walking with friends on the South Downs or in the Peak District. The previous autumn he had sold his flat and moved into a terraced house in Crouch End. He was bringing his new girlfriend to Gareth's thirtieth birthday celebration and Olivia was looking forward to meeting her.

Tom and Nat were driving through the grey and brown February countryside. Though they had set off early from London for Suffolk, they were running late because, after they had travelled a mile or so, Nat had realised she had forgotten to bring the birthday present she had made for Gareth. Tom had had to do a U-turn and head back to the street in Camden where she lived, where he parked illegally on a double yellow, keeping an eye out for police and traffic wardens. Eventually she reappeared, triumphantly waving at him a bright pink macramé pot plant holder and a crumpled piece of wrapping paper.

Tom had met Nat three months ago at his workplace in the City. It had been the end of the day and he had been on his way out, hurrying to catch a train to Sheffield, when the lift had jammed between floors. The only other person in the lift had been a young woman wearing an orange raincoat and a long, stripy knitted scarf. Her short brown hair was parted in the middle; he noticed, when she turned to him, that her eyes were a very dark brown. 'Do you think we should press the alarm button?' she had asked him, and he had said, 'Yes, I suppose so,' and had done so. Espying an OS map of the Peak District in his pocket, she had struck up a conversation about walking routes round Edale and Mam Tor. By the time the lift shuddered into life fifteen minutes later, Tom had learned that she loved walking, that she had been temping at Collins Roper for the past fortnight, and that she preferred to work for arts organisations or cooperatives but had accepted this post because the pay was good and Christmas was coming up. And that she was the same age as him, twenty-seven, and her name was Natasha Fetherston.

That had been how it started. Tom couldn't remember the lifts at Collins Roper ever jamming before. As he got to know Nat better, he noticed that things happened when he was with her. A woman fainted on the pavement in front of them and had to be scooped up and driven to her home in south London, and it took hours in choking traffic crossing the Thames back and forth before Tom was able to return to his home in Crouch End. On their second date, Nat had rescued a budgerigar she had found in the doorway of an Islington pub; she had taken the cold, bedraggled bird back to her room in Camden while he had scoured the streets for a shop that sold birdseed on a Sunday afternoon. Their third, they had been wandering along High Holborn after having had lunch when a man had beckoned to them to tell them about a concert that was about to start. Tom, who had imagined a quiet afternoon ironing shirts, had instead found himself sitting beside Nat in a chilly stone chapel, listening to a beautiful Chinese woman play the Goldberg Variations.

It was disconcerting. In Nat's company today, might he accidentally join a circus or take up hot air ballooning?

Glancing at the clock on the dashboard, he saw that they had made up ten minutes. He hated being late. Nat sat beside him, her work bag on her lap, her fingers busy with a crochet hook and a ball of turquoise wool. Tom had hesitated before asking her to Gareth's thirtieth birthday party because he hadn't been sure if she would want to come, or whether they had known each other long enough – they had only been dating for six weeks. Or whether, indeed, it was a simply terrible idea because contact with his family might put her off him for good. The only thing he had been certain of was that the occasion would be so much more enjoyable if she was there.

They drove through Halstead in Essex, heading north. He knew that his decision to introduce Nat to his family might prove to be a mistake. They might behave appallingly and then she would be horrified, and he would never see her again. If Lorcan and Dad had already reached Gareth's house, they might have clashed before Tom and Nat even arrived.

He said, 'It could get a bit sticky today.'

Nat looked up from the woollen thing she was constructing. 'Your family?'

'My parents can be prickly with each other.' He had told her about the divorce and about Dad's remarriage to Serena and the subsequent birth of his half-sister, Amelia. Nat's own father had died when she was twenty-one years old.

He said, 'If Lorcan has a few drinks he can get a bit loud.'

He might have added that Cleo would try too hard to make the occasion go perfectly and then feel disappointed when not everything went to plan. And if there was a disagreement, then Gareth would defend their father, and that would wind Lorcan up.

Nat made a disparaging sound. 'You haven't met the Fetherstons. Barking mad, the lot of us.'

'Damn.' Tom braked. Ahead of them lay a ford, brimming with water after recent heavy rainfall.

'Take a run at it?' Nat suggested.

'It might be too deep.' He twisted in his seat to get the AA map from the back. 'I'll have to find another route.'

'If you go back to the village we've just come through and take a left turn, that should work.'

'You know this area?'

'My family are from Norfolk, not that far from here. We used to come on day trips here.'

'I didn't know.' He put the car into reverse. 'Where in Norfolk? Norwich?'

'No, in the countryside, a few miles from Swaffham.'

Tom swung the car round and they headed back towards the village. Nat put her crochet back in her bag and took out a packet of crisps. As she pulled it open, fragments of crisp flew into the footwell. Tom had hoovered the Ford's interior the previous day in preparation for the journey.

'Oops, sorry,' she said. She offered him the packet. 'Honestly, Tom, whatever your family are like, I bet they're not half as tricky as mine. Take a left here.'

'You're sure?'

'Course I am.' She gave him one of her warm smiles, which touched her eyes and seemed to make him melt inside. 'Almost sure. And if I'm wrong, it'll be an adventure, won't it?'

Iris said, 'Have you remembered the Cosy Toes?' and Lorcan said, 'We won't need it, will we?'

'We might go out for a walk. And the rain hood for the pushchair, too.' In Cambridge the sky was a pale, crystalline blue, but that didn't mean it might not be raining in Suffolk. Florence, who was four and a half months old and liked to see what was going on, was happier in the pushchair than the carrycot.

She had fallen asleep as they were packing the car, thank goodness. Iris looked round for Magnus, who had been there a moment ago. She didn't want to leave Florence in the front garden while she searched for her son, and she didn't want to put the carrycot in the car before Magnus was immobilised in his seat because he might wake his sister climbing into the vehicle. Florence was easily disturbed and a poor sleeper. Once woken, she might cry for hours, and Iris, who was very tired, who had been tired since Florence was born, wasn't sure if she could bear that.

Lorcan came out of the house with the Cosy Toes and plastic rain hood. Iris asked him to find Magnus.

'He might be in the cupboard,' she suggested.

'Which cupboard?'

'The one under the stairs.'

Magnus's latest fad – mentally Iris skirted round the word *obsession* – was to imagine that he was a squirrel. The under-stairs cupboard was his drey. At mealtimes he bunched his hands together and made a squeaking noise to ask for food. The squirrel thing had been going on for a couple of months. She wondered whether it was connected to the birth of his sister, whether being a squirrel seemed a more attractive prospect than being the elder brother of a tiny, squalling human being.

Iris packed items they might need for the journey into the remaining spaces in the car – nappies, spare plastic pants and Babygros and a pink cardigan (Florence spat up a lot of her feed), bottles of sterilised water and a tin of baby milk. She had recently started topping up Florence's breast feeds with a bottle in the hope that she might sleep better. Another bag held a cup of juice for Magnus along with a change of clothes, some books and a cuddly toy, and a plastic bag and old towel in case he was travel sick.

In the wing mirror she caught sight of her reflection. She hadn't got round to putting on make-up and her hair needed washing. The shadows beneath her eyes looked as if they had been sketched on with a piece of charcoal. Cleo would look immaculate, as would Oscar and Hazel. How Cleo succeeded in making her two appear as perfect as if they were modelling for a children's clothing catalogue Iris had no idea. She had once asked her, and Cleo had looked surprised, as if having neat children was a normal thing. As Lorcan and Magnus came out of the house, Iris saw the orange streak down the front of her son's brown jumper, a remnant of his breakfast egg. She picked at it with a fingernail, unable to face the battle of persuading him to put on a different one. Since becoming a squirrel, he had been resistant to wearing any jersey but the brown one.

She gave herself a mental shake. She wasn't going to let herself plummet down the all too familiar rabbit hole of anxiety and despondency. Not today. It was a beautiful day, and she was looking forward to going to Cleo and Gareth's house, with its spacious, pale interiors and large windows that looked out over the soft green Suffolk countryside. Magnus would play with his cousins, and there would be plenty of Flynns to cuddle Florence if she was grouchy. Iris was looking forward to not having to cook for an entire twenty-four hours. Perhaps all the attention and country air would tire Florence out and she would sleep through the night for the first time.

She coaxed Magnus into his seat, and then Lorcan, behind her, said, 'Do you think you could carry this on your lap?'

She looked round. Lorcan was holding an enormous bouquet of flowers. 'What's that?' she said.

'They're amazing, aren't they? I picked them up first thing from the florist on Bridge Street.'

'Lorcan . . .'

'They're for Cleo.'

'I thought the champagne was our present.' She stared at the flowers, then at him. 'I can't possibly hold that for the entire journey. I need my hands free in case Florence wakes up or Marcus needs anything.'

'Okay.'

Lorcan lifted the carrycot into the back and fixed it in place with the seat belt. Iris moved her own seat forward so that the flowers could fit in the footwell behind her. At last, only half an hour later than planned, they set off.

Iris's mood, precarious since the birth of Florence, had been shaken by the sight of the bouquet. What was Lorcan doing spending money on a lavish gift without consulting her, when only a week ago they had talked about cutting down on expenditure? Since then, she had been trying to economise, checking the price of groceries and trying not to indulge herself with cups of coffee in cafés. Now she questioned whether Lorcan was remembering to do the same. She thought of asking him how much the bouquet had cost but decided not to. She was afraid to. In her brief glance she had seen roses, orchids and snapdragons . . . in *February*.

After having Magnus, Iris had returned to work at her former job with a pharmaceutical company, but the juggling of family and work obligations had been a constant battle. There had been no provision for part-time working and no flexitime, so Magnus had been cared for by a patchy series of nannies and au pairs. Iris herself had been one of only a handful of female scientists in her department. She had had to use her annual leave to be with Magnus whenever he was unwell or needed to see a doctor or have an inoculation, and she suspected it had been noted to her detriment that she never stayed late to finish a piece of work as her male colleagues did. Men who had once been junior to her had been promoted ahead of her. All her superiors had been male.

She had given in her notice when she was six months pregnant with Florence. She had woken up one morning in a cold sweat, having pictured how impossible her life would be with a full-time job and two infants. She and Lorcan had discussed it, and they had agreed that she would give up work to look after their young family. It would only be for a few years; they would save money on childcare, and as soon as Florence went to school, Iris would return to work, even if it meant starting again from the lowest rung. Meanwhile, they would economise.

Lorcan said, 'You don't mind, do you, love, about the flowers? Cleo always makes such an effort. I wanted to show her how much we appreciate it.'

She felt a surge of love for him. From the early days of their relationship she had adored him for his kindness and generosity. She squeezed his hand. 'Of course I don't mind. It was sweet of you to think of it. And Lorcan, you promise—'

'Not to get into an argument with Dad.'

'And go easy on the drinking, please.'

He grunted. 'Christ, though, if Serena keeps banging on about the kid going to a private school . . .'

'*Lorcan.*'

'Don't tell me it doesn't drive you nuts as well. Sweetheart, I'll behave myself. It'll be fine. Don't worry.'

Iris glanced over her shoulder at the children in the back. Magnus had stopped making squirrel noises and was singing to himself and Florence was still asleep.

'Perhaps we should go out for drives more often,' she said. 'Flo always sleeps better in the car.'

They had left the city behind and were heading through flattish Cambridgeshire countryside. Jackdaws rose from a leafless tree in a ragged black cloud and beneath the birches the snowdrops shone like stars. And at last Iris began to relax.

Olivia was in her bedroom at Greengage Cottage, getting ready for Gareth's birthday party. She inspected her reflection in the mirror. Her navy-blue jersey dress had originally been bought for a literary function of George's, but it still fitted and flattered her figure. So much of her time was spent in her gardening clothes – corduroy trousers, an old jumper and a Barbour jacket. It was nice to wear something more glamorous.

First thing that morning she had nipped over to the Hayloft to wish Gareth a very happy birthday and to offer to help with the preparations for the party. Cleo had been decorating a cold baked salmon with slices of cucumber and lemon while Gareth had been turning out a game pie onto a platter. Olivia had peeled potatoes, prepared vegetables and whipped up a meringue. By eleven o'clock, the arrangements were well under way, so she had taken the children to the play park in the village to let off steam. While they were out, Gareth and Cleo had added the finishing touches to the birthday cake.

She glanced at her watch. It was a quarter past twelve. Through the window she could see the gravel area in front of the Hayloft. The only vehicles parked there were Gareth's van and Cleo's Fiesta, which meant that the rest of the family had not yet arrived. The day was crisp and cold, the sun a bright silver ball, quite low in the sky.

In the kitchen, she took the trifle she had made the previous day out of the fridge and beat up a carton of cream into pillowy white clouds.

It was unlike Tom not to be bang on time. When Olivia had spoken on the phone to him the previous week, she had sensed hesitancy on his part about inviting his girlfriend to the party. 'I want her to have a good time,' he had said, and Olivia had known that what he was really saying was, 'I don't want Lorcan to drink too much and get touchy with Gareth. And I don't want Dad to put his foot in it and spark off a row.' As she spread the cream on top of the trifle, she gave a small inward sigh. Tom's concerns were not unfounded. Still, she was hopeful that everyone would be on their best behaviour today and the occasion would go smoothly.

Grating chocolate on top of the cream, her thoughts turned to Lorcan and Iris. With three sons, Olivia found that at any given time there would often be one she was worrying about most, and at the moment that son was Lorcan. She tended to think of him as her most complicated son. His natural optimism could be punctuated by periods of moroseness; his pride led him to tip too easily into defensiveness and self-doubt.

On visits to Cambridge since the birth of Florence, Olivia had noticed how Lorcan and Iris seemed to move within a cloud of confusion. They would run out of milk for the baby or Calpol for Magnus, or there would be no clean sheets, or the guinea pigs would escape their hutch and they would have to scour the garden searching for them. All these things were to be expected in any household with very small children, but recently she had detected an underpinning of precariousness and pent-up emotion. Lorcan was short-tempered and Olivia had more than once found Iris in tears.

Her daughter-in-law in particular could do with an enjoyable weekend away. Though Olivia completely understood her reasons for giving up work, she suspected that Iris, who was a thoughtful, considered and intellectual woman, missed it. She remembered how, when at home looking after three children, she herself had longed for sensible adult conversation and the pleasure of single-mindedly concentrating on one task at a time, ordinary activities made impossible by the presence of infants, delightful though they were. And how, when she had embarked on her teaching career, she had felt her sense of self, which had been consumed by the needs of her children and the demands of George's career, return.

Twenty months ago, Lorcan and Iris had moved from their flat into an Edwardian house in north Cambridge. It was a beautiful house, spacious and elegant with high-ceilinged rooms and a multiplicity of original features, but they had stretched themselves to buy it. The loss of Iris's income must mean that finances were tight; mortgage rates were rising in an alarming fashion. Olivia, who had lived in a series of homes in need of constant repair and renovation, knew all too well that old houses, however charming, cost money. And Lorcan had never been good at economising. Big-hearted and generous, he liked to surprise friends and family with splendid gifts. He would see it as an admission of failure to cut back on buying the food and drink for a party.

Catching sight of Oscar slipping through the gap in the hedge between the two houses, Olivia went out to meet him.

'Hello, gorgeous boy.'

'Mummy says is the trifle ready.'

'Let's go and get it, shall we?' She took his hand, and they went into the cottage.

Lorcan was the first to arrive, which surprised Cleo. It was usually Tom who turned up first. Gareth commented on this as he ushered Lorcan, Iris and the children and their paraphernalia into the house.

'Perhaps it's the new girlfriend,' he said. 'Perhaps she'll get Tom into the habit of turning up for a party ten minutes late, like a normal person.'

Lorcan put the box of champagne on the side table, wished Gareth a happy birthday and hugged him and then Olivia.

He offered Cleo a huge bouquet. 'These are for you.'

'They're gorgeous. Thank you, Lorcan.' Cleo kissed him.

Olivia said, 'How was the journey?'

'Not too bad. Florence slept.' Lorcan was helping Magnus out of his jacket.

The baby was writhing and making complaining noises. Olivia said, 'May I?' and lifted Florence out of the carrycot and joggled her up and down.

'Would you like to feed her, Iris? The little sitting room is nice and quiet. I'll get you a cup of tea.'

'Thank you, Olivia. Could you make up a bottle for me?' Iris extracted a bottle from a bag, gave instructions to Olivia, then took her daughter, who was by now red-faced and howling, and disappeared into the sitting room.

Cleo suggested to Oscar that he take Magnus to play with his train set, but Magnus hid behind his father's legs, his thumb in his mouth, looking alarmed, as if playing with his cousin's Brio trains was a dreadful ordeal.

In the kitchen, Cleo glanced at the clock. It was ten to one. She disliked unpunctuality, believed it born of lack of consideration, and was worried that the lunch would spoil. For all his faults, George generally turned up on time, and as for Tom, as Gareth had pointed out, he had a habit of arriving early, while they were still washing the lettuce or she was putting on her lipstick. They were all curious to meet Natasha. Tom had never introduced a girlfriend to the family before.

The food was ready, and the children would get fractious if they had to wait much longer for their lunch. Olivia was obviously thinking the same, because from across the kitchen she caught Cleo's eye and tilted her head in the direction of Oscar, Magnus and Hazel. Cleo nodded and gave an inward sigh. If the three cousins had their lunch now, that would mean Amelia would end up eating with the grown-ups, which she had been trying to avoid. Serena didn't appear to believe in teaching her child table manners, and Amelia would pick at other people's plates and chew with her mouth open.

Cleo knew why she was feeling on edge today. It was because of the enormous, life-changing decision she and Gareth had finally arrived at last night. It was also because of the slight bickering disagreement that had followed it. They were not given to stormy arguments. Having both witnessed too many altercations during their childhoods, they prided themselves on rarely exchanging a cross word. So even this, a failure to agree on a detail, on the best time to inform his family of their decision, had left her feeling deflated and jumpy.

They thought the same about all the important things – how to bring up the children, what to spend their money on, where to live and where to go on holiday – and Gareth was, in general, easy-going, so Cleo found any divergence of opinion unsettling. She still thought he was wrong. Surely it was best to get tricky discussions over with as soon as possible. It would be best, too, to tell the family when they were all together – and who knew when that would happen again? Cleo was certain that once they got used to the idea, the Flynns would share their excitement.

Olivia said, 'Is that a car?'

Gareth opened the front door. 'It's Tom,' he called back. He went outside.

The kettle had boiled. Olivia made a mug of tea and put it on a tray alongside a warmed bottle of milk and a plate of biscuits, then took the tray to Iris, who was feeding her daughter. Florence was a notably beautiful baby, bright and lively and healthy, but poor Iris hadn't yet been able to get her into any sort of routine. Olivia was extremely fond of Iris, and it troubled her that in the hallway, as the baby had begun to howl, she had seen tears in her daughter-in-law's eyes. She remembered how tough she herself had found the first six months of each of her sons' lives, and how she had seemed to stagger from crisis to crisis in a fuddle of tiredness. Compared to that, teaching in a primary school or running a gardening business was a piece of cake.

'How's she doing?' she asked.

'Better.' Iris pulled down her jumper. 'She's calmed down a bit.'

'Hello, beautiful. She is the most gorgeous baby, Iris. You've done so well with her. Would you like me to see if she wants the bottle? You have your tea.' She held out her arms for Florence, who beamed at her.

All three Flynn brothers were good-looking in different ways, though in Nat's opinion, Tom, with his narrow, high-cheekboned face, chiselled features and straight dark hair, was the handsomest of the three. He had introduced her to his mother, Olivia, as soon as they had arrived. If Olivia Flynn had been in a crowd of people, Nat would have worked out straight away that she was Tom's mother. Nat's own mother would have said they were like peas in a pod.

While the children were having their lunch at the kitchen table, the adults were ushered into a large, L-shaped living room for hors d'oeuvres of blinis, vol-au-vents and champagne. The floorboards were waxed, the walls painted a soft apricot. A navy sofa stood to one side of the room, and down the centre of it ran a long pine table, laid for nine. Glass patio doors looked out to a terrace and lawn and then beyond to a jigsaw of field and trees and a stream that glittered in the winter sunshine. A breeze moved the buff feathery flags of the reeds edging the water. *Wow*, Nat thought. She felt as if she had walked into a photograph in an interior design magazine.

Bottles were uncorked and birthday toasts raised to Gareth. Soon, Nat had the pleasant, dazed feeling that comes from having drunk a couple of glasses of champagne while not having had much to eat. She hadn't had time for breakfast that morning so was surviving on the crisps she had eaten in Tom's car.

It took her a while to realise that Gareth and Cleo had no clutter. A glass bowl stood in an alcove and there was a single, shiny copy of *House & Garden* on a coffee table. But where were the stacks of newspapers and magazines, the baskets of knitting wool and fabric scraps, the clothes for mending and the heaps of paperwork, unopened letters and flyers? Had the Flynns bundled everything into a cupboard, or did they have a special room for their belongings, on which they shut the door when guests appeared?

Tom's eldest brother, Lorcan, came to talk to her. Nat scanned the room. 'It's so *tidy*. Imagine living like this, in a house like this.' She looked up at him. 'Or perhaps you do.'

He laughed. 'I'm afraid not. I like to imagine this place slips into chaos as soon as we've gone.'

Two little boys, making squeaking noises, hurtled into the room and ran round the table.

Lorcan raised his voice. 'Magnus! Slow down a bit!'

Magnus, a tall, gangly, black-haired boy, was leading the charge. His glasses were perched at a perilous angle halfway down his nose as his cousins chased after him. Oscar had on a silver plastic breastplate over striped dungarees, and his little sister, Hazel, was wearing a white dress appliquéd with strawberries.

'He's a cutie, your Magnus,' Nat said.

Lorcan smiled. 'We think so.'

He asked her how she and Tom had met, and Nat told him about the lift breaking down. Lorcan said that he had met Iris at a cricket match, where she had tended his broken nose. He ran a fingertip down it to show her the bump.

Tom came to join them. He put his arm round Nat's waist. 'Are you okay?'

'I'm great. What a beautiful house.'

'It's quite something, isn't it?'

Lorcan said, 'Where the hell is Dad? I can't believe he's not here yet.'

Tom frowned. 'Maybe they got a puncture.'

Lorcan made a contemptuous snorting sound. 'We've got time to open one more, then.' He began to tease the foil top off another bottle of champagne.

'It's odd that they haven't phoned,' said Olivia.

Cleo was fretting. 'If everyone has too much to drink now, they won't enjoy the lunch.'

Gareth was checking something in the oven. 'I don't think we can wait much longer, love. Why don't we go ahead and serve the first course?'

'Because they'll turn up just as I've got the food on the table, I know they will.' Cleo sounded on edge. 'There'll be a lot of fuss, because there's always a lot of fuss with George, and Serena will go on about her diet, and I'll have to go and make her herbal tea and a cup of warm milk for Amelia.' She gave an exasperated little shrug. 'Okay. The potatoes are soggy anyway.'

Cleo had made name cards, each with a different pen-and-ink illustration. Olivia's had a charming little sketch of an avocet. She helped Gareth and Cleo bring in the serving bowls and platters. While Gareth sliced the ham and Cleo cut up the game pie and people helped themselves to cold salmon, Olivia offered round vegetables. Cleo was right, the potatoes were soggy.

They had just started eating when the doorbell rang. Cleo muttered, 'Good grief, bang on cue, would you believe it?'

Gareth went to answer the door. Shortly afterwards, George came into the dining room. He still knew how to make a dramatic entrance, thought Olivia. He was wearing his long black overcoat, and his wild silver hair was windswept. At much the same time as acquiring a new wife, he had bought a sports car.

She gave him a smile and said hello. George flung his coat onto the sofa and sat down in one of the empty seats. Cleo rescued the coat, to hang it up presumably, while Gareth poured his father a glass of champagne. Magnus and Oscar were running round the table.

Cleo shooed the boys out of the room. She said to George, 'Where are Serena and Amelia?'

'They couldn't make it.'

She pursed her mouth.

Olivia said, 'I hope they're not unwell.'

'No, no. How is everyone? In good health, I hope. May I have some of that very impressive pie?'

Tom said, 'How was your journey, Dad? Nat and I had to take a detour because of the floods.'

'It wasn't too bad at all.'

'Hazel will be disappointed Amelia isn't here,' Gareth said.

'Gareth, happy *thirtieth* – good grief.' George raised his glass to his middle son. 'Congratulations.'

There was something he wasn't telling them, thought Olivia. Today he looked every day of his sixty-seven years. Beneath the tan, his skin was pallid and papery, and the energy and bounce that were characteristic of him were absent.

Sometimes she wished she could rid herself of her understanding of him. She would have preferred to be ignorant of his needs and his moods, but their marriage had lasted for twenty-seven years, and it wasn't possible to turn him into a stranger. She had, however, learned from her mistakes, and knew now to do her utmost to keep George and his emotional states at arm's length.

Lorcan, who had been fetching a clean cardigan for Florence, came into the room. 'Where's Serena?'

'I'm afraid she couldn't be here.'

'She didn't want to bother?'

'No, Lorcan.' George stared down at his plate.

'More game pie, Dad?' asked Gareth.

'What, then?'

'Lorcan,' Iris said quietly. He sat down.

Olivia said, 'Are you all right, George?'

'Very well, thank you.' His smile took in the entire family. 'Wonderful talk at the British Library yesterday evening. Delightful audience. And I've been talking to Macready, in Edinburgh, about a residency.'

Cleo said, 'Isn't Amelia about to start school? Would Serena really want to uproot her?'

George didn't reply. He poked at the game pie with his fork.

Lorcan said, 'Dad? What's going on?'

The clatter of cutlery faded and silence fell. George said, 'Actually, Serena and I have decided to call it a day.'

Gareth, looking bewildered, repeated, 'Call it a day?'

'Yes.'

'You mean . . .'

'Serena and I . . . by mutual agreement . . . perfectly civilised . . . no animosity . . .' George's phrases scattered and collided like floes of ice breaking off from a glacier. He looked deeply uncomfortable.

Cleo said, 'George, are you telling us that you and Serena have split up?'

'You're dumping her?'

'Not *dumping* her, Lorcan. We've agreed to separate.'

'Sounds like dumping to me.'

'Lorcan, please . . .'

'Good God.' Lorcan gave his head a vigorous shake.

'Dad . . .' said Gareth.

Olivia spoke crisply, needing to be clear. 'This . . . this separation, George . . . do you expect it to be permanent?'

'I think so.' He added tiredly, 'Serena has spoken to a solicitor. She and Amelia have moved out of the flat.'

'You must be kidding.'

'I would never joke about something so serious, Lorcan. I understand how it must appear to you, but—'

'Do you, Dad? Do you understand?' Lorcan rose, planting his hands flat on the tabletop. 'See, the way I'm looking at it, you wrecked our family, and now you're telling us you're finishing with wife number two. How long has the marriage lasted? Five years? Christ, it isn't even that.'

Gareth muttered, 'For crying out loud, Lorcan, can't you shut up? You're not helping.'

'When was this, George?'

'A couple of weeks ago.'

'It might have helped if you'd let us know before today.' Cleo had gone pink. 'It's Gareth's birthday. This is supposed to be a celebration.'

'It's okay, love. These things happen.'

'No, it isn't okay. Actually, it isn't at all okay, Gareth. I hate this, I hate it.' Cleo's voice shook. Hearing a sudden loud cry, she looked around. 'Oh God, that's Hazel. I thought she was in here . . .' She hurried out of the room.

'You're unbelievable, Dad,' said Lorcan. 'And Cleo's right, you know, Gareth. It isn't okay, not at all.'

'I said, shut up.' Gareth's voice was silky and dangerous.

'What?' Lorcan leaned towards his brother. 'Are you telling me you're fine with this? That despite Dad's appalling behaviour, everything is hunky-dory?'

'Leave it, Lorcan, please.' Iris had the baby balanced on her hip. She put her free hand on her husband's arm.

'Yeah, leave it, Lorcan.' Gareth stared at his elder brother. His eyes were cold. 'Don't mess up the whole bloody day. Not again.'

'Let's just eat this lovely lunch and talk about it later . . .'

'Such a complete *arse* . . .'

'Gareth, Lorcan, that's quite enough. It's a shock for us all, but—'

Though Olivia had raised her voice, Lorcan spoke over her. 'You've made it perfectly – *tediously* – clear whose side you're on, Gareth.'

'It's not a question of sides. It's about trying to keep the family together. But for God's sake, I don't know why I bother.' Gareth had clenched his fists. 'All the effort Cleo and I have made . . . all the times we've invited you in the hope that you'll start behaving like a civilised human being . . .'

'Well, we won't have to do that much longer, will we, Gareth?'

Cleo had come back into the room. Hazel was in her arms, taking little sobbing breaths, and Cleo was holding a flannel to her forehead.

'Jesus.' Gareth sprang up. 'What happened?'

'She bumped her head on the chest of drawers.'

'Is she all right?'

'I think so. But there's a lump.'

'Let me take her.'

She passed Hazel across. Then she addressed Lorcan. 'Don't worry, you won't have to endure any more family parties here.' Cleo, who hardly ever lost her temper, sounded furious and upset.

Then she addressed the entire table. 'Gareth and I have something to tell you all. We hadn't planned to give you our news today, but now seems as good a time as any.'

'Cleo, please.' Gareth spoke softly. 'We agreed.'

'You may have agreed, Gareth. I didn't.'

'Not now, love, please.'

Olivia said, 'Cleo? What is it?'

Cleo's gaze swung round the table, coming to rest on each of the Flynns in turn. 'You remember Peter Ryan, who Gareth used to work for? You know that he went back to Australia about eighteen months ago? Well, he recently got in contact with Gareth. Business is booming out there and he could do with more help. He's asked Gareth to join him. Eventually he should be able to become a partner in Peter's construction company.'

Olivia said, 'Cleo, where? Where is it that Peter wants Gareth to work for him?'

'In Sydney. Gareth has decided to accept the offer. It's a wonderful opportunity. In a few months' time we'll be moving to Australia.'

Iris said, 'Australia . . .'

Natasha said, 'Wow. Cool.'

It wasn't possible, thought Olivia. It couldn't happen.

Then Lorcan spoke. 'What? You're leaving Mum? You got her to move all the way out here and now you're swanning off and abandoning her in the middle of nowhere? How unbelievably and lousily selfish of you, Gareth.'

Chapter Fifteen

1978, Suffolk

It was as if, thought Olivia, none of her family were able to bear the sight of each other. They had scattered throughout the house and garden, Gareth and Cleo to Hazel's bedroom, to read her a story and calm her down, Natasha to take Magnus and Oscar, who had chosen their moment to hurl themselves back into the room and run about under everyone's feet, out into the garden. Tom had at some point during that disastrous lunch left the room and was now pacing about the lawn, searching the sky with binoculars. Iris had dragged Lorcan out of the house and the two of them were standing on the gravel, Iris holding the baby, while Lorcan made angry gestures. Olivia could tell by their expressions and movements that an argument was taking place.

At lunch, Iris and Cleo had had to separate the two brothers. Eventually Lorcan had apologised for losing his temper. Gareth's acceptance had been a stiff, silent nod.

Olivia went into the kitchen and began to clear up. Her trifle, a lemon meringue pie and a plate of fairy cakes still stood on the counter. The birthday cake was untouched in the fridge. She tried not to think about what Cleo had said because such a thing – *Australia!* – was too much to take in. She stacked plates and cutlery in the dishwasher, then began to rinse the large platters under the tap.

George came into the room. 'It was Serena who decided to end the relationship, not me,' he said.

I don't care. She wanted to say it, but instead dried her hands and gave George a hard stare. He didn't merely look tired, she thought, he looked ill. He was huffing and puffing, as if he had been running, and he had put on weight since she had last seen him. Well, Serena's excellent cooking shouldn't be a problem any longer, she thought, rather waspishly.

Stifling a sigh, she said, 'Sit down, George. I'll make you a coffee.'

He sat down at the table and put his head in his hands. 'Oh God.'

Olivia filled the Cona jug with water and put it on the hob. 'You don't look well.'

'I haven't been sleeping. There's been so much toing and froing, what with Serena clearing out her things.'

Olivia spooned ground coffee into the glass funnel. 'I'm sorry,' she said. 'It must be difficult.'

'Things hadn't been right between us for a while, but I thought . . . I hoped . . .'

'I don't want the details, George. It's a shame the relationship hasn't worked out for you, but I really don't need to know.'

He rubbed his forehead with his fingertips. 'No, of course you don't. Sorry. Sorry about everything. I've made such a mess of things.' He looked up, his eyes haunted. 'Do you think Lorcan will ever forgive me?'

'It's been a shock. You need to give him time.'

'Yes. Yes, I see that.'

George fell silent. He sat hunched in the wicker chair. He seemed to have shrunk. The hair on the top of his head had thinned, revealing freckled scalp.

He said, 'Australia . . . Do you think it's my fault?'

'No,' she said firmly. 'Don't be silly, George. I expect they like the idea of an adventure. Not everything is to do with you.'

She began to grind the coffee beans and the kitchen filled with delicious fumes. A part of her clung to the hope that Cleo had said that on the spur of the moment because she was (perfectly understandably) angry and fed up with the Flynns for spoiling Gareth's birthday party. Or that she, Olivia, had got the wrong end of the stick and Gareth and Cleo were *thinking* about going to Australia but hadn't yet made up their minds and would drop the idea once they reflected on it. The mere thought of them going to live so far away made her feel utterly bereft.

She gave George a cup of coffee, then put a slice of lemon meringue pie in front of him. 'You should eat something.' She patted his shoulder. 'I'll go and see if the others want anything.'

'Thank you.'

Through a side window, she saw that Tom's girlfriend was pushing the boys on the swing. She prepared a tray of coffee and fairy cakes and took it outside.

'It's good of you to keep an eye on them, Natasha.'

'It's Nat, please.' She smiled at Olivia. 'The only person who calls me Natasha is my sister Morwenna when she's cross with me. We've been having fun, haven't we, boys? Okay, Oscar, it's Magnus's turn.'

She was such a pretty girl, thought Olivia, all huge dark eyes and heart-shaped face. Oscar slid off the swing and Olivia offered him a fairy cake. He began to nibble off the icing.

'I thought you might need a coffee, Nat.'

'*Desperate* for one. Thanks.'

'Do you have just the one sister?'

Nat shook her head. 'Three, and a little brother. It goes Morwenna, me, India, Petra, then my brother, Russell, who's twelve and a pain in the neck.'

'Goodness. I envy you, being part of a big family. I was an only child. I do like your jumper. Did you knit it yourself?'

Nat, who was blowing on her coffee to cool it, nodded, then called out, 'Sit on the swing properly, Magnus. If you twist round like that, you'll whack your head and crack your skull and end up in hospital. I'm knitting a hat to match the jumper. I made the skirt, too.'

'I love that combination of turquoise and lime green.'

'I'll send you the pattern, if you like.'

'Thank you, Nat, that would be great. I used to sew a lot. My mother taught me. When I was very young, in the late thirties, I worked for a London dressmaker.'

'Wow, what a fabulous job. I love those gorgeous evening dresses they wore then. I once found an evening dress by Worth in a charity shop and I wore it till it fell apart. I felt so glamorous in it.'

'One of the dressmaker's clients was a woman called Grace Ruthwell. To me, she was the epitome of glamour.' Olivia smiled, remembering. From Grace she had learned how a woman could change her appearance through her clothing and jewellery, and how she could be inconspicuous or the centre of attention. Though Grace had never been inconspicuous. She had always drawn the eye.

Nat called out, 'Oscar, you can have a go now!'

'I must apologise for that scene, Nat. What you must think of us. I would say we're not usually like that, but I'm not sure that these days that's true.'

Nat, who had just, like Oscar, bitten the icing from the top of a fairy cake, turned her dark brown gaze on her. 'Honestly, Olivia, I've seen worse,' she said solemnly. 'Much, much worse.'

The sky was dimming, casting shadows, so that from a distance the hollow in which Oscar and Magnus were playing appeared to be filled with dark water. The boys showed Tom their treasures: a magpie's feather, a rusty tin can, a snail shell swirled with iridescent stripes. Then they went back to walking round stiff-limbed, pretending to be robots.

'I'm sorry,' Tom said to Nat.

'What for?'

'Inflicting that on you. Lorcan gets so angry about everything.'

'Honestly, it's fine.' Nat squeezed his hand. 'Your brothers haven't killed each other or anything, I suppose?'

'Not yet.' He gave her a slanting smile.

'My sister Petra once tore up all my clothes and threw them out of the window. The only ones I had left were what I was wearing at the time. Now, I can't even remember what we were arguing about.' Seeing that he was upset, she gently brushed back his hair from his forehead. 'Your dad, though. Not a great moment to choose to drop news like that.'

'His timing's never been great.'

'That coffee's for you, love.'

Tom took the mug from the tray. 'Thanks.'

They followed Oscar and Magnus through the garden, then through the hedge that divided the Hayloft from Greengage Cottage and into the woodland. A gust of wind chased over the brow of the hill, its path made visible by the movement of the grass and a rustle of dead leaves. They stood side by side watching the boys rampage.

'You look so beautiful,' said Tom. 'I was afraid we might have put you off.'

'Put me off?' She considered him. 'You mean put me off *you?*' She touched her lips against his. 'This is how much I'm put off, Tom Flynn. And this.'

'I'd have said no to Peter if I'd thought you weren't happy here, Mum,' Gareth said.

They were in the kitchen. On the worktop were mugs and the glass jug with a black slick of coffee in the bottom of it, and the wreckage of trifle and lemon meringue pie. Olivia began to scrape the leftovers into the bin.

She said, 'Gareth, you must do what's best for your career and your family, I understand that. And yes, I've settled in well here.' She didn't say, but if you go, I will miss you so much, because that would make it real, and she didn't want it to be real. She also knew it was her job to set her children free to pursue their dreams and ambitions rather than tether them to the ground with a sense of duty and responsibility. The last thing she ever wanted to be was a burden.

'You'll come and visit us, won't you, Mum? It sounds such an amazing country, so different to here. You'll love it.'

Olivia pictured great heat, deserts, sharks, poisonous spiders and jellyfish, all of which she had heard Australia had in abundance. 'I'm sure I will.'

Gareth was unloading the dishwasher. She could tell how much he wanted her to be happy and excited for him.

'If you're certain it's what you both want, love, then I'm delighted for you. And the job sounds great. Congratulations, you deserve it, you've worked so hard.'

'It'll be a big increase in salary. And to tell the truth, it hasn't been working out that well with Rich.' Since Peter Ryan had left for Australia, Gareth had been working for a construction company owned by a man called Rich Taylor. 'We don't really see eye to eye.' He took out the dishwasher filter. 'Rich likes to cut corners. We've had a few disagreements about it. Even if Peter hadn't got in touch, I'd have been looking for a new job.'

'What about Cleo? Does she want to go?'

'She can't wait. When you come to see us, you must stay as long as you like. We'll make sure we get a house with plenty of room for all of us. We're planning to travel about and see the country. It would be great if you were able to come along with us.' As he ran the filter under the tap, he said, 'I didn't mean you to find out like that. I'd meant to choose a better time.'

There was never a good time to be told that your family was about to go and live on the other side of the world. 'Gareth, love, truly I understand,' she said firmly. 'And if you're going to live abroad for a while, then it's best to do it while the children are small. But it's a big step.'

'It isn't a spur-of-the-moment decision. Cleo and I have been talking about it for months.'

This was another shock to absorb, that a conversation had been going on of which she had been completely ignorant. And some of her dismay must have shown on her face because Gareth said, 'I wasn't certain it would happen. I didn't want to say anything before I was sure it was going to work out.'

She hung a saucepan on a hook. 'When are you thinking of leaving?'

'In a couple of months, I hope. It's all organised at the other end. Peter will try to find us a flat for the first few weeks. As soon as we've caught our breath, we'll start looking for a house.'

A couple of months . . .

'What about Cleo's work?'

'Peter says there'll be plenty of opportunity for her. It'll be a great experience for her to work in another country.' His voice was muffled by the interior of the dishwasher. 'And I promise we'll let this house out to someone nice.'

Olivia concentrated on putting cutlery into a drawer. Vigorously she polished spoons with a tea towel and slotted them in place. It hadn't occurred to her that Gareth would let the house, that a stranger would come to live at the Hayloft, but of course that would make financial sense.

He emerged from the dishwasher. 'Do you think Dad and Serena have really split up? Permanently, I mean?'

For once, it was a relief to talk about George. 'It sounds like it.'

'I mean, for God's sake,' he said witheringly. '*Jeez*. That didn't last long, did it? And to spring it on us like that . . . It spoiled the whole bloody day.'

'I don't think he meant to tell you today.'

'Doesn't matter. He should have thought a bit more about it. Did he think we wouldn't notice when he turned up without Serena and Amelia?' Gareth dried his hands. 'I can't imagine Dad on his own, can you? Will he be okay, do you think?'

'I'm sure he'll be fine,' Olivia said briskly. 'He has lived alone before, you know, back in the thirties, between Oxford and the army. Though goodness me, that was a long time ago. Maybe he'll take that residency he was talking about. Gareth, love, is Cleo all right?'

'She's giving the children their bath.'

'That was a nasty bump on Hazel's head. You go and give her a hand. I can finish off here. And I'm so sorry about today, about the way it's turned out, after both of you worked so hard. And on your *birthday*.' She hugged him.

Before he left the room, Gareth looked back. 'Lorcan winds me up,' he said. 'He thinks I don't mind about things, but he has no idea how I feel. I'm sick of it.'

Olivia tidied crackers and digestive biscuits into a tin. How long would it take her to recover from today's events, if indeed she ever could? To distract herself from the shocks and upsets of the day, she turned her mind to the project she and Margot were working on for a new client, a Mrs Astill, who had recently moved into the village. It was a complete redesign of her neglected garden on a tricky north-facing L-shaped plot.

Iris appeared with Florence in her arms. 'George is heading off,' she said.

Olivia let out a breath. 'Thank goodness.'

'I'll make us some tea,' said Iris. She passed Florence to Olivia.

Olivia sat down on a bench with her granddaughter on her lap. 'She's almost sitting up on her own.'

'I know. Magnus took for ever to learn. Do you remember I had to prop him up with cushions?'

'Magnus is adorable. They're both adorable.'

'Lorcan knows he shouldn't have lashed out earlier.'

Iris took mugs out of the cupboard. 'He's apologising to Cleo.'

'Will you stay tonight?'

She shook her head. 'We're going home. Gareth and Lorcan aren't really speaking to each other and I'd hate to outstay our welcome. I haven't drunk anything, so I can drive.' She kissed the top of the baby's head. 'Please come and see us soon, Olivia.'

'I will do.' Florence had seized Olivia's beads in a chubby hand and was inspecting them with great seriousness. Olivia sighed. 'I suppose I should say goodbye to George.'

'Don't. You sit here with Flo, have a break. The rest of us can see him off.'

A little before nine o'clock, after both Lorcan and Tom had driven away and the clearing up was finished and Oscar and Hazel were in bed, Olivia slipped back to her cottage.

Aeons seemed to have passed since she had left it that morning, Oscar in one hand, a trifle in the other. Still in her coat, she drew the curtains, put more coal in the Rayburn, then splashed water into a glass of whisky. Though she took out her pad of graph paper and pens, she quickly discovered she hadn't the focus to work.

She went outside and walked to the woodland at the side of her house. Though it was small, it had a magic of its own. Standing in the heart of it, in the shelter of a tall beech tree, she breathed in the chilly, earthy air and listened to the sounds of the small creatures that lived there. The light of her torch picked out fallen branches, which she'd stacked up to make a home for hedgehogs and beetles. When she looked back, she saw how the crescent moon lit up the gap in the hedge between the two houses.

Coming to live next door to her son and daughter-in-law, Olivia had known that she must tread carefully. Just as a woman might fear being a bad mother, so could she also miss her step as a mother-in-law. She must not intrude, and she must not give unsolicited advice, especially about her grandchildren. She must avoid being intolerant or nosy or bossy. She must offer the right amount of help and no more.

Yet the companionship of her daughters-in-law and the gift of grandchildren more than consoled her for the tightrope she sometimes felt she had to walk. Bringing up her own sons, she had been the lone female in an all-male household. Iris and Cleo were generous with their friendship and affection, and she loved them for their brightness and humour, their intelligence and beauty.

Today, Iris had looked exhausted. Florence wasn't yet sleeping through the night, and how could anyone function rationally after months of broken sleep? As for Cleo, she needed her own space. Her relationship with her mother was difficult, though this was not a subject she and Olivia had talked about at any length. They ambled round antique shops together and visited open gardens; their conversations were a sharing of interests rather than explorations of feeling. Today must have been a wretched experience for Cleo, who hated disagreement and disorder, and Olivia's heart bled for her.

She went back inside the house and dialled Louise's number. When her friend picked up the phone, Olivia said, 'I thought you might be out, painting the town red.'

'Jeremy had to cancel at the last minute. An emergency at the hospital.' Louise's latest boyfriend was an orthopaedic surgeon. 'How did the party go?'

'Oh, Louise, it was a complete disaster.' Olivia sketched

out the day, feeling a heaviness lift from her shoulders as she shared her fears and anxieties with her oldest friend.

Louise said, 'Is the move to Australia definite?'

'It rather sounds as though it is. Cleo and Gareth aren't ditherers, are they? And when I think of the way Lorcan and George behaved today, who can blame them?' She flopped onto the sofa. 'Every now and then, Lou, George throws a grenade into our lives. And he's still doing it.'

'George must deal with his own problems. They're not yours, Olivia.' Louise spoke crisply, using what Olivia mentally termed her senior civil servant voice.

'I know. But it's hard to see why Cleo, particularly, should wish to spend time with a family riven by these eruptions.'

'I think it's far more likely that they see Australia as a wonderful opportunity.'

'And I'm proud of them for that, for being so intrepid.' She supposed eventually the dust would settle. Though it hadn't so far.

After she and Louise had finished talking, Olivia went back to the table and began to sketch out initial ideas for the new client's garden. Much of the work she and Margot took on involved routine tasks, so it was exciting to embark on a bigger project. Now and then her thoughts intruded. They wouldn't really go to Australia, would they? Her son and daughter-in-law and her grandchildren Oscar and Hazel, whom she loved beyond measure, they couldn't move so far away. It was inconceivable.

Chapter Sixteen

1978, Suffolk, Cambridge and London

Gareth, Cleo and the children left England on a misty Monday at the end of April. Their journey would take a day and a half, with stops in Bahrain and Singapore to refuel. The evening before they went away, the family had supper at Greengage Cottage, where they were to stay overnight, their belongings having been either packed up for storage or shipped to Sydney. The cases and bags they were taking with them on the plane stood in the front room.

The house was being let furnished. Over supper, Gareth spoke briefly about the new tenant, a Mr McQuinnan, but then conversation lapsed and everyone was thankful for Oscar's chatter.

Early the following morning, Olivia drove the family to Heathrow. They said their goodbyes in Departures, and she blew kisses as they headed away towards Passport Control. She watched them for as long as she could – Oscar was easy to spot because he had insisted on wearing his red sunhat, and Hazel was clutching the teddy bear Olivia had made for her first birthday. When they were out of sight, she found a quiet corner to weep in. Once she had got herself together, she drove back to Suffolk, where the moist air lingered, blurring the fields and the stands of trees.

In the afternoon, she headed to Mrs Astill's garden on the outskirts of Holfield St Peter. A fortnight ago, they had started work to clear and level the substantial plot.

Margot was attacking a bed of nettles. She was tall and big-boned with a ruddy, cheerful face and an unruly mass of blondish hair. She was wearing corduroy trousers and a T-shirt, an outfit she varied only mildly, adding a jumper when it was cold or a waterproof when wet, and exchanging the trousers for her late husband's khaki army shorts when summer's temperatures peaked.

She came to meet Olivia. 'Did they get away all right?'

'Yes, fine. I didn't wait to see the plane take off.'

'No, I wouldn't have either.' Margot propped her hoe against the fence. 'I can't bear long-drawn-out partings, can you? Tea?' She took a Thermos flask out of a capacious tartan bag and poured Olivia a cup.

'Thanks.'

'Have you heard about Ralph?' Ralph was Holfield St Peter's choir's musical director.

'No. What's up?'

'He's got shingles.'

'Oh Lord, Margot, poor Ralph.'

'Dot says he has terrible blisters. He'll be out of action for weeks. Mary Shaw said she'd have a go at the piano at choir tonight. Ben offered to conduct.' Margot, who was persuading a ladybird from her T-shirt onto the leaf of a dogwood, looked dubious. 'Is the new tenant in yet?'

'Mr McQuinnan? It doesn't look like it.'

Olivia chopped through the last of the bramble roots with a spade. She found herself pouncing upon the twining fronds with a certain amount of savagery. She wasn't disposed to like Mr McQuinnan, whom she saw as an interloper, though she knew that was unreasonable. It was hardly his fault that her son, daughter-in-law and grandchildren were at that moment in an aeroplane, flying off to live thousands of miles away.

The air warmed and the mist cleared and the sun came out, and some of the heaviness of the morning's parting lifted. At choir that evening, Mary Shaw, who ran the village shop and who sang alto, thumped out the melody lines one-handed while her husband, Ben, a solicitor, beat time. Everyone was determined to work the pieces up to a good standard for Ralph's sake, but the session felt unsatisfactory, and his expertise was much missed.

After the rehearsal, Olivia walked home. As she passed the Hayloft and saw its darkened windows and undrawn curtains, the house seemed to have already taken on the lifeless aspect of an empty dwelling, and the treacherous tears stung her eyes once more. But that, she said to herself firmly as she let herself into the cottage, was because she had been up since five that morning and could do with some sleep.

After they finished clearing the Astill plot, they marked out the beds and paths. This was the part of any large project that Olivia loved most, when the new garden began to emerge from the blank canvas.

It drizzled all day. They stopped work at six, and she loaded her belongings into her car and headed home. As she drove past the Hayloft, her eye was caught by a small grey van standing on the gravel forecourt. A man was unloading boxes from it. He was tall and slim and clad in jeans and a navy-blue roll-neck jersey.

Olivia parked the car and walked to the boundary hedge. 'Hello?' she called out. 'Mr McQuinnan?'

He spun round. 'That's me, yes.'

'I'm pleased to meet you. I'm Olivia Flynn, your neighbour.'

He crossed the garden to her. There was a hedge between them, and he was clutching a cardboard box, so it was impractical to offer him her hand.

'I hope the move's going smoothly,' she said.

'Fine, thank you.'

A silence, which she filled by saying, 'Do let me know if you need anything or if you can't find where anything is. And I will fill in this gap in the hedge and tidy it up, I promise.'

His eyes, which were a deep, clear blue, settled on the privet and hawthorn. 'I'd be glad of that,' he said. 'If you'll excuse me, Mrs Flynn,' and he walked away.

Taken aback by the abrupt ending of their conversation, Olivia stared after him. Then, with a soft, disapproving tut, she gathered up her belongings and let herself into the house.

She took off her wellingtons and hung up her jacket, all the while mulling over her exchange with her new neighbour. Awful, awful man. She disliked thinking of him living in Gareth and Cleo's house. She imagined him looking at the rooms, so familiar to her and so much loved, with those disdainful blue eyes and finding them not up to scratch. He hadn't even told her his Christian name. Here she was, living next door to him with no other houses in the vicinity – he could be anyone, an axe murderer even! Though probably not that, she acknowledged. She shouldn't let her imagination run away with her. He had looked normal enough, if rather distant and curt.

She decided to go to the garden centre in the morning and buy hedging plants to block up the gap. Mr McQuinnan didn't want his garden to be accessible to his neighbour, which was fair enough, and she would prefer to see as little of him as possible. Heading upstairs, she caught sight of her reflection in the hall mirror. She had a smear of mud across one cheekbone and the day's rain had plastered her hair to her skull. She rubbed at her face with damp fingers. No wonder he had taken fright.

In the bathroom, she stripped off her clothes and had a long, hot shower. Afterwards, she wrapped herself up in a towelling robe and began to sort out the items in the laundry basket for washing. At the bottom she came across a tiny pink sock, and she had to sit down on the edge of the bed, the sock clutched in her hand, floored by the sight of it, almost done in.

When she returned home from the garden centre, Olivia noticed that on the Hayloft's gravel frontage a lorry had taken the place of the grey van. Its rear doors stood open and a man in brown overalls was talking to Mr McQuinnan.

She began to prepare the ground for the young hedging plants. Sounds from next door made her glance up now and then as she worked. One of the men was unloading some boxes from the lorry, while three others were dismantling the patio doors. Olivia removed the hessian wrappings from the bay and the viburnum. She kept glancing up, trying to make out what was going on. The patio doors had been taken out of their frame and all four removal men were unloading from the lorry a large object swathed in dust sheets. By the shape of it, it could only be a grand piano. Mr McQuinnan was hovering around, keeping an eye on the process. As the instrument was slowly carried towards the aperture, he darted ahead, presumably to check for obstacles.

She was unable to resist watching as the piano was slowly and carefully eased through the doorway. The house swallowed it up. A murmur of voices echoed, among them Mr McQuinnan's baritone, and it struck her how quickly one learned to recognise the timbre of a voice. She checked that the holes were dug deeply enough for the root balls of the saplings. From the Hayloft she heard shouts to watch out as the patio doors were rehung, then a series of clunks as the heavy glass slid into place. Feet crunched on gravel, doors slammed, and the lorry's engine started up.

She looked round for the stakes she had chosen to support the hedging plants. Mr McQuinnan was standing on the gravel, one hand lifted in farewell as the removal van drove off. Then he went back inside the house. A flurry of scales and arpeggios, fast and liquid, poured through the open patio doors. Olivia stopped, spade in hand, and listened. Eventually the scales were abandoned, and she heard instead a fragment of melody. Haunting and stately, it seemed to tear at her heartstrings.

Then silence. With the absence of music, the air seemed empty. Olivia returned to backfilling the holes. A sound made her look up again, and she saw that Mr McQuinnan had stepped through the patio doors onto the gravel. She watched him stand motionless, then look round and sway. He made a sound, a little *oof*. And then, as if he was a puppet and someone had cut the strings, he flopped onto the gravel and lay still.

Dropping the spade, Olivia pushed through the hedge towards him. By the time she reached him, he was stirring. 'It's okay,' she said, kneeling beside him. 'No need to move.'

A long tear – no, a cut – ran down the lower left leg of his jeans. Blood was soaking through the fabric.

He groaned. 'I fell over.'

'Actually, Mr McQuinnan, I think you fainted.'

'Luke,' he said. 'My name's Luke. Sorry . . . I'm sorry about . . .'

'What happened, Luke?' She peered at the wound.

'I was using my penknife to open a box, to get through the tape. I couldn't find any scissors. I expect they're in one of the boxes.' He groaned again. 'My hand must have slipped.' He hauled himself into a sitting position against the wall of the house. His face was white. 'I think I stabbed myself.'

'Sit still while I have a proper look at it. I promise I'll try not to hurt you.'

Olivia ripped through the hem of the jeans with her pruning knife so that she could see the injury. A deep cut, six inches long, ran down his shin and was bleeding copiously.

'That looks nasty. You're going to be fine, though.' She took off her cotton scarf, folded it into a pad and pressed it firmly against the wound. He winced, but didn't complain. 'Can you hold that in place? We need to stop the bleeding. Yes, that's it. I'm going to go and get something to bind this up. I'll be back in a sec. Don't move.'

She fetched a clean tea towel, a length of bandage and a safety pin and bound up his leg. While she worked, he murmured a stream of apologies.

'Such an idiot . . . interrupting your work . . . so clumsy of me.'

'It's okay.' She pinned the bandage in place, sat back on her heels and gave him a comforting smile. 'You're going to need some stitches in that, I'm afraid. Are you registered with a doctor yet?'

Screwing up his eyes, he shook his head. 'I haven't got round to it. It's on the list.'

'I'll drive you to mine. I'm sure they'll be able to find someone to sort you out.'

'I wouldn't dream of it. I can drive.'

'No, you can't,' she said firmly. 'I'll go and get my car.'

Olivia parked her Hillman Imp on the Hayloft's gravel area. 'Where are your house keys, Luke?'

'In the pocket of my jacket. Which is . . . hanging on a hook by the front door.'

Olivia went inside the house. 'I've got them,' she called back to him. Through the open living-room door she could see the piano, huge and black and gleaming.

She locked up and helped him into the car. They rattled through the sappy bright greens of late April, between hedges where May blossom had begun to erupt, heading for Lavenham, where her doctor was based.

He said, 'All these little winding roads. It'll take me months to find my way around.'

'You'll soon get the hang of it. Where have you moved from?'

'London. Teddington.'

'That's quite a change.'

She expected him to offer some sort of explanation, but he didn't. In profile his features were regular: high forehead and heavy-lidded, deep-set eyes, a long, narrow Roman nose and level brows several shades darker than his thatch of untidy light brown hair.

'How are you doing, Luke? Does it hurt a lot?'

'It's not too bad. I feel a bit muzzy.'

'That'll be shock and blood loss. Try to relax if you can. Have one of these.' She took a packet of fruit bonbons out of the glove box and offered it to him. 'The sugar will help with the shock.'

'You know a lot about first aid.'

'I'm the mother of three sons – I've seen a lot of cuts and bruises in my time.'

Slowing for a crossroads, she asked him how he was settling in.

'It's a nice house. I expect, when everything is put away, it'll be peaceful.'

'Is that why you moved here, for the peace and quiet?'

'Pretty much, yes.'

Glancing down at his leg, she saw that a red stain had begun to show through the white bandage. He still looked very pale. 'Not far now,' she said encouragingly, and chattered on to keep his mind off the injury.

'I'm a gardener, so if you need any help with the garden, just ask. Me and my friend Margot, we mostly do routine work, weeding and pruning, but now and again we design a garden from scratch. We started work on a new garden this week for a lady in the village, Mrs Astill.'

This seemed to capture his interest. 'Are you involved in the design?'

'I do most of it, yes. Margot's specialism is the planting.'

'How do you begin?'

'With this garden, we've kept several mature trees, so I work round those. But otherwise, it's pretty much a blank canvas.'

'Do you find that daunting?'

'To begin with, but it's exciting, too. It's an L-shaped plot, which I like, because I can create a different mood in the two parts of the garden. Are you a musician, Luke?' When his gaze swung to her, she prompted, 'The grand piano.'

'I am, yes. Mostly I teach.'

They had reached the centre of Lavenham, where half-timbered medieval buildings jostled crookedly against each other like houses in a fairy tale. They turned off up a side street and Olivia found a place to park. Before Luke opened the passenger door, he said, 'I'm afraid I was rather unfriendly yesterday.'

'It doesn't matter.'

'I think it does. I had some things on my mind, but that's no excuse and I apologise.'

'It's okay, honestly.'

They climbed out of the car. Luke murmured something about getting a taxi home. Olivia ignored him. 'I'll wait for you. Is there anyone I can call for you?'

'No, thanks. Oh Lord, Annie . . .'

'Annie?'

'My daughter. She's visiting this afternoon. She's going to make a fuss about this.'

She offered him her arm, and together they made their slow, limping way into the building.

The next day, while she was working in the greenhouse, a young woman put her head round the door. 'Olivia?'

'Yes.'

'I'm Annie McQuinnan. Oh dear.' As she came into the greenhouse, Annie dislodged a plant pot with her elbow. Olivia caught it before it tumbled to the ground.

Luke McQuinnan's daughter had curly light brown hair, her father's blue eyes and a cheerful smile. They shook hands.

Olivia said, 'How is he?' At the clinic, the nurse had stitched up the wound, lent Luke a pair of crutches and instructed him to rest.

'He's looking better today. He keeps trying to do things, but I'm nagging him to sit still. Thank you so much for looking after him.'

'It was no trouble. How long will you be staying, Annie?'

'A couple of days, then I have a rehearsal, so I'll have to get back to London.'

Olivia scribbled on a piece of paper. 'Here's my phone number. I'll check up on your father now and then, but if you have any concerns, give me a ring.'

'Thank you. You're so kind.' Annie smiled. 'I wonder if it's all a bit mad, Dad coming here where he doesn't know anyone. But I do understand, honestly, I can see why he wants to give it a go. He'll be fed up if it doesn't work, though – he says he won't, but I know he will. Oops.' She righted a pelargonium. 'Sorry, almost brought this to a sticky end.'

Since Gareth and Cleo's departure, both Lorcan and Tom had phoned Olivia frequently to chat, and with invitations for her to visit. She suspected the two of them had talked to each other and were trying to fill the gap left by their brother's absence. Their thoughtfulness touched her.

The weather turned wet and cold and the Astill plot became a quagmire. Surveying the puddles, Olivia and Margot decided to stop work at midday to give the ground a chance to recover.

She was driving home through a curtain of rain when she recognised a tall, slender figure slowly limping up the road ahead of her. Drawing up, she wound down the passenger window.

'May I give you a lift, Luke?'

'Um, I . . .'

'Hop in, it's pouring.'

As he climbed into the car, the stick he was using tipped over and they both grabbed at it at once. His hand brushed against hers. He had nice hands, she noticed, strong-looking and long-fingered with well-shaped nails.

He apologised for dripping over her car. 'I thought it was easing off,' he said. 'I've been trying to walk a bit further each day. I should have taken an umbrella.'

'How's your leg?'

'Much better, thanks.'

Over the last couple of days, an idea had been brewing in Olivia's mind. They had almost reached the Hayloft when she said, 'I wonder whether you might be able to help me out, Luke. I belong to a village choir in Holfield St Peter. We meet once a week in the church hall. We sing a variety of music – Gilbert and Sullivan, pop songs and folk songs and some classical. But the man who teaches us has fallen ill.'

He did not respond, so she went on to explain about Ralph's severe case of shingles and their lack of a skilled pianist. Still nothing, no murmurs of sympathy or expressions of interest, though she thought she saw in his eyes a guardedness.

She ploughed on. 'Ralph had started teaching us Pergolesi's *Stabat Mater*. He wants us to sing it at our next concert. But the last couple of sessions have been hopeless – every time we have a go at it, we fall apart. And I wondered, as you play the piano . . . you said you were a music teacher . . . whether you would consider playing for us. Just for a few weeks, till Ralph gets better. It would be so . . . so . . .'

The words dried up. She knew before he spoke that he was going to refuse.

'I'm sorry,' he said. 'But I'm afraid I can't help.'

He said this so firmly that Olivia immediately let the subject drop. She drew up outside the Hayloft. Luke climbed out of the car, and they exchanged quick, embarrassed goodbyes.

Letting herself into Greengage Cottage, she was relieved that she was going away the following day to stay with Iris and Lorcan in Cambridge, and would thus be spared the possibility of further awkward encounters with Luke McQuinnan, for a while at least.

It was eight in the evening, and Olivia had just made another attempt to settle Florence. She and Iris were taking it in turns. She was at the top of the stairs, about to creep down silently, when Lorcan came home from work. He dropped his keys onto the side table in the hall, and then, after a quick look at the letters left there, swept them into his pocket.

Seeing him glance up the stairs and catch sight of her, Olivia made a soft shushing sound and put a finger to her lips.

Lorcan tiptoed up the treads. 'Florence?' he whispered.

'I think she's settled.' She hugged him. 'Good day?'

'Fine.'

Iris was in the living room, lying on the sofa. She jerked up as Olivia came into the room. 'Has she gone down?'

'Fingers crossed. Don't get up, Iris. Have a rest.'

Olivia began to pick up the Duplo that Magnus had scattered liberally and lethally over the hall and stairs. Lorcan came down and began to help, but she shooed him off and he went to greet Iris.

Their voices drifted to her from the living room.

'How it's been, love?'

'The usual. Flo wouldn't go down for her morning nap. If she gives it up for good, I don't see how I'll ever get anything done.'

'Shall I go and get us a Chinese takeaway?'

'It's okay, your mum's cooked us something. You're late, Lorcan.'

'I had a few things to do.'

Olivia scrabbled for the bricks beneath the hall table. She heard Iris say, with a rising, agitated inflection, 'Have you been drinking?'

'A half in the pub, before I caught the train. Work thing, someone was leaving. I couldn't get out of it.'

Olivia put the toy basket in the hall cupboard, then went into the kitchen to check the casserole. After a few minutes, Lorcan appeared. He took a bottle of red wine from the rack and glasses from the cupboard. His back to her, he poured a large glass and gulped down half of it.

'Glass of wine, Mum?'

'Thanks, that'd be great.' The casserole was almost ready; she slid it back into the oven.

Lorcan swallowed the remainder of his wine, then poured two more glasses, passing one to Olivia. After he had taken Iris her drink, he returned to the kitchen to refill his own glass, knocking it back quickly.

Olivia said, 'Who was leaving, love?'

'Oh . . . no one important.' He reached for the bottle again.

'Lorcan . . .'

'What?'

'Ease off, maybe?' She kept her voice light.

'For God's sake, Mum, I can handle it,' he said irritably.

They both heard the baby's cry from upstairs. '*Christ*,' Lorcan muttered. Then, 'I'll go, Iris!' Olivia heard him bound up the stairs, two at a time.

After leaving Lorcan and Iris, Olivia travelled on to London, to visit the Clairmonts. She and Dinah were in the elegant dark green and white kitchen, preparing an early supper of chicken paprika followed by a lemon tart. Afterwards, the three of them, Olivia and Dinah and Tony, were going to the theatre to see *A Little Night Music*.

She was telling Dinah about Luke McQuinnan's accident. 'I dropped round a couple of times in the week to make sure he was all right. I took him a casserole and some home-made soup.'

Dinah, who was making pastry, raised her eyebrows. 'What's he like? Is he handsome?'

'Not bad. Tall . . . fit-looking.' Olivia caught her friend's expression. 'Oh, Di, *don't*. Do you seriously think I'd consider for a single moment another man who's precious about his art? And hamfisted to boot.'

'Is he?'

'He's certainly hamfisted.' Grating a lemon, Olivia exhaled. 'Except when he plays the piano. As for the rest of it, I expect I'm being unfair.' She explained about Luke refusing to accompany the choir. 'I felt a bit fed up with him at first,' she added. 'But I've heard him playing, Di, and it's rather wonderful. You simply have to listen. So when he said he teaches, I don't suppose he meant getting little kids through their Grade One piano. I shouldn't have asked him. I'm afraid I put my foot in it, and honestly, when he said no, I wanted to curl up and die. He's my neighbour now, after all, and we had rather a sticky start and were just about managing to get on.'

Dinah beat an egg yolk with chilled water. 'He's on his own, you said?'

'He appears to be. I met his daughter, Annie, who said something a bit odd – that he would be fed up if coming to live at the Hayloft didn't work.' Olivia cut the lemons in half to squeeze them.

'What did she mean?'

'I've no idea.'

'How strange. Do you think it's time for a Martini?'

'Definitely.'

Dinah left the kitchen, coming back a few moments later with a bottle and two glasses. 'What did you think of the daughter?'

'Rather scatty, like her father. But likeable. I couldn't help warming to her. Dinah, stop it, honestly, *no*.' Olivia flicked open the bin and dropped in the lemon rinds. 'Apart from anything else, he stabbed himself by accident. So no thank you.'

Taking tonic from the fridge, Dinah gave her a severe look. 'I'm merely hinting that it's about time you managed more than a couple of dates with a man, Olivia.'

'I'm perfectly happy as I am.'

'Are you?'

'I'd never marry again. Not after George. Never.'

'I didn't say a word about marriage. Here.' Dinah put a glass in front of her. 'Have you heard from Gareth and Cleo?'

'They phoned. They were in a hotel for the first few days, but now they've moved into their flat. It sounds nice.' The line had been crackly, and it had been hard to make out what Gareth was saying. Oscar had refused to say anything at all and Hazel had just shrieked. All the same, it was a relief to know they were safe and well and settled in their new home.

What she had longed for was to touch them, to hold them, to breathe in the soapy, biscuity scent of Oscar's skin and to stroke Hazel's soft, silky hair. This yearning had seemed to come not from the brain, but from the heart itself.

'That's good news,' Dinah said. She looked round the kitchen. 'There. Almost done. Let's go and sit in comfort. Oh, and I don't think George's problem was his creativity. It was his egotism.'

Shortly after Olivia returned to Greengage Cottage on Monday evening, there was a knock on the door. Opening it, she saw Luke McQuinnan.

'I've been trying to catch you,' he said.

'I've been in London. Come in, Luke.'

'Thanks, but no, I won't take up your time. I wanted to apologise for not being more help the other day. And for being abrupt with you.'

'It's fine.' She was mortified that he had noticed she minded. She would have preferred him to have forgotten the incident.

'I don't think it is,' he said. 'I'd like to explain.'

'You don't need to. I shouldn't have asked. I understand completely.'

'I don't think you do, Olivia.'

'You're a professional musician and it's just a little village choir, I see that.'

'You thought I refused out of professional pride?' He gave a slight smile. 'It wasn't that. I would help you if I could, but I can't. I mean, I physically can't.' A pause during which he seemed to be searching for words. Then he said, 'Six years ago, my wife, Harriet, died in a car accident.'

Appalled, she said, 'Luke, I'm so sorry . . .'

'I'm okay. But I haven't played in public since then. I tried giving a concert a few months after it happened, and it was a complete disaster. I couldn't play a note. Hundreds of people were watching. We were halfway through a cycle of Benjamin Britten songs – *The Holy Sonnets of John Donne* – and I just . . . I had to go backstage and throw up. And then they kept asking me if I was okay to try again, but I couldn't. I couldn't even remember what it was I was supposed to be playing. Just . . . a blank. The poor tenor had to struggle on without me.'

'I'm so sorry. How dreadful for you.'

'A psychiatrist told me afterwards that it was a version of stage fright. A couple of months later, I thought I was okay and I gave it another go – conducting, not playing, that time – and the same thing happened. I just seemed to freeze. After that, it seemed sensible not to go on courting humiliation.' He shuffled, looking away. 'It's the standing-up in front of people. I can't seem to cope with it. I go to pieces. So I've accepted that that part of my career is over. I still teach, and I enjoy that very much.'

'Luke, I didn't mean to pry. I'm sorry if I was tactless.'

'You weren't. And don't feel sorry for me, please, Olivia. Teaching is rewarding. I'm lucky to be able to make a living out of doing something I love.'

He was standing in the shadow of the porch. It occurred to her that if he ever got as far as coming into the cottage, she would have to watch him constantly to make sure he didn't hit his head on the low lintels.

She said, 'I did wonder why you came to live here.'

'I used to compose, but after I lost Harriet, that dried up too. Recently, though, I've had this idea in my head for a composition – just a fragment, but it wouldn't let me go. After a while, I thought I'd give it a try. Put my teaching on the back burner for a few months, set myself a time limit and see if I can make anything of it. If so, then great, and if not, if it doesn't work, then I'll accept that. I knew I needed to find somewhere quiet to work, where I'd be able to write without friends dropping round and tradesmen turning up, all the usual distractions.' His face lightened in a grin. 'So I had to bury myself in the middle of nowhere. It's a sort of last-ditch attempt.'

'Is it working?'

'I feel as if I'm getting somewhere. It's amazing, after all this time . . . it's as if a closed door is beginning to creak open.' He raked back his hair with his fingers. 'It's a weird feeling.'

'A good one?'

'Oh yes.' His voice was fervent.

'My ex-husband, George, is a poet. He used to go and sit under a tree when he needed inspiration.'

He laughed. 'Maybe I'll try that. No shortage of trees round here.' He gave her a piercing look. 'George Flynn? You were married to George Flynn?'

'I was, yes.'

'I hope it isn't driving you crazy, hearing the same phrase over and over again.'

'Not at all.'

'And I hope you find someone more suitable to help out your choir.'

'And I hope it works out for you, coming here.' She had the impulse to hug him, to wish him luck, but said instead, 'Early days, Luke.'

'Yes, early days.'

Their argument the previous evening had been about money. Their disagreements were becoming more frequent and almost always started off being about money. Lorcan had spoken of booking a summer holiday, in Spain perhaps, and Iris had pointed out that he himself had said they needed to economise. Had that altered? Sulkily, he admitted that it had not. Though they had slept in the same bed that night, they had not touched. Hurt and ill-humour made an invisible fence between them, and Iris had dozed only fitfully.

The next day, Florence wouldn't settle. Iris took her out in the pram and walked three times round Midsummer Common before at last her daughter drifted off to sleep. Later, changing her nappy, she saw a pearly mark on the baby's upper jaw and berated herself for not realising she was teething.

Shortly afterwards, Olivia arrived. Lorcan had asked her to stay for the weekend so that she could babysit tomorrow night, Saturday, to allow them to go out for dinner. Olivia played with Florence so that Iris could give Magnus some attention, and she felt herself begin to relax a little.

She kept expecting Lorcan to appear – he usually aimed to get home promptly on a Friday night – but he didn't, and inexorably her anxieties returned. As she and Olivia bathed the children and put them to bed, then tidied up, Iris wondered where he was. And who he was with. She kept looking at her watch, feeling increasingly upset and frazzled.

She heard the front door open and went downstairs. Lorcan was letting himself into the house.

'Where were you?' The words burst out of her.

He looked furtive. 'I had some things to catch up on. And the trains were messed about. I've brought you some flowers.' He brandished a bunch of peonies, looking pleased with himself.

'I don't want flowers!' she hissed. 'I want you home, making me a cup of tea or reading Magnus a story! Not doing whatever it is you're doing in London! How can you be so utterly clueless!' She grabbed her denim jacket from the peg. 'I'm going out,' she muttered. 'I need some fresh air.'

Olivia followed her out into the garden. 'Would you like some company?' she said quietly, and Iris nodded, unable to speak, afraid that if she did, she would either scream or burst into tears.

They walked along the towpath that led beside the Cam into the city. The May evening was warm and sunny, and as she distracted herself by looking at the college eights and the people fooling round in punts on the river, Iris began to feel calmer.

Olivia said, '*Oh!*' and patted her pocket and drew out a Kit Kat. 'Look what I've found.'

'Do you always have a Kit Kat on you, Olivia?'

'Useful bribes for grandchildren.'

They sat down on a bench and Olivia divided the biscuit between them. Iris said, 'You must miss Oscar and Hazel.'

'I do. So much.'

'All of us do.' A crowd of hopeful ducks waddled towards them, quacking, espying the Kit Kat. Iris said, 'Did you know that Lorcan didn't even say goodbye to Gareth? I tried to make him change his mind because I knew it would only make him feel worse if he let his brother leave for Australia without saying goodbye, but he wouldn't listen.'

'I'm sure he misses him,' said Olivia.

'Of course he does, though he'd never admit it. And he's still furious with George. It makes him so moody. I daren't even try to talk to him about it.' Recently, Iris had stopped mentioning his father to Lorcan. It only set him off, and she simply hadn't the energy to deal with that because the children used up all that she had.

She crumbled the last chunk of biscuit for the ducks, and sighed. 'Lorcan and me, we seem to be stuck . . . we keep going round and round, making the same mistakes and never resolving anything. One of us loses our temper and then we yell at each other and then we feel terrible about it, and eventually we make up. It's exhausting.'

Olivia squeezed her arm. 'Early parenthood is pretty relentless,' she said. 'It will get better. In a little while, when Florence is sleeping through the night and Magnus starts school, it will begin to seem easier, I promise you. And then you can think about what you want to do. Whether you want to go back to work, all those decisions.'

'Sometimes I wonder if Florence will ever sleep through the night! And Magnus . . . I'm afraid I'll forget to talk like a normal person, spending my days with a baby and a small boy who prefers to be a squirrel.' Iris gave Olivia an anxious stare. 'Do you think that he's . . . that he's a bit . . . well, *odd?*'

'Iris, Magnus is fine.' Olivia spoke firmly.

'I'm afraid he behaves the way he does because of us, because me and Lorcan are at each other's throats.'

'Magnus is a bright, imaginative little boy. It's tiresome, this stage he's going through, I agree, but it's normal.'

It reassured Iris that Olivia, who had taught at a primary school for decades, should say this. 'Do you think so?'

'I'm certain of it. Iris, love, you're just tired. That's why you're having these gloomy thoughts.'

Iris caught sight of a blob of porridge on her skirt, spat there by Florence at breakfast, and scraped it off. 'I'm not even sure I want to go out tomorrow,' she muttered. 'I haven't washed my hair for days and I've a spot on my chin. And I've nothing to wear. Nothing fits.'

'Give it a go.' Olivia's voice was gentle. 'It'll make you feel better to get out of the house. Lorcan and I can look after the children in the morning so you can have a lie-in and a shower. What do you think?'

'Okay.' Iris smiled. 'Thanks, Olivia.'

They walked back to the house. Already Iris felt bad about her disagreement with Lorcan. She remembered the beautiful pink peonies he had bought for her and was ashamed of herself for lashing out. Really, she could hardly blame him if he had the odd drink with a good-tempered, cheerful colleague after work, perhaps one of the many young, pretty secretaries at the BBC. And yet the thought of it seemed to gouge out her heart.

Chapter Seventeen

1978, London, Suffolk and Cambridge

Olivia was staying with Tom for the weekend. Tom's small two-bedroom terraced house in Crouch End, in north London, was immaculate, with nothing out of place. His sitting room was sparsely furnished, with plain curtains and no cushions; on the shelves were books by Asimov, Moorcock and Ballard and the *Whole Earth Catalog*, as well as volumes of George's poetry. The sleek, modern kitchen was equipped with the latest gadgets – an electric mixer, a yoghurt maker, a pressure cooker.

Tom and Nat were cooking supper, spaghetti bolognese followed by an elaborate French dessert. Nat was looking charming in a short tawny-orange linen dress. She had tied an emerald-green silk scarf round her head. Olivia had been instructed not to do anything and was sitting on a stool sipping a glass of wine and eating peanuts.

Tom finished off the bolognese sauce while Nat cracked and separated eggs. 'Oh God,' she said, as an egg white slithered to the floor. 'Missed.'

'No problem, plenty more.' Tom wiped up the mess. 'Did you talk to your mum?'

'I phoned her last night.'

'Was she all right?'

'Yeah, she was okay. We couldn't talk for long. There was a queue outside the phone box. She said India had offered to sort out the boxes and things in the Enchanted Land.'

Tom explained over his shoulder to Olivia, 'Nat's father was a magician.'

'Goodness, Nat, how amazing.'

'He used to put on shows in the barn at our house. People would come from all over the place.' Nat dabbed a fingertip into the concoction she was making to taste it. 'And we had a museum of magic and a shop selling magic tricks and things. Dad called it the Enchanted Land.'

'It sounds wonderful.'

'It was. But Tom, Mum wouldn't let India do anything.'

'Okay. Any particular reason?'

Nat paused, looked away, then said casually, 'Oh, you know. It's hard for her, going through Dad's things. Can you give me a hand with the custard part of this? I usually use Bird's.'

Tom put a lid on the pan of mince, then washed his hands. 'You can always phone home from here, you know, sweetheart.'

'Thanks, but it's fine. Mum's not a great one for the phone. She prefers writing letters.'

Olivia said, 'Where does your mother live, Nat?'

'In Norfolk, a few miles from Swaffham.'

When the milk had come to a simmer, Tom poured half of it over the egg mixture while Nat whisked.

She said, 'Did we put the vanilla in?'

'With the milk, yes.'

'You're an amazing cook, Tom.' Nat stood on tiptoe to kiss him.

'I just follow a recipe. You can make a meal out of nothing, I've seen you. I could never do that.'

'I'm a good plain cook, that's what my mum says. I make treacle pudding, not *îles flottantes*.'

They wound their arms round each other's waists. It comforted Olivia, after her recent stay with Iris and Lorcan, to see Tom and Nat so happy, so well matched. She had in the past worried that Tom's desire to avoid conflict and emotional intensity might lead to him steering clear of involvement altogether. He stroked the nape of Nat's neck. In turning to kiss him again, she sprayed the front of her dress with the whisk. Egg mixture dappled the linen.

Olivia rose from the stool. 'You'll need to soak that . . .'

Nat threw Olivia a grin. 'I know all about getting stains out of things, believe me.'

She dashed upstairs. Tom said, 'Nat used to help her mother make the costumes for her father's shows. Sometimes she was his assistant on stage.'

'Have you met her family?'

'Her elder sister, Morwenna, once, in Covent Garden, for a quick drink.' A slight frown crossed his face. 'I haven't been to Norfolk. I haven't met her mother.'

Nat came back into the kitchen wearing jeans and an oversized pale blue shirt, presumably one of Tom's. She said, 'I've put it to soak in the basin.'

She took over making the pudding while Tom went outside to water the garden. The plants he grew were of all shades of green and differing shapes of leaf, giving the tiny urban plot a subtropical appearance and the feel of a cool, verdant cave.

Nat wiped up a splash of egg from the worktop with her sleeve, and then, remembering that she was wearing Tom's shirt, said, 'Oops,' and ran the cuff under the tap.

She was stirring the pan when she said suddenly, 'Olivia, do you think a tidy person and an untidy person can ever live together?'

Startled, Olivia considered. 'Couples often view these things differently, it's true. But you tend to knock the sharp corners off each other once you've been together for a while.' Though when she thought of Lorcan and Iris, or even of her own marriage to George, she felt less confident of that statement. 'You can be tidy and tolerant,' she said, after another moment's thought. 'Tom is tidy, but he's a very tolerant person.'

'I don't mean a bit messy. I mean . . . keeping everything, never throwing anything away, never going through stuff and sorting it out. I'm untidy, but I know people who are much, much worse.' Nat's gaze evaded Olivia. 'Sometimes I wonder if I'll end up like that. Whether it's something that just happens to you.'

Olivia wondered who Nat was thinking about. A family member, perhaps – one of her sisters, or even her mother.

'I think that if you love each other, you can work things out,' she said firmly. 'That's what matters most. Do you want a hand with that, Nat?'

'Please.'

Olivia went to stand beside her. 'Everyone has different aspects to them, don't they? You would think, if you didn't know Tom well, that he'd be the sort of person who'd have neat rows of alyssum and begonias in his garden, but it isn't like that at all.'

'But you'd only think that,' Nat said, frowning fiercely while she stirred, 'if you didn't really understand him at all.'

The phone was ringing as Olivia unlocked the cottage's front door. She dashed inside and grabbed the receiver.

'Hello?'

'Olivia?'

Though she had not heard his voice for years, she knew it instantly. Her heart skipped a beat. 'Rory,' she said. She sat down on the sofa.

'I hope you don't mind me calling you.'

Did she? A part of her did. The last time they had spoken had been the short phone call she had made to end the affair after Tom had fallen ill with appendicitis.

She said, 'It's rather a surprise.'

'Yes, I'm sorry. Maybe I should have written, but that seemed, I don't know, a little cowardly. How are you?'

'I'm very well. And you?'

'I'm fine. I'm sorry to spring this on you out of the blue, but I was wondering whether I could talk to you. In person, preferably. You're living in Suffolk now, aren't you? It would be great if I could drive over and we could chat. I could take you out to lunch, if that worked for you.'

Olivia wound the flex of the phone round her hand. 'Talk about what?' she said.

'The Ruthwells. I'm researching a book.'

'British fascism before the war.'

'You remembered.'

I have an idea for a book, he had said. *Not this one, and I suspect not the next one. It's been brewing for a while.* That conversation had taken place in Rory's flat seven and a half years ago.

She said, 'What is it you'd like to know?'

On a fine Saturday in late May, Olivia walked to the village pub, the Fox, which was low, thatched and washed in Suffolk pink, to meet Rory Madden.

The garden was busy. She caught sight of him sitting at

a table in the shade of a birch tree. He rose, seeing her, and she waved. His lips brushed her cheek; she hugged him.

'Thank you for coming,' he said. 'It's good of you.'

'How are you, Rory?'

'Very well. You look wonderful.'

'You don't look so bad yourself.'

She sat down. She watched him as he went inside the Fox to buy drinks and order ploughman's lunches. Sunlight filtered through the pale, spindly branches of the birches.

The first moment of meeting was over, and that could only be a relief. During the past week, recalling the two previous episodes in which Rory had been a part of her life – the heady joy of first love and the elation of their short-lived affair – she had wondered how they would manage, the two of them, and whether there would be any awkwardness or self-consciousness between them. But she had sensed in him no acrimony and no regret. She thought him little changed. He had more than a sprinkling of grey in his hair now, and a line or two round his mouth, but to her he looked the same as he always had. Perhaps those people one has known and loved for a lifetime forever remain young. Because she still felt love for him, though that love had a different quality to what it had once had. Passion had softened into friendship, but she valued that no less.

He came back with the beers and food. She said, 'How did you trace me?'

'Through your ex-husband's publisher. I told George Flynn we were old friends, and I was a historian and I wanted to chat with you about your life in London before the war.' He looked across the table to her. 'We are, aren't we, Olivia? Old friends?'

She recognised the uncertainty in his eyes. 'We are, yes.'

'I'm glad of that.' He raised his glass. '*Sláinte*.'

'Cheers.'

Without further preamble, he said, 'I don't know if you saw the article in the *Observer*, but there have been investigations into that last place Claude Ruthwell sent Frankie to.'

'The school? I didn't know.'

'It was called Allershaw. It's closed now. And I'm not sure that you'd call it a school; it was more of an institution for boys who were thought to be backward or disabled in some way. There were quite a few establishments like that back then. There was a belief that it was better for children with problems to be educated away from their families, so that they could have specialist care. Institutions like Allershaw tended to be very regimented. The theory was that children with behavioural or physical problems responded better to a strict regime. But it sounds as though the place went beyond being simply spartan. The boys were mistreated. It was abusive.'

'Oh, Rory.' She looked away. 'Poor Frankie.'

'It's hard to think of him sent away from his home to somewhere like that. There's an ongoing investigation. A journalist has got her teeth into it and seems to have made it her mission to expose the abuses. And after I read the article, it got me fired up to get on with the book. I'd let it slip, rather.'

'I remember you telling me you kept coming up against barriers.'

He frowned and tapped the table for emphasis. 'Think, Olivia. Say you're one of the great and the good. Say you're used to a certain amount of social standing – respect, even. You're not going to want it to be known that back in the thirties you thought Hitler and Mussolini were jolly fine fellows. So none of this has been easy or straightforward. I kept on hitting the buffers and, as I said, I let it slide for quite a few months. Then I read about Allershaw, and some of the questions I'd had for years came flooding back. Did Claude Ruthwell use the place as a dumping ground for a son he saw as . . . substandard, an embarrassment? Did he place Frankie in the institution so that he could wash his hands of him?'

'Was he aware that with chronic asthma, Frankie might not survive?' It was the first time she had voiced the thought aloud.

'That occurred to you too.' She saw the interest in his eyes.

'It crossed my mind. You'd never be able to prove it, Rory.'

'No . . . but neglect, that might be possible to prove. So I went through all my old notes and started from scratch. I made a list of names, and I've been trying to get in contact with them. Alice Ruthwell – Alice Hain – was top of my list.'

'Alice married Michael Hain.'

'She did, yes. She lives in Hampshire. I offered to drive there to talk to her. I wanted to know whether Grace had left her any letters or diaries.'

She looked at him sharply. '*Left* her them?'

'Grace is dead.' He shot her a glance. 'You didn't know?'

'No. Oh, Rory. When was this?'

'A month or two ago. She was in her late seventies, a good age. I wrote to her, to her home in France, asking her if I could speak to her about Claude. She'd had a friend living with her for the last half-dozen years. The friend wrote back and told me that Grace had passed away.' He buttered a chunk of bread and scowled. 'The frustrating thing was that I'd tried to speak to her when I was over there a few years ago, researching my book on the Maquis, but she was out of the country then, travelling. And after that, I kept intending to get in touch, but . . .' He spread out his hands. 'I didn't get round to it.'

'What did Alice say?'

'She won't talk to me. She refuses point-blank.'

'Do you know why?'

Rory shook his head.

Olivia sipped her beer, thinking. 'And Claude Ruthwell? Is he still alive?'

'Still going strong. I approached him.' There was something cold and reptilian about Rory's smile. 'I received a solicitor's letter by return of post, threatening all sorts of things.'

'I don't imagine that put you off.'

'No, I took it as encouragement, a sign that he had something to hide. I've spent the past few weeks looking into Ruthwell's little ultra-right-wing group. They kept themselves well under the radar, and managed to avoid getting interned during the war.'

Olivia thought about the Ruthwells and the time she had spent with them. All those parties, at both Hinton Place and Paper Buildings. She took an envelope out of her bag and passed it to Rory.

'I've written down some names and dates, everything I can remember. I don't know how much use it will be. It's odd that Alice won't talk to you. Those couple of times I saw her, she was perfectly friendly.'

'Her husband died about eighteen months ago, so maybe it's something to do with that.'

'Oh, that's sad.' She remembered the pleasant, kindly-looking man she had met at another party, the one in Bedford Square. He had been somewhat older than Alice.

She said, 'Alice loved him very much. The way she spoke of him . . . They couldn't marry until the mid sixties, after she divorced Ivo Mortimer. It's a shame they didn't have longer together. She hasn't had an easy time of it, Rory. You can see why she might not want to dig up the past.'

'It's frustrating, though. If Grace kept a diary or had hung on to her letters, it might have given me a breakthrough.'

Olivia remembered Grace's writing desk in the Hinton Place morning room. She remembered the love notes she had delivered to Sammy Ellwood. She said, 'People wrote a lot of letters back then.'

'I'd love to get my hands on them. There's always a point at which I know I have enough material to make a start. There's a feeling of excitement because I can envisage what the book's going to become. But I'm not there yet. It feels too thin.'

'You'll get there, I know you will.' She smiled at him. 'You have a dogged determination, Rory. And a sort of ruthlessness.'

'I'm not sure you're flattering me.' For a moment he looked troubled. He said quietly, 'What I felt for you was genuine, Olivia. I wasn't just playing the field, if that's what you thought. But our timing was never good, I'll give you that.'

She put her hand on his sleeve. 'It's okay.'

'I was sorry to hear about your divorce.'

'Don't be. It was probably overdue. I thought I was doing the right thing, being there for our sons, staying with George, but maybe I wasn't. Maybe I was living a lie, and they saw that.' She had tried to keep the family together, but perhaps in doing so she had unwittingly helped drive them apart. Perhaps a bad marriage had been worse than no marriage and had done harm.

He said, 'Divorces are messy. You'd have done your best, Olivia, I know you would. The point is, are you happy here?'

'Very much so. And you?'

'I've met someone. I know, I know . . .' Amusement sparkled in his eyes. 'I never thought I would. Gillian works in the history department too. We've known each other for years and we've been friends for a long time. And then, one evening, everything changed.'

'Does your daughter approve?'

'Naomi? Yes, thank goodness.'

Olivia thought back to all the moments when her life had intertwined with his. She said, 'I don't regret anything, do you, Rory?'

He touched his glass against hers. 'No, not one single moment.'

Later, walking home, she thought not about Rory Madden but about Grace Ruthwell. She pictured Grace in her cyclamen-pink dress, dashing out of the house after Frankie that first day they had met. Grace sitting on the sofa in the chartreuse bedroom, filled with fear that she might one day lose her son. Lastly Grace in the gold ivy-leaved gown, shimmering like a flame. Meeting Grace Ruthwell had been part of what had formed Olivia. She would not have been the woman she had become without her. She did not mourn for her, because she knew that whatever hardships and grief she had endured, Grace was a woman who would have lived her life to the full.

Her thoughts turned to Alice. She wondered why Alice had refused to speak to Rory. Perhaps the loss of a mother and a much-loved husband was too recent, too painful.

But a memory nagged at the corners of her consciousness, and she felt as if she was about to detect at last a solution to an old puzzle. Though she teased away at it, trying to expose it to the light, she was unable to grasp it, and the flicker of intuition vanished, drifting on the air like the scent of honeysuckle in the hedgerows.

Tom said, 'How are you, Mum?'

'I'm very well, love. What about you? Have you had a good week?'

'Fine, it's been fine.'

Olivia was in Greengage Cottage's sitting room, phone in hand. It was early Friday evening and she had come home from work, showered and changed into a summer frock. It was very warm in the house and she was barefoot.

She said, 'Have you heard from Lorcan?'

'Not recently. Have you, Mum?'

'Not for a while. How's Nat?'

'She had to go home. Her brother, Russell, sent her a postcard telling her that her mum's hurt her ankle. She's damaged a ligament and can't get about. Russell's only twelve, so he needs someone to keep an eye on him.'

'I'm sorry to hear that, Tom. How difficult for Nat. What about her job?'

'She had to throw it in. She was temping. She never stays in the same place for long. I heard of a post available at the Royal Court and thought she might want to apply for that, but now this has happened . . .' Olivia heard the concern in his voice.

She said, 'Does she know how long she'll have to stay at home?'

'She wasn't sure. A few weeks, maybe a month. Oh, and I'm looking after Stanley.'

'Stanley?'

'The budgie we found in the street a while ago. He chucks seed everywhere.' There was a silence, during which Olivia made out from the other end of the line the muted hum of a radio, along with a faint squawking – the budgerigar, perhaps.

Tom said, 'I offered to run her to Norfolk, but she didn't want me to.' He sounded bewildered.

'I expect she didn't want to put you to any trouble.'

'I've plenty of leave owing. I wouldn't have minded at all. I like driving. I would have liked to help her out.'

'You could always pop up and see her.'

'I might do. It would only be an hour or so from you, Mum, so I could call in on the way.'

Later, Olivia ran through their conversation in her head while she padded round the kitchen. Tom and Nat had been going out for over six months, but Nat hadn't yet introduced him to her family. Several perfectly reasonable explanations sprang to mind. Nat might have been too busy, or a visit may not have been convenient for her mother. And Olivia completely understood why a woman might not choose to meet her daughter's boyfriend for the first time while hobbling about on crutches. But the omission was plainly troubling Tom, who was prone to self-doubt. He might wonder if it was due to a lack of commitment on Nat's part. This seemed very unlikely to Olivia, when she thought of the two of them in Tom's kitchen, making floating islands. They had seemed so happy, so well suited.

She opened the fridge and cupboard, thinking about supper. She was looking forward to a quiet evening pottering around, tidying up, doing some knitting or reading a book, perhaps. Through the kitchen window, she caught sight of the gravel area in front of the Hayloft. The grey van was not there; Luke McQuinnan had been away for the past week. In his absence, Olivia missed the sound of music.

The phone rang again. Munching an apple, she went back into the sitting room and picked up the receiver. 'Hello?'

'Mum . . .'

She frowned. 'Is that you, Lorcan?'

'Yeah.' His voice sounded odd. There was a crash, followed by a muttered *Christ al-bloody-mighty*.

'Lorcan?' she said. 'What's going on?'

'Dropped the bloody phone . . . Why we have it stuck in this stupid corner of the room . . . The damned lamp's smashed . . .' The words were thick and indistinct.

He was drunk, she realised. Very, very drunk. 'Lorcan,' she said sharply.

A silence.

'Talk to me. What's happened?'

She heard his heavy breaths, and then a sort of gulp, as if he was trying to stifle a sob. A pit seemed to open up inside her.

'Lorcan? *Please*. What is it?'

'Iris has left me,' he said.

Shortly afterwards, Lorcan ended the phone call. Olivia glanced at the clock. Half past six. A moment's thought, and then she dashed round the house, throwing a few items into a bag, closing windows and locking doors. Within half an hour of speaking to Lorcan, she was in her car, hurtling across rural Suffolk. Catching sight of the Hillman Imp's speedometer, she made herself slow. George always said that she drove like someone who had learned to drive on a tractor.

She reached Lorcan and Iris's home in north Cambridge

shortly after eight o'clock. After a lot of knocking and bell ringing, the front door opened and her son's bleary face appeared in the aperture.

'Lorcan,' she said.

'What are you doing here, Mum?'

'I wanted to make sure you were okay.'

Slouching across the doorway, he gave a sour smile. 'I haven't topped myself, if that's what you're worrying about.'

'*Lorcan*,' she hissed. 'Don't be flippant!'

He shrugged and looked away. He was barefoot and wearing a baggy T-shirt and a pair of jeans with paint stains. His hair looked unbrushed, he hadn't shaved and his eyes were puffy and bloodshot.

She said, more gently, 'How are you doing?' and his gaze slid slowly in her direction.

'My wife's left me. She's taken my kids and gone to stay with her parents. How do you think I'm doing?'

'I'm so sorry, love. May I come in?'

For a long, awful moment she thought he might refuse, but then he stood aside.

She wanted to hug him but sensed that he would reject her. Instead, following him into the house, she said, 'Why don't I make coffee? I'm sure we could both do with some.'

In the kitchen, unwashed dishes were piled in the sink and on the worktops. Empty wine bottles stood on the draining board. She opened the back door, and a waft of spring scents replaced the stale fug of cigarette ash and alcohol. Lorcan went outside and stood on the terrace, smoking, as the coffee brewed. Olivia rinsed some mugs.

She went into the garden. A child's tricycle stood on the terrace and a yellow plastic duck on wheels lay on its side on the lawn. 'Here.' She handed him a mug of coffee. 'When did she go?'

'A few days ago.' He gave a loose flap of his hand. 'I thought . . . I kept hoping she'd be back when I came home from work.'

'Have you spoken to her?'

'I tried.' He tapped ash off the cigarette, then gave a short laugh. 'It didn't go well. But then nothing's gone well for ages.'

Beneath his dishevelled appearance, he looked exhausted. She wondered whether he had slept or eaten since Iris had left home. She said, 'Have you had any supper?'

'I'm not hungry.'

She made to go back into the kitchen, but he snapped at her, 'Mum, for God's sake, I'm not ten years old! I can look after myself. None of this is your business!'

The expression in his eyes made her recoil. She sat down on a rusty metal seat, trying to compose herself. The roses were coming out, the jasmine just starting to bloom; there was still light, and the day's warmth lingered. She tried to concentrate on these things. One of them needed to remain calm, and that person must be her.

'Sorry,' he muttered. 'Sorry, Mum.' He held out a hand to her and she squeezed it. His anger and pride dropped away and she saw beneath them his vulnerability.

'I shouldn't take it out on you,' he said. 'It's just . . .' He flicked the cigarette butt into the flower bed and let out a breath. 'I don't blame Iris for going. I've loused everything up. It's all my fault.'

She said carefully, 'What happened?'

'She got fed up with me.'

'You quarrelled?' Perhaps that was all it was. Lorcan and

Iris had argued, and he had lost his temper and Iris had walked out. They would talk and sort it out.

But he said, 'It hasn't been good between us for months. And then something happened, and . . . *whoosh*. It all seemed to go out of control.' His expression was grim. 'I was trying to make things right again, but I've made such a hash of it.'

It was on the tip of her tongue to ask him what, exactly, had happened, and what he had been trying to make right, but she knew she should not. As Lorcan had pointed out to her, he was no longer a ten-year-old to be consoled with a hug and a chocolate biscuit. He was an adult, and his problems were complex, and unless he volunteered to share them, they were his and Iris's alone.

She said, 'You have to talk to her, love. And you have to sort yourself out.'

'What's the point?' He made a wild gesture. 'We'd still be in the same state. Nothing would have changed. And as for sorting myself out, I wouldn't know where to begin.'

'You need to cut down on the drinking.'

Anger flared in his eyes. 'Christ, Mum.'

'It's not helping.' She steeled herself for his response.

But then he seemed to deflate, and he said quietly, 'I know. I'll try. But I'm afraid it won't make any difference. I'm afraid it's too late.'

'You need to give Iris time. She's had a tough few months. You both have.' She stood up. 'I'm going to make us something to eat. I haven't had any supper yet, and I'm ravenous. Lorcan?'

He nodded. They went into the kitchen. Lorcan took out eggs and bacon from the fridge and he washed up the dirty dishes while she cooked.

Olivia was lifting the eggs out of the pan when he said, 'You say give her time, but what if that doesn't work, Mum? I love her. What if she's just had enough of me? What am I supposed to do then?'

The house in which Iris and her younger brother had been brought up, though neither pretty nor smart, echoed the Jacksons' scientific interests. There was a home-made propagator in the kitchen, pen-and-ink sketches of flowers and seedheads hanging on the walls, and collections of shells and fossils in cabinets and on mantelpieces. Arriving there a few evenings ago, relief had flooded through Iris as she had felt herself enfolded in the familiar, slightly scruffy warmth.

In part, she had fled to Much Hadham simply because of her desperate need for sleep. And that had worked, because on her first night back in her childhood home, she had slept for the longest uninterrupted stretch since before Florence had been born. Flo had woken for a feed at two in the morning, as she always did. At six o'clock, Iris's mother, Julia, had given her a bottle, and afterwards she had gone back to sleep. As soon as Magnus had woken up, his grandfather had taken him to play with the train set that occupied the entire upper floor of the garage. Iris had seen little of the two of them since, except at mealtimes, during which Magnus had not squeaked like a squirrel once and instead had talked non-stop about the new railway station he and Grandad were constructing.

For the last two nights, Florence had slept through till six, a feat that seemed to Iris both miraculous and transformative. Julia gave her granddaughter her breakfast and then took her out in the pram for a walk round the village

– she was a staunch believer in infants getting plenty of fresh air. All this had meant that Iris was able to have a lie-in followed by a long, leisurely shower. The blissful shock of having slept properly made her feel heavy-eyed and rather as if she was moving through warm, seaweed-filled water, but the fraught, jangling agitation that had become a part of her began to retreat.

Her mother wouldn't let her help with housework, so she spent the mornings sitting on an old blanket in the shade of the garden, leafing through magazines and playing with the baby. Sunlight gleamed on the blades of grass. Now and then she scuttled after Florence, who had become an expert crawler, and stopped her eating a daisy.

With time to reflect and the ability to think clearly, she was able to acknowledge that lack of sleep wasn't her only problem. She might prefer to avoid thinking about the evening she had fled her marital home, just as she might prefer not to dwell on her discovery of the letters and bank statements that Lorcan had hidden in his sock drawer, and which she had, in the course of attempting to tidy the house, discovered. She had been trying to sort out the most pressing of her problems – get Florence sleeping through the night, tidy rooms that were sinking ever deeper into chaos, and repair her relationship with Lorcan. In pursuit of the second aim, she had ironed shirts and paired socks.

It had been when she was putting the socks away that she had discovered the letters. A whole bundle of them, from the bank and the building society. Bewildered, and with a sick feeling inside her, she had begun to read. *Dear Mr Flynn, I thought you would wish to be informed that your overdraft is currently standing at the sum of £281.99 . . . Dear Mr Flynn, I am contacting you about your mortgage arrears . . .*

Lorcan had come home from work. A terrible quarrel had ensued, during which Iris had vented her fear and anger on him. It came to her now, as she sat beneath her mother's much-prized *Magnolia grandiflora*, that in getting married, in having children and giving up her job, she had lost her independence, had lost control of her life, and she hated that. The only income she could truly call hers was the family allowance. Otherwise, she was entirely financially dependent on Lorcan, who, it had to be recognised, was not good with money.

And it was she herself who had let that happen. The children had absorbed her energy, and tiredness had meant that her anxiety had slipped out of control. She had left the management of their finances to Lorcan, and that in turn had led to disaster. He was not the only one to blame. She had abnegated responsibility.

Iris had always been careful with money, had eked out her small grant to cover each university term, and when working had lived frugally but well. She had never until now been in debt. The thought of the sum they owed the bank frightened her. Most alarming of all was her discovery that they had fallen behind with the mortgage payments.

At midday, with her daughter sitting on the blanket beside her, she was idly scanning an article on quick, economical family suppers when her mother and Olivia came into the garden. She sprang up, thinking of Lorcan, of accidents and illnesses.

Julia Jackson said, 'Why don't I give Florence her lunch? You two can have a chat out here. It's such a beautiful sunny day.' She scooped the baby off the rug and went into the house.

Tucking her cotton skirt beneath her, Olivia sat down on the blanket. 'How are you, Iris?'

'Better, thanks.'

'I've just been to Cambridge, to see Lorcan.'

'Is he all right? Is he looking after himself?'

'I stayed overnight. He's fine now. He wasn't in the best of moods when I arrived, I'll admit, and the conversation certainly wasn't easy, but basically, Iris, he's okay.'

'Thank goodness.' She felt relief wash through her.

Olivia frowned. 'He told me not to meddle. I hope *you* don't think I'm meddling, coming here.'

'No, of course not. It's good to see you.'

'How are the children?'

'They're fine.'

Iris heard herself. It wouldn't do. Only that morning she had promised herself she would face up to problems, that she would no longer evade uncomfortable conversations or put off difficult decisions. Or what was the point of coming here?

'They miss their daddy,' she said. 'Magnus is confused. He struggles with sudden changes. Thank goodness for Dad's train set.' Looking Olivia in the eye, she explained, 'The other night, Lorcan and I were arguing about money. And, I don't know, it got out of hand, and I couldn't bear it, so I came here. And I don't regret it. At least I can *sleep* here.' She smoothed and folded Florence's cardigan. 'It's not only the money. He gets so *angry*. I love him, but I'm not going home, not until I'm sure things are going to be different. It's not just him; I've got to think what I need to do as well. But Lorcan needs to change, and to tell you the truth, Olivia, there have been times when I don't know if he's capable of it. So it's up to him now.'

Magnus and her father were emerging from the door at the back of the garage. Iris waved, and Magnus ran across the lawn to her.

Mrs Astill's garden was taking shape. An order of roses had arrived that afternoon from Peter Beales' nursery, and Olivia and Margot were moving them about the garden, working out which plant should go where. Olivia heard a car draw up by the back gate. A door closed and a latch was lifted. Looking up, she saw her youngest son.

'Tom!'

'Hello, Mum. Sorry to barge in. That guy in Gareth's house told me you were working here.'

Several things registered at once: that Luke McQuinnan had been listening when she had blethered on about her work to take his mind off his injured leg. And that of all her sons, Tom would not have come here while she was at work without good reason.

She straightened. Her mouth had gone dry. She said, 'Is it Lorcan?'

'Lorcan?' Tom looked confused. 'No, Mum, it's not Lorcan. It's Dad, I'm afraid.'

Chapter Eighteen

1978, Cambridge and Suffolk

After his mother broke the news to him that his father had had a heart attack, all Lorcan could think of was how much he longed for Iris to hold him and tell him it was going to be all right.

Iris had taken the car when she had fled Cambridge with the children. Public transport to Much Hadham would be non-existent at this time in the evening, so, unable to see her in person, Lorcan phoned the Jacksons' house.

Iris said, after he had told her about his father's illness, 'Lorcan, I'm so sorry, how awful. How is he?'

Lorcan was sitting on the rug in the front room, the phone in his hand, a glass of beer, a packet of Embassy Regal and an ashtray beside him. He said, 'Mum said the doctor told her it was a mild heart attack. She and Tom saw him for a few minutes. She said he looked very tired, but he was awake, and he talked a bit.'

'That sounds hopeful, love.'

He lit a cigarette. 'I don't know what to do.'

'You don't have to do anything now. This must have been

a terrible shock, so give yourself a moment to take a breath.'

'I want to go and see how he is.'

'You can do that tomorrow.'

'I can't. It would be so bloody hypocritical after . . . after everything.'

'Lorcan.' He knew that Iris was choosing her words carefully. 'I don't think it would be hypocritical at all, but even if it was, would that matter? In the circumstances, would that matter at all?'

'I'm not sure I've forgiven him – you know, for everything – so how can I go along there and pretend that I have?'

'Do you have to forgive him first?'

'Don't I?'

'Not necessarily. You must have all sorts of complicated feelings, I see that, but surely the only thing of importance now is that your father knows you love him. Which you do, don't you?'

He drew on the cigarette, then said, 'Yes. But that's the trouble.'

'You mean that he let you down.'

He stretched out his legs and leaned his back against the armchair. Hearing her voice made him feel calmer, less hopeless. He said, 'He did, didn't he? I used to worship him, and then I got fed up with him, and then so angry. I thought he was such a fraud.'

'You're right, he did let you down. But none of us gets it right all the time.'

'Dad got it rather spectacularly wrong.' But Lorcan's thoughts turned towards the heap of letters and financial statements in his sock drawer.

He heard Iris say, 'I've got so much wrong.'

'Rot. It's not your fault, it's all mine.'

'No, that's not true, Lorcan. I've been thinking about us a lot. I think part of the problem is that I've hated not going to work. I thought I'd love being at home all the time with the children, but the truth is I don't, and I've known that for a while. I was afraid that made me a lousy mother, so I didn't say anything. But I don't think it does. There are different ways of being a good mother.' A pause, then she said, 'I was afraid you were seeing someone.'

'Seeing someone? What?' He was startled. 'You mean a woman?'

'Yes. I was so tired and miserable I would hardly have blamed you – except that I would have, I'd have hated it.'

'Good God, Iris . . . What on earth made you think that?'

'You kept coming home late. And I could tell you'd been drinking.'

'I was in a pub, yes, and I'd had a pint, but I was writing stories.'

'Stories?'

'Science fiction stories. I've been trying to earn some extra money, to help with the mortgage. I thought I'd give it a go. I can't write at home, it's too, too . . .'

'Noisy,' she said. 'Chaotic.'

'Pubs are noisy too, but it's not a noise I have to do anything about.'

She laughed. 'I know exactly what you mean.'

'I didn't tell you in case it didn't work out.'

'Have you sold any?'

'Three,' he said. He felt a faint sense of disbelief – and a flare of pride – in that. 'And I've started writing a novel.'

'Lorcan, that's amazing.'

'It won't pay the bills, I'm afraid. Iris, I love you. I love you so much. I would never even look at anyone else.'

'Oh.' The sound was little more than a sigh. 'I love you too. I miss you.'

Lorcan heard distant noises from the other end of the phone line. Chinking and clunking – a table being cleared, perhaps. A baby's coo. He missed the children so much. He let his gaze drift round the room. The previous evening, he had tidied up. It had been odd to come home from work today and find the room still orderly, no toys and tiny garments and sucking cups and beakers scattered about. He hated it.

He said, 'When I was about Magnus's age, Dad made me this papier-mâché island. We painted it green for the land and blue for the sea. I loved it. I used to make up stories about the people who lived there. When I was older, I was rubbish at football and Dad spent ages trying to teach me how to kick a ball. And when I crashed the car one night, he didn't tell me off, he just put his arms round me and hugged me. I miss him, Iris. I miss him a lot.'

There were tears in his eyes. He took a shaky inbreath, then had another swallow of beer. 'I'm so sorry about everything,' he said.

'Go and see your dad, Lorcan.' Iris's voice was gentle. 'He needs you, and so does your mum. Just go and see him.'

Olivia stayed with Tom so that she could visit George at the hospital in the afternoons. Tom went to see his father in the evenings, after work. When Lorcan turned up, Olivia claimed that she needed to stretch her legs. As she left the ward, the two of them began to talk; by the time she returned, half an hour later, George had fallen asleep and Lorcan was sitting beside him, holding his hand. Out of the shock and anxiety of the last few days, healing had begun, and she took comfort in that.

George was discharged from hospital on the understanding that he rest and receive care during his recovery. Olivia suggested he come home with her so that she could look after him. There was, simply, no one else. Tom and Lorcan had jobs to do and Gareth was in Australia, and as for Serena, she had turned up at the hospital one afternoon with a bunch of carnations and a determined expression on her face. Olivia had waited in the corridor while she had paid George a brief visit. Emerging from the ward, Serena had described, pointedly, the one-bedroom flat in which she and Amelia were now living and had then made her exit in a cloud of long, floaty chiffon scarves and Revlon perfume.

George began to regain his strength only slowly. Always previously physically fit, he railed against the limitations his illness had enforced on him. His doctor had instructed him not to smoke or drink, to avoid vigorous exercise and emotional outbursts; he found all these strictures irksome. He had always enjoyed company, and while some of his friends made the journey to Suffolk to visit him, he inevitably had to spend time on his own. Once he was on his feet more, he fell into the habit of following Olivia round the house, engaging her in conversation or listing his symptoms. Though she felt sympathy for him for having been wrenched from the life he knew, there were times when she found herself longing for her own space.

At the weekend, Lorcan and Tom visited. They were on the terrace at the back, chatting to their father, when the doorbell rang. Olivia went to open it. Seeing Gareth, she screamed with joy, then flung her arms round him.

'I came as soon as I could,' he said. 'I've been so worried, Mum. How is he?'

Lorcan said, 'I'm sorry I was such a dick,' and Gareth, handing him a Coke, said, 'S'all right.'

'No, really.'

'It's okay.' Gareth sat down between Lorcan and Tom. The three brothers had walked down the hill to the Fox, in Holfield St Peter, because their father had fallen asleep in an armchair and their mother looked like she could do with a quiet hour. They were sitting at a table in a low-ceilinged alcove.

'I'm used to you being a dick, Lorcan.' Gareth took a mouthful of beer. Then he said, 'Maybe I could have handled it better.'

'Good grief,' Lorcan said, faking astonishment. 'Gareth admitting he's less than perfect.'

Gareth grinned. 'Make the most of it. It might not happen again.'

Lorcan knew he still needed to try to make amends. 'We've missed you.'

'Cleo and I have missed you lot as well,' Gareth said casually. 'We'll stay a couple of years or so in Australia, long enough to see some of the country, and then we'll come home. Cleo agrees. How's Iris?'

And it was that easy, Lorcan thought. An apology, an acknowledgement, an expression of affection, and he felt as if a weight had been lifted from his shoulders.

'We're talking.' He shuffled awkwardly. Why did he find it so difficult to speak of emotional matters? He felt this inability to be pathetic; he knew it to be destructive, because it had led to misunderstandings and hurt. 'We're working it out. We're trying to do better.' He doodled in a splash of beer on the tabletop. 'Iris says she won't come home until I've sorted things out.'

Tom said, 'What sort of things?'

'Our finances, mostly.' Lorcan grimaced.

'What's the problem?'

'We owe rather a lot of money.' The mere thought of his indebtedness made his spirits plummet.

'Can you see what your money's going on, and where you could cut back your expenditure?'

The previous night Lorcan had stayed up late, going through bills and bank statements. 'I mean, I can see we've spent too much money, but I don't know what to do about it. I don't think saving a few pounds on booze and groceries will cut it. Jeez, just to *think* about it. I wish I still smoked.' He had thrown his half-finished pack of cigarettes into the bin after visiting his father on the cardiac ward. At the same time, he had given up drinking, for a while at least. He didn't like the person he became when he drank too much. At some point in the future, when he was sure he could handle it, he might go back to having the odd glass of beer.

'I'll get some crisps,' Gareth said.

While Gareth was at the bar, Lorcan said to Tom, 'I think what happens is that I believe that by spending money I'll keep the family together. That I'll make us all happy again. Oh, and spending money cheers me up. I can see now how stupid it was.'

'Not stupid,' said Tom. 'Misguided, maybe. I'll give you a hand, Lorcan. Finance is my area of expertise, after all.' He glanced at his watch. 'Did you say you were heading back tonight? I'll drive to Cambridge with you and look through the paperwork if you like.'

Gareth dropped three bags of crisps onto the table. 'I thought you'd be dashing off to London to see the beautiful Natasha.'

Tom gave a half-smile and ripped open a packet.

Gareth sat down. He said, 'All I could think of when Mum told me about Dad was how *colourless* we'd all be without him. I mean, you can never accuse him of sinking into the background, can you? Dad's at the centre of everything. Do you remember some of those weird characters who used to stay with us when we lived at Goldscombe? How they worshipped him? How, whatever oddities he'd collected, we'd all somehow gel and the evening would turn into a party?'

In the kitchen of his house in Cambridge, Lorcan put the sheaf of bills and bank statements on the table in front of Tom. 'I didn't open them for ages,' he admitted. 'I stuffed them in a drawer. I couldn't face it.'

'Why don't you make us some coffee?' Tom knew he wouldn't be able to concentrate with Lorcan hovering around, peering over his shoulder. 'It shouldn't take me too long to go through these. You're sure this is the lot?'

Lorcan nodded, then said, 'We're behind with the mortgage.'

Tom extracted a piece of paper from the pile and studied it. 'Four months. Have you talked to your building society?'

'Not yet.'

Scanning columns, Tom frowned. 'Your expenditure looks rather high.'

Lorcan snorted. 'That's the understatement of the month.'

'You okay? You look jittery. We'll find a way round this and work out how to deal with it. Now, make some coffee, please, Lorcan.'

Tom put the statements in date order, then went through the bills. He made notes on a piece of paper and checked any entries he couldn't make sense of with Lorcan, who still looked twitchy and alarmed.

'What's happened with Nat?' Lorcan said, as he was refilling the coffee mugs.

Tom took off his glasses and rubbed his eyes. 'Nothing.'

'Rot. You've hardly mentioned her. A while back, you'd say her name every other sentence.'

Tom put down the pen. A couple of evenings ago he had spoken to Nat on the phone. Once again he had offered to visit her in Norfolk; once more she had put him off, leaving him confused and low.

He said, 'I haven't seen her for a while. She had to go home. Her mother tripped and hurt her ankle and can't get about.'

'I liked her,' Lorcan said. 'And she was good with the kids.'

'She doesn't want me to visit her. It would be easy enough to drive there from Mum's house, but every time I suggest it, she comes out with some reason why I can't.' Tom hadn't meant to tell Lorcan that; it just came out.

'Do you know why?'

'Not really. I assume . . .' He polished the lenses of his glasses with his handkerchief. 'I assume she's had enough.'

'Of you? Did she say that?'

'No, but what other explanation could there be?' Tom watched Lorcan putting saucepans and utensils into cupboards. 'I mean, I'm hardly . . . She's so beautiful and lively and fun. I expect she got bored with me. I mean, "fun" isn't the adjective you'd choose to describe me, is it, Lorcan?' This was the conclusion he had arrived at after thinking it through: that Nat was dropping him because he was too staid. Their relationship could never have worked out. He had tried to console himself with the thought that in time it would become less painful, but so far that wasn't working at all.

'Go and see her,' Lorcan said.

'Haven't you been listening? She doesn't want me to.'

'Tom, just *go*.'

'Leave it, won't you?' There was an edge to Tom's voice.

Lorcan sat down at the table opposite his brother. 'I grant you, I'm hardly the person to give advice. And you might not always be fun, Tom, though you often are in your own way, but you have other attributes. Look at you now, taking the time to go through this mess. I thought Nat was great, and she seemed really keen on you. And what's the worst that can happen? She can only tell you to push off.'

Ignoring him, Tom went through the remaining pieces of paper. Then, taking off his glasses again, he said, 'Okay. I think I've got it straight.'

'So what's the verdict? Debtors' prison?'

Tom knew that Lorcan was trying to make a joke of it.

'I think,' he said, looking his brother in the eye, 'that you may have to sell the house.'

In the afternoons, when George was resting, Olivia worked on Mrs Astill's garden. While she had been staying in London, Margot had completed the planting. They had reached the tweaking stage, Margot declared one afternoon, as she brushed the earth from her palms. The two of them were standing at the right angle of the L. In the weeks and months to come, nature would take over and the plants would flourish and create their own colours and vistas.

Olivia walked home. Tomorrow they would transport the pots of ornamental flowers that she and Margot had nurtured in their greenhouses and put them in place. And that would be it, their final day of work on the garden. She enjoyed the sense of satisfaction that came with the completion of a large project.

As she approached the Hayloft, she heard music sweeping through the open window. Luke must have come back to the house, and that realisation magnified her happiness. He was playing the piano, and the plaintive tune was now stitched above a slow, stately rise and fall of chords. She listened as the music ebbed and flowed, noticing the small adjustments of time and pitch that told her he was experimenting, trying to decide what worked best. Then she prised off her boots, took a deep breath, opened the door and called out a hello to George.

Tom's godmother, Dinah Clairmont, said much the same as Lorcan. She had on hearing about his father's illness offered to take Tom to lunch. They were in the Punjab, in Covent Garden, because they shared a fondness for Indian food. Dinah, who was wearing an emerald-coloured dress and a chunky black necklace, had tucked her half-dozen shopping bags beside the table. Tom explained to her that his father was on the mend, though he still looked pretty awful. He added, 'He doesn't look like Dad, really.' Dinah made some comforting remarks.

Then he found himself telling his godmother about Nat.

'It's easy to assume the worst,' Dinah said, when he had finished. 'And then often find one is completely mistaken.'

Tom smoothed a poppadum crumb from the white tablecloth and said, obstinately, 'What if I'm not?'

She raised her eyebrows at him. 'Believe me, there are all sorts of reasons why a girl might not want the boy she's fond of to see her family home. For instance, her relatives might be an embarrassment. They might have outlandish or unpleasant opinions. Or they might simply be dull. And there's money, too, Tom. We often tend to underestimate the importance of money in relationships. Nat's family might not be as well off as yours. She might feel that as a couple, you are unequal. Or she might be afraid you would look down on her.'

'I would never do that.'

'I know you wouldn't.'

'Maybe *we* put her off – the Flynns, I mean.'

'I doubt that.' Dinah gave him a benevolent smile. 'I held you when you were a tiny scrap of a thing, Tom, only a few minutes old. I've never spoken to you about how I felt then because I don't wish to embarrass you, but I could tell from just looking at you that you were sweet-natured. You've grown into such a fine young man. If your Nat is the woman you say she is, then she'll be missing you. You need to trust her, Tom. Go and see her. Talk to her.'

Walking back to the office, he reflected on what his godmother had said. Six months ago, Nat had come into his life like a whirlwind. She had shaken him out of his pleasant, tidy, controlled existence. Life was unpredictable when she was around – could he live with that? Was that what he wanted?

As he swung through the glass doors of the office building, he acknowledged that in the course of this year he had changed. He, Tom Flynn, was the sort of person who planned a hike in the Peak District when stranded in a lift with a stranger. He was the sort of person who asked his girlfriend to a birthday party on the spur of the moment. He had become more open to emotional involvement and more accepting of life's ups and downs. This other side of him had been there all along, but it had been Nat who had shown it to him.

Olivia came back into the house after taking down the washing from the line. George had put on the radio, and Wagner was playing very loudly. He had got packets and jars out of the cupboard and was liberally dusting the counter and floor with flour.

She said, 'What are you doing?'

'Making flatbreads. Do you have any Turkish chilli flakes?'

'The village shop doesn't run to Turkish chilli flakes. There should be some paprika. Could you turn it down a little?'

He adjusted the radio a fraction, then launched into a critique of an opera he had seen a few months ago at the Coliseum. When he paused for breath, Olivia said, 'I'm going outside to get on with the new flower bed. Don't tire yourself out, George.'

She had got out of the habit, she thought, of living with another person. Or perhaps she had got out of the habit of living with George. The opening scene to *Götterdämmerung* flowed through the open living-room window.

Hearing a voice call out a hello, she looked across to the Hayloft and saw Luke McQuinnan.

'I'm sorry about the noise,' she said, walking to the hedge. 'I'd forgotten how loud my ex-husband likes to have the radio on.'

'Not a problem. How is he?'

'Much better, thanks. Talking non-stop. That must mean he's getting better.'

'Could you do with a drink? I've just opened a bottle.'

She laughed. 'Yes, why not? It would be lovely to escape for ten minutes.'

She looped round the lane to the Hayloft. As Luke showed her into the house, he said, 'How's the choir?'

'Battling along.'

'What's so frustrating is that I can play at home or when I'm with a pupil, but any sort of audience and I go to pieces.'

'Luke, honestly, I understand.'

In the room where Gareth and Cleo had once held their family celebrations, the grand piano now dominated the space. Against the walls were free-standing bookshelves bearing stacks of sheet music. It felt odd to see on the mantelpiece framed photos that were not of her own family, as they had once been, but of Luke's: Annie McQuinnan playing the flute; a dark-haired boy standing on a hilltop, buffeted by the wind; a portrait of a beautiful woman sitting beside a rock pool, smiling at the camera – Harriet, presumably.

'It looks so different,' she said.

'Not in a bad way, I hope.'

'No, not at all. Do you feel more settled, Luke?'

'Very much so. It's an easy house to live in.'

The room was ordered and uncluttered. 'I like the shelves,' she said.

'I made them.' He ran a hand along a smooth-grained surface. 'I like making things now and again. Don't worry, I was careful with the chisel, so no more accidents. This house belongs to your son and daughter-in-law, doesn't it? Where have they moved to?'

'Australia. Sydney.'

'Permanently?'

'I don't think so. They think they'll be back in a year or two.' It had been a great comfort to talk to Gareth on his brief visit home to see his father, and to know that they were happy, and that Cleo and the children were thriving. Olivia had bought a dozen small gifts for them, which Gareth had squeezed into his case before heading back for Heathrow.

'Will you visit them there?'

'Yes, I think so. They've asked me to. Have you ever been to Australia?'

Luke shook his head. 'The States, yes, on a concert tour some time ago, but no, never Australia. I'd like to, though.' He handed her a glass of wine.

'Are you celebrating?'

'I've finished writing the first part of the work.'

'Wow. Brilliant.' She raised her glass in a toast. 'Congratulations.'

They went to sit on the terrace. Fat, billowing clouds, shaded on the underside with grey, scudded over fields marked out by the puffy dark green lines of hedgerows. She sat on one of the wicker chairs, a foot tucked beneath her. The wine tasted crisp and delicious.

'I took this house because of the view,' he said. 'That first day I moved in, that time I was a bit off with you, I was thinking how much Harriet would have loved it here.'

'What was she like?'

'Bright . . . funny . . . very talented. She was a professional flautist. And she was kind and gentle and she had a sort of serenity. If I was nervous before a concert, she could always make me feel better.'

'She sounds lovely.'

He smiled. 'She wasn't so great at practical things. She

couldn't boil an egg – literally. I wasn't much of a cook back then either, so we sort of limped along. And she was a lousy driver. The night she died she'd been visiting a friend in the countryside. It was dark and wet, and the police reckoned she must have misjudged the bend in the road. Her car collided with a lorry. Afterwards, I felt I should have been there, that I should have been the one driving in bad weather, not her.'

'Some things just happen, Luke,' she said gently. 'Awful things can just happen.'

'I don't know if that makes it any easier to accept. The suddenness, the randomness feels unbearable. Maybe we'd rather find something to blame, even if that means blaming ourselves.' He sat down. 'It took me years and a succession of shrinks and therapists to unpick all that. At the time, whatever I felt had to be put aside because of the children. I had to make their lives as normal as possible. Back then, Jake was still at school and Annie was at college.'

'I admire your fortitude.'

He made a brushing-away gesture. 'You do what you need to do, don't you? How's it going with your ex?'

Olivia glanced over to Greengage Cottage. There was no sign of George, so he must still be indoors, laying waste to her kitchen.

'You should come and say hello,' she said. 'He'd enjoy talking to you. He can be good company, though he's rather down in the dumps just now.'

'I'll drop by. I'd like to meet him.'

'It's been such a shock to him. George was always the sort of person who is hardly ever ill. I miss my quiet moments, though. I miss not bothering with cooking if I don't feel like it, and I miss being able to go out whenever I want. I feel guilty for saying it, but the truth is I'll be relieved when I've got the house back to myself.'

'It's not easy, adapting to living with someone else, even if you know them well.'

Sometimes, she thought, it was especially tricky if you knew them well. She took another mouthful of wine. She could feel herself relaxing, the stresses of the last few weeks melting away.

She said, 'I'd hate to think I've become more intolerant as I've grown older.'

'I'm sure you haven't. I think it's that we have more people to please. My ex-girlfriend made it her mission to organise me. Invite people round to dinner, book theatre tickets, buy me new socks, that sort of thing. Nothing *wrong*, and it was good of her to bother, but . . .'

'Not what you wanted.'

'Not what I was looking for.'

'Was that why you finished?'

'That, and Annie didn't take to her.'

She raised her eyebrows at him. 'That would be a problem.'

There was a wry twist to his mouth. 'You could say that. When you get to our age, you have a history.'

She understood what he meant. 'Grown-up children . . . friends . . . neighbours . . . colleagues . . . a life.'

'It's asking a lot of anyone to step into that.' He topped up their glasses. 'Not that Carlotta and I would have lasted anyway. When I told her I was leaving London to come here, she accused me of being self-indulgent and romantic.' A quick spark of a grin lit up his eyes. 'Those are, by the way, qualities she disapproves of, though I hadn't realised until then quite how much.'

She said, with some mockery, 'But Luke, what is life without music?'

He raised his glass. 'Couldn't agree with you more.'

'Seriously, we all need some creativity and pleasure in our lives.' She glanced over to the cottage. 'That's why I bought the woodland.'

'That patch on the other side of your house? What do you plan to do with it?'

'I've hacked back a lot of the brambles and nettles. I've left some for the butterflies and to make jelly, but they'd nearly taken over the plot, so they needed getting under control. If you look on the sunnier side . . .' She went to the edge of the terrace and pointed. 'I planted some apples, mostly crab, but a few for eating, and I'm trying out a couple of pears. And I put in a rowan on the far side, for good luck.'

'And has it brought you good luck?'

'Time will tell. The truth is, Luke, there have been rifts within the family. I feel more optimistic than I did a while ago, but there's still a part of me firmly keeping my fingers crossed. You can never be sure. So recently, I've *really* needed that rowan to do its stuff.'

He was looking at her, amusement in his eyes.

She shrugged. 'Yeah, I know, I'm a bit of an old hippy.'

'I suspect a lot of us are, at heart.'

She was aware of his height as he stood beside her. She was five foot six, but he must have been at least six inches taller.

'I bought the wood on impulse,' she said. 'It was up for sale at the same time as the cottage and I couldn't resist it.'

'Maybe we should all do something impulsive once in a while.'

She noticed the warmth in his voice and in his expression. It seemed a while since she had relaxed and chatted with a man. Since her divorce, friends had invited her to dinner parties to which they had also asked along a single man, in the glaringly obvious hope that something might come of it. She was not looking for anything other than friendship. She disliked being set up and had never felt the smallest flicker of attraction to any of those dinner party guests.

The realisation, as she stood beside him, that she was attracted to Luke McQuinnan jolted her. She wondered whether these feelings were in reaction to the weeks she had spent caring for a cantankerous ex-husband, and whether anything would feel pleasant compared to that. But in her heart she knew that such an assumption was facile and false.

He said, 'Another glass?'

'Thanks, but I'd better not.' She needed to think, to be alone, to mull over this discovery. 'George is cooking. I keep thinking I'll see smoke coming out of the windows.'

He was showing her out of the house when he said, 'What happened between you and your husband? Did you just drift apart?'

She looked back at him. He said quickly, 'Sorry, shouldn't have asked. No business of mine.'

She shook her head. 'I'll tell you what happened, Luke. George has great gifts and many talents. But faithfulness wasn't among them. And though it took me a while, eventually I realised I couldn't live with that. He's feeling much better now, but he needs to return to his own flat. I'm afraid he's getting a little too comfortable here. Thanks for the drink.' She kissed his cheek. 'I enjoyed it.'

She walked away. After a moment or two, she heard his footsteps on the gravel. When she looked back, he was leaning against the gatepost. 'If you ever want to escape again, you know where I am,' he called out. 'Or even if you just fancy a drink at the pub.'

'Good offers, both of them! I might take you up on it.' There was an inflection of interest, of flirtation even, in her voice, and she smiled to herself as she let herself back into Greengage Cottage.

Lorcan and Iris were walking through Much Hadham. Lorcan was pushing the pushchair with Florence in it, and Magnus was skittering along the verge, pretending to be a steam train.

Lorcan said, 'Tom went through all the statements from the bank and building society. We had a long talk about it.'

Before he could go on, Iris said, 'I think we should sell the house.'

He stared at her. 'What?'

'It isn't practical, us living in Cambridge. When we bought it, I was working there, but then I stopped, and now it doesn't make any sense. Your commute's too long, Lorcan. We should move closer to London.'

Lorcan yelled, 'Brakes on, Magnus! We're coming up to a road!' He lowered his voice. 'But Iris, I thought you loved the house.'

'I did, I adored it, but I'm not sure I love it now. I've seen what it's done to us.' Iris hunched her shoulders. 'And it was too expensive in the first place. I shouldn't have persuaded you to buy it. I think we should look for somewhere smaller, a three-bedroom semi, something like that. We'd manage perfectly well. When we have people to stay, we could put the children in together.'

Iris took Magnus's hand to cross the road. Lorcan said,

'Tom said we should think about selling.' He had been dreading telling Iris that. Her words had lifted a weight from him.

'There you are, then. Tom's always right about financial matters.'

'You're certain you don't mind?'

'Completely. And . . .' Iris retrieved Florence's toy bunny from where it had fallen on the pavement, dusted it off and gave it back to her. 'And I think I should keep an eye on our finances in future.'

'Yes. Can't argue with that.'

She threaded her arm through his. 'If we moved here, to somewhere around Much Hadham, Mum and Dad would be able to help with the children. Then I could go back to work. There are part-time scientific jobs – not many, but there are some. Companies are starting to realise they need to hold on to their female staff. I've been talking to some friends from university who work in pharmaceutical companies round here and I've got some names. I've written letters of application. I need to work, Lorcan. I'm not happy if I don't work.'

'I know.' He put his arm round her waist. They had reached the entrance to the park. Magnus tore onto the grass and Florence bounced up and down in the pushchair, making whooping noises.

Lorcan said, 'When you're a head of department or whatever, I'll give up my job and stay at home and look after the kids and write science fiction novels.'

'Maybe they'll be bestsellers.'

'Maybe they will.' He took her in his arms and kissed her. 'I miss you so much. I love you so much. Come home, please.'

How would he bear it if she refused him again? He would keep trying, he thought. He would change and be better and keep trying.

But she said, 'I'm longing to come home. Tonight? Shall we pack the kids into the car and drive home tonight?'

George said, 'Maybe we should try again,' and Olivia, who was washing up, managed not to drop the glass she was handing him to dry.

'George, *no*.'

He rubbed at the glass with a tea towel. 'Why not? We get on with each other. We work well as a team.'

'We would drive each other barmy within a week.' She scoured a saucepan. '*Think*, George, you know we would.'

He sighed. 'I suppose so.'

'You're on your best behaviour now, and you're still a little, a little . . .'

'Crushed,' he said mournfully. 'You've missed a bit.'

She hacked at the lump of scrambled egg. 'Under the weather, I was going to say. I was also going to suggest that maybe it's about time you thought of going back to your flat.'

'I suppose I should.' Then he said, 'I hate it. I hate getting old.'

'I know you do.'

'I can't trust my own body. I'll always be thinking it will do something unpredictable and wretched.'

She rubbed his shoulder in the way she might have when comforting Magnus or Oscar. 'It must be hard. But the doctor said you were doing well.'

'Rest and recuperation. Healthy eating, no smoking and watch the booze,' George quoted grumpily. 'Lose weight, gentle exercise, never do anything fun.' He put the glasses in a cupboard.

'You'll survive, George Flynn. You're as hard as nails.'

'I survived Dunkirk. If you can get through that . . .'

'Exactly.'

'I've always wondered . . .' His brow creased.

'Tea? Coffee? What did you wonder?'

'It had better be tea. That blasted cardiologist told me not to drink strong coffee. And what, I ask you, is the point of weak coffee?'

Olivia noticed that he did not, as he invariably had when married to her, fling the damp tea towel anyhow on the work surface, but hung it neatly from a peg. Living with Serena had taught him something after all.

He said, 'When I was there, at Dunkirk, praying to be rescued, I remember how the instinct for survival kicked in. How when a boat came in sight and I waded through the sea to try to reach it, I had to fight against the urge to push weaker men out of the way. It's a powerful urge, that, to grasp at life, at the chance of life.'

'You've hardly ever talked to me about Dunkirk.'

'I can't. Even me . . . there aren't the words to describe such an experience. Or if there are, I don't have them. I've always tried to keep those memories out of sight. Eventually a vessel came within reach, and I grabbed at it. And I think I've gone on grabbing at whatever comes up ever since. Living through that made everything that followed seem fragile in some way. As if I can't be sure that anything will last. And I think I've felt, well, if that's how it is, why not take whatever's on offer? I'm not making excuses, Olivia. I know that my behaviour was appalling and that I hurt you a great deal. I was a fool.'

She passed him a mug of tea. She said, 'It wasn't all bad. We had some good times, didn't we?'

'We did. And we produced three wonderful sons. So, as you say . . .' He smiled. 'We didn't get it all wrong.'

There had been a time when she had worried that the divorce and the rows and silences that had preceded it had done irreparable harm to their children. When Gareth had left the country and Iris had left Lorcan, and even Tom had stepped back from his Natasha, she had worried for them. But the process of repair had begun. Olivia remembered that joyous day when Gareth had come back from Australia. Later, she had stood on the verge in the twilight, waiting for the three of them to come home, looking out for them. Eventually she had seen her sons walking back from the pub: Lorcan, Gareth and Tom, side by side, laughing and joking, in step.

'I'm enormously proud of them, aren't you, George?' she said. 'I don't think we did too badly at all.'

Tom had offered to take George back to London. He arrived at Greengage Cottage to pick up his father and his belongings shortly after two on Saturday afternoon. They were in the sitting room, and George was going through the shelves, checking he hadn't forgotten anything, when Tom said, 'I saw Nat this morning.'

Olivia was folding a jumper that belonged to George. She looked up at him. 'Do you mean in Swaffham?'

'Yes.'

'She invited you?'

Tom had a cheese sandwich and a black coffee in hand and was perched on the windowsill. 'No, I just went. The house is in the countryside. Pretty remote, no neighbours. It reminded me of Goldscombe.'

'Ah, Goldscombe,' said George, with a smile. 'Happy days.'

'How was Nat?'

'She's okay. It hasn't been easy for her, though. Her mother's not well.'

'You said she'd hurt her ankle.'

'She was hobbling about. But that's not what I meant. The house . . . it was in a state. So much stuff in the rooms. And not useful stuff . . . there were cardboard boxes and empty soup tins and hundreds of old copies of the *East Anglian Daily Times*. Nat said she'd done a lot of sorting-out, but some of the rooms I caught sight of it would be hard to walk through. She can't just chuck it all in the bin, you see. She has to go through each item one at a time, or her mum gets upset.'

George said, 'I had a great-aunt like that. After she died, I cleared out her house. She appeared to have kept every envelope, every tea and biscuit packet she had ever owned.'

Recalling her own conversation with Nat in Tom's kitchen – *do you think a tidy person and an untidy person can ever live together?* – Olivia said, 'That was why she didn't want you to go there.'

'Yes. She was afraid I'd be disgusted by the state of the house.'

She said gently, 'And were you, Tom?'

'To be honest, yes, I was, at first. Her little brother, Russell, offered to make me a mug of tea.' He exhaled sharply, a small, plosive sound that indicated, Olivia felt, all the difficult emotions he must have struggled with at that moment. 'I didn't want to drink it. The thing is, when a house is that messy, it isn't clean either. And there were pets – cats and guinea pigs – in the kitchen. Lots of them. But Mum, it was okay. I thanked Russell and I drank the tea because I knew it would upset Nat if I didn't. That was what mattered.'

'The things we do for love . . .' George looked at his son fondly.

'Nat and I talked about everything. And I met her mother, who is lovely, funny and bright and welcoming. So,' Tom said with a frown, 'I think we're all right again.'

'Is this mine?' George brandished a book.

'I think so, George. I'm so glad, Tom. Nat's a wonderful woman.'

'She is. She's thinking about restoring the Enchanted Land, getting it going again. That's the family business, Dad. Nat knows all about the magic side of it and I could help with financial matters, if she'd like me to. She's mulling it over.'

'Magic and finance,' said George. 'There's a poem there, I'm sure of it.'

'You can stay with me tonight, if you like, Dad.'

'Thanks, but no, I should get back to my flat. John Farley said he'd drop round for a drink this evening.' George caught Olivia's eye. 'Tea,' he said, with a sigh. 'Best behaviour, I know.'

There had been a moment when he had wondered whether he could bear it, when he had thought he had made a mistake in going there. Nat's brother had let him into the house. Russell was a smallish twelve-year-old, with nut-brown hair stuck up in tufts and tortoiseshell NHS glasses that rested at an angle on his snub nose. On each tread of the stairs had lain books and magazines and items of clothing and balls of wool with needles protruding from them like colourful porcupines. On the quarry tiles in the hall, between hillocks of junk mail and unopened letters, he saw muddy football boots and plimsolls, a discarded anorak, a duffel bag.

He had followed Russell through a living room, taking a path that wound between towers of yellowing newspapers. Clothing, for washing or ironing or repair, he guessed, nestled on the sofas and armchairs and snaked together in bags and wicker baskets.

In the kitchen, Russell chatted to him as the kettle boiled. Nat was upstairs, helping his mum dress, he told Tom. He liked Nat being at home because she made shepherd's pie and toad in the hole. When his mum was ill, they sometimes had Weetabix for supper. He, Russ, was helping Nat sort out the Enchanted Land.

The kitchen smelled of guinea pig and cat. Russell was balancing the mugs on the edge of the sink because the worktop was crammed with stacks of old soup cans, empty cereal boxes and wrappings. Nat must be trying to do some housework, because plates and bowls were draining on the rack.

A voice from behind him exclaimed, 'Tom!' and he spun round.

'Hello, Nat.'

'You didn't tell me you were coming . . . Russ, you shouldn't have just . . .' Nat looked deeply upset.

'Here you are, Tom.' Russell handed Tom a mug.

'Thanks, Russell, just what I needed.' He took a mouthful. 'Good tea,' he said.

The boy looked pleased with himself. 'Shall I make you one, Nat?'

'I'm okay. Can you make some tea and toast for Mum and take it upstairs?' Nat turned to Tom. She still looked distressed, but he could tell that she was trying to hold herself together. 'Let's go outside.'

For the next hour they sat in the shade of a spreading horse chestnut tree. They talked and Nat cried a little, dashing away the tears on the sleeve of her blouse. 'I didn't want you to see this place,' she said to him. 'I didn't want you to see how my family lives. Your family and mine . . . we might as well come from different planets. I tried to talk to you about it, Tom, I tried so many times, but I couldn't make myself. I've missed you so much. I've hated being so far away from you.'

He held her in his arms and told her he loved her. She explained about the episodes of depression her mother suffered from, which had worsened after Nat's father had died, and the hoarding that accompanied them. He described Goldscombe, and how sad he had felt when his family had moved away from Devon.

After a while they went for a walk in the meadows and copses that surrounded the house, and then Nat showed him the Enchanted Land. The barn's cavernous interior was crammed with stalls bright with gold leaf and colourful exhibits. 'I used to love it here.' Nat stroked a swagged velvet curtain that framed a small stage. 'It was my favourite place on earth.'

The day after Tom drove George back to his Hampstead flat, Olivia and Luke McQuinnan went out for the day to Walberswick. They tramped along the pebble beach to Dunwich, where they ate fish and chips. Afterwards, they stood on top of a sandbank, looking out over the North Sea. Luke said that they should try to make out the shapes of the eight churches that had over the centuries been lost beneath the waves in a succession of storms, so they stared at the grey-blue water, which was glazed with sunlight. They strained to pick out from beneath the crash and hiss of the waves the chime of submerged church bells.

Clambering down the sandbank, he gave her his hand, and it seemed easy and natural to go on holding it as they walked back to Walberswick. Olivia was drawn to this arc of the Suffolk coast for its bleak, uncompromising beauty and for the strength and savagery of a sea that drowned towns and harbours and tore the foundations from beneath houses.

Both long-legged, they walked in step, talking non-stop. He had grown up in London, Luke told her. Neither of his parents were professional musicians, though his mother had been a keen and talented amateur. As a boy, he had sung in a cathedral choir, where a teacher had nurtured his talent for composition. He had read music at Cambridge and had continued to study both piano and composition there because he had never been able to decide between the two. Much of his work was written for sacred settings. Though he would not describe himself as religious, he had always been interested in the spiritual.

By the time they returned to Holfield, Annie's car was parked outside the Hayloft. Standing on tiptoe, Olivia kissed Luke's cheek and they said goodbye.

In the porch of Greengage Cottage, she discovered that the postman had left a parcel for her. Indoors, she kicked off her gritty sandals and hung up her jacket. The weather was hotter inland than on the coast, and warmth had gathered in the house. Though she opened the windows to let in air, the rooms felt only marginally cooler. Slipping out of the back door, she saw that Luke and his daughter were sitting on the Hayloft's terrace. Annie was waving her arms around as if conducting an orchestra and Luke was laughing. Olivia's gaze lingered on his tall, slim form.

When she took a second look at the parcel, she saw that the sender had printed her name – Alice Hain – on the back of the brown paper, above a Hampshire address. Surprised and curious, Olivia cut through string and Sellotape and peeled back wrapping paper.

Nestling inside the layers of tissue paper she found a small pale green and silver box. Inside it was a platinum bangle, art deco in style, set with red and purple stones as smooth and oval as boiled sweets, and in a breath she was transported back to the summer of 1939 and Grace Ruthwell's bedroom in Hinton Place. Grace had been dressing for a luncheon engagement and she had asked Olivia to help her select which jewellery she should wear. This was the bangle she had chosen.

It's a favourite of mine, Grace had said. *Here, try it on.*

Now, forty years later, Olivia slid it once more onto her wrist. Sitting down at the kitchen table, she turned her hand this way and that, watching how the coloured stones seized the sunlight, intensifying it within them. She thought of all that had passed since that day, and the girl she had once been and the woman she had become, and of everything she had achieved and endured. She had overcome the dangers and deprivation of war and she had coped with marriage to a man who, though he had great gifts, had also had his demons. She had cherished her many long friendships and had pursued fulfilling careers that had allowed her to grow. But her greatest achievement had been her family, her sons and her grandchildren. Scattered over the globe they might be, but they would always come home.

Music drifted across from the Hayloft. She went to sit on the terrace, listening to it. Piano and flute were playing together the lilting, haunting melody she had become familiar with. Olivia ran her thumb over a ruby. The faint, salty scent of the sea lingered on her skin and on the hems of her jeans. She remembered how easily her hand had fitted into Luke's, and how natural it had felt at the end of a glorious day to kiss him goodbye. She had never lost her capacity to love. It burned inside her, along with the flame of optimism and the thirst for adventure she had carried with her all those years ago to London.

The heat, and the events of the day, meant that she slept only intermittently that night. And there it was again, when she woke in the early hours of the morning, that glimmer of understanding, of intuition, that bobbed like a piece of thistledown caught on a breeze before darting away, just out of reach.

She went downstairs and reread the note Alice had put in the parcel.

My mother left this to you. She always wanted you to have it.

Outside, a current of cool air rose from the stream that ran along the lowest part of the field. She walked to the wood. And she remembered. She remembered how Grace had let her try on the bangle, and how she had said, *It suits you. You have such slender hands.*

On her return, she fetched a pen and notepaper and sat at the kitchen table and began to write a letter. She thanked Alice for sending her the bangle and expressed condolences on the death of her mother. *Perhaps we could meet up when you are next in town,* she added. *Do please let me know a time and date that would be convenient for you.*

Sealing the envelope, she felt as if she was about to watch a drop of water fall into a pond; she imagined how the ripples would spread across the surface so that its appearance would soon be entirely changed.

Chapter Nineteen

1978–9, Suffolk and London

On Monday evening, in the church hall in Holfield St Peter, Olivia's choir attempted for the third time the opening of Pergolesi's *Stabat Mater*. For the third time, the sopranos came in late, and the voices fractured and faded.

The door opened and Luke McQuinnan came into the hall. He approached the small stage and spoke to Ben, who was conducting, and who said, 'Yes *please*. Thank *God*,' and stepped aside. Ben's wife, Mary, darted away from the piano, back to her place with the altos.

Luke sat down at the piano. He said, 'I'll play the full intro. Firsts, you come in on the first beat of the bar, seconds on the third. I'll cue you in and give you a hand with the tricky bits.'

The stretch of silence before the music began seemed unbearable to Olivia. She saw how his hands hovered over the keyboard, saw their slight tremor. *It's the standing-up in front of people, I can't seem to cope with it. I go to pieces.* She willed him to play.

The opening chord rang out and she was able to breathe again. As the intro developed, mournful and quiet, she saw the expression of calm concentration on his features and then an intentness as he stood, continuing to play one-handed, bringing the voices in, the lower line first and then the upper, perfectly on the beat. When they threatened to falter, he sang with them, his rich baritone helping them gather confidence until the voices wove together in exultation, threading in and out in an intricate pattern before combining into a glorious whole. And she no longer needed the sheet music, because she found that she knew it by heart, and she focused only on the melody as it rose and fell, the phrases echoing, filling the room, rising into harmony before dying away, so that in the end, when at last the singers fell silent, the only sound that remained was the reverberation of the final chord.

It was dusk, and long purple shadows pasted the road as they walked up the hill together. She said, 'You were wonderful. So calm. So professional.'

'I was terrified. I nearly ran out of the room.'

'You didn't, and that's what matters.'

'It's a decent little choir.'

'It is. I enjoy it. I didn't know . . . You didn't say, Luke.'

'I wasn't sure, and then, well, I've been in London for a couple of days, teaching and meeting up with people, and on the train coming back, I knew I had to do it. I've missed that part of my life so much, Olivia. I had to try again. In the end, you have to face up to things. I couldn't go on for the rest of my days with that part of me missing.'

She squeezed his hand. 'Did it feel good?'

When he turned to her, she saw that his face was lit up with joy. 'Oh, it felt like coming home.'

Then he kissed her. His mouth brushed against hers with slight hesitancy to begin with, and then, seeing her acquiescence, he kissed her again and she could think of nothing but the touch of his lips and the strength of his embrace. She closed her eyes and the rest of the world receded, and everything but his warmth and the slight roughness of his skin and the ripple of his muscles beneath his shirt was as nothing.

The sound of a car heading along the road made them break apart. Arm in arm, they reached the Hayloft. He said, 'Do you fancy a drink?'

'Please.'

They went into the house. She made to take off her jacket, but he kissed her again. And then they were climbing the stairs and she was kicking off her shoes and unbuttoning his shirt, and somehow they were in the bedroom and her dress was on the floor, a pool of blue and white, and his arms were around her and she was coming alive again, every part of her yearning for his touch.

Sunlight pouring through the open window woke her. She was lying in his arms and the sheet was tangled around them. Luke murmured a good morning, and she yawned and stretched luxuriantly and then, propping herself up on her elbows, kissed him.

'What's the time?'

'Just gone eight.'

'Oh God, I'm supposed to be working.'

'Five minutes won't make any difference.' His blue eyes were alight with humour and desire.

'I suppose not.' She didn't care if it did. She could be late for once. When he ran his palm from her waist to her hip, she gave a soft groan and welcomed him into her.

It was, thank heavens, an easy day's work – the routine fortnightly tidying of two gardens in Lavenham – and by three she was free to go home. The grey van was standing in front of the Hayloft. In Greengage Cottage, she had a shower and put on a sleeveless dress. It was still hot, so she went round the house opening windows on the shady side. She was towelling her hair when the doorbell rang.

Luke was standing in the porch. 'Am I disturbing you? I can come back later.'

'Not at all. Come in. Mind your head, the lintels are low.'

She liked the sight of him in her kitchen, his lean, rangy figure as he rested against the sink while she took a jug of chilled lemonade out of the fridge and poured them both a glass. Though he was tall, he wasn't the sort of man who took up all the space. He gave her time to think, to speak. He seemed to make the room complete.

'Great place,' he said, looking round.

'Thank you.'

'It's the sort of house I'd pictured you having.' He scanned the room. 'Family photos and nice old pieces of furniture and plenty of flowers.'

'What have you done with your own house, Luke, the one in Teddington?'

'Annie's living in it, so it's a bit of a wreck.'

She laughed. 'You're very brave, handing over your home to your daughter for months on end.'

His expression altered slightly. 'That's what I wanted to talk to you about.'

As they took the lemonade out to the terrace to sit in the shade, she was aware of some small part of her closing off, protecting itself, like the petals of a flower folding up.

He said, 'Last week I decided not to renew my tenancy on the Hayloft.'

'I see.' But she didn't see at all. Surely what had happened last night had been as important to him as it had to her. Their lovemaking had been more than a bit of fun, a celebration of the events of the evening.

'No, I don't think you do.' He took her hand. 'Listen . . . about last night. I've wanted that to happen for so long. I care for you, Olivia. I fancy you like mad, too, but it's more than that. I think I've fallen in love with you, but as things stand, I have nothing to offer you.'

'Luke, that's not true.' Her voice was hoarse. His words rang through her head, full of hope and joy and promise.

'I need to go back to London to get my career – my life – going again. I can do it now. You've helped me do it. I couldn't have got to this point without you.'

She pressed his hand between hers. 'You're going to start working again? Performing in public?'

'Yes. My oratorio is almost finished. I'd like to conduct the first performance myself and I can hardly expect to just waltz in after years and assume that's going to happen. The last time I was in London, I talked to some contacts. I've been offered a job. I haven't committed yet, but that's the next step.'

She drew his hand to her mouth and kissed it. 'You know that I wish you every bit of luck in the world, don't you?'

'Thank you.' Her stroked her hair, still damp from the shower. 'And you know that I'll miss you so much, and that this isn't the end for us.'

'I do, yes.'

'I'll come back for you. And when I do, I hope there'll be a place in your life for me.'

Towards the end of July, she met Alice in the Harrods Tea Rooms. A waiter was serving tea and scones; catching sight of Olivia, Alice said to him, 'One moment, please. Tea, Olivia? Or coffee?'

'Tea, please.'

As the waiter left, Olivia sat down opposite Alice. 'Thank you for agreeing to meet me. And thank you for sending me your mother's bangle. It means a lot to me. I can't tell you how touched I was to know that Grace had thought of me.'

'It's a pleasure. You're looking well, Olivia.'

'Thank you. And you? Are you well?'

Alice, who had always been slender, had lost weight. Her blue eyes had darkened over the years; they had greyed and lost their jewel-like quality.

She made a dismissive gesture. 'It's been a difficult couple of years. First Michael, then Mummy.'

'I was so sorry to hear of the death of your husband,' said Olivia. 'You must miss him so much.'

'I do. Every moment of every day.' A wariness crossed Alice's features. 'How did you know about Michael?'

'Rory Madden told me.'

The waiter reappeared with tea and scones for Olivia. When he had gone, Alice said, 'Michael was the love of my life. Do you know when we first met?' A smile touched the corners of her mouth before she continued. 'I was a debutante, before the war, at a party in Gloucestershire. Oh, how I detested those parties! One would be abandoned by one's mother, sometimes in the middle of nowhere, amid a group of people one neither knew nor cared for. I've always enjoyed walking and riding, thank goodness, so that part of the weekend was bearable, but the rest of it, the dreary suppers and the dances with clumsy youths who stood on your toes and the silly, girlish frocks one was obliged to wear . . . I loathed every minute of it. And then I met Michael. An awful boy was pestering me, so I escaped to the library. Michael was sitting by the fire, reading a book about wild birds, and we got talking. And we just talked and talked.' Alice split a scone in half, then looked up. 'I don't know if you know how these things work, Olivia.'

'Not at all.'

'The same group of people are invited to all the events, so one would see the same men over and over again. So Michael and I, we saw each other in Devon and in Sussex and in London, of course. And if he was there, I had a lovely time. And when he wasn't, I simply longed to be with him.'

Olivia said, 'Shall I pour you some tea?'

'Oh, yes. Please.' Alice waved her fingers. 'That's enough. I like plenty of milk.'

'What happened?'

'With Michael?' She glanced aside to the next table, where three women in their forties were comparing diaries. 'My mother found out. We were in love, and I suppose that made us stupid and careless. She told me I mustn't see him again.'

'Why not?'

'Oh, Olivia.' Sadness veiled Alice's finely cut features. 'Because he wasn't the sort of man I was supposed to marry. Because he wasn't wealthy enough, and because, even though he came from a good family, he wasn't sufficiently well connected to satisfy my mother's ambitions.'

'And Ivo Mortimer was?'

Alice shrugged. 'Ivo had a town house in Knightsbridge and an estate in the country. How could Michael, who was training to be a barrister and living in digs, compare with that?' Her voice was bitter. She looked away. 'I remember imploring her, trying to make her understand, and do you know what she said to me? She said, we all think we're in love when we're nineteen years old, but it never lasts. She made me write to Michael and tell him that the understanding we had between us was over.'

'Was that why you took your mother's letter?'

Alice stilled. She put down her cup. It was possible, thought Olivia, that she might storm out of the restaurant, or even have the waiter throw her out. It was also possible that she herself was mistaken.

Alice did neither of those things. Instead, she said quietly, 'Yes, it was.' There was a silence. Then she said softly, 'I didn't mean . . . I didn't *intend* when I took it . . .'

'You were angry with Grace.'

'No, I hated her.' Alice ran a hand over the starched white tablecloth, smoothing out a wrinkle. 'I wanted to punish her. I'd gone into the morning room to look for a stamp and I saw the letter on my mother's desk. I read it. I was shocked. Every move of mine was policed, while all the time she was having a love affair! I remember thinking how hypocritical she was, and how disgusting it was that a woman of her age, of Mummy's age, should write such stuff.' She gave her head a little shake. 'We are so intolerant, so uncomprehending, when we're young.' Her voice dropped. 'I thought back then that *love*, passionate love, was the preserve of the young. What a fool I was. I heard my father in the corridor, speaking to his valet, and I gave him the letter. I didn't think twice about it.' She raised her eyebrows, put her head to one side and gave a little shrug. 'I wanted to punish my mother, but I think I also wanted my father to notice me. As a child, I often felt overlooked. Mummy always gave far more attention to Frankie than to me, and as for my father, he was never interested in either of us.'

'And did it work?'

'Oh, yes. For a while, at least. When I gave him the letter, he smiled at me. Do you know, I think I could count on the fingers of one hand the number of times he'd smiled at me. And he was pleased with me when I agreed to marry Ivo.' Alice looked up, meeting Olivia's eyes. 'I've regretted what I did. I've regretted it so much. Frankie was sent to that awful place because of me.'

'No, Alice. Your father chose to do that.'

'But I made it easy for him.'

Olivia shook her head. She had thought about this since receiving Grace's bequest. 'If your father hadn't dismissed Rory then, he would have left the family's service a few weeks later anyway. Once war broke out, he would have had to join the forces. I doubt if another tutor could have been found. And because of the Blitz, Frankie couldn't have stayed in London. Your father was responsible for what happened, Alice, not you. He chose to send his son to that institution.'

'I read about it,' Alice said softly. 'I read about that place, Allershaw. It made me cry.' Her face was white and pinched. 'Perhaps you're right.' She fumbled inside a leather handbag for cigarettes and a lighter. 'Still, I wish Frankie was still here. I wish none of it had ever happened.'

The waiter returned to ask them if they needed more hot water, but Alice waved him away.

'Do you have children, Olivia?'

'Three sons.'

'How wonderful.' There was a wistful note in Alice's voice. 'Ivo never wanted children and it didn't work out for Michael and me. I was in my mid forties when we married. I suppose I was too old. I would have loved a child – a son or daughter, I wouldn't have minded which. I wouldn't have brought them up as I was brought up. I'd have made time for them

. . . I would have . . .' Her eyes were shining with tears.

'Loved them,' Olivia said gently, and Alice nodded. 'Your mother loved *you*, Alice. She cared about you.'

'Then she wasn't very good at showing it. Not while I was young.'

Though Grace had wanted the best for Alice, perhaps Frankie, with his brightness and spontaneity and vulnerability, had been the child of her heart.

Alice went on, 'We got on better, Mummy and I, when I was older. I used to go and stay with her in France every summer. She looked forward to me coming, I know she did. Her friend Nancy, who lived with her, told me so.' She crumbled her scone between her fingers. 'I always wondered whether Mummy guessed about the letter. She never said anything to me. We both had regrets, I think. But I believe that we came to understand each other better.'

'Your mother assumed that one of the servants had taken it.' Though it occurred to Olivia that Grace, like she herself, might have worked it out over the years.

Her own plate lay untouched in front of her. 'Do you still see your father, Alice?'

'Not often. Weddings and funerals, that sort of thing. I can't bear his wife, and anyway, Daddy and I don't have much to say to each other.' Alice flicked her lighter and inhaled the cigarette. A malicious smile played about her mouth. 'His son, my half-brother Justin, must be a dreadful disappointment to him. He appears to be spending his inheritance on drugs and women.'

She looked up at Olivia. 'I expect you've come here to ask me to let Rory Madden see my mother's diaries and letters.'

'Would you?'

'I posted them to him this morning, on my way to the railway station.'

'Thank you. Rory will appreciate it.'

Alice glanced at her watch. She dropped her lighter back into her handbag and stood up. 'I must go. I have an appointment. I know what Michael would say if he were here. He would say that when one has done wrong, one must find a way to atone. And he would have said . . .' Her voice fell and a smile played about the corners of her mouth. 'He would have said that there is relief in confession. And he was right about most things. I've been trying to make up for what I did.'

On impulse, Olivia hugged her. After a moment, Alice returned the embrace.

'Will you be all right, Alice?'

'I'm fine.' She smoothed back her pale hair, glanced at her reflection in a hand mirror, then snapped it shut. 'I shall go home this evening. I prefer the country. I'm quite content – I have my horses and the dogs for company. Goodbye, Olivia.'

After she left the department store, Olivia walked the mile to Mayfair, and Hinton Place. The square had recovered from the depredations of war and the passing of time had returned it to its former glory. In the central garden, the trees were in leaf. Gleaming black railings had been restored to the frontages of the houses.

On this fine summer's day, the windows were open in the upper storeys of the Ruthwells' house. Blinds made of a fashionable floral print maintained the privacy of the lower part of the building, and two cars, a Bentley and a sports car in British racing green, were parked outside. Olivia imagined how excited Frankie would have been to see the cars, and how he would have added them to his drawing book. Her life had in many ways been shaped by the events that had taken place in that house before the war. In her heart, she wished Alice well.

Her thoughts turned to Luke. He was living in London during the week. He had applied for the position of musical director of a chamber choir as well as continuing to teach and compose. He was considering playing in a few amateur concerts – he was, he had written to her, easing himself back into his career.

She was seeing him that evening. They were to have supper together and then go to a concert at the Wigmore Hall. There were so many decisions they must make, all the complications that introducing a new person into an established family entailed.

But she was optimistic that it would work out in the end. They were both patient people, and they would wait for each other. And after all, she had plenty to occupy herself. A new garden had recently been commissioned. She had ordered saplings to plant in the woodland in the autumn. And there was a trip to Australia to plan.

Briskly she headed for the Underground station.

Through the window she caught sight of Lorcan and Iris's car, slowing as it approached Greengage Cottage. Olivia brushed her floury hands on her apron, then went outside, stepping carefully on the paving stones because that spring it had been raining for ever and the woodland and garden were awash. She waved madly as the Cortina slowed.

Iris wound down the window and looked out. 'Where shall we park, Olivia?'

'Just here, in my place. I've put my car outside the Hayloft.

Doreen and Ravi are away this weekend and they said I could use it.' The couple currently renting the Hayloft were retired doctors in their sixties.

Lorcan let Magnus out of the car. He ran towards Olivia and flung his arms round her waist. She gave him a big hug.

'Can I play in the den, Granny?'

'Of course you can. You need to put on your wellies first.'

Iris was carrying a cake tin. Lorcan had Florence in his arms. They all went inside the cottage. Olivia said, 'How's the decorating going?'

Lorcan and Iris had sold their Cambridge house and had three months ago moved into a spacious semi-detached on the outskirts of Much Hadham. Lorcan was stripping off old wallpaper and repairing plaster, arts he had learned, he had reminded her, during family house moves.

'The living room's almost finished.'

'I chose some fabulous Laura Ashley wallpaper,' Iris said. 'It looks very smart. You must come over soon and see it, Olivia.'

'Tom gave me a hand with the pattern-matching.' Lorcan sat his daughter on the kitchen work surface and handed her a scrap of pastry to play with. 'Wallpapering is very mathematical.'

'They're coming to lunch, aren't they?' Iris said.

Olivia glanced at the clock. 'They should be here any time.'

'I can't imagine Tom living in the country, doing accounts for farmers and landowners.'

'I can,' said Iris. 'He'll love it.'

Tom had given his notice at work and put his house on the market. He was planning to start up his own accountancy business in the east of England.

'Tom was never a London person.' Olivia put the pastry shell in the oven. 'He was the only one of you three born in Devon, remember. He's never happier than when hiking up a hill.'

Lorcan snorted. 'Not many of those in Norfolk.'

Some of the Flynns had been taken by surprise when, a few weeks ago, Tom had told them that he and Nat, who were now engaged to be married, were looking for a house in Swaffham. They should not have been, thought Olivia, because Tom wanted to be near Nat, and Nat had decided to stay in Norfolk to help her mother look after Russell, who, as she had recently pointed out to Olivia, might be perfectly biddable now, at the age of thirteen, but as he approached the more difficult teenage years would need someone to keep an eye on him. 'I was a tearaway when I was sixteen,' she had added. 'If Russ is like me, then heaven help us. Anyway, Mum's happier when I'm not too far away.'

Iris said, 'I'm so looking forward to the wedding.'

'Me too.' Olivia was helping Nat make bridesmaids' dresses for Morwenna, India and Petra. She began to slice leeks. 'How's the job going?'

Towards the end of the previous year, Iris had started to work three days a week at a pharmaceutical company in Welwyn. By then, Magnus was attending a primary school in Much Hadham. Iris's parents looked after Florence two days each week; on the third, the little girl went to a local childminder. Olivia helped with childcare at half term and in the school holidays.

'It's going well. Linda has suggested I work with another team for a few months, to broaden my experience.' Iris looked round the room. 'Where's Magnus?'

'Magnus!' Lorcan roared. 'Have you put your boots on yet?' He dropped his voice. 'I'll take the kids to play in the woods.'

'Lorcan,' said Iris, 'have you told your mum . . .'

'Oh.' His smile was triumphant. 'I've some news, Mum. I had a letter yesterday. I think I've found a publisher for *Memo From a Dying Sun*.'

'Lorcan!' Olivia threw her arms round him. 'That's wonderful! Your first novel – I'm so pleased for you!'

'I haven't signed a contract yet, so it's not quite definite.'

Iris ruffled his curls. 'He keeps saying that, and I keep saying that they wouldn't have told him they loved it if they weren't intending to publish it. I bet George says the same.'

'George?' Olivia looked up.

'He's coming today, isn't he?'

'He hasn't said anything to me.'

'I think he is, Mum.'

'I thought he was in Edinburgh . . .' She felt an all too familiar flicker of exasperation. 'Are you sure, love?'

'Pretty much. We spoke on the phone a couple of days ago and I mentioned we were coming here today. Apparently he's been travelling round the country and he's had some events in the east of England. He said something about catching us all at the same time.' Lorcan scooped Florence off the worktop. In the doorway, he looked back. 'He said he might bring someone.'

'*Someone?*'

'A friend,' Lorcan added, a touch of mockery in his voice. 'Best of luck with that, Mum.'

He left the room to wrestle Florence into her wellies and waterproof suit. Olivia and Iris stared at each other, and then Iris gave a snort of laughter.

Olivia sighed. 'I hope George isn't assuming he can sleep here. There's isn't any room.' Lorcan, Iris and the children were staying the night.

'There's always the sofa,' said Iris. Her eyes were bright with laughter.

Olivia wouldn't be surprised if George turned up with a tent and expected to pitch it in her garden. Then she would worry about him catching a cold and getting ill again.

Iris said, 'Doesn't the pub have a couple of rooms?'

'It does, yes, you're right. Goodness.' Olivia shook her head as if to clear it. 'Could you peel a few more potatoes, do you think, Iris? Just in case.'

She put the quiche in the oven and took a packet of sausages out of the fridge. Would there be enough food to go round if two extra people turned up? It would be fine, she told herself. Most of the Flynns' parties went well in the end.

Iris ran water into the sink. 'Have you heard from Luke?'

'We talked on the phone last night. He's doing well. He's conducting a series of concerts in churches in Sussex for a centenary. Quite small affairs, so nothing too daunting.'

'Sensible.'

'I think so.'

'I think Luke is great,' said Iris gently. 'And Lorcan does too.'

'Thank you.' Olivia smiled. 'So do I, actually.'

Iris hugged her. 'That, Olivia, is obvious to us all from the expression on your face whenever you say his name.'

And Luke appeared to feel the same about her, which was perfect, and just as well, because there was so much that must be decided. Where they should live and how they could see each other and accommodate their careers at the same time, for a start. But she knew they would find a way.

Iris said, 'That's a car, isn't it?' and Olivia went to look out of the sitting-room window. She recognised Tom's Volvo; she saw a bright flare of pink raincoat as Nat climbed out of the passenger seat.

Chapter Twenty

1979, Suffolk

During the night, a storm swept through East Anglia. In the early hours, Olivia was woken by lightning that flashed through the curtains, and then a hammering of thunder. The rain began to batter against the window panes like a living creature seeking to find a way into the house. She lay awake, thinking about Luke.

He was due to return to England in a couple of days' time. For the past four weeks he had been touring Europe with his chamber choir. Among the works they had performed had been his oratorio, which had been well received. He had sent her postcards, and they had exchanged letters and phone calls.

More than a year had passed since he had left the Hayloft to pick up the threads of his career. They had, during that time, come ever closer to each other. They would keep both their houses, they had decided, his in the city and hers in the country, for now at least, because a sturdy web of family, friends and work bound them to both London and Suffolk. As the moment of his return approached, her longing to see him, to touch him, intensified, and hours seemed to pass before she was able to go back to sleep.

In the morning, the garden of Greengage Cottage was glazed with puddles and scattered with a tawny and crimson confetti of fallen leaves. The wind had blown over the bird table and knocked the prop from the washing line. The clouds were retreating, grey and heavy as they rumbled towards the North Sea coast, and in their absence the sky sparkled, a pale and diaphanous blue, as if it had been scrubbed clean.

She put on her boots and waxed jacket and set to work in the woodland. A slanting autumnal light fell between the trees and the air was cold and pungent with the scent of wet soil and fungi and leaf mould. Leaves like silver pennies had been torn from the white poplars, leaving their branches bare, and a circle of fly agaric, the red and white spotted toadstools of fairy tales, had sprung up overnight beneath a pine. Drops of rain strung themselves like diamonds on the cobwebs that festooned the brambles.

She began to gather up the twigs and branches that the storm had scattered over the forest floor. She would dry some to burn in the sitting-room fire; the remainder she would put aside for a bonfire on Guy Fawkes Night. She had an axe with her to chop up the branches, and she worked hard through the morning, as if to tire herself out, looking up now and then, on edge, as if she were waiting for something to happen – or someone to appear. A prickling of her skin, a taut anticipation in her stomach: and yet Luke was not due to fly home until later today, and even then he would go first to Teddington, where he would stay overnight before driving to Suffolk tomorrow morning. That was the plan.

As the hours went on, the wind returned, making spiteful little darts that swirled the fallen leaves and tangled her hair and showered her with raindrops when she brushed against an elder bush. A large branch had been ripped from a willow; strips of pink wood and grey bark tied it to the trunk some way above her head. She gave the branch a cautious shake, but it did not come away from the tree. She thought she would go and fetch a saw and stepladder and cut it off cleanly.

Something made her look down the road. A man was walking up the slope from the village, towards the Hayloft and Greengage Cottage. Her heartbeat hurtled as he seemed to solidify, to become real. Luke McQuinnan emerged from the shadows of the trees that edged the lane, tall and lean, in jeans and a navy-blue peacoat, his brown hair ruffled and slightly untidy, as always.

She took a small indrawn breath. Then she called out, 'You're early!'

'I managed to catch an earlier plane! And then I came straight here.' He was smiling. 'Trains and buses . . . I've lost count of them. I couldn't wait, Olivia, I've missed you so much!'

Dropping the branch, she ran to meet him, and he swept her up in his embrace.